THE DRAGON HEIR

THE DRAGON HEIR

CINDA WILLIAMS CHIMA

Indigo

The right of Cinda Williams Chima to be identified as the
author of this work has been asserted by her in accordance
with the Copyright, Designs and Patents Act 1988.

First published in Great Britain in 2011 by Indigo
An imprint of the Orion Publishing Group
Orion House, 5 Upper St Martin's Lane,
London WC2H 9EA
An Hachette UK Company

A CIP catalogue record for this book
is available from the British Library

ISBN 978 1 78062 053 4

3 5 7 9 10 8 6 4 2

Printed in Great Britain by Clays Ltd, St Ives plc

The Orion Publishing Group's policy is to use papers
that are natural, renewable and recyclable products and
made from wood grown in sustainable forests. The logging
and manufacturing processes are expected to conform to
the environmental regulations of the country of origin.

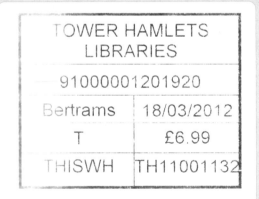

www.cindachima.com
www.orionbooks.co.uk

For Eric and Keith—who believe in dragons

❧ ACKNOWLEDGMENTS ❧

A book is like a ship. It requires a host of people to launch one. Some help with the structure and design, others provide the financing, some cheer from the shoreline, while others put their shoulders to the keel and push it free from its moorings.

I'm grateful to all the talented people at Hyperion, especially my editor, Arianne Lewin, who made me rewrite the whole thing and make it a better book. Thanks to Elizabeth Clark, who, along with artist Larry Rostant, is responsible for those gorgeous covers. Thanks to Angus Killick and his team, who put my books into the hands of teachers and librarians. (And thanks also to those teachers and librarians who put my books into the hands of readers.)

Bless you, Christopher Schelling. In addition to being a stellar agent, he regularly convinces me, rightly or wrongly, that I'm not crazy.

Thanks to the genius Pam Daum, for the gorgeous photographs. Writer, artist, forever friends. I miss you.

Thanks to my generous colleagues in Hudson Writers and Twinsburg Writers for providing the gift of loving, specific critique. Thanks especially to Marsha McGregor, who endured some rather incoherent phone calls and talked me down.

I owe a heartfelt thanks to Rod, who provided moral, emotional and technical support (Website, photography, layout and design, printer diagnosis and treatment) while enduring the occasional rant and doing more than his share of housework and relationship maintenance. (Those birthday cards that went out—wasn't me.)

Finally, thanks to my early readers, Eric and Keith, who started it all.

THE
DRAGON
HEIR

Fog clung to Booker Mountain like an old ragged coat. The pickup's chancy headlights poked frail tunnels through the mist. Although the road was narrow and treacherous, Madison didn't worry. Her grandmother Min could find her way blindfolded and sound asleep.

Min rammed the truck into low gear as the grade steepened. Her face was set in hard, angry lines, but Madison knew Min wasn't mad at her. She felt rescued, cocooned in the pickup with John Robert on her lap and Grace jammed between her and the door. Grace was sleeping, her head braced against the window, her hair hanging in knots around her face. Min hadn't taken the time to comb it.

"Won't Mama worry when she comes home and finds us gone?" Madison asked, speaking softly so as not to startle John Robert, who was sucking his thumb with that drunk-baby look on his face.

"Carlene could do with a little worrying, if you ask me,"

Min said. "The idea, leaving a ten-year-old in charge of a baby and a toddler for two days."

"Somebody probably called off," Madison suggested. "Or maybe Harold Duane asked her to work late."

"The tavern's only open till two. She had no business staying out all night."

"I'm real grown up for my age, Mama says."

Min snorted and rolled her eyes. "I know you are, honey. You're more grown up than your mama. You were born wise."

They swept past the brick-and-stone wall and lighted gateposts that marked the Roper place. Min made a sign with her hand as they passed the broad driveway.

"What's that for?" Madison asked, knowing it was a hex.

Min didn't answer. Min always said good Christians didn't hex people.

"Why do you want to hex the Ropers?" Madison persisted. Brice Roper lived there. He was in her class at school. He had this glow around him like light through rain-smeared glass— the kind of glow rich people had, maybe. Brice had four Arabian horses, and he'd let you ride them if he liked you.

Madison had never been riding at the Ropers.

"The Ropers want our mountain," Min said.

Madison blinked. Booker Mountain? What would they want with that? "But their place is much nicer," she blurted out.

If you liked fancy stone houses with pillars and grassy lawns and miles of white fence. And Arabian horses.

"Coal," Min said bluntly. "Bryson Roper can't get the rest of his coal out of the ground without going through Booker Mountain. And that belongs to me."

They rounded the last curve, past the mailbox that said M. BOOKER, READER AND ADVISER. The pickup rattled to a stop at the foot of the porch steps.

Madison carried John Robert and Min carried Grace. Madison walked flat-footed across the weathered planks of the porch, so she wouldn't get splinters in her bare feet. By the time they'd climbed the steps and crossed the porch and carried the kids to the back bedrooms, Min was breathing hard, her face a funny gray color.

Madison felt the cold kiss of fear on the back of her neck. "Gramma? You all right?"

Min only waved her hand, too breathless to speak. She clawed open the neck of her blouse, revealing the opal necklace she always wore. The one she sometimes let Madison try on.

Once they had the young ones settled in bed, Madison built a fire in the stove and made coffee for both of them. Min didn't even complain about how she made it, which was worrisome.

"It's going to be a cold winter," Min predicted, settling into the only chair with arms, and wrapping a shawl around her shoulders. Some of her color had come back. "More snow than we've had in a long time. A dying time."

When Min predicted anything, it was best to listen. Still, Madison was old enough to wonder how a person who could foretell the future could run into so much bad luck.

Madison liked sitting at the table in the front room, drinking sweet coffee with Min. The stripey cat lay purring in front of the fire. Only one thing would make it better, if Min would only say yes.

"Read the cards for me, Gramma!" Madison begged. Reading the cards was a serious business, her grandmother always said, and not done for the entertainment of young girls.

But Min studied Madison a moment, her pale blue eyes glittering like moonstones, her capable hands wrapped around her mug of coffee, then nodded. "All right. It's time. Fetch the cards from on top of the mantel."

"You mean it?" Madison scrambled down from her chair before Min could change her mind.

Min kept two decks of cards in a battered wooden box with a cross carved into the top. She called them "gypsy cards," but they looked like regular playing cards to Madison, with a few extras. The box also held a leather pouch full of pebbles and little bones, but Madison had never seen Min use those.

Min handed her the thicker deck. Madison shuffled the cards awkwardly, cut them three times, and shuffled again.

"Lay them out in three rows of three," Min said, and Madison did.

Her grandmother flipped them over, the cards slapping softly on the weathered wood of the table.

"Madison Moss." Now her voice was a stranger's, the voice of the reader. "Would you hear the truth?"

"Yes, ma'am," Madison answered, swallowing hard, hoping there wouldn't be anything scary.

Min studied the cards, pushed her glasses down on her nose, and studied them some more. Madison leaned forward, squinting down at them. The center card in each row was a dragon with snaky eyes and a long, twisting tail, brilliant with color, glittering with gilt.

Abruptly, Min scooped them up and handed them back to Madison. "Shuffle again."

Mystified, Madison shuffled and spread them. Dragons again. Min frowned at them. Moved them about with the tips of her fingers. Pulling the leather pouch from the box, she emptied it into her palm. Tossed the pebbles and bones down onto the table. Raked them up and threw them down, muttering to herself.

"What's the matter?" Madison asked, disappointed. "Aren't they working?"

"Oh, child," Min said, shaking her head. The color had left her face again. She extended her trembly hand toward Madison, then drew it back as if afraid to touch her. "Never mind. Let's try something else." Min handed her the smaller, thirty-two-card deck, sevens and up.

Madison shuffled the cards again and set them out in the familiar gypsy spread, three rows of seven cards in pairs. Past, present, and future.

No dragons.

Personally, Madison wasn't all that interested in the past or the present. But she had hopes for the future. She leaned forward eagerly as Min flipped the cards over one by one. Min whispered her reading, as if unsure of herself.

"A squabble over money," she said, turning over the seven of diamonds. In the next pair, the nine of spades lay over the queen of clubs. "The death of a wise woman." A three of diamonds placed over the other two. "A legal letter and a bequest."

Madison was bored by the notion of squabbles about money and legal letters. "Will I ever have a boyfriend?" she demanded. She was already old enough to know she didn't care much for the boys of Coal Grove.

Min turned the face cards up. Two kings. King of clubs

and king of spades. Jack of diamonds. She flipped up the modifiers, stared at them a moment. Seemed like she didn't like what she was seeing. Min gripped both of Madison's hands, leaning in close, her blue eyes like windows to a younger Min enclosed in wrinkly skin.

"Maddie, honey, listen. Beware the magical guilds," she whispered. "Especially wizards."

"Gramma, I don't know any magical gills," Madison said, floundering for understanding.

"Brice Roper," Min said. "He's a bad one. Ain't nothing good about him."

Madison blinked at her. "Old Brice or young Brice?" she asked.

"Young Brice," Min said, which surprised her, because old Brice was scary and mean, and everybody said young Brice had a way about him. People buzzed around young Brice like yellow jackets around lemonade.

"Do not mingle with the gifted, Madison. Do not mess with magic. It's meant nothing but trouble for our family. Swear you won't truck with them."

Min sounded almost like the preacher in the Quonset hut church Madison went to once, who talked about those who trafficked with the devil. "But, Gramma. Aren't the cards magic?" Madison ventured.

"Swear it!" Min squeezed her hands so hard that tears sprang to Madison's eyes.

"All right, I swear!" she said, blinking fast to keep the tears from escaping her eyes and running down her face. She didn't think the Ropers wanted to truck with her, anyway.

Min released Madison's hands. "My wisdom is wasted on

you, child." She looked more sad than mad.

Her gramma looked back at the cards. "I see four pretty witch boys coming. Two will claim your heart in different ways. Two are deceivers who'll come to your door, one dark, one fair. All of them have magic . . ."

By then, Madison had kind of lost track of who was who. Still, this was a *wonderful* fortune, with four pretty boys to dream on.

Min caressed the tiny portraits of the kings with the tips of her fingers. "But, remember this, Madison Moss: they have no power that you don't give away."

❧ CHAPTER ONE ❧
RAVEN'S GHYLL

The wind shrieked down out of Scotland, over Solway Firth, and bullied its way between the peaks and fells of the Cumbrian lakes, driving snow before it. Jason Haley hunched his shoulders against the sleet that needled his face and hands.

Raven's Ghyll spread before him, alternately hidden, then revealed by swirls of cloud and ice. A treacherous sheep path, pricked by cairns of stone, descended toward the valley floor.

His wizard stone thrummed within him, responding to the proximity of the Weirstone. The massive crystalline stone gleamed like a sapphire against the flank of the mountain known as Ravenshead. Blinking snow from his eyelashes, Jason peered up at it. Also known as the Dragon's Tooth, the Weirstone was the source of power for all of the magical Weirguilds.

It had been six hours by car from London to Keswick, over increasingly hazardous roads, fighting the weather and the weird British custom of driving on the left side of the road. By the time he reached Keswick, Jason's eyes were twitchy from peering through the swirling flakes and his arms and shoulders ached from gripping the steering wheel.

That was the easy part.

He'd made the long climb to the top of the ghyll, his feet sliding on the weathered stones despite his spiked climbing boots. He'd had to slide between the sentries posted by the Roses on the surrounding hills. The Wizard Houses of the Red and the White Rose had laid siege to Raven's Ghyll after the lord of the ghyll, Claude D'Orsay, betrayed them on the island of Second Sister.

At least Jason was in good shape, better than he'd ever been. Most wizards were soft, since they used magic to do the heavy lifting. Jason, on the other hand, had been training under the tender hand of Leander Hastings, who favored five-mile runs before breakfast. Jason was only seventeen and Hastings had been around for more than a century, but it still wasn't easy to keep up with the lean wizard.

Turning his back to the wind, creating a small shelter with his body, Jason lit a cigarette. Hastings was always on him about the smoking. But the risk seemed small compared to the danger he was in, here on the edge of the abyss.

He'd be lucky to make it to eighteen. For one thing, there was a good chance Hastings would kill him when he found out what he'd been up to.

Somewhere down below was D'Orsay, renegade wizard and holder of the fraudulent Covenant signed at Second Sister—the document that threatened to enslave them all.

D'Orsay was everything Jason was not: he was a cake-eater, born to privilege, former Master of the Game, heir of an aristocratic Wizard House. Jason was an underpowered street punk, a mixed-blood orphan holding a grudge.

Hopefully D'Orsay had no idea that bad news was coming down the hill toward him. Hopefully no one would expect an intruder on a night like this. Hopefully he could locate the Covenant and be away with it before anyone knew he was there.

If he couldn't find the Covenant, he'd look for D'Orsay's legendary hoard of weapons—the last legacy of Old Magic. That rumor was the only thing keeping the Roses at bay.

At the very least, he'd scope out D'Orsay's fortifications and find out how many wizards protected the ghyll. If he could succeed at any one of those things, Hastings might give him a longer leash.

At least he was *doing* something. Maybe Hastings was content to hang out in London, watching and waiting for somebody to jump. But there was nothing more boring than watching the Roses watch D'Orsay.

When Jason finished his cigarette, he shrugged into his backpack and began the painfully slow descent to the floor of the ghyll. To call it a trail was a stretch—he'd chosen it for its obscurity. D'Orsay couldn't possibly monitor every overgrown sheep track and hiking path that led into the ghyll.

Jason had hoped the weather would let up once he got below the shoulder of the peak, but the biting wind still slammed snow into his face and tugged at his extremities, threatening to rip him off the mountain.

Ahead, a yellowish mist shrouded the trail, close to the ground, strange for the weather and time of day. An odd color for any season. Jason eyed it warily, extended his gloved hand, and spoke a charm. Nothing. He didn't know if the problem was in the charm or in himself. Wasn't that Shakespeare?

He tried a couple more charms without success until the mist grudgingly yielded to his magic, dissolving to shreds that the wind carried away.

By now it was dark in the ghyll below, the peaks around him gilded with the last of the light. Lamps kindled in Raven's Ghyll Castle, at the far end of the valley. The dark shape of it bulked through the swirls of flakes and blowing snow.

He was able to move with greater speed as he neared the bottom, since the sharp verticals gave way to more gradual switchbacks. Until he rounded a corner and blundered into a mess—like a giant cobweb made of thick, translucent cords—nearly invisible in the failing light.

It was a Weirnet, a magical web made to capture the gifted. He tried to back out of it, but it was incredibly sticky, and every move embedded him further.

So much for a surprise attack. Jason forced himself into stillness, moving only his right arm, which he used to fish for his knife. Gripping the hilt, he pulled it free and sliced carefully at the tendrils within reach. The net parted reluctantly. It was designed to resist magic, and he wasn't doing much better with an actual blade.

Something bright streaked across the sky like a comet, then detonated at the height of its arc, flooding the ghyll with phosphorescent light.

Now the fun begins, Jason thought.

It took ten precious minutes to cut himself free. Even then, the opening was just broad enough to slide through.

He knew he should ditch the mission and get out while he could. But his entire life had been a string of bad decisions. He had no desire to slink back to Hastings with the same bad taste in his mouth he'd had since Leicester and D'Orsay killed his father.

He thrust his body through the breach. As he emerged, volleys of wizard flame erupted from the hillside above, and he flung himself sideways. He scrambled on hands and knees into a grove of trees, then turned to look.

All around him, black-clad wizards slipped through the forest, directing withering fire toward the tear in the web.

Jason considered his options. If D'Orsay was smart (and he was), he would stay barricaded inside the hold until the all-clear. D'Orsay's hoard of magical pieces would be in the keep, too. Along with the Covenant that made D'Orsay ruler of all the magical guilds.

To the castle, then. But best not to be noticed.

Jason stuffed his fingers under his coat and pulled out a circlet of dull stone engraved with runes. It was a *dyrne sefa*, meaning secret heart, an amulet of power. Despite the cold, it was hot to the touch, steaming in the brittle air, drawing power from the nearby Weirstone. Stroking the surface with his fingertips, he spoke a charm.

Now rendered unnoticeable, Jason threaded through the woods and across the open meadow of the valley floor toward the castle. Away from the shelter of the ghyll walls, the wind assaulted him again. But now he was impervious to the cold, ignited with power and determination.

The meadow was studded with wind-seared brush, powdered with fine, dry snow, and fissured with ravines. The need to mind his footing warred with the desire to peer about like a tourist.

These must be the tournament fields.

Here the blood of generations of warriors had been shed

in ritual battles that allocated power to the Wizard Houses.

Here the warriors Jack Swift and Ellen Stephenson had fought the tournament that broke the original Covenant and challenged the power of the Roses.

Here the sanctuary of Trinity was born.

More than anything, Jason wanted to make the same kind of mark on the world.

Wizard flares rocketed into the air, lighting the ghyll as if it were midday. Trees went up like torches, sending smoke roiling into the sky. Jason guessed he should be flattered at the intensity of the response to his trespassing. It was like using a shotgun against a gnat. Still the snow fell, glittering in impossible colors as the light struck it.

Ahead loomed the castle, a forbidding stone structure that might have been hewn from the side of the mountain. Terraced gardens surrounded it, littered with the skeletons of winter-dead plants, like the leavings of a failed fair-weather civilization.

Squadrons of wizards charged up and down the valley, magical shields fixed in place, splattering power in all directions. Some passed within a few feet of him, glowing white ghosts in hooded, snow-powdered parkas. Jason continued his stubborn march on the hold.

He'd hoped they'd give up, assuming their intruder had fled. But no. D'Orsay's wizards gathered near the castle, forming a broad phalanx of bristling power. Charms were spoken, and a great wall of poisonous green vapor rolled toward him across the meadow.

Chemical warfare, wizard style.

Swearing softly, Jason disabled the unnoticeable charm so he could use other magic. He extended his hand and tried to reproduce the charm he'd used on the yellow mist. Either he got it wrong, or he simply wasn't strong enough. The cloud kept coming, relentlessly swallowing trees and stones and fleeing animals. There'd be nothing left alive in the ghyll by morning.

His only hope was to get above the cloud. Jason turned, sprinted for the Ravenshead, and began to climb. As the way grew steeper, he had to reach high to find handholds above his head, desperately hauling himself up by insinuating his body into crevices and wedging his feet into the imperfections that marred the stone face of the mountain.

About the time he thought his lungs would burst, he reached a ledge just below the Weirstone and shoved his body up and over. He lay facedown in the snow until he caught his breath, then pulled himself to his feet.

The ghyll below was a sea of mist, a vast polluted cesspool that lapped higher and higher on the surrounding slopes.

Then the earthquakes began. Thunder rumbled through the ghyll, and the stones under Jason's feet rippled like an out-of-control skateboard. The mountain shifted and shuddered, trying to fling him off. Boulders crashed down from above, shaken loose from ancient perches high on the slopes, bouncing past him and disappearing into the sea of mist at the bottom. This was more than wizard mischief. It seemed . . . apocalyptic.

Jason crouched back against Ravenshead, his arms wrapped around his head to fend off falling debris, his gaze drawn back to the blue flame of the Weirstone.

It loomed above his head, a faceted crystal the blue-green color of the deepest and clearest ocean. With the stone so near, blood surged through his body, intoxicating him, heating him down to his fingers and toes. Power battered him from all sides, vibrating in his bones like a crashing bass from a magical band.

As he watched, a jagged crack opened in the solid rock face above him. It yawned wider and wider, a raw gash in the shadow of the stone. Small stones and grit stung his skin and he squeezed his eyes shut to avoid being blinded.

Gradually, the earth quieted and the stone dimmed. Jason opened his eyes. He crept forward and peered over the edge of the rock. The green mist was still inching up the slope.

He sat back on his heels, eyeing the new-made cave. Cool air, flowing from under the Weirstone, kissed his face. Maybe he could worm deeper into the mountain until the mist subsided. Seeing no other choice, he plunged into the opening.

The air was surprisingly fresh to have been bottled up in the mountain for so long. Jason collected light on the tips of his fingers, a makeshift lamp to show the way. As he snaked back into the rock, it became clear that the quake had reopened a cave hewn out of the mountain in centuries past. Scattered across the stone floor was evidence of prior occupation: the bones of large animals, shards of pottery, and metal fittings.

Jason pushed on, the cave wind blowing against his face. Good, he thought. That might keep the mist at bay.

The passage ended in a chamber the size of a large ballroom. Far above, the wind whistled through an opening to the outside. That, then, was the source of the fresh air. Jason tried to push light to the ceiling, but the dark vault soared high overhead, beyond the reach of his puny lamp. The Weirstone glittered, a long shaft driving far into the mountain.

Soot smudged the walls all around, as if from the smoke

of thousands of ancient fires. In one corner bulked a great raised platform, eight feet off the floor. Jason found finger-holds and scrambled to the top.

Here were fragments of fabric: velvets and satins and lace that disintegrated when he touched them. More large bones lay piled neatly in a corner, including what might have been human skeletons. Human and animal skulls grinned out from niches in the wall. He was in the lair of some great predator or the site of a long-ago battle.

At the far end of the platform was a massive oak door.

Jason eyed the door. In a movie, that would be the door you shouldn't open.

But of course you would.

By now, the ghyll, the mist, and the wizards searching for him outside seemed a distant threat. He had to get past that door. Something drew him forward.

Jason pulled the *dyrne sefa* free once again. Using it like an eyepiece, he scanned the entry. It was covered with a delicate labyrinth of glittering threads, invisible to the naked eye. Another kind of web.

Extending his hand, he muttered, *"Geryman."* Open. The door remained shut.

Jason looked about for tools. Lifting one of the long leg bones, he came at the door from the side, extending the bone and poking cautiously through the web of light.

With a sound like a gunshot the door exploded outward in a blast of flame. Had he been standing at the threshold, he would have been incinerated. As it was, he almost wet his pants.

When his rocketing pulse had steadied, he approached the doorway, again from the side, and peered through.

Beyond the entrance was yet another door, set with six panels of beaten gold, each engraved with an image. It took a moment for Jason to realize what he was seeing.

Each engraving depicted one of the Weirguilds. A beautiful woman with rippling hair and flowing robes extended her hands toward Jason, smiling. She obviously represented the enchanters, who had the gift of charm and seduction. A tall, muscled man in a breastplate and kilt charged forward, swinging a sword. That was the warrior, who excelled in battle.

In another scene, an old man gazed into a mirror, tears rolling down his wrinkled cheeks. He must be a sooth-sayer or seer, who could predict the future, though imperfectly. In the fourth, a woman ground roots with a mortar and pestle. She was a sorcerer, expert in the creation and use of magical tools and materials. Finally, a lean-faced man in a nimbus of light manipulated the strings of a marionette who seemed unaware of the puppeteer.

Well, there's the wizard, Jason thought. The only one of the lot who could shape magic with words, and for that reason most powerful.

The center panel, the largest, was engraved with a magnificent dragon, clawed forelegs extended and wings spread.

The legend was that the founders of the magical guilds had originated in the ghyll as cousins, slaves to a dragon who ruled the dragonhold. Eventually, by working together, they'd managed to outsmart the dragon. In some versions they killed it, in others they put it into a magical sleep. They'd renamed the valley Raven's Ghyll, preferring to forget that the dragon had ever existed.

Then four of the cousins were tricked into signing a covenant that made them subservient to the fifth cousin.

The wizard.

By the sixteenth century, the hierarchy of the magical guilds was well established. The ruling wizards had organized themselves into the warring houses of the Red and the White Rose, whose incessant battles decimated the houses over time. The system of tournaments known as the Game had been launched to limit bloodshed among wizards. The Dragon House, to which Jason belonged, harked back to a time before wizards assumed their dominant role.

Jason studied the engraving of the dragon, knowing such pieces often held important clues. The work had been done by Old Magic, using an artistry lost to time. Power seemed to ripple under the dragon's metal scales, and humor and intelligence glittered in its golden eyes. An elaborate cloak poured in glittering folds down the dragon's back, to be caught in the arms of a lady who stood just behind the beast.

The lady was well-dressed for a servant, if that's what she was. Her hair was carefully arranged and she wore a necklace with a single glittering gemstone set into the metal. Although she was tiny next to the dragon, she seemed unafraid. She rested one hand on the dragon's leg in an affectionate way and the dragon's head arced down toward her as if to continue an intimate conversation.

In a faint continuous script around the center panel ran the words, "Enter with a virtuous heart, or not at all."

Well, that shuts me out, Jason thought. Though by wizard standards he might qualify.

Who would have made something so cool and then hidden it in the mountain to be found only by chance? And what lay behind it?

It's no use. You're going in. You can't resist.

Taking a deep breath, extending his hand, he whispered *"Geryman"* again, expecting another detonation.

This time, the double doors swung silently in.

Once again, he used the *dyrne sefa* to examine the entrance for magical traps. And found none. Leading with the leg bone, waving it like a sword, he advanced through the doorway.

It was a storeroom, lined ceiling-high with barrels, chests and casks, strongboxes and coffers, baskets and bins.

He stood blinking stupidly for a moment, then dropped the bone and pried the lid off the nearest barrel. Recklessly thrusting his hand deep, he let the contents trickle through his fingers.

Pearls. In all colors, from precious black to creamy white to pale pink and yellow. Large and round and perfect. These must be worth a fortune, he thought.

He lifted the lid on a small brass-bound chest. Emeralds, in a deep green with fiery hearts. A small gold coffer was filled with diamonds so large that anywhere else he'd assume they were fake.

There were stones in all colors, spools of gold chain, both loose gems and jewels in medieval settings. Coins engraved with the portraits of long-dead kings and queens. Bolts of velvet and satin shrouded in sleeves of sturdy linen. Cabinets filled with parchment scrolls, fragile with age, and books in leather bindings. Paintings in gilded frames were lined four-deep against the walls.

In some of the large baskets he found the best treasure yet: talismans for protection, amulets for power, inscribed with spell runes in the mysterious languages of magic. Many were crafted from the flat black stones familiar from his own collection, the magical pieces he'd inherited from his mother. Others were made of precious metals—devised by methods now lost to the guilds.

They were carelessly jumbled together, and he sorted them into piles, his fingers itching to put them to use. Jason was not particularly powerful, but with these at his disposal, even Raven's Ghyll Castle might fall.

Was this the legendary hoard of weapons? It seemed unlikely. The hoard was said to be a living arsenal, regularly added to and used by the D'Orsays. These things looked like they'd lain untouched for centuries. While some of the *sefa*s could be used as weapons, this was mostly fancy work—jewelry, books, art, gemstones.

Was it possible that D'Orsay didn't know this was here? Totally possible.

Jason leaned against the wall, rubbing his chin. Well, now. It wouldn't do for the Roses or D'Orsay to get hold of it.

He couldn't haul everything out in one trip, but he couldn't count on coming back, either. He might not make it out alive this time. And if he were caught, they'd quickly force the cave's location out of him.

He'd have to focus on smaller items, and choose carefully. He zipped open his backpack and set it on the cave floor.

The magical artifacts were the first priority. He and Hastings and the rest of the Dragon House were in this war for survival. Anything that kept the other Wizard Houses away from the sanctuary at Trinity was golden. The rebels could use these amulets to make the price of conquest too high for Claude D'Orsay or the Roses.

Jason methodically worked his way through the vault, torn between a growing claustrophobia and the fear he'd overlook something critical. He wrapped some of the more fragile and dangerous-looking pieces in strips of cloth he ripped from the bolts of fabric. Then he shoveled magical jewelry, crystals, mirrors, and scrying stones into the backpack, trying to be careful, hoping he wouldn't break anything or inadvertently set something off. It was like loading pipe bombs into a shopping cart.

At the back of the cave, a sword in a jeweled scabbard stood alone, as if its owner had leaned it against the wall, meaning to come back and retrieve it. He gripped the hilt gingerly. The metal tingled in his hand, a kind of magical greeting.

"What have we here?" Jason muttered, feeling a rising excitement.

The hilt and crosspiece were of rather plain make, embellished with a Celtic cross on the pommel, centered with a flat-petaled rose. It was somehow more beautiful for its simplicity. Jason was no warrior, but he recognized quality when he saw it. As he drew the blade from its covering, it seemed to ignite, driving the shadows from the corners.

Could this be one of the seven great blades?

Of the seven, only one other was known to exist: Shadowslayer, the blade carried by Jason's friend, the warrior Jack Swift, of Trinity. Stroking the glittering metal, Jason wished he could marry himself to a weapon the way Jack did.

But, no. Always better to be a wizard than a warrior in the hierarchy of the magical guilds.

Sliding the blade back into its scabbard, he carried it forward and set it next to the bulging backpack. Now what else? he queried the room.

Niches lined the back wall, in the blue shadow of the Dragon's Tooth. Some were empty, some displayed treasures, some were mortared shut. Reasoning that the closed niches might contain the most valuable contents, he took the time to break them open with cautious bits of magic. The mountain shuddered uneasily under the assault. Dirt from above trickled onto his head and shoulders.

A battered wooden chest covered with a tracery of runes stood in an open niche just under the Weirstone. Jason lifted it down to the floor of the cave and pried at the lid. Inside was a collection of scrolls, bound together with linen twine, covered with writing he couldn't decipher. And a large book secured with a jeweled lock.

Jason wasn't much for books, and this one looked awkward and heavy, and who knew if it was worth carrying back with him? Then again, someone had taken the trouble to lock it.

The lock fell apart in his hands, and the ancient binding protested with a crackling sound as he opened it. This was almost too easy. The text was written in a flowing hand by a scribe or scholar. On the title page was scribbled, *Of the Last Days of the Glorious Kingdom and How it Passed Into Memory: A Tragedie.*

Spinning light off his fingers, Jason scanned the first few pages.

It was a journal, kept by the attendant to some ancient ruler, written in the Language of Magic. He almost closed the book and set it aside, but something kept him reading.

My Lady Queen Aidan Ladhra greeted the kings of Gaul in the great keep! How she glittered in the firelight, her jeweled armor burnished bright by my hand. Her terrible beauty transfixed our guests and struck them dumb with awe. They fell on their faces, and only rose when she begged them to do so in the most gentle voice.

They dined with us, and I must say, my Lady was most disappointed in their conversation. She was gracious as always, but her guests were impossible! She brought in musicians, and they ignored them, eating and belching and singing bawdy songs and slipping silver into their pockets. She spoke of art and sorcerie, and they were only confused. They know nothing of magic. . . .

Jason jumped ahead in the text.

My Lady Aidan sent a kind invitation to the Kings of Britain, inviting them to attend her at her winter court. But they came with armies, and with battle machines of all kinds, and sent an envoy demanding her surrender. It was a patronizing message; clearly they thought her to be stupid and incapable of negotiation. I am afraid my Lady was so nettled that she killed the messenger on the spot and ate him for supper. Then destroyed the armies that came after.

Whoa.

Jason skipped forward again.

Failing in her attempt to find friends among the existing kingdoms, and discouraged by their responses to her friendly overtures, my Lady Aidan has decided to create her own community of peers, artists and scholars gifted with the use of magic, a talent that will pass to their children. I have seen the future in my glass, and I've told her this is risky, but my Lady is lonely with only my poor self for companionship. As for me, I require no gift other than her presence.

The mountain groaned and shifted overhead. Although it was cool in the cave, Jason blotted sweat from his face with his sleeve. Conscious of passing time, he hurriedly turned over the fragile pages, his damp fingers leaving spots.

My Lady Aidan tires of the constant disputes among those she has gifted with power. Where she sought companionship, she has gained only troubles. Priceless talents she has given to all, yet they each are jealous of the others. I fear they are conspiring against her, particularly the wizard Demus, who shapes magic with words. I see them cast envious eyes on the treasure she has accumulated. But she will have none of my warnings. She considers these squabblers her children, rightly or wrongly, and will hear no evil about them.

Somewhere along the underground passage, Jason heard rock crash against rock. It was time to go, and he still didn't know if the book was worth taking. He flipped to the back, looking for the last entry. It appeared to have been scrawled in haste, the pages stained and blurred, as if spotted with tears.

It has happened, as I predicted. Demus and the other ungrateful vipers have poisoned us. My Lady retreated to the great hall in Dragon's Ghyll to die. I tended her as best I could, but there was nothing I could do. She expired a few hours ago.

She dies childless. Before she passed into sleep, she gave into my hands the Dragonheart, which is now the source of power for all the magical guilds. Despite all, she still has hopes for them. Over my objections, she named me Dragon Heir, and charged me and my descendants to hold the guilds in check and prevent them from visiting destruction on each other and the world. I promised I would to ease her passing, though I am dying myself. I have no love for this task. I would wish that my children have nothing to do with the gifted.

When I hold the Dragonheart stone in my hands, it is as if my mistress still lives. The flame of her spirit burns at its center, safer in this vessel than in any fleshly home, powerful enough to destroy all of her enemies. I only wish I were strong enough to use it.

The dragonhold is surrounded. My children have scattered to the four winds. I dare not send a message to them lest it be intercepted, tho' I have sent along some small items of value by trusted courier.

Truly, I harbor the bitter and rebellious hope that they thrive and prosper in ignorance of their charge.

Before I die beside my mistress, I will bury the Dragonheart stone in the mountain with such protections as I can lend it. Perhaps chance will put it into the possession of one with the heart and desire to release its full power. That person will seize control of the gifts that have been given. That person will once again reign over the guilds. Or destroy them, as they deserve.

Jason rested the book on his knees. Was this just another of the fantastical legends created to explain a rather twisted heritage?

He set the book aside and peered again into the hollow in the rock, illuminating the niche with the light at his fingertips.

At the back of the niche stood an elaborate pedestal of intricately worked metal, topped by an opal the size of a softball. Gingerly, Jason reached into the niche and lifted the stone off its base.

Jason sat back on his heels, cradling the stone between his hands. It was ovoid in shape, glittering with broad flashes of green and blue and purple fire. It was perfect, crystalline, no flaws in it that he could see. It warmed his fingers, as if flames actually burned at its center, and seemed to hum with power. Long minutes passed while he gazed into its heart, mesmerized. A pulsing current seemed to flow between the stone in his hands and the Weirstone in his chest, reinforcing it. Like the Dragon's Tooth set into the mountain, only . . . portable.

A performance enhancer? Exactly what he needed.

Leaning forward again, he pulled the metal base from the niche. It was a tangle of mythical beasts, or maybe one mythical beast with multiple heads. Dragons.

Feeling a little giddy, Jason dumped agates from a velvet bag and dropped the stone inside. Ripping a piece of crimson velvet from a bolt, he wrapped the stand carefully. He stuffed them into his backpack. This is mine, he thought.

Sorting quickly through the jewelry, he chose several interesting pieces, including a large gold earring for himself; a Celtic star. He poked loose jewels and jewelry into the empty corners of the bag, then zipped the pack shut. He slung the backpack over one shoulder, listing a little under the weight. He hung the sword in its scabbard over the other shoulder and slid the massive book under one arm. He wished he could carry more.

Around him, the mountain grew increasingly restless, groaning as rock slid against rock, sifting sand and pebbles onto the stone floor. It was as if the Ravenshead recognized the thief at its heart and meant to stop him. Jason was overcome by the notion that he had stayed too long.

He stepped out between the double doors, and they slammed shut behind him.

Great cracks fissured the stone vault overhead, spidering out ahead of him.

Uh-oh.

He charged back toward the entrance to the cave, leaping over debris, dodging falling rock and gravel, twisting and turning down the narrow passageway, feeling the pitch and shudder of the rock beneath his feet. Ahead he saw light, meaning he was almost through.

The mountain shimmied, shivered and quaked. Slivers of stone stung his face. Up ahead, he was horrified to see that the two great slabs of rock that had split to open the cave were sliding, slumping toward one another. The wedge of light was disappearing. He'd be trapped inside the Ravenshead.

He squeezed himself through the collapsing entrance, sliding like an eel, clutching the book close to his body, scraping his elbows and knees, smashing his hands, twisting to free the loaded backpack, dragging the sword after him, metal fittings sparking against stone.

And then he was out, clinging to the icy ledge at the entrance to the cave as the mountain snapped shut behind him.

Jason lay on his face on the rock—the sword, the book, and the backpack beside him, his battered hands leaving bloody smears in the snow.

He allowed himself a few more minutes rest before he levered himself into a sitting position and snuck a look over the edge.

The one-sided battle seemed to be over. The greenish mist was dissipating, shredding into long streamers that swirled away on the wind. The forest still smoldered on the slopes of the ghyll. Wizard fire was notoriously hard to put out.

Jason leaned back against Ravenshead and pulled out another cigarette. He had trouble lighting it. His hands were shaking, and not from the cold. The stone in his backpack provided all the warmth he needed. Somehow, he had to get it out of the ghyll.

Using bungee cords, he bound the book to the outside of the backpack, distributing the weight as best he could. Then he lay down and slept restlessly, the magical stone illuminating his dreams.

* * *

Jason waited until the darkest hour before morning, giving the deadly mist more time to clear. Then he crept down the rockface, fighting the weight of his awkward burden, the sword catching in underbrush and crevices. He breathed out a long sigh of relief when he reached the valley floor.

Raven's Ghyll Castle was still brilliantly lit, and Jason could see dark figures moving along the walls, no doubt on the alert for a possible attack. Jason weighed the risk of going back the way he came against finding a new way out. He decided to take his chances on the path he knew.

Jason made himself unnoticeable and picked his way up the valley, the weight of the backpack becoming more and more apparent as he struggled along. Every so often the sound of quiet conversation or a faint light through the trees told him there were wizards keeping watch in the woods around him. When he reached the base of the trail, he turned upslope, walking even more carefully. He squinted against the wind, searching the inky shadows under the canopy of pines.

He was so numb with cold, he scarcely felt the trip wire when he brushed it. He was immediately engulfed in a bright, glittering cloud, his formerly unnoticeable self totally revealed, in brilliant outline.

"Ha!" The voice came from behind him.

Acting totally on instinct, Jason dropped the unnoticeable charm and threw up a shield in time to turn a gout of blistering wizard flame. He swung round to confront his attacker.

It was a boy, younger than him, thirteen, maybe, almost pretty, pale blue eyes behind wire rim glasses, snow powdering his blond curls.

Well, crap, Jason thought. The *plan* was to get out without being spotted.

"I knew you must've gone unnoticeable," the boy crowed. "There's no way you'd have got through Father's guards otherwise."

Jason had stepped off-trail to circle around this new obstacle, but the boy's words stopped him. "*Father's* guards," Jason repeated. "Who the hell are you?"

"I'm Devereaux D'Orsay," the boy said. "I live here. Who are you?"

"Geoffrey Wylie," Jason said, producing the first wizard name that came to mind. The Red Rose wizard could use a little street cred, anyway.

"You are trespassing, Mr. Wylie," Devereaux D'Orsay said. He extended his hand imperiously. "Hand over the sword and the backpack."

"Ri–ight," Jason said. He went to turn away and Devereaux flung out an immobilization charm that Jason managed to deflect, though it left him stunned and reeling. The kid had talent. Unfortunately.

The boy frowned, drawing himself up to his puny height. "You. Come with me. I'm taking you down to the hold. Father and I will interrogate you and find out what you are doing here and for whom you're working."

Jason sighed, releasing a plume of vapor. He and Seph McCauley had killed Gregory Leicester in self defense. He figured he could kill Claude D'Orsay without losing any sleep over it. But not a thirteen-year-old kid. And that meant he'd be leaving a witness behind.

"Just go away, okay?" Jason said, wearily, "and let's forget this ever happened."

This seemed to enrage Devereaux D'Orsay. He flung himself at Jason, managing to penetrate his shield and knock him off his feet. They rolled together into a small ravine, a cartoon tangle of arms and legs. Devereaux ripped at him, pulling on the cords around the backpack until the book came free and tumbled loose into the snow.

Jason punched the kid in the nose and blood poured out, distracting little D'Orsay enough so Jason could lay an immobilization charm on him. He managed to extricate himself and stood, looking down at Claude D'Orsay's immobilized son, wishing he could make him disappear.

"Say hi to Claude for me," he muttered. "Tell him I'll stop by again." There was no time to look for the lost book. Their magical fracas wouldn't have gone unnoticed. Energized by the desire to stay alive, Jason loped up the trail, heading for the road back to Keswick, conscious of the mysterious stone in his backpack.

Behind him, the great shoulder of the mountain lay shrouded in unbroken darkness. The flame at the heart of the Dragon's Tooth had gone out.

↫ CHAPTER TWO ↬
SANCTUARY

Madison Moss picked her way across the icy street, clutching her portfolio close to her body so it wouldn't catch the wind. The "uniform" she wore for her waitress job at the Legends Inn—a long swishy skirt and lacy Victorian blouse—was impractical for navigating small town sidewalks in a north-eastern Ohio winter.

Over top, she wore a fleece-lined barn coat she'd found at the Salvation Army, and on her feet were a pair of tooled red leather boots she'd bought at a sidewalk sale downtown. That was in September, when she'd felt rich.

Now she had $10.55 in her coat pocket. Her book and supply list for spring semester totaled $455.79 plus tax. She could've probably ordered online for less, but her credit card was still maxed out from fall.

Back in her room was a bill for health insurance—$150—required by Trinity College. The kinds of jobs her mother, Carlene, could find didn't offer benefits.

What else? The transmission in Madison's old pickup was going. She could still get it moving by gunning the engine and shifting directly into second gear from a dead stop.

If she was at home, she'd talk some shade-tree mechanic into fixing it. He'd be afraid to say no. Afraid his shop or house might burn down with his family inside of it.

There were some advantages to being named a witch.

Madison's stomach clenched up in a familiar way until she could push that thought out of her mind. She was trying to keep too many worries at bay. It was like one of those games at the arcade where the alligators pop up and you slam them with a mallet before they can bite you.

Even with the state paying the tuition for courses she was taking for college credit, and even though she was living with her cousin Rachel for free, and even though she was working as many hours as Rachel would give her at the Legends Inn, she was broke and getting broker. Christmas was coming and she didn't have any presents for Grace or John Robert or Carlene.

Or Seph.

She glanced at her watch and walked faster. Trinity Square was a holiday postcard from the past: snowy commons surrounded by the weathered stone buildings of the college, bows and greenery draped over the old-fashioned street lamps. Quaint storefronts glittered with their holiday offerings and shoppers hustled by with bundles and bags.

Totally perfect.

Totally annoying.

But better than home. Back in Coalton County, she was the subject of sermons in hangdog little churches where sweaty-handed preachers used her as a bad example. "Witch," they shouted. And whispered, "Firestarter." People crossed the street when they saw her coming. They collected into prissy little groups after she passed by, like gossiping starlings.

Trinity's sidewalks were crowded with glittering people whose magic glowed through their skins like Christmas lights through layers of snow. They were mostly Anawizard Weir—members of the non-wizard magical guilds who'd taken refuge from the war in the sanctuary of Trinity.

It was a war unnoticed by the Anaweir—non-magical people—but the bloodletting had spread all over the world. It was a running battle between shifting factions of wizards, the nightmare the Covenant had been intended to prevent. Those in the underguilds who refused to participate had fled to Trinity—and were deemed rebels because of it.

Madison didn't shine, so they never gave her a second glance.

The scents of cinnamon and patchouli teased her nose as she stepped into the warm interior of Magic Hands, the consignment art shop on the square. Iris Bolingame was at her worktable in the back, soldering glass. Iris was a wizard with stained glass. Literally.

"Hey, Maddie," Iris said, setting down her work and washing the flux from her hands. "I have to tell you—people love your work. It's been attracting a lot of interest."

Madison fingered the beaded earrings hanging from the Christmas tree on the counter and gazed longingly at the jewelry in the glass showcase. "I was just—you know—I wanted to see if any of my pieces sold."

"Hmmm." Iris came forward to the counter and riffled through the card file. "Let's see. Three prints, one watercolor, four boxes of notecards." She looked up at Madison. "Wow. In just two weeks. That's great, huh?"

"I was wondering if I could get the money now."

Iris hesitated. "We usually wait until the end of the month and process all the checks at once, but if it's an emergency . . ."

"Never mind," Madison said, pretending to examine the kaleidoscopes on the counter. "I was just going to do some shopping is all." Traitorous tears burned in her eyes. I hate this, she thought, and I've done it all my life. Scraping, scrimping, making excuses.

"Are you all right, honey?" Madison looked up and met Iris's worried eyes.

"I'm fine," she whispered, willing Iris not to call her on it.

The wizard impulsively reached out for her, then yanked her hand back at the last moment, pretending to fuss with the ornaments that dangled from her long braid. Iris hadn't been at Second Sister, but she'd certainly heard about it. Wizards were wary of a person who could suck the magic right out of them.

It's like I have an incurable disease, Maddie thought, and no one knows how contagious it is. Not even me.

"If you have anything else you'd like to place here . . ." Iris's cheeks were stained pink with embarrassment.

Madison straightened, lifted her chin, cleared her throat. "Actually, there's something I'd like to take back, for now, anyway." Madison shuffled through the bin of matted drawings, pulled one out, and slid it into her portfolio. She brought the sticker to Iris, who noted it on Maddie's card. "I have a few other prints back in my room. I'll bring them in tomorrow."

She left Magic Hands and turned down Maple, kicking

at chunks of ice thrown up by the snowplow, heading for the high school.

With any luck, she'd bring in some tips that evening at the Legends. Business was usually slow in the winter, but not this year. This year Trinity was like Aspen at the holidays. That's what cousin Rachel said, anyway. She'd been there, once, at an innkeepers' convention.

Classes were just letting out at Trinity High School, and students were clattering down the steps, splintering off into adjacent streets and climbing onto buses. A few of them waved—it was a small town, after all, and they'd seen her with hometown boy Jack Swift and his friends Harmon Fitch and Will Childers.

Some of the girls studied her appraisingly, no doubt wondering what the exotic Seph McCauley saw in her. But most of the faces were empty of opinions about her. Trinity might be a small town, but compared to Coal Grove, it was a metropolis.

Clutching that welcome cloak of anonymity around her, Madison cut through the school's crowded lobby to the main office.

She pulled a manila envelope out of her portfolio and handed it to the secretary. "For Mr. Penworthy," she said. "Progress reports from Dr. Mignon for the grading period."

"Dr. Mignon is supposed to send those directly to me, Miss Moss," Mr. Penworthy said from the doorway of his office. "I've told you that before."

The Trinity High School principal wore high heeled boots, a Western belt with a silver buckle, and a string tie. Madison glanced down at her own fancy boots and shrugged. It was all about scale and context. That's what she told herself, anyway.

Madison paused before she spoke, afraid of what would leak out. "I . . . I'm sorry, sir," Madison said. "She insisted I give this to you. Said she wanted me to be in the loop. Said to call her if you had any questions."

The principal hadn't liked the idea of supervising Madison's post-secondary program from the start, even though all he had to do was handle the paperwork.

Mr. Penworthy snatched the envelope away from his secretary and waved it at Madison. "How do I know your grades haven't been tampered with?"

Madison bit back the first words that came to mind. "Well. Um. I guess you could call her. Sir." She practically curtsied as she backed out of the office.

You can't afford to get into any more trouble, she said to herself. You came up here to make a fresh start.

It had started at Coal Grove High School, with notes left on her locker and slipped into her backpack, and text messages flying around. Stories that claimed Madison Moss was a witch. Not the white witch or granny woman traditional in those parts. No. Maddie was an evil, diabolical harpy who would suck your soul out through your ear and hex your garden or ensnare your boyfriend.

She had no clue where it was coming from, but the gossip was widespread and persistent. Kids made signs against the evil eye in the hallway when she passed. Girls tried to get a lock of her hair to use for love charms. Boys dared each other to ask her out.

It wasn't even like people still believed in that kind of thing. It was more like everybody was moonstruck or something. Madison tried to ignore it, hoping it would wear off or that some other scandal would come up to talk about.

Then the fires started. At first, it was tumbledown barns, sheds, and haystacks that went up like tinder, all around the county. Later, it was occupied barns and hunting cabins and country churches. There was no putting the fires out. Everything burned to the dirt. The perpetrators marked each site with a witchcraft symbol—a pentacle, an elven cross, a chalice. Madison didn't even know what they meant until she looked them up at the library.

Fear swept across the county, and suspicion focused on Booker Mountain, fed by the rumors that had gone round before. The police came out and looked for clues, though they didn't seem sure what to look for. Someone left a cauldron filled with blood in the barnyard. People left threatening messages on their phone (when they had a phone.) Someone sneaked into the family graveyard on Booker Mountain and broke some of the headstones, scribbled threats and profanity on others. A delegation from the Foursquare Church performed an exorcism in front of their gate until Madison brought out Jordie's shotgun and waved it at them.

That didn't help.

It was a nightmare that got worse and worse. Carloads of thrill seekers started following her around, hoping to catch her in the act. People refused to serve her in restaurants, and refused to be served by Carlene. What friends she had melted away.

Carlene was finally moved to action when it looked like she'd lose her job. She called Rachel, and Rachel offered Madison room and board and a job in Trinity. And her art teacher, Ms. McGregor, told Madison how she could use college credit to graduate from high school. Madison left Coalton County at the end of her junior year.

And just like that, the fires stopped. Which confirmed her guilt, some said.

Her gut twisted up and she shoved the memory away. She was done with that.

The hallways had cleared by the time she left the office, and the busses were gone. She eyed the students hanging out on the front steps, thinking she might see Seph's tall, spare form among them. But no. He'd said he'd meet her at Corcoran's and she was already late. Luckily, it was just down the block. She crossed the parking lot and headed up the street.

She stamped the snow off her boots in front of Corcoran's Diner, glaring at the plastic reindeer mounted on the door, its lighted nose glowing cheerfully in the waning afternoon light. The bells mounted on its collar jangled as she pushed the door open.

Corcoran's was jammed with the usual after-school crowd. Madison scanned the room—the red leatherette booths along the side, the battered stools at the soda fountain.

No Seph.

Madison checked her watch. She was twenty minutes late. Maybe he'd come and gone? She flipped open her cell phone. No messages.

Harmon Fitch and his girlfriend, Rosie, were huddled over Fitch's laptop at their usual table in the front window.

Fitch looked up. "Hey, Maddie. Pull up a chair."

He turned the laptop toward Rosie, who flung back her long dreadlocks and began typing furiously. Probably hacking into the Pentagon.

Madison shook her head. "Thanks. I can't stay. I have to get to work." She shifted from one foot to the other.

Rosie passed the notebook back to Fitch. He studied the

screen and grinned savagely. "Brilliant. Let's try this." His fingers flickered over the keyboard, entering strings of letters and numbers.

"Um. Have you seen Seph?" She tilted the portfolio toward Fitch. "He was supposed to meet me here. I have something for him."

Fitch's fingers never stopped moving. "Last I saw him was second period, sleeping through class, as usual. He cut Calculus this afternoon."

"He what?"

Fitch left off typing and leaned back in his chair, regarding her thoughtfully. "He didn't show for Math, and he wasn't on the absent list. You been keeping him up late or what?"

Madison flinched, feeling the blood rush to her face. "Wasn't me." Then who? She fought back a wave of jealousy. She'd been avoiding Seph, making excuses. She couldn't complain if he hung out with someone else.

Fitch shrugged and leaned over his computer again. "Anyway, he's in trouble. Garrity was pissed. It's the third time this semester."

Fear pricked at her, warring with guilt. It wasn't like him to miss class.

Maybe he was sick.

Even worse, maybe he was sick because of her.

But how could that be, when she hadn't seen him in days? He'd texted her yesterday, asking for help with an art project. He wouldn't ask unless he was desperate. She couldn't say no.

"Well, if he comes in, could you tell him to call me?"

She tried his cell phone, but it went to voice mail. She left a message.

Where else could he be? Could he have forgotten?

In desperation, she walked all the way to Perry Park, though it was little used in the wintertime. Seph was nowhere to be seen, but she came upon the warriors Jack Swift and Ellen Stephenson, drilling their ghost army in a secluded clearing in the woods.

She found them by following the sounds of combat. Jack had put up one of those wizard enclosures to keep nosy people away, in the unlikely event that nosy people were out walking in the woods in mid-December. But Madison was an elicitor. Magic and its illusions didn't work on her. She just sponged it up, then it dribbled back out, totally out of her control.

There in the meadow was Jack Swift, his long gold-red hair tied back with a leather strip, leading two dozen warriors across the snowy field in a howling charge. To be met by Ellen Stephenson and *her* two dozen, a bristling wall of swords and shields.

There was no sign of Seph.

It was a motley collection of soldiers, with armor and weaponry drawn from two centuries of warfare. Their weapons glittered in the frail winter sun, their breath was pluming into the cold air. The warriors collided with a bone-shattering thud into a melee of arms and legs and deadly weapons. Blood splattered across the snow, and vintage curses and challenges in a half-dozen languages rang through the trees as individual warriors tried to free themselves from the press of bodies so they could use their swords.

Jack extricated himself, clearing a great space around him with his sword, Shadowslayer. The blade flickered like a flame in the gloom under the trees. Ellen spun in under his reach, her sword somehow finding an opening in his defenses. The flat of her blade slammed into his ribs, raising a spray of snow.

"A hit!" she crowed. "A palpable hit. Do you yield?"

"*Barely* palpable," Jack growled, driving her back furiously. Sparks flew as their blades collided and their heated bodies steamed in the frigid air. Their boots churned the meadow into a thick pudding of mud and ice.

Madison was fascinated in spite of herself. Tall, muscular Jack was a pleasure to watch any time. He and Ellen were longtime dancing partners whose bodies moved to a savage melody no one else heard.

It was like a lifesize video game, a gut-wrenching bout between the living and the dead. They might be injured—even mortally during these skirmishes—but everyone rose whole at the end of the day, if not without aches and pains.

Finally, Jack pivoted and struck Ellen's sword a massive, two-handed blow, sending it flying out of her hands. Jack came on, grinning, sword extended, backing Ellen into a tree. "So, Warrior, do *you* yiel . . . hey!" he yelped as Ellen let fly with her sling, and a fist-size rock struck him on the shoulder.

Ellen hated to lose.

Jack finally noticed Madison, lurking in the fringes of the trees. "Madison! Where'd you come from?" Side-stepping a tall warrior in buckskins who lunged at him with a hatchet, he raised his hand. "Hold!" he shouted.

The fighting dwindled into late hits and skirmishes, then subsided.

The spell was broken. Madison jammed her hat down over her ears. "Don't let *me* interrupt."

Jack and Ellen looked at one another, as if each hoped

the other would speak. Madison didn't approve of any of the frenetic preparations going on in Trinity, and they knew it. The gifted were a club from which Madison was excluded.

Jack cleared his throat. "We're, you know, drilling. In case the other Wizard Houses try to break into the sanctuary."

Madison hunched her shoulders like she could disappear into her coat. "They're *not* coming here. They wouldn't."

"They're fighting other places," Ellen pointed out. "Kidnapping sorcerers to help in the war. Stockpiling weapons."

True. But. Madison jerked her head at the motley army. "If the Roses do come—which they won't—what are you going to do? Do you really think you'll be able to hold them off with *this* sorry lot?" As soon as she said it, she regretted it. Her mother, Carlene, always said Madison's manners were two steps behind her wicked tongue.

Like Carlene was an example for anyone.

"Well," Jack said. He and Ellen exchanged glances again. "We have to try."

"Maybe you should buy some assault rifles, then," Madison suggested sarcastically. "And rocket-propelled grenades."

"Assault rifles don't work against wizards, unless you take them by surprise," Ellen said. She'd been raised by wizards, outside of the usual teen social circles, so sarcasm often went right by her. "Their shields can totally turn non-magical attacks. But a warrior can take a wizard in a magical battle on a level playing field."

"Well, I think it's a waste of . . ." Sensing a presence, she swung around. The buckskin-clad warrior was right behind her, rudely eavesdropping on the conversation. "Did you *want* something?"

He swept off his hat and managed a creditable little bow. "My name's Jeremiah Brooks, ma'am," he said. "I don't believe we've been introduced."

Madison squinted up at him. He was very tall and smelled of sweat, leather, and gunpowder.

"I'm Maddie Moss."

"Pleased to make your acquaintance, ma'am. If I may say so, you just might be the prettiest girl in town." Jeremiah Brooks smiled, a long, slow, droop-lidded smile.

"Jeremiah lived near here in the 1780s," Jack explained. "He was kidnapped by the Roses and died at Raven's Ghyll in 1792."

"Is that so, Mr. Brooks?" Madison asked, for lack of anything else to say. Of course it was so. Mr. Jeremiah Brooks was a ghost. She was being hit on by somebody who'd been dead for more than 200 years. These sorts of things were a dime a dozen in Trinity, Ohio.

Brooks dismissed his death with a wave of his hand. "Miz Moss, if you'd care to go dancing with me tonight, you'll see there's some life left in me yet."

"I don't date dead people," Madison said, glaring at the ghost warrior. "That's where I draw the line." These ghosts were just a little too substantial as far as she was concerned. They ate, drank, fought . . . and danced, apparently. Except for their odd mode of dress and the weapons they carried, you couldn't tell them from live people.

Jack grinned. "Better watch yourself, Brooks. Maddie's going out with my cousin. The most powerful wizard I know."

Brooks paled under his stubble of beard. "I'm sorry, ma'am. No offense meant. You didn't seem like the kind to . . . I had no way of knowing that . . ."

"We're not going out." Madison scowled at Jack, who shrugged and raised his eyebrows at Ellen.

Madison tried again. "I mean, we're just . . . friends. Good friends. To be honest, I've barely seen him lately." *You're running on at the mouth. Stop it.*

Brooks lifted an eyebrow. "Well, watch yourself, Miz Moss. I don't know that you can be friends with a wizard. They've been known to take advantage of young ladies. If you take my meaning."

Madison gave him a look, then turned to Jack and Ellen. "*Anyway.* We were supposed to meet an hour ago. You haven't seen him, have you?"

Jack shook his head. "I don't see him anymore, either. He and Nick are totally caught up with maintaining the boundary."

While the warriors played their war games, the wizards of Trinity had established an invisible barrier to suppress attack magic within the sanctuary. The maintenance of it seemed to demand a huge amount of energy. And time.

"I still don't get why we need a special boundary now, when we never did before," Madison said.

"Well, the ban on attack magic is written into the Covenant, but I guess now nobody knows whether it's in force or not," Jack said, "or when D'Orsay might consecrate his new Covenant. Things are kind of up in the air."

Madison stamped her feet, finding that her fancy boots were not much protection against the cold. "Well, I was supposed to help him with an art project, but he didn't show."

Jack and Ellen shifted their feet in the beaten-down snow, obviously eager to get back to their scrimmage. "If we see Seph, we'll tell him you're looking for him," Ellen offered.

Madison jammed her hands in her pockets, trying to warm them. "It's getting late anyway. I need to get to work. See you."

The clatter of fighting resumed before she made it out of the clearing.

Now she had only an hour before her shift started. She'd try Seph's Aunt Becka's, then move on to the waterfront. If he wasn't at either of those places, she'd have to go on to work.

Nothing could have happened to him. He'd just gotten hung up. Like usual. He had to be safe within the sanctuary. There was a boundary up, after all. No attack magic.

All the while knowing that, within the sanctuary at least, the biggest threat to Seph McCauley was Madison Moss and the magic that leaked from her fingers.

A memory surfaced, the battle at the inn at Second Sister, a scene painted in lurid orange hues. Gregory Leicester smiled, extending his wizard hands, launching flaming death at Seph. Maddie had stepped between them, catching the full force of the attack. She'd reeled in the magic while the wizard struggled on the end of her line like a bluegill at Jackson Lake. Leicester had fallen, along with all of his captive wizards.

She'd been left contaminated. The bitter taste of hex magic lingered on the back of her tongue and seeped out through her pores, a virulent and deadly poison made just for Seph.

After their return from Second Sister, he'd complained of

headaches, stomach pains, fatigue. He broke out in welts and rashes, and grew thin and pale and hollow-eyed, as if he had some wasting disease.

At first Madison thought it was the aftermath of the ordeal on the island. She assumed time would heal him, but he only got worse. His hands shook and his changeable eyes went cloudy and dull and twice he fainted at school.

Seph's parents took him to England for Christmas and he seemed to improve, but took ill again when he came back to Trinity. His mother, Linda, fussed over him and called in the healer Mercedes Foster, who prescribed fresh air and sun-shine and good food and potions and amulets that did no good. When Mercedes finally put him to bed, Madison spent long hours sitting with him, reading to him, holding his hand. She guessed she wasn't much of a nurse, because he only seemed to grow weaker.

Then Madison went home for a week during fall break. When she came back, Seph was out of bed and feeling bet-ter. He looked like a different person, more like his old self.

But not for long. And that was when she knew.

Sometimes she wondered if she was possessed. She could feel something evil inside her react to Seph's presence, like a serpent uncoiling. Her touch was toxic. No one else seemed to make the connection, least of all Seph. And if they found out . . .

So she began avoiding him, avoiding his touch especially, making excuses. And dying inside every time.

Madison turned onto Jefferson Street, negotiating the icy bricks. Jefferson was lined with tall oaks and gracious "painted ladies." That's what they called these Victorian houses iced with turrets, spindles, and wraparound porches.

Jack shared an elegant green-shingled Queen Anne with his mother.

Jack's mother, Becka, and Seph's mother, Linda, were sisters in a family full of secrets. Linda was an enchanter, a master of charisma—seduction, some said. Becka was Anaweir—she wasn't magical, and she knew nothing about the magic going on all around her.

Madison paused at the foot of the driveway. Seph's car was parked next to the side entrance.

She knocked on the screen door. No answer. Pounded on the inside door. Nothing. She tried the knob, and it was unlocked.

"Anybody home?" she called, pushing the door open and poking her head into the foyer.

He was in there somewhere. She could feel his presence in the acceleration of her heartbeat, a faint vibration in her bones.

Witch boy.

She crossed the foyer and passed down the hallway to the family room at the rear. And froze in the doorway.

Seph lay sprawled on the rug in front of the hearth. His face beneath the dark curls was pale and chiseled as porcelain, save the dark smudges under his eyes. He was frowning, lips parted, as if he'd succumbed between two words. For a terrible moment, she thought he was dead, until she saw the faint rise and fall of his chest.

"Good day, Maddie." The wizard Nick Snowbeard half-rose from his chair in the hearth corner and draped a quilt over Seph, then settled back into his seat by the fire. "It is a pleasure to see you, as always."

She dropped to her knees next to Seph, her heart

clamoring in her chest, worrying she was somehow responsible. "What happened? Is he . . . ?"

The old caretaker tilted his head, looking surprised. "Why, my dear, he's sleeping, of course, though he isn't particularly happy about it."

Madison looked at Seph, as if he might have a comment, then back at Snowbeard. Worry turned to irritation. "He's taking a *nap*? We were supposed to meet two hours ago."

"The boy is exhausted. He's overextended himself, maintaining the boundary twenty-four hours a day." The old wizard pressed his fingers between his briared eyebrows, as if he had a headache. Old Bear, the gifted called him, or sometimes, the Silver Bear. He did resemble a slightly rumpled bear rousted from his den in midwinter.

"It was a breakdown in communications," Snowbeard went on. "Too much to do, and too few people to do it. Hastings is away, and I was . . . unexpectedly delayed. I had no idea he'd been on his own so long, and it's not in his nature to ask for help. But now I've relieved him, and I put him to sleep, over his protest."

Madison leaned forward, clutching her skirts in her fists. "He's always falling asleep in school. Plus, he missed a lot of school back in the fall, when he was so sick." *And whose fault was that?* "I didn't think you were allowed to work somebody to death like this. I guess there aren't any child labor laws for wizards."

Snowbeard lifted a teacup from the side table and took a long swallow. He set it back on the saucer with trembling hands, china clattering against china. "My dear, I am . . . sorry. Although he is young, he is the most powerful wizard we have at our disposal, aside from his father and me. Iris is willing, but she just isn't strong enough to manage the boundary for long. It's incredibly draining. There are others who are not particularly trustworthy. Most wizards have sided with the Roses or D'Orsay. Many of the Dragon partisans don't consider the sanctuary to be a priority, now that the war's broken out."

"But you do."

"I think we need a place of safety, yes, or we'll be ground to dust between the stones of wizard ambition. Have you noticed that the town is full of gifted refugees?"

Of course she'd noticed. These were well-educated people, people with money, gifted artists who moved into shops around the square. The Wizard Houses considered them rebels for their refusal to support the war. And the more non-wizard Weir crowded in, the more Trinity seemed like a target. Which didn't fit in with Madison's plans at all.

She sat next to Seph with her back against the hearth, conscious of maintaining some small space between them. The snow from her boots melted into puddles on the hard-wood floor. "I wish you wouldn't let all those people in here."

"You can hardly blame them for seeking sanctuary," Nick said. "Wizards are snatching up the non-wizard Weir all over the world, recruiting them for the war effort. They need sorcerers to build weaponry, warriors to wield it, seers to look into the future and plan strategy, enchanters for espionage purposes."

He sighed. "This can only spell disaster. For centuries, wizards haven't dared to openly war on each other, for fear of breaking the Covenant and rousing the dragon that sleeps in Raven's Ghyll. I suppose wizards don't believe in dragons—or the Covenant—anymore." The old man's voice trailed off.

Madison struggled to keep the skepticism off her face. Dragons. Right. There were plenty of real-life monsters to fight.

Madison looked down at Seph. His face was a work of art that required intensive study. She was glad to be able to do it when he wasn't looking back with those green eyes that missed nothing. She resisted the temptation to trace his cheekbones and strong nose with her forefinger. If Seph had some kind of reaction in front of Nick, it would be all over for sure.

She'd met Seph for the first time on the Lake Erie beach. He'd been hanging around her for days, watching her in that entitled, rich boy, wizardly way. Like he could crook a finger and she'd come running. She'd had enough of that from Brice Roper back home.

But Brice was simple—beneath that handsome surface he was about an inch deep. There was a complexity in Seph that fascinated her. His eyes were like the green, shaded pools of Booker Creek that changed with the light. Though he was young, his face already bore traces of history and loss. She'd sketched him repeatedly, trying to capture his intensity and power with line and color.

When Seph saw her drawings, when he realized she saw the magic in him, he'd thought she was working for the Roses. He'd used Persuasion on her, the power sizzling through his fingers. She'd drawn in his magic, rich and sweet, and he'd fallen, stunned, to the sand. For days afterward, she'd felt giddy, like she'd drunk from some magical cup of joy.

So different from now. She shuddered.

Nick cleared his throat. She looked up from her reverie to find the old man watching her. Min always

She stumbled into speech. "I was supposed to help him with an art project that's due tomorrow. He's way behind on all his work, and he won't have enough credits for graduation, if he doesn't pass his courses. He . . ." Her voice trailed off. Nick was staring into the distance, his weathered face drawn down into long lines of guilt and sorrow.

"What about when he goes away to school?" she said softly. It will be better when he goes away, she told herself. You won't have to see him every day.

"To be truthful, my dear, I'm not sure he should leave the sanctuary at all. It might put him in danger."

"But why would they go after him? He's just seventeen!"

"Wizard politics," Nick replied. "He's a target, by virtue of who he is. This is not the kind of conflict in which it is possible to remain neutral. Most wizards hate his father for supporting the other guilds against the Wizard Houses. And now that they know that Linda is one of the masterminds of the rebellion . . ." Nick shrugged. "They've been recruiting him furiously, you know. The Roses. D'Orsay. Making all sorts of offers I'm not supposed to know about."

"Do they really think he would . . . go over to the dark side?" Madison's cheeks burned as the blood rushed to her face.

"Based on usual wizard practice, they assume it's a matter of price, or leverage." Nick rubbed the side of his nose with his forefinger. "He's made an impression. D'Orsay and Leicester would have won at Second Sister, had it not been for Seph and Jason . . . and you, my dear," he finished, delicately.

At Second Sister, she'd seen wizards casting spells and

conjuring images of dragons, and doing murder with magic. She'd seen Seph flinging flame from his fingertips, battling for his life. Had seen the greedy Wizard Houses circling when they realized how powerful he was.

She'd finally understood the stakes. And now she saw nothing ahead but catastrophe. She was no good for Seph. He was no good for her. Madison had to get away from this magical business. She had to. She reached up and fingered Min's opal, hanging from a chain around her neck. "Do not mess with magic," Min had said. "It's meant nothing but trouble for our family."

The old wizard cleared his throat. "You know, Madison, given your gifts, you could have a role to play."

"No!" Madison was suffocating, her lungs clamping down on each breath. "This is not my fight. I'm not a member of any of your guilds or Houses or . . . or anything." She folded her arms across her chest, tucking her hands away. "There's no magic in me." She closed her mouth firmly on the lie.

"We don't really understand what happened when Leicester and his linked wizards flamed you. Did the power just . . . dissipate, or . . ."

"It really doesn't matter, does it? The point is, I don't want to be part of this."

She'd come to Trinity to shake off the taint of magic. And yet it seemed to coalesce about her wherever she went.

"My dear Madison," Nick said, and paused, clearly unused to this sort of persuasion. "We could use your help. We wouldn't ask you to do anything you aren't comfortable with. Hastings and I could work with you to . . ." His voice trailed off when he saw Madison's expression.

"I want to be the first in my family to go to college. By the end of this semester, I'll have a year of credits. But, it's all I can do to get my schoolwork done and get in my hours at the Legends."

She glanced at her watch and groaned. "I have to go. I'm late already, and I need this job." Shifting up onto her knees, she unfastened her portfolio and pulled out a matted charcoal sketch, the one from Magic Hands. It was Trinity Square at dusk, snow sifting down through the great trees, puddles of lamplight and shadow on the snow-covered grass.

It was not what Seph wanted from her, but it was something. A small offering that represented a dream she had, once.

"When Seph wakes up, could you give this to him? Tell him it's from me."

She stood, zipped up her coat, and stashed her portfolio back under her arm. On the way down the driveway, she kicked the brick wall that lined the garden.

❧ CHAPTER THREE ❧
BANISHED FROM THE SCEPTRED ISLE

Jason preferred the snows of Cumbria to the winter rains of London. It was only a brief splash across a cobbled street from the cab to the pub, but he still got drenched to the skin. He ducked beneath a wooden sign bearing the legend, THE PENNY WHISTLE and into a gloomy interior that smelled of tobacco, malt, and decades of fried fish. It was an old place, with brick floors and a tin ceiling. Tom the bartender claimed the building dated from the 1600s.

Nodding to Tom and holding up two fingers, Jason passed through the pub and into a private room in the back. Tom never carded him. The drinking age for wizards was kind of flexible. Like in medieval days.

The fireplace in the back room shared a chimney with the hearth in the front. With a gesture, Jason kindled the heavy logs on the grate and sat at the table nearest the hearth. He set his backpack on the floor between his feet, feeling jumpy as a terrorist with a bomb hidden under his chair.

Totally aware of the hot proximity of the stone.

A few minutes later, Tom set two pints of dark ale in front of Jason.

"Thanks, Tom." Closing his eyes, concentrating, Jason forced the water from his clothing.

"You're steaming."

Jason opened his eyes to find Tom gone and Hastings standing over him. He must have fallen asleep. He'd not really slept since hiking out of the ghyll, save a few accidental minutes on the train.

Hastings could ghost around like a demon. Sometimes it seemed the wizard could walk through walls. Rubbing his gritty eyes, Jason looked around. The door to the outer bar was shut, and the borders of the room had the smudgy look of magical barriers. They were secure.

Hastings sat down across from him and studied him from under heavy black brows. It was spooky how much Hastings and Seph favored each other, with their thick, curling hair, high cheekbones, prominent noses and green eyes (though Seph's eyes tended to change color hour to hour and day to day, no doubt courtesy of his enchanter mom).

"These both for me?" Hastings asked wryly, inclining his head toward the pints on the table.

"One's for you." Jason shoved one glass in Hasting's direction and reached for the other.

Hastings gripped Jason's wrist before he could raise the glass to his lips. "Not a good idea. You need to stay sharp. Just because you *can* get away with something doesn't mean you should."

You like *your* pints, Jason thought, but knew better than to say it. He shrugged and let go of the glass. "Bloody filthy weather, as the locals say."

"Pronounce it more like blue-dy," Hastings corrected him, taking full possession of Jason's pint. "You still sound American."

Must've saved up lectures while I was gone. "I *am* American."

"It makes you stand out. It makes people remember you."

Hastings just didn't get it. Jason *wanted* to be remembered.

"Where have you been? I told you to stay put." Hastings was never one to waste time on pleasantries.

There was no point in holding out on Hastings. He'd have it out of him soon enough, anyway.

"I decided to check out Raven's Ghyll."

"You *what*?" The wizard didn't raise his voice, but it seemed loud just the same.

"You were gone. I had some time." Jason took a breath and forced himself to look into Hastings's eyes.

"I told you to watch and let me know if Jessamine Longbranch returned to London. That was your assignment."

"That's make-work," Jason protested. "Her place has been shut up for months. There was nothing to do."

"Oh?" Hastings lifted an eyebrow. "She's been back now for at least three days. And I have no idea what's gone on since her return."

"Wylie was there yesterday. And a bunch of others. They've been meeting every day." Jason slid a paper across the table at Hastings. "I . . . um . . . persuaded the neighbors to keep track while I was gone."

Hastings tapped his long fingers on the battered tabletop. "I did not give this assignment to the neighbors. What did you hope to accomplish? In Raven's Ghyll, I mean."

"Well. Everyone's afraid to go in—the Roses, the—ah—

everybody." Jason focused on the table. He'd been arguing for an attempt on the ghyll since he'd arrived in London, and Hastings had refused.

"We've discussed that. You knew the ghyll was likely to be heavily fortified. There was little to gain and a lot to lose by going in. If you'd been captured, the consequences would have been dire. I've been to the cellar of Raven's Ghyll Castle, and it's not a place I'd want to revisit."

"I figured that one person, alone, could probably slip in unnoticed."

"And did you? Slip in unnoticed?"

I bet he already knows the answer to that, Jason thought. He cleared his throat. "No. They—ah—noticed."

"So what happened?"

"Well. It was like kicking an anthill. He has an army up there, and they all turned out. I went unnoticeable and headed for the hold."

Hastings frowned. "You should have left immediately when you knew you were outed."

Right. I bet you'd have stormed the castle with your bare hands, Jason thought. "I figured that's what they would expect me to do." He realized his foot was jittering and consciously stilled himself. "Then D'Orsay—or somebody—flooded the ghyll with Luciferous mist."

Hastings swore. "You're certain? I didn't think anyone still knew how to make it."

"It was that, or something like it. I left off making for the castle and headed for higher ground. I climbed up Ravenshead as far as the Weirstone. Then there was this earthquake."

"And fire and pestilence as well, I suppose," Hastings said dryly.

"Ha. Anyway, a big crack opened up on Ravenshead, just below the Weirstone. I hid there until the mist cleared." Jason lit a cigarette, connecting on the second try, then blew out a stream of smoke.

"Were you seen? Were you recognized?" Hastings waved away the smoke, making no effort to hide his disapproval of Jason in general and his smoking in particular.

Jason hesitated. "I was seen," he admitted. "I don't think I was recognized."

"If you were seen, you will be identified. You made quite an impression at Second Sister." Hastings slammed his hand down on the table. "Despite your unrelenting thirst for confrontation, going after D'Orsay doesn't really help us. At least he diverts the Roses' attention. We need to get hold of the Covenant and destroy it before someone tries to ram it down our throats."

"What if D'Orsay has the Covenant?" Jason countered stubbornly. After all, the former Master of Games had disappeared from the ill-fated meeting on the island of Second Sister along with the document the guilds had signed under duress.

"Maybe he does," Hastings growled. "But I don't think so. Else he'd have called in his allies and held a big ceremony in the ghyll consecrating the document and declaring himself ruler over all of us."

"I didn't find the Covenant, all right? But there's this." Jason lifted the backpack from between his feet, unzipped it, and dumped the contents onto the table—everything except the opal and its stand, which were hidden in the side pocket. He hadn't exactly decided whether to share that with Hastings.

Hastings looked down at the loot on the table and up at Jason, raising an eyebrow in inquiry.

"I found this stuff in a cave behind the Weirstone."

Hastings raked through the mixture of gems and jewelry and magical artifacts on the battered wooden table, held some of them up to the light so he could read their inscriptions, looked up more than once as if to make sure the door remained secure.

It seemed that, for once, Jason had impressed the unimpressible Leander Hastings.

Finally, Hastings spoke. "Is this all of it?"

Jason shook his head. "It was all I could carry out. The mountain was still unstable. The entrance caved in around me as I was leaving," he added. Why did he always feel like he had to defend himself?

"Do you think D'Orsay knew about these things?"

"Nah." Jason shook his head. "It looked like nothing had been touched in centuries. Plus, I mean, wouldn't he have used this already, what with the fix he's in?"

"How did you decide? What to take, that is."

Jason shrugged. "My mom taught me a lot about amulets and talismans. So I chose the pieces that seemed most powerful, either by their inscriptions or the—you know—the vibes. I took mostly magical pieces. Plus a sword," he added.

The wizard's head came up. "A sword?"

"I left it back in my room. I didn't think I should cart it through the streets of London. It was hard enough smuggling it down here on the train." He'd used a golf bag. Come to think of it, a ski bag would have been more in keeping with the season.

"Right," Hastings said, taking natural command. "Let's pack these things up." He reached for the backpack.

Jason held on to it. "Oh, yeah. I almost forgot. There's this other thing." Jason fumbled in the front pocket, pulled out the opal and handed it to Hastings.

The wizard weighed the bag in his hand, then undid the drawstring and dumped the opal out onto the tabletop, corralling it with his arms. The faint glow from the stone threw the wizard's planed face into high relief.

"What *is* this?" Hastings whispered.

"It's a *sefa*, I guess," Jason replied. "I thought maybe you could teach me how to use it."

Now that it was free of its velvet covering, the stone seemed to yank at his insides. Images of a broken landscape brushed his consciousness, like wings. A seductive voice whispered in his ear, but he couldn't make out the words.

Hastings quickly put the stone back in its bag, drawing tight the cord. "We've got to get this . . . all of this . . . to a safe place. And that's nowhere in Britain."

Jason was pleased by Hastings's reaction, but confused by his words. "What do you mean? Why?"

Hastings didn't respond immediately. He sat thinking, drumming his fingers on the tabletop, green eyes glittering in the firelight.

"We'll take this lot to Trinity," he announced finally. "It's the safest place, because we're already maintaining a boundary around the sanctuary, and no one will ask questions about increased security."

"Trinity?" Jason squinted at Hastings. "I thought you and I could use some of this stuff to go after D'Orsay. And the Covenant."

"Claude D'Orsay is not our first priority," Hastings said, biting off each word. "I want Nick Snowbeard to take a look at these things. And Seph, since he's involved in maintaining security in Trinity."

Seph. Of course. Jason fought down a surge of jealousy.

"I thought maybe we could . . ." Jason began, but Hastings raised a hand to shut him up.

"I'd like to see the sword, but I don't think we can risk being seen together. Go straight back, collect the sword, and catch the first plane back to the States."

Jason's weary mind stumbled. "You want me to carry this stuff back to Trinity *myself*?"

"Well, yes," Hastings replied, as if Jason was impossibly slow. "It has to be you. The fewer people who know about this, the better."

"But I don't want to go back," Jason protested. "Give me another chance, and I know I can get into the ghyll on my own. If I can't find the Covenant, I'll look for the hoard. Maybe I can get back into the cave."

"You'll never get in again, especially not after a failed attack."

"Who else is going to do it? You? Everybody knows who you are. Everybody knows your face. You won't get within miles of the ghyll. The Roses will murder you, even if you're supposed to be their ally against D'Orsay."

"I am not allied with the Roses," Hastings said stiffly. "Even if our interests temporarily coincide, we'll end up fighting them in the end."

"So this is what I get for failing," Jason said bitterly. "I'm out."

Hastings drained his glass and slammed it back down on the table. "This is what you get for taking a foolish chance for no good reason. Do you think *your* face isn't known? D'Orsay's no fool. Do you think I advise a nondescript appearance because I'm a bloody *conservative*? You're overconfident, Jason, and you're flamboyant and careless, and that combination is going to get you killed. I don't want to be responsible for the mess you leave behind."

This was ironic coming from a man who had one of the most memorable faces and personages of anyone Jason had ever known. Whose daring escapades were legendary.

Jason leaned across the table. "Listen to me. I'll lose the earring." He touched his earlobe. "I'll lose the plumage." He sluiced his fingers through his bleached hair. "I'll wear a bloody tweed and ascot if that's what you want. Just let me stay and work with you."

Hastings sighed. "Don't think this means it's all gone wrong." He rested his hand on the backpack. "This is a tremendous find. Sometimes I'm not very . . . liberal with compliments."

"I don't want compliments. I want to stay here. I want to *do* something."

"And I want someone I can trust to take these things back to Trinity before D'Orsay manages to track us down. Do you think he's not looking?" Hastings sat back, extending his long legs. "It's not enough to do *something*. It's important to do the *right* thing."

"I know it is," Jason said, trying not to sound sullen. "But nothing's going to happen in Trinity."

"Don't be too sure. I have a feeling that the pieces you found are important. The battle may well turn on them."

"Then why take them to Trinity? You'll put the whole town in danger."

"That is exactly why no one must discover where they are. And, bear in mind: if we lose this war, Trinity will be destroyed along with everything else."

Jason stood and began pacing, pivoting at each end of

the room. "Can't you at least try to understand?"

"I understand you better than you realize."

"Why? The Roses killed your father and sister a hundred years ago so you understand how I feel about Leicester and D'Orsay murdering my father?"

"Because I know what it's like to want to prove yourself so badly it destroys everything else that matters," Hastings replied, gazing into the fire. "Sometimes it's just an excuse to avoid dealing with your own demons."

So now Hastings was a psychiatrist, in addition to being a wizard and warriormaster. Jason bit back a hot reply. "Look. I'm an orphan. Like you were. No one cares what happens to me. It's my choice. Mine."

"I assumed responsibility for you when I brought you to Britain."

Jason noticed that Hastings didn't claim to care about him. "Please. I want to help." He was perilously close to begging. "Jack and Ellen are out drilling their warriors. That's what they're good at. Seph is maintaining the barrier. I can't do any of that. I want to be where I'm useful."

"The most useful thing you can do for me now is to get the sword and the rest back to Trinity," Hastings said, without looking up. "Have Nick take a look at the blade. It may very well be one of the seven. If it is, pass it along to Ellen. She deserves a weapon worthy of her skills. She and Jack may play a critical role if it comes to a war."

Nick. Ellen. Seph. Jack. All important to the Cause. Everyone was except him.

Jason knew the argument was over. His mistake was thinking Hastings was actually participating. He slumped back into his chair. "When will you come back to Trinity?"

The wizard shrugged. "Soon, I hope. I'm going to try to find out what's going on at Raven's Ghyll. Whether it's been noticed that things have gone missing, and whether they may be on your trail. Maybe I can muddy the water a bit. Draw them off."

And that, as they say, was that. Jason's brief career as operative for the Dragon House was over.

Jason fell asleep on the tube on the way back to his apartment, missing the Mornington Crescent station and getting off at Camden Town. He walked back through the city streets to clear his head. On his way, he stopped in at an Internet café and booked a flight from Heathrow to New York that departed the following morning.

So the man loitering near the Underground exits at Mornington Crescent with a photograph of Jason Haley didn't spot him there.

Jason stopped in to see a girl who lived in the building next door to his own. They ordered pizza and he stayed late. By then, it was sleeting. The buildings were set atop a common cellar, so he passed through the laundries into his own building without going outside.

So the woman sheltering in the entryway of Jason's apartment building didn't realize her fox had gone to ground.

Back in his room, Jason packed up his meager belongings. He'd planned to take the train from Euston, but now Hastings had gone and made him jumpy. In the end, he called a car service and booked a car to pick him up at 4 a.m. He gave his name as Bob Roberts and didn't name a destination. He'd bring his backpack as a carry-on, and convince the airline to let him gate-check the golf bag with the sword in it.

Golfers were funny about letting go of their clubs, weren't they?

He'd only been in the UK for a few months. He hoped his banishment wouldn't last long.

Leesha Middleton shook the snow from her curls and extended her frozen hands toward the fire. Why couldn't Claude D'Orsay den up in Belize for the winter, like any sane person?

She glanced around the parlor with an educated eye. Everything had a stuffy, old-money look, like the museum rooms at her grandparents' estates. They smelled the same, too—like cigars and leather and old men's musty wool cardigans. Leesha ran a finger under her high-necked sweater and touched the gold collar—the torc—that circled her neck. Touching it was becoming a habit.

"Who are you?"

Leesha jumped and turned round.

The boy had slipped up behind her. He was slender and bookish-looking, with blond curls, a fair complexion, and eyes that were such a pale blue—behind frameless glasses—as to be almost colorless. He might have been fourteen, too

young to be interesting, though Leesha was only seventeen
herself. He was almost pretty, but the effect was marred by a
black eye and a nose that had been recently broken.

"I'm Alicia Middleton," she said, seeing no reason to
lie.

"Devereaux D'Orsay," the boy replied, standing rather
too close and staring fixedly into her face. "Father didn't
mention we were expecting guests."

"Didn't he?" It hadn't been easy to get this invitation. A
fax of the last page of the Covenant signed by the guilds at
Second Sister had done the trick. She'd ordered her grandparents' chauffeur, Charles, to drive her here from their estate
in Scotland. If she could manage to live through the day and
avoid being grounded, she'd be very very lucky.

"Would you care for something to drink?" Devereaux
asked, nodding toward the sideboard, where there was an
array of bottles and cans of soda.

Leesha shook her head. "No, thank you."

The boy leaned against the sideboard. "We've more of
a selection down in the cellar," he said. "Would you like to
see?"

"No, I'm quite all right, thank you." Looking to change
the subject, she said, "Who beat you up?"

That struck a nerve. "No one beat me up, Miss
Middleton," the boy said, straightening, his fair face flushing
dark rose against the bruises. "From a power standpoint, I
totally had the advantage. Had it not been for . . ."

"Devereaux."

Now it was the boy's turn to jump and look guilty.

Claude D'Orsay stood framed in the doorway, dressed
in wool trousers, cashmere sweater, and tweed jacket. The

wizard's hair was dark and close-cropped, his face fine-boned and aristocratic.

"Miss Middleton, a pleasure to see you again. I see you've met my son."

"Yes," Leesha replied. "I wouldn't have known it from his looks."

"He favors my late wife." D'Orsay came into the room and extended his hand to Leesha. His grip was cool and dry, with a wizard's electrical sting.

"You didn't tell me anyone was coming, Father." Devereaux still looked sullen. "How was I supposed to know who she was?"

"It was rather short notice, Dev," D'Orsay replied. "Miss Middleton requested a meeting." He studied Leesha appraisingly. "I believe the last time we met was here, at Raven's Ghyll, at the last tournament."

"That was a disaster," Leesha said bluntly.

D'Orsay didn't disagree, but nodded toward the sideboard. "Would you like something?"

"No, thank you," Leesha replied, wondering how many times she was going to have to refuse refreshment before leaving.

D'Orsay gestured to one of two chairs by the hearth. "Please. Sit. Make yourself comfortable."

Leesha sat, not particularly comfortably, and D'Orsay sat down opposite her. Devereaux slouched onto the hearth itself, clearly intending to listen, if not to participate.

Leesha nodded at Devereaux, and raised an eyebrow.

"Dev can stay. I value his opinion." D'Orsay paused. "So. Are you here representing Jessamine Longbranch?"

"Why would you think that?"

"I believe you were working for her last year when you—ah—brought those two young men here as hostages during the last tournament. Friends of that bizarre mongrel warrior she created. Jack Swift. Now *that* was a disaster."

"Must've seemed like a good idea at the time," Leesha said. "Anyway, I'm not working for her anymore."

"Ah, yes. Didn't I hear you'd fallen in with some traders? I don't imagine Jessamine approved."

Leesha examined her nails. "You can't believe everything you hear."

"But you're working with someone."

"Uh-huh."

"Who?"

"My partner wants to remain anonymous until we're sure we can do business."

D'Orsay sat back in his chair and smiled like a cat with a bird between his paws. "We can be very persuasive."

Leesha's heart flopped wildly but she managed to keep her voice steady. "My partner wouldn't like it if anything bad happened to me."

"Did you bring the document with you?"

"Do I look stupid or what?"

D'Orsay shrugged. "One can never tell by appearances. Where is it now?"

"You should be thinking about what kind of deal you're willing to make."

"I could offer to trade you for the Covenant."

Leesha sighed. She groped in her bag for her compact and reapplied her lipstick, trying to keep her hand from shaking. Playing for time. "I'm just the hired help, you know? I can be replaced. But my associate might be annoyed enough to decide to sell the piece to someone else."

"No one else would want it."

"Please. I'm a trader. I know who wants what. The Roses want to destroy it because it takes power out of their hands and puts it in yours. The underguilds want to destroy it because it keeps them subservient to wizards. You want to consecrate it and enforce it. I bet we could get a three-way auction going."

D'Orsay raised his hand. "I hardly think that's necessary." He smiled, as if acknowledging defeat. The man was a charmer, no doubt about it. And good looking, for someone so totally old.

D'Orsay rose, laid another log on the fire, and returned to his seat, taking his time. "Has your associate given you leave to negotiate the sale?"

"He has."

"Then I assume he's shared with you what offer he might be willing to accept?"

"He has."

"And . . . ?"

"He wants to be written in."

D'Orsay shoved back his sleeves. "Excuse me?"

"The new Covenant states that all of the magical guilds including the Wizard Houses will be ruled by you and Gregory Leicester and your heirs. Leicester is dead, and he has no blood heirs. My partner wishes to be named legal heir to Gregory Leicester and so, coruler of the guilds."

"Your partner is out of his mind," D'Orsay said pleasantly.

Leesha took a deep breath, cursing the day she'd become entangled in this. "That's his price. Take it or leave it."

"Who does he think he is? Does he really think I would

bring him in as a full partner? Leicester and I worked on this project for years."

"Look at it this way. What can you offer that the Roses can't? I'm sure they can come up with more money than you, if everyone puts in. Plus, if they destroy the Covenant, then my associate doesn't have to worry about living under *your* rule, which, having read the document, seems risky. The only way to ease his mind is to allow him to come in as an equal."

D'Orsay pressed his fingertips together. "If I knew who I was dealing with, if I knew we would be compatible . . ."

If you knew if he'd be easy to kill, Leesha thought. No doubt both partners would be hiring assassins before the ink on the agreement was dry. With any luck, they'd kill each other.

"This is my inheritance, too," Devereaux said, leaning forward. "Let's take her to the cellar. We can *make* her tell us whatever we want."

Getawayfrommeyoumiserablelittlecreep, Leesha thought, perspiration trickling between her shoulder blades. She made a show of looking at her watch.

"Let me handle this, Dev," D'Orsay said. The wizard massaged his forehead, as if it hurt, then turned back to Leesha. "Perhaps we could negotiate a private sale, you and I."

Leesha considered this. In fact, she'd considered this long before she ever entered the Ghyll. "I don't actually hold the original."

"Perhaps you could obtain it."

"That would be . . . difficult." Impossible, actually, with things as they were, but she wouldn't tell him that.

"Your partner could meet with an accident."

Leesha liked that idea a lot. "He *could*, but I couldn't be connected with it in any way. Plus it would have to be a completely . . . um . . . *permanent* accident. If you know what I mean."

"Ah." D'Orsay smiled. "You might be able to provide an opportunity, yes?"

"Maybe."

"And what would you want in return?"

That would be enough. Getting free of Warren Barber. Getting free of this whole business. But it wouldn't be wizardly to say so. "Oh, I don't know. Money is nice. Or maybe I'd like to be written in myself," she added. They'd expect that, of course.

D'Orsay smiled back. "Very well, then. I think we can come to an arrangement." Meaning they'd stab each other in the back as soon as they could. "But, tell me. How did your employer come by the document? As a sometime buyer of antiquities and art, I know that the provenance of a piece often speaks to its authenticity."

Leesha rolled her eyes. "Now that would be too much like a clue."

D'Orsay's smile disappeared. "There can no deal between us without a name."

"And if he finds out I told you?"

"My dear young lady, he won't find out from me. That would not be in my self-interest. I cannot go after your partner if I don't know who it is. Hmm?"

Leesha took a deep breath and resisted the temptation to finger her neckline again. "It's Warren Barber."

D'Orsay raised his eyebrows skeptically. "Who?"

"Warren Barber," she repeated.

The eyebrows stayed up. "And who, may I ask, is that?"

Old Warren doesn't move in your circles, I guess, Leesha thought. Mine either. She shivered, then turned it into a shrug. "He was one of Leicester's students at the Havens. Sometimes called the Spider."

"The . . . Spider." D'Orsay tapped his elegant forefinger against his chin, looking amused. "You're saying this whole scheme's been organized by *teenagers*?"

"Well. No offense, but the old people don't seem to be doing so great."

"Perhaps not." D'Orsay inclined his head graciously. "But I've not heard of Barber."

"He does Weirwalls. Supposedly he was the one that spun the wall around the inn at Second Sister to keep the guilds from escaping the conference before the Covenant was signed." Leesha hadn't been there, thank god, but she'd heard all about it.

"I see." D'Orsay's eyes glittered. "Then he must have been the one who *failed*, who let McCauley and Haley and the girl into the hall."

Barber hadn't mentioned that. Ha. "Anyway, when he saw what was happening, when McCauley showed up and Leicester got killed, Barber went and stole the document."

"How . . . resourceful." D'Orsay sighed, as if mourning the duplicity of man. "Now, then. What manner of paperwork would satisfy young Mr. Barber?"

"I have something with me." Leesha pulled a folder from her portfolio. "These attest that, for purposes of the Covenant, my associate to be named later is the heir of Gregory Leicester, and assumes all privileges and rights, blah, blah." She handed it across to D'Orsay. "Once these are signed and properly processed, the ... ah ... revised Covenant will be made available for consecration in the ghyll before the Weirstone." Naturally, details of that were rather sketchy.

A peculiar expression flitted across D'Orsay's face. Followed by a calculating one. "Ah. Well. The Weirstone."

"Is there a problem?"

"Well, there may be. There was an intruder in the ghyll a few nights ago." D'Orsay smiled thinly. "He attacked my son, and I believe he might have carried away something important."

Leesha glanced over at Devereaux's battered face. "What makes you think that?"

"The Weirstone has dimmed. In fact, it appears to be ... extinguished."

Leesha shuddered, the reaction of any reasonable wizard to a threat to their heritage of magic. "What do you think that means?"

"Difficult to say what it means in terms of the consecration of the Covenant. The Roses and the rebels assume we hold it. Perhaps that was the intent of the raid, to make it impossible for us to enforce it."

"But that would ruin everything!"

"Precisely. Therefore, now that our interests so closely coincide, perhaps we could ask Mr. Barber to contribute to the success of this enterprise in a material way."

"Excuse me?" He'd lost her after *precisely*.

"As an act of good faith, I am asking that you and your partner bring the perpetrator back here, alive, along with whatever he took from here."

Great. She knew who would get *that* assignment. "How ... how is Barber supposed to find this person," Leesha said, irritably, "when we don't even know for sure if he took any-thing?"

D'Orsay smiled. "We can help you there. We now know who it was, and we have some idea about what's missing."

"Why should we go out hunting your burglar?"

D'Orsay waved the papers under Leesha's nose. "As soon as I sign this, Barber has as much interest in seeing the Covenant consecrated as I do. But I'm rather pinned down here. If I leave Raven's Ghyll, the Roses will be on me before I'm out of Cumbria. And in my absence, they might seize control of the ghyll. Which, again, would be inconvenient if we wish to access the Weirstone. Barber, on the other hand, can follow this Jason Haley to America, and . . ."

"Who's Jason Haley?" Leesha interrupted. "I never heard of him."

D'Orsay stood and crossed to the desk, choosing a folder from a pile. He pulled out a color print, returned, and handed it to Leesha. "Dev didn't have any trouble identifying him from our database of rebels and troublemakers."

To Leesha's surprise, Jason Haley looked to be a boy about her age, dressed in jeans and a sweatshirt, with brilliant blue eyes and a sardonic grin.

"He shouldn't present any difficulty for someone like Barber. From what we gather, he's a minor operative and sneak thief. . . ."

"Who managed to sneak in here and steal something out from under your nose."

D'Orsay nodded. "True. And he's also the boy who teamed up with McCauley in the attack at Second Sister. He's aligned with the riffraff in Trinity."

"Riffraff like Leander Hastings and Nicodemus

Snowbeard? *Them*, I've heard of. I'd rather not cross paths with them again." *Oh, God, no.* Her former partners were still buried under the Trinity High School parking lot.

"That's the field we're playing on, my dear."

Leesha sighed. "Do you think he's gone to Trinity?"

"I suspect so."

Too many people knew her in Trinity. "What did Haley take?"

Devereaux opened his mouth as if to speak, but D'Orsay cut in. "We believe it's a *sefa* stone of some kind, small enough to hold in your hands, with a flaming center. Useless on its own, we believe, but, somehow, here in the ghyll . . ." D'Orsay shrugged.

That wouldn't be easy to find, even in Trinity, Leesha thought glumly.

"So," D'Orsay said cheerfully. "Send Barber after Jason Haley. Perhaps they'll kill each other and you can collect the stone. Meanwhile, do keep in touch about Barber's whereabouts and we'll look for an opportunity to eliminate him. Do we have a bargain?" D'Orsay asked.

"That depends. Are you going to sign this or not?" Leesha said crossly. "I have to take something back to Barber." She was tired of being everyone's servant.

D'Orsay crossed to his desk, found a pen in the drawer, and signed the paperwork with a flourish, scribbling an addendum in the margins. He handed it to Leesha. "I'll have your driver bring the car round for you, then. I look forward to a long and prosperous relationship. Assuming you or Barber bring back Jason Haley and the Covenant, we'll be seeing more of each other."

★ ★ ★

After the girl had gone, Dev crossed to the shelf next to the fireplace and lifted down the book Haley had dropped in the snow, struggling a little with the weight of it. Dev sat down on the hearth and began leafing through. They'd both read it two or three times, debating its meaning.

Dev began to read aloud, his blond head still bent over the book. *"I will bury the Dragonheart stone in the mountain with such protections as I can lend it, in the hope that chance will put it into the possession of one with the heart and desire to release its full power. That person will seize control of the gifts that have been given. That person will once again reign over the guilds. Or destroy them, as they deserve."*

He looked up at D'Orsay. "So you think Haley took the Dragonheart."

"I think he must have, Dev." D'Orsay felt positively betrayed. If Haley found this thing called the Dragonheart in the ghyll, *where* did he find it? And how did he find it so fast? These were D'Orsay's ancestral lands, after all. They'd been in his family since—well—since the property had been called Dragon's Ghyll. If there were magical artifacts in the valley, they belonged to him and his heirs.

Dev set the heavy book aside, stood, and paced restlessly back and forth. "I should have stopped him. I let him get away."

"Dev. He's a vicious street hoodlum. Just look what he did to your face."

It was true. Jason Haley was little more than an under-powered punk with a talent for illusion, but he and Hastings and McCauley had already brought down a conspiracy that had been years in the making.

The scene at Second Sister played over in D'Orsay's head,

like the ever-repeating trailer of a bad film. He blocked the scenes, picked over and tallied the players on screen.

He and Leicester had engineered a meeting of all the magical guilds and the Wizard Council on the island of Second Sister. Leicester's slave wizards immobilized everyone in the room. They'd forced the guilds and the council to sign D'Orsay's Covenant, naming them rulers over the guilds. That much had gone according to plan.

Haley and McCauley must have been hiding in the room all along. Haley's fake dragon appeared, a thirty-foot-tall glamour that dazzled and distracted all the wizards in the hall while McCauley opened fire against Leicester. Leicester lured McCauley into the open. And then, *something* happened.

A girl had appeared out of nowhere, a girl with the singular name of Madison Moss. How she'd come to be at Second Sister, D'Orsay had no idea. When Leicester flamed McCauley, the girl stepped in front and took the hit. Leicester went down, his wizard slaves with him. And Haley and McCauley had killed him.

Who was this girl? She was not from any of the major families, or he'd have recognized her. He'd searched the online genealogies, his agents had inquired. As far as they could tell, she was a nobody.

Pausing at the hearth, D'Orsay gripped the poker with its emblems of roses and thrust it into the flames. The log dissolved to ash and sparks flew upward.

Devereaux spoke, startling him out of his reverie. "I don't understand why you're dealing with them, Father. Barber sounds like a common thief. And we don't want him to get hold of the Dragonheart."

"There is a saying, Dev. It takes a thief to catch one.

Besides, what I said was true. It would be difficult for me to leave the ghyll to go after Haley, and I don't want to involve anyone else."

"I could go. It's my fault Haley got away."

D'Orsay patted Dev's shoulder affectionately. "My enemies would be just as happy to get hold of you, as leverage."

Dev glowered and clenched his fists, a stance familiar from childhood. "I can protect myself."

"You *are* a prodigy, Devereaux, but I think you're a little young to go up against the Roses." D'Orsay chose not to mention Jason Haley, who'd already given Dev a beating. Dev was just beginning to recover his self-confidence.

"That girl, that Alicia Middleton, is very pretty."

"Don't go falling for her. Alicia Middleton is the kind of girl who'll eat you alive."

"But you're partners with her."

"For now, Dev. For now. Let's hope she betrays Warren Barber and gets us the Dragonheart. I suspect she'll be easier to handle than him." D'Orsay smiled and ruffled Dev's hair. Dev flinched away, a familiar sulky look on his face.

D'Orsay sighed. "You've got to get out more, Dev. Make some friends. I'm afraid that's my fault. I just don't want anything to happen to you."

"Do you really think Haley is a small-time thief?"

D'Orsay paused to think before answering. "I'm not sure if Haley is very clever or very lucky. He's gotten in my way too many times to be ordinary. If we're lucky, young Miss Middleton and Barber will take care of him. Or he'll rid us of them, which wouldn't be all bad. Except that leaves us without the Covenant, and without a functioning Weirstone."

"You don't know there's anything really wrong with it. I mean, just because it's dark, that doesn't . . ."

"Can't you *feel* it?" D'Orsay had grown up with the stone, situated as it was on his ancestral lands. All his life, it had been like a magnet that pulled at the poles of his heart. The call of the Weirstone meant home to him, and, just now, the call was very faint.

❧ CHAPTER FIVE ❧
TO CHURCH

The sound intruded into Madison's mind, a faint and persistent tapping, like something pecking on the outside of her skull. This was followed by the sense that she was suffocating.

She opened her eyes, squinting against the overhead light. The giant *Arts of the Eastern Civilizations* textbook lay open on her chest, which explained why she couldn't breathe. She'd fallen asleep studying again.

She pushed the heavy book aside and sat up. The clock on the bedside table said 2:48. So the test was less than ten hours away.

She heard tapping again. Throwing back the comforter, she slid from the high Victorian bed, her bare feet thudding on the wood floor. She shivered in her cotton nightgown. The Legends Inn was beautiful, but, like most Victorian buildings, it was not well-insulated, especially up on the third floor.

She crossed to the door, undid the chain, pulled it open. And was ambushed.

It was Seph McCauley, snow powdering his jacket and sparkling in his curls, smelling of fresh air and magic. Her heart floundered frantically in her chest, as if it meant to escape.

"Oh!" she said.

"Hey, Maddie," he said softly, stepping inside and pulling the door shut behind him. "Oh, I'm sorry. Were you asleep?" he added, grinning, looking her up and down.

"Do you know what time it is?" she mumbled, forcing her fingers through her tangled hair. She hadn't seen him for three days (not that she was counting), and now when he did come, she was all baggy-eyed and cranky. "Rachel will skin you alive if she finds you here at this hour."

"Oh, I don't think she'll notice," he said, touching the amulet that hung around his neck. "You're shivering." He grabbed up her shawl from the foot of the bed and draped it around her shoulders, reeling her in like a fish in a net. When there were inches between them, she pulled free, wrapping the shawl around herself for protection.

He looked away and stuffed his hands into his pockets, a faint release of breath signaling his frustration. He wasn't used to being rebuffed. He didn't understand—he would never understand if she could help it. Most guys gave up after a try or two. But Seph was persistent, and she didn't know how long she could continue to keep him at arm's length.

"What are you *doing* here?" Madison demanded, her own frustration sharpening her tongue. She was not so much surprised by the hour of his appearance as by the fact that he was there at all. These were the hours Seph liked to keep. He was a city boy who came alive at night. "Who's minding the boundary?"

"Nick's in charge tonight. Get dressed. Let's go out."

"It's three o'clock in the morning," she protested. "I have an exam tomor . . . today."

"It's only for a little while. Jason's back."

Madison stopped fussing with her hair and stared at Seph. "What's he doing back? I thought he was gone for good. I mean, he dropped out of school and all."

"He brought some things back from Britain for safekeeping. We're supposed to meet him to look the stuff over. Please come." Seph looked into her eyes, as if searching for hopeful signs.

Madison wavered. It wasn't like she'd be any use when it came to magic. But it seemed safe enough, and it was hard to say no to Seph for reasons that had nothing to do with wizardry. Plus she couldn't help wondering what had brought Jason home.

"All right. But I can't stay long." Grabbing up her clothes from the chair beside her bed, she carried them into the tiny lavatory and locked the door. Shedding her nightgown, she pulled her jeans on, following with a sweatshirt, heavy socks, and her red boots. Armoring herself for the personal battle ahead.

When she came out, the phone rang, jarringly loud in the quiet inn. Madison ignored it, shrugging on her barn coat and tying a handwoven scarf around her neck.

"Aren't you going to get that?" Seph asked, nodding toward the phone.

"The machine'll pick up. It's Mama. She's the only one besides you who calls me in the middle of the night."

The answering machine clicked on. "You've reached Maddie Moss. Leave a message." There was a beep and then her mother's voice, all husky from cigarettes. "Baby girl, I know you're there. I need to talk to you. It's about Grace and John Robert. Pick up the phone!" There was a long pause, and then, "Fine! Go to hell!" And the phone banged down.

Madison jammed her brimmed hat down on her head. "Let's go."

"Why won't you talk to her?" Seph asked, as they passed through the dark hallway and descended the stairs.

Madison put her finger to her lips. "Shhh. I do talk to her. Just not every time she calls."

They slipped out the front door, crossed the porch, and turned down Lakeside. It was very cold, despite the proximity of the lake. The snow crunched under their feet like shards of glass.

"What does she want?" Seph asked. "Your mother, I mean."

"She wants me to come home and watch my brother and sister. She needs a babysitter, and—guess what?—she can't find anyone else who'll work for free and keep her hours and is available at a moment's notice."

Seph looked at her quizzically. "But you're in school. She knows that, right?"

This was so far off Seph's experience, he couldn't possibly understand. "She knows that, but she doesn't specially care. She'd understand if I were studying dental hygiene or computers. But I could do that at the community college at home. As far as she's concerned, I already know how to paint pretty pictures. I always take the ribbon at the county fair." Madison shrugged. "She also might need money."

"But you don't make that much," Seph replied, the understatement of the year. He steered her south on Church Street with a hand on her elbow. She relaxed fractionally. It seemed okay. She couldn't feel the wizard heat of him through three layers of wool.

"Mama knows I'm living with Rachel for free. She doesn't understand that my books cost a hundred and fifty dollars apiece."

Madison wanted to change the subject. She wasn't like Carlene, who was always just about to move to Las Vegas or Paris, France, or join up with a country band, and somehow believed every story she told. Madison wouldn't pretend she had a different kind of family. She couldn't pretend that things could ever work out between her and Seph. But that didn't mean she wanted to talk about it.

"Where're we meeting Jason?" Madison asked, knowing nothing was open in Trinity, Ohio, at three in the morning on a Tuesday.

"St. Catherine's."

Madison missed her step and Seph deftly caught her about the waist. She pulled free quickly, feeling his hot fingers through her coat, feeling the wicked power inside her respond. "We're meeting him in *church* in the middle of the night? Who picked that?"

"Jason did." Seph shrugged. "I don't know why, but I guess we'll find out." Seph attended Mass at St. Catherine's regularly. He wore a Celtic cross on a chain around his neck, alongside the *dyrne sefa*. His Catholic faith was the rock he'd stood upon through a lonely lifetime.

I wish I believed in something, Madison thought. I wish I belonged somewhere.

The church stood amid tall trees on a campus that included the Catholic grade school and high school, along with a small cemetery. Seph had keys to the side door of the church.

The sanctuary was chilly and dark, lit only by the sconces along the walls. The light that usually poured through the great windows was hours away. Madison flinched when something moved in the shadows up by the altar. Two tall figures materialized and came toward them. Jack and Ellen.

"Jason here yet?" Seph asked.

They shook their heads. "I hope he gets here soon," Ellen said. She yawned and sat down in one of the pews, drawing her knees up and pillowing her head on her arms. Unlike most girls her age, Ellen always seemed totally at home in her body. Madison stared down at her own traitorous hands.

A slice of light spilled into the nave as the side door opened and closed. A ripple of power washed over Madison before the intruder spoke.

"Friend or foe?" someone whispered. "Weir or Anaweir?"

It was Jason.

He came forward into the light, wearing only a leather jacket against the bitter cold. He carried a duffle, and a backpack was slung over one shoulder, a golf bag over the other. He was grinning, that grin that always had an edge to it, as if he didn't trust the world or himself.

Power fountained off him with an intensity Madison had never seen in Jason before, contrasting with his travel-beaten, haggard appearance. There were dark circles under his blue eyes, and his face was unevenly stubbled over.

"How are things in the UK?" Jack asked. "Did you look up any of our old friends from Raven's Ghyll?"

Jason's head snapped up, but then he settled back and sort of smiled. "Nah. Maybe next time."

"How's my father?" Seph asked.

"Your old man's all right," Jason replied, fussing with the buckle on the back pack. "I saw him in London two days ago."

"What's in the bag?" Jack asked, gazing curiously at the golf bag.

"You've got us all intrigued," Madison drawled.

"Me most of all." Nick Snowbeard appeared from behind the altar, leaning heavily on his staff. "Which should be obvious from the fact that I'm here. Old men aren't used to gadding about in the middle of the night."

Madison squinted at Nick, surprised. Seph had said that Snowbeard was maintaining the boundary, yet the old wizard was still able to function. Seph was always visibly distracted, almost impaired, when he was on duty.

Jason laid the golf bag on the floor and knelt next to it. "First. A present for Ellen." He unzipped the bag and lifted out a sword in a scabbard, presenting it to her with both hands, reverently, like a courtier to his queen.

Ellen blinked at him, stunned speechless, as if no one had ever given her a present before. Then she took the sword from Jason and drew it slowly from its scabbard. The blade illuminated the entire nave of the church with blue light. The cross on the hilt blazed brightest of all.

"Maybe you won't be able to tell what it can do inside a church, but . . . ." Jason's voice trailed off as Ellen went through a series of stances, her face fierce and focused. The blade hummed as it cut the air, and the candles on the altar guttered and flamed higher than before. Jack stood watching, balanced lightly on the balls of his feet, body tilted forward, eyes following the arc of the sword like a child on the playground who longs to join in the game.

Finally, Ellen completed the sequence, cheeks flushed, eyes shining. She grinned, allowing the tip of the blade to drift to the floor. Then looked around at the circle of faces, fastening on Jason's. "Whoa! Really? This is for me?" as if she couldn't quite believe it. "This is so . . . cool," she finished lamely.

"May I see the blade, my dear?" Nick extended his weathered hand. Reluctantly, Ellen passed him the sword. Nick turned it over in his hands, studying the crosspiece, the layered metal blade, the cross emblazoned on the hilt. The old wizard blinked slowly, like a blindsided owl.

"Where did you get this?" he asked Jason, an unusual edge to his voice.

"At Raven's Ghyll. In a cave in Ravenshead, under the Dragon's Tooth. You know. The Weirstone."

Nick frowned. "In a cave under the Weirstone? I'm quite familiar with the place, and there is no cave there these days."

"It opened in an earthquake," Jason explained. "I guess D'Orsay and the others didn't know it was there, either."

"I daresay." Nick eyed him keenly for a moment. "The cave is open, is it?"

"Well. Maybe not. It kind of caved in when I left."

Nick took a quick breath, as if he wanted to ask more questions, but instead turned to Ellen. "Has your weapon told you her name?"

She nodded. "Waymaker," she whispered, glaring around at the others, as if they might argue.

"Ah. I thought so." The old man nodded. "Waymaker,

wrought by sorcerers in Dragon's Ghyll under the rule of the Dragon Aidan Ladhra. One of the seven great blades." Snowbeard closed his eyes for a long moment, then sighed and opened them and handed the blade back to Ellen. "It's fitting that Waymaker fight next to Shadowslayer in the hands of the last heirs of the Warrior Guild."

"Maybe we're not the last." Jack looked uncomfortable at the idea of being the last of a dying breed. "Maybe there are others we don't know about."

"If there are," Ellen said, strapping on the scabbard and cinching it around her hips, "they can find their own swords."

"Wait till you see the rest of this," Jason said, lifting his backpack onto the front pew and unzipping it. He dumped the contents onto the weathered wood seat and stood back, allowing the others to crowd in. Only Ellen stood aside, caressing Waymaker's hilt, a distant expression on her face.

Madison picked through the jewelry. She'd always loved shiny things. There were gold and silver medieval pieces, set with precious and semiprecious stones: brooches and necklaces and bracelets and hair adornments. Her fingers itched to sketch the designs. She gathered her mass of hair into a gold net and set a jewel-encrusted tiara on her head, stuck three rings on each hand, and admired the result. "I always wanted to be a queen," she said wistfully.

Queens never had to worry about finding money for tuition and books.

Her eyes kept straying to the backpack. Jason had set it aside in one of the pews. Something glittered in the back of her mind, a light in the darkness, like a painting she'd not yet splashed onto the canvas.

Seph had collected a pile of objects in front of him. Some were dull black rocks, totally unimpressive, others were crafted in precious metals, engraved with mysterious designs. Some were mounted on chains or set into jewelry. He sorted through them with his long fingers, turning them to catch the light so he could read the inscriptions on them, murmuring magical words under his breath.

Jack tried on a pair of gauntlets in a lightweight silver metal, extending his arms to check out the effect.

"And these all came from the same cave, I assume?" Snowbeard said.

Jason nodded. "This wasn't even half of it, but I tried to take the best, as far as I could choose. Hastings told me to bring all this stuff back here and hide it, and not to let anyone know it's here. That's why I'm back." He half-mumbled the last part, like he didn't want to say it out loud.

Madison sat down in the pew next to the backpack. It was illuminated, pulsing with magic, and she realized that the power that had seemed to emanate from Jason was really coming from it. Before she knew what she was doing, she'd lifted it onto her lap, cradling it in her arms.

"Hey!" Jason jerked the backpack out of her hands. "Careful."

Madison was mortified. She wasn't usually a grabby person. "I—I'm sorry. But, you know what? Something's still in there," she said. "It's like . . . I don't know . . . *important.*"

Suddenly, it was like everybody in the church had stopped talking and focused on them.

"*Is* there something else, Jason?" Nick asked into the silence.

Jason's face hardened, and his eyes narrowed, like he

might refuse to answer. He looked from Nick to Madison, then sighed and groped in the front pocket of his backpack. He brought out a velvet bag embroidered over with symbols in a darker thread. "It's some kind of *sefa*," he said, shrugging. "I . . . ah . . . picked it out for myself." He handed it to Nick.

The old man weighed the parcel in his two hands, as if he could discern its essence by touch alone. "This is very old," he said thoughtfully. "And yet, somehow new. Familiar, yet strange. It has a potential for power that is truly amazing, yet not quite manifest. Something I've never encountered before."

He opened the bag and drew out a large, slightly ovoid stone. They all gathered around it, like planets around a new sun.

"Mère de Dieu," Seph muttered. He always lapsed into French when he got excited. "What is it?"

"I think it's called the Dragonheart," Jason replied, his eyes on the stone." Then he shut his mouth, as if he'd said too much.

Nick's head came up. "The Dragonheart? Really? What makes you think so?"

"There was a book in the cave. I read some of it. It talked about a stone like this. Called the Dragonheart."

"Do you have the book?" Nick asked, his black eyes glittering with interest.

Jason shook his head. "No, I—ah—lost it on the way out."

"What else did it say about the stone?" Nick's voice had sharpened considerably.

"I don't remember exactly," Jason said sullenly. "Something about taking control of the magical guilds or destroying them. Like it was a weapon or something. I was kind of in a hurry."

"That's a pity." Nick stroked the surface of the stone with a wrinkled finger. "Even here in church, you can feel it." The glow from the stone lit the wizard's face, accentuating the lines of age so that he looked like the oldest of prophets. "Madison is right. This *is* important."

"I don't know about *important*," Jason said, clearly worried that his prize might be confiscated. "But I thought it looked cool." He pulled out a dangerous-looking metal stand, all sharp edges and sinuous monsters. "This came with it."

Madison was fascinated by the stone in Nick's hands. Broad flashes of blue and green surfaced as he turned it, like the scales of some brilliantly colored fish surfacing in an exotic tropical sea.

Not that she'd ever seen an exotic tropical sea.

It was more than her usual fascination with shiny things. She was always conscious of the presence of power, drawn to it, in fact, but this beat against her senses and clamored in her ears, impossible to ignore.

Ambushed by a rush of desire, Madison reached out a finger toward the stone. The stone kindled, illuminating the entire church, and a small tongue of flame erupted from the center to lick the surface, as if seeking a connection. She jerked back her hand without making contact and retreated a step, gripping the side of the pew to steady herself.

No. No more. She was done with that. She drew a shaky breath and looked up to see Jason watching her.

"You okay?" he asked, laying a proprietary hand on the stone. Madison nodded mutely.

"I would like to study these objects," Nick said, frowning. "It would help if Mercedes Foster could take a look at them, as well, since they're the work of sorcerers, for the most part. Though the more people who know about this, the more difficult it will be to keep it a secret."

Jason nodded. "Hastings said to hide this stuff somewhere secure. So I thought of the church, because—you know— churches suppress magic. Maybe these things wouldn't be so obvious to someone who's looking for them. Seph belongs here, and has a key, so he could go in and out pretty easy."

"Why? Is someone after you?" Madison asked, trying to shake off the influence of the stone. "Does anyone know about this?"

Jason looked away from her. "As far as I know, I got away clean." Something told Madison he was lying.

"But there are people in here all the time," Ellen objected. "What if we need to get to . . . get to these things, and a Mass is going on? Besides, where would we hide it? We can't just shove it under a pew."

"There's the mourner's chapel," Seph suggested. "People don't go in there unless there's a funeral, and not a lot for that, since it's tiny. It's downstairs, next to the crypt. And there's a secret entrance."

"There's dead people in this church?" Madison shivered. She preferred that bodies be buried out in the churchyard, so their spirits could roam free if they liked.

Seph nodded. "It was built by the Presbyterians, but it was taken over by European Catholics more than a hundred and fifty years ago. They liked to be buried out of the weather, I guess. Come on. Bring the stuff. I'll show you."

Seph led them through a doorway at the front of the

sanctuary and down a narrow, dimly lit flight of stairs.

The crypt lay on one side of the stairs, the chapel on the other. The chapel was just big enough for a family to gather privately. At one end a stone was set into the wall, engraved with the name and dates for one JAMES MCALISTER 1795 TO 1860.

"Seems like a strange resting place for a Presbyterian, but McAlister was also one of the region's leading abolitionists," Seph said. "Watch."

He pushed the stone and it pivoted silently on an invisible hinge, revealing a rough opening the width of a man's shoulders. Air whistled through, bringing with it the scent of water and stone.

"This was a station on the Underground Railway. There's a tunnel that runs all the way to the lake. Escaped slaves would hide in the church basement, then meet boats on the shore and travel across to Canada. Not fun to crawl through, these days. If ever."

The crypt housed several rooms lined with vaults, most of them occupied for more than a century. Jack walked down the row, scanning the names on the vaults in a businesslike fashion until he came to the one he was looking for. "Here we go," he murmured, pointing at an inscription. "Perfect."

Madison peered around him to read, J. THOMAS SWIFT, ESQ. There were no dates.

"Who's that?" she asked.

"That's my dad," Jack replied. "Or, it will be. This was my dad's church, on Christmas and Easter, anyway. He bought this vault when he lived in Trinity. Before the divorce."

Madison eyed it doubtfully. "You're saying it's empty?"

Jack nodded. "Yeah. I mean, he's still alive, right? So,

unless you think it's too obvious because he's related to me, we can stash the stuff in there."

"And we can get at it pretty much whenever we want, without going through the main church," Seph added. "People never come down here. Most of the people buried here died a hundred years ago."

"I'll keep the Dragonheart with me," Jason suggested. "Seph's house is totally warded, so it should be safe."

He wants the stone, Madison thought jealously, recognizing the same strange lust in herself. Was this like one of those magical objects in stories that people fought and died over?

"*All* of the items will be safer here, in the sanctuary, with the proper warding," Nick said, frowning at Jason. "Harder to find, and easier for us all to examine. Once we know more, we can make a decision about their final disposition."

Jason dropped the subject, though Madison noticed his eyes straying to the Dragonheart as they opened the vault and concealed the jewelry and artifacts inside. Jason, Seph, and Snowbeard made arrangements to meet regularly and examine and experiment with the talismans and amulets in the vault. They seemed almost giddy in their optimism that Jason's treasure would offer them an advantage in the war that everyone seemed to think was inevitable.

Madison was less enthusiastic. The Dragonheart still glittered enticingly in a corner of her mind, one more thing she'd have to try and ignore. The presence of this treasure in Trinity did not make her feel safer. In fact, she felt like Trinity had become a target that would be noticed, sooner or later, by those who would destroy everything she cared about.

❧ CHAPTER SIX ❧
PASSAGES

Well, thought Jason. Jack is the talk of the town. I'm glad it's not me.

Jack's dad, Thomas Swift, had returned to Trinity for Christmas, determined to show off to the locals by throwing the party of the year.

Word on the street was that Daddy had hired a party planner, who'd been working on the thing for months. He called it a Midwinter Solstice party, but it was more of a debutante party for Jack, if they had that kind of thing for guys. Thomas had brought a small contingent of business associates and social climbers and preppy kids from Boston, so Jack could "network," he said.

The local guest list had started out to be just as exclusive, but Jack had turned it into an open house by passing out invitations at school. In fact, he'd begged all his friends to come, so he wouldn't be marooned with a crowd of old people and East Coast lawyers.

The Lakeside Club was totally fancy—a huge Victorian palace with a ballroom set next to the lake. Tiny lights embroidered the dock and gazebo, glittered on the snow, and flickered in the winter-stripped trees. There were huge wreaths over the fireplaces, and bells and greenery on all the tables.

It would have been even nicer in the summer, when the party could spill out onto the terrace by the lake and they might have been a little less fussy about the dress code.

Even Hastings had returned from Britain for the party. Jason spotted the wizard several times over the course of the evening, cruising the room with a glittering Linda Downey at his side. Jason had hoped to take him aside and get some news from Britain, but the wizard and enchanter were always the center of a crowd.

Jason felt sorry for Jack. Thomas worked the room like a life insurance salesman at a funeral, towing his reluctant son along. Jack towered over the big shots in his custom-tailored suit, since nothing off the rack would have fit him. His hair was tied back neatly because he'd refused to chop it off for the occasion.

The place was packed, of course—Jack was the home-town Mr. Popular. And the food was incredible—shrimp and little crabmeat pies, fruit towers, and platters of desserts.

Jason thrust his fingers into his neckline, loosening the tie Linda had inflicted on him. He guessed the spectacle was worth putting on a jacket—temporarily, at least.

He drifted into the bar, thinking he might find it unattended, and found Becka Downey and Thomas Swift, Jack's parents, nose to nose, arguing.

Battle of the litigators. Jason withdrew into the shadows, but he could still hear everything.

"I have to say, I'm worried about Jack," Thomas said.

"Really? You've hardly spoken to him since Christmas."

"Well, I assumed you were handling things. With his grades, he shouldn't have any trouble getting into an Ivy League school. I offered to pull some strings if there's an issue. And yet, he's seriously considering going to Trinity?"

"Trinity is one of the best liberal-arts schools in the country. And he can go there for free."

Thomas waved his hand, dismissing *free*. "I told you I would finance his education. Maybe his undergraduate school doesn't matter. But, frankly, he seems totally clueless about what he wants to do. He has to start strong, you know, or he'll never get into a good law school."

Becka lifted her chin. "Did he tell you he wants to go to law school?"

Thomas ignored this. "I found him a summer job with a firm in Boston, but he says he'd rather stay around here. Working at the docks is all well and good while you're in high school. Now it's time he thought about his future. I mean, he looks like a bodybuilder, for God's sake."

At least no one's fighting over *my* future, Jason thought. He drifted back out into the main hall, which was packed with Jack's family and friends, people he didn't know. He hadn't been born and raised in Trinity. Although he was (reluctantly) back in school, he tended to hang out with Seph and Jack and Ellen and Madison. Otherwise, he felt like a total outsider.

There were some girls he'd gotten to know, though. Maybe he could make some plans for later on. He passed along the buffet table, loading a small plate with desserts.

"I can't believe how cold it is," someone behind him said.

He swung around. It was a girl, small and shapely, with full red lips and masses of dark curls spilling down her back. She carried herself like a rich person. Or a wizard. Or both. He didn't remember seeing her before.

He studied her with interest. "It tends to be cold here in the winter. So I hear."

"Well, duh. How could I forget?" She shivered, despite the high-necked sweater she was wearing. Jason was no fashion expert, but it seemed like an odd choice for such a glitzy party.

"I used to go to high school at Trinity," the girl said. "But I don't remember you."

Jason leaned back against the wall. "I've only been here a year."

"I'm Alicia Middleton," she said, sticking out her hand. "Leesha, I guess."

"Jason Haley." Jason took her hand, feeling the power in the grip. A wizard, and she was juiced, compared to him. Her and everybody else.

There was an awkward pause as Leesha no doubt made her own comparisons, and then Jason said, "So you know Jack from school?"

"Actually, I used to go out with him."

"Really?" Huh, Jason thought. Jack went out with a wizard? She must be pre-Ellen. Nobody with any sense would try and get between those two. "So you moved away or what?"

"We broke up," she replied, answering his unspoken question. "And then I moved away."

"Well," Jason said. "Cool that you're still friends. I mean, that Jack invited you and all."

"Oh, he didn't really invite me," Leesha said. "I just

moved back to town, and I saw the party was an open house, so I came. I figured I'd see a lot of people I know." She paused, then rushed on. "But I guess the people I hung out with aren't here."

"That always happens," Jason said.

She opened her mouth as if to say more, but then her eyes fixed on something behind him. She went pale to the hairline, her eyes widened and she took a step back, one hand at her throat.

"Leesha! *What the hell* are you doing here?"

Jason swung around. Jack Swift was bearing down on them like a thunderstorm over the lake. Ellen, Will, and Fitch were right behind him.

"H-hey, Jack." Leesha continued to backpedal until she bumped up against the wall. "What's up? I mean—well—look, chill out, will you? I only wanted to say happy birthday." Her voice rose into a kind of frightened squeak as Jack invaded her space.

"Now, why is it I don't believe you?" Jack said. "You've got a hell of a lot of nerve."

"The girl must be looking for another hot-fudge shower," Ellen said. Then she, too, advanced on Leesha.

"Hey," Jason said, thrusting himself in front of Leesha. "Take it easy."

Jack glared at him as if he'd taken leave of his senses. "I guess you two haven't been properly introduced," he growled.

"This is Alicia Middleton, trader and renegade wizard," Ellen put in. "She used to go to school here, until she and some traders kidnapped Jack, so they could sell him to the highest bidder. So wizards could play him in a tournament."

"Then she snatched me and Fitch from a train station in

Carlisle so Dr. Longbranch could use us as hostages to make Jack fight," Will added, a frown clouding his usually friendly face.

"The only nice thing she ever did was break up with Jack," Fitch said. "That was awesome, really."

Leesha looked around the circle of scowling faces, yanking at the neck of her sweater as if she were suffocating. "We've all done things we'd rather forget about. I mean, Ellen came to Trinity to *kill* Jack."

"It's not like I had a *choice*," Ellen muttered.

Leesha was definitely playing to a hostile audience. "Look, I know I've made some bad decisions."

Ellen rolled her eyes and mimicked Leesha, fluffing her hair and mouthing *I know I've made some bad decisions*. "So why are you here?"

Leesha hesitated, biting at her lip. "Well, I've got both Wizard Houses pissed at me now. A sanctuary seemed like a good idea."

"Well, maybe you should've thought of that before you made so many enemies," Jack said, looking totally unsympathetic.

"I thought we could—you know—help each other," Leesha persisted. "I know something about the Roses and D'Orsay and . . ."

"Like we could trust you," Ellen muttered. "How do we know you're not here as a spy? Like before?"

Jeez, Jason thought. Give the girl a break.

"Come on," he said to Leesha. "Let's get your coat and I'll walk you out." He took her elbow and steered her toward the door, feeling Jack's hot glare between his shoulder blades.

Leesha handed her valet ticket to the attendant and they

sheltered in the entryway against the raw northwestern wind. Close to shore, the lake was larded over with ice. Further out, the wind raked it into a dark chop. Jason expended a bit of power to take the edge off the cold.

"Well," Leesha said. "They didn't seem glad to see me."

Jason snorted. "What'd you expect?"

"You make a few *teensy* mistakes . . ." Leesha said, pouting. "That's the thing about small towns, they never forget a *thing*."

Jason laughed. She had attitude, he had to admit.

"Are you staying with family, or what?" he asked.

"With my great aunt," she said. "She's like, half deaf and three-quarters blind. That's how I ended up here before. My parents are wizards, but they're sort of always on the move, you know? And really busy." Her voice trailed off. "So. Whenever they get busy or I get in trouble, I have to come live with my Aunt Millisandra. It's like the worst punishment they can think of, sending me to live in the Midwest."

"And is it?"

She shivered. "There's worse things. I didn't actually get kicked out of school this time. Jessamine Longbranch—d'you know her? Warriormaster for the White Rose? She was the one who planned to play Jack in the Game. That thing with Jack at the high school—Longbranch had recruited me to spy on Jack, but I kind of went out on my own.

"So. She has this big grudge against me. It took her a while, she's been distracted, but anyway, I came home one day to find two assassins waiting in the residence hall." Leesha stared glumly out at the frozen lake.

"And?" Jason prompted, when he finally caught up and realized she hadn't finished the story.

"Well, they're—you know—*dead*, of course," she said, shrugging.

Okaayy, Jason thought, studying her with new respect and not a little apprehension.

"But it could happen again, and I didn't want to be looking over my shoulder all the time. So I came here."

"So how long are you here for?"

"Long as I can stand it, I guess. This town's really changed. It's like a fortress. How does the sanctuary work, anyway? Is there really some kind of rule against attack magic?"

"More than a *rule*," Jason said, figuring Leesha wasn't into following rules. "It's enforced with magic. Hexes, attack magic, curses, black magic *sefa*s—anything stronger than Persuasion—they don't work in here."

Leesha stared at him in disbelief. "Really?"

"Really."

She smiled, pressing her fingers into her neckline. "Cool." She stepped close and looked up at him with wide eyes. "Who enforces it, anyway? I mean, must be someone with a lot of talent."

He took a quick step back, remembering who he was talking to. "Must be. Well, here's your ride, I think." It was just a guess. The valet had pulled up in an Audi TT. Jason went to turn away.

She gripped his arm, sending a current of Persuasion up into his shoulder. "I really need to stay here. I know I've done some bad things in the past, but people change." She searched his eyes.

"I'm not the one you have to convince," Jason said. "Maybe you should start with Jack."

She wrinkled her nose. "Jack's been mad at me ever since I broke up with him. And after that whole deal with the traders, I don't think that's going to change."

"Then talk to Hastings."

She flinched. "He's so scary, you know?"

He did know. Hastings gave the impression he could see right through you. Which might be a good thing where Leesha was concerned.

Jason figured she wouldn't stay in the sanctuary long if Hastings didn't want her there. But would he really make her leave? Especially since she couldn't use attack magic.

Still, Persuasion in her hands might be weapon enough, he thought.

Leesha's hand was still on his arm. "Maybe you could talk to him for me?" She gazed up at him. Her eyes were a kind of violet gray, like smoke on the horizon.

Jason had his own petition to deliver. He took back his arm. "Sorry. I can't help you. I just don't have that much influence." Jason backed away like a courtier from a queen, then turned and headed inside.

He looked over his shoulder, once, and saw Leesha still standing next to her car, her hair a cloud around her head, looking small and vulnerable and very much alone.

❧ CHAPTER SEVEN ❧
A CHANGE OF PLANS

By 10 p.m., the contingent from Boston had either left or retired to the bar. A DJ had set up in the ballroom, and music pounded out over the lake. Jack and his friends gathered in a windowed sitting area off the ballroom. A fire crackled on the great hearth, and they dipped hot chocolate out of great silver tureens. The jackets and ties came off as soon as the chaperones faded.

The Weir were well represented: Jack Swift, Ellen Stephenson, Seph McCauley, and Jason Haley. Plus Will Childers and Harmon Fitch, who were kind of honorary members of the guilds. And Madison, who was something else entirely.

She recalled Min's warning, years ago. *Beware the magical guilds. Promise me you'll stay away from them. Swear.*

Maddie had sworn, and yet, here she was. I can't help it, Gramma, she thought. You'd understand if you were here. She was wedged into an elegant loveseat beside Seph, conscious of his hip pressing against hers, the soft buzz of power flowing through. She tried to ignore it.

He seemed totally at home at these dress-up affairs—not stuffy, but in context. He still looked dressed up, even though his jacket was off and his sleeves rolled, long legs extended and crossed at the ankles. His shirt was so white it hurt her eyes, his collar starched, the crease in his trousers still perfect.

Madison had found a vintage emerald silk dress at the consignment shop, bias-cut, with seaming at the hip and gores that flared out from the knee, and a black crocheted shawl with long fringe and tiny beads and sequins. It had cost all of fifteen dollars, which she couldn't afford. It was kind of low cut, which made her fuss with the straps and pull the shawl closely around her shoulders. Her strappy sandals were silly in the snow, but then she wasn't known to be practical.

Some of the East Coast boys had asked her to dance, and she declined. She wasn't going to say yes to them when she had to say no to Seph. Seph was a great dancer, but one slow dance with Madison might sicken him for days.

Still, she couldn't help tapping her foot to the music and wishing they were out on the dance floor. Also, if she were dancing, she wouldn't have to hear about the traitorous wizard Leesha Middleton all night. She was already tired of the subject.

"Leesha's up to something," Jack said. "Otherwise she'd never come back to Trinity. She used to complain there was no place in Ohio she could buy cute shoes."

"I have that problem, too," Fitch muttered, to general laughter. "No, really, I mean, you try and match an outfit . . ."

Despite his jokes, Madison couldn't help thinking Fitch

looked a little twitchy—with good reason. Leesha *had* kidnapped him and Will.

"She'd better not come near any of us," Ellen said. Meaning Jack, no doubt. She paced restlessly around the elegant room, picking up objects and setting them down again. "I kept hoping Hastings would come out and say something, but he and Linda didn't stay too long."

Seph straightened, as always, quick to defend his father. "Look, Leesha's just not a priority for him. There's not much she can do, not with the boundary up. She can't use attack charms here."

"You don't know her like we do," Ellen said, scowling.

"I know her well enough," Seph said, scrubbing a hand through his hair. "We met in a club in Toronto. She slipped wizard flame in my drink."

"What?" Madison stared at Seph, suddenly more interested in the subject of Leesha. "I didn't know that."

"She seems really scared," Jason said.

Everyone turned to look at him.

"What? Don't tell me you *believe* her." Jack made an irritated sound. "Are you crazy?"

"She says both Wizard Houses are after her," Jason said, leaning against the brickwork around the fireplace. "And that they'll kill her if she leaves the sanctuary."

"When did you have this little talk?" Jack rolled his eyes. "I mean, she just got here, and you're already best friends?"

"I didn't say that," Jason replied, looking mulish. "I ran into her by the desserts."

"You don't just *run into* Leesha Middleton," Fitch said. "I've found that out."

"Whatever." Jason flipped his hand, dismissing the subject,

and turned to Seph. "I'm hoping your dad'll take me back to Britain with him. Maybe you could say something?"

Seph shrugged. "I guess. I've barely had a chance to talk to him. I'll probably see him tomorrow."

Jason pushed away from the wall. "Well, I'm going. I'm meeting some people."

"Hope it's not Leesha," Seph called after him, grinning. Jason batted the comment away with a rude gesture and disappeared around the corner.

"I think I'll go, too," Madison said. Will and Fitch seemed comfortable enough, but these days she always felt edgy among Seph's gifted friends—afraid the hex magic might suddenly surface and give her away.

It'll be better in the fall, she thought. He'll be safe away at school. He'll be away from this whole magical battle/siege mentality.

He'll be far away from me, she thought, and it felt like something was stuck in her throat that she couldn't swallow down.

"I'll walk you home," Seph said, standing and helping her to her feet, not giving her a chance to decline.

When they arrived back at the inn, the parking lot was nearly full. It hadn't been easy to get the night off for Jack's party, and Madison hated to give up the tips.

They circled around to the less-traveled side entrance. Seph followed her onto the porch. "Mind if I come in for a while?" he asked, looking down at her. His eyes darkened to a deep blue green.

Seph had a way of watching her with those witchy eyes that made her stumble over words and into walls. He could suck all her breath away and set her heart hammering without so much as touching her. It was dangerous to be alone with Seph McCauley—not because of what he might do, but because of how she might react.

"Well . . ." She hesitated. "For a little while," she whispered, her resistance evaporating. She was weak, that was all there was to it. "We can go sit in the parlor," she added primly. The parlor was a safely public place.

"The *parlor*?" Seph raised an eyebrow. "I thought maybe we . . ."

"Come on," she said. "We'll have to be quiet or Rachel will kick us out."

Shaking his head, Seph followed Madison through the kitchen with its hulking commercial range and loaded pantry, crossed the center hall, and entered the parlor. The room was furnished with marble-topped Victorian tables and curved-back chairs, and lined with bookshelves. A cheerful fire burned on the hearth, and bottles of wine, a tea service, and trays of cookies were set out on the sideboard for guests of the inn. Rachel's presence making itself felt.

They settled into the chairs, side by side, like two nineteenth-century sweethearts in the presence of a chaperone. Seph covered her hand with his on the delicate armrest, brushing his thumb over her tingling skin. The hex magic within her uncoiled, alerted by his presence, and rippled into her extremities. Her pulse began to hammer and she slid a glance at him. How could he not notice?

"Whoa," he said, massaging his temples with his other hand. "I was fine earlier, but now I'm getting the mother of all headaches."

"Maybe you'll be less busy this summer," she suggested, withdrawing her hand as soon as she could and tugging at her shawl. "With . . . with the boundary and all, I mean."

He stared moodily into the flames. "I don't know. I can't see things changing, unless they get worse."

"You should try and relax a little. Have a little fun before you go away to school."

Seph cleared his throat. "I've been meaning to talk to you about that."

"About what?"

He took a deep breath, as if anticipating the battle ahead. "I've decided to put off Northwestern for awhile."

"What?" She twisted in her seat. "Why?" Like she had to ask.

"What with everything going on and all. I just think it would be better if I stayed here."

"Who talked you into that? Nick? Your father?"

He shifted his shoulders unhappily. "I decided on my own."

"I'll just bet you did." The words tumbled out, hard and furious.

"We could see each other more. I thought you'd be happy." He looked over at her, then away. "Guess not."

Madison hadn't meant it to turn into a fight. Why couldn't she talk to people about things without getting all raggedy mad? "I don't see you now, and you're right in town."

"Do you even *want* to see me?" He paused, and when she didn't reply, he continued. "Ever since Second Sister, you've been . . . different." His voice broke with frustration. "It's like . . . you're scared of me. You flinch when I touch you. It makes it really hard, okay?"

Typical. Seph McCauley chose to confront the elephant in the parlor when she'd just as soon walk around it.

Seph barreled on. "I know you can't forget what happened last summer. At Second Sister. But it's been six months. If you'd just talk about it, I think it would help."

He'd given her this tiny opening, an excuse for her crazy behavior, and she seized on it. "I'm *trying* to forget," she said. "But I can't. Those people getting burned up and ripped apart. And I know Leicester was . . . evil, but when you and Jason . . ."

"That's not who I am, Maddie. Leicester tortured me for months." He held up his maimed hand. "He did this to me. He killed Jason's father, and I thought he'd killed mine.

"I'm not saying you were wrong. Killing him, I mean." Maddie stared down at her lap. "It's my problem, not yours." That part was the truth, anyway.

"But it *is* my problem. Sometimes . . . the way you look at me, I think it's going to be all right. And then . . . I never know, from day to day, where I stand. If I've been staying away from you, it's because it's too hard." He reached out and touched her hand. "I miss you."

"I'm just . . . it's hard for me, too." She kept her gaze downcast, afraid to meet his eyes. "I need some space, okay? Can you just . . . give me some time?"

"I don't know how much time we have. I don't know what's going to happen." When she said nothing, Seph went on. "It would be easier for me to go away, and then I wouldn't have to see you all the time. But I have to stay. If we lose this war, we lose everything."

"I don't see why winning the war is up to you."

"It's not all up to me. But I have to help." He leaned his head back, closed his eyes, the lashes dark against his bloodless skin. "I'm sorry, Maddie," he whispered. "I don't know what's wrong with me lately. I don't feel so well."

She pulled her hand free. It was happening again. His undiluted presence was having its usual effect. She could feel power rising inside her, coalescing under her breastbone. She was leaking magic, despite all her efforts to contain it. Like she had any idea how.

She tried naming colors in alpha order, a trick from when she was little. Azure. Blue. Citrine. Dark Green. Eggplant. Fuchsia. But it was no good. Her skin flamed and her hands and arms tingled and burned. She knew what that meant.

"Seph, listen, I better . . ." The telephone rang, somewhere close by. She heard running footsteps, Rachel's business voice, "The Legends. Rachel Booker."

Moments later, Rachel appeared in the doorway to the parlor, extending the phone toward Madison. "It's for you. Your mama."

Madison couldn't very well refuse to speak to her mother, with Rachel standing right there. So she took the phone reluctantly. "Mama?"

Carlene's voice reverberated in her ear amid a cloud of static. "Madison? What's wrong with the phone?"

Madison struggled to control the power that threatened to pour out of her body. The static cleared.

"Oh, Madison, honey, thank God. I've been trying to reach you for days. I don't know what to do." Her mother's voice was thick with tears and several beers, if Madison was any judge. And she was.

Madison sighed. "I'm kind of busy, Mama. What's going on?"

"They've took the kids."

"What do you mean? Who?"

"Grace and John Robert. The county."

"The county's took . . . taken Grace and J.R.? Why?"

"You remember Sheila Ann White? She married Tom Harper but they're separated now. She works at the bank and sometimes fills in at Charley's."

Madison struggled to keep her voice in check, pulling patience from some unknown source. "What does Sheila Ann White Harper have to do with Grace and John Robert?"

"I worked a double shift on Friday. She promised to watch the kids when she got off at the bank. But they called her into work at Charley's and she forgot completely."

"Why didn't you call off when Sheila Ann didn't show?"

"Well, see, I was already at work. She was coming to watch them for second shift."

"You left them home alone all *day* while you worked a double?" Madison's voice rose.

"Gracie is ten years old," Carlene said defensively. "She can watch John Robert in the daytime."

I'll bet the county doesn't agree, Madison thought. "Didn't Grace call you when Sheila Ann didn't come?"

"Well, we don't exactly have phone service right now. I got behind in my payments again."

Madison sighed. "How did the county hear about it?"

Long pause. "The shed caught fire."

No. It was happening again, and she wasn't even there to be blamed. "How did the shed catch fire? Are things catching fire again? Did . . . did somebody set it?"

"I don't know. Brice Roper spotted the smoke and drove up there."

"Brice Roper?" Her insides twisted, knotted up. Suddenly, she was back at school, facing down Brice and his leering, jeering friends. "Right. I bet he just happened to see it. Probably sneaking around up there."

Another pause. "Well. He and his daddy took the kids into Coal Grove and turned them over to the county. I about went crazy when I came home and found them gone."

Madison looked up to find Seph watching her. She closed her eyes, wishing him gone. He didn't need to hear this.

She lowered her voice further. "When did all this happen?"

"A week ago."

"A week ago!" Static crashed in her ear again and she held the phone at arm's length, took a deep breath, let it out, brought it back to her ear. "Mama, where are they?" Madison pictured Grace and John Robert locked up in some kind of home for wayward kids. Grace would be having a fit. J. R. would cry.

"They're in foster care. There's a hearing scheduled. I have Ray McCartney representing me. But, the thing is, he don't think they'll give the kids back to me."

"Why not?"

"This ain't the first time the county's been out." Carlene rushed on, so Madison couldn't get a word in. "You know they've been hassling us ever since Min died. Ray wants you to come back for the hearing. He says they might let the kids go if the county knows you'll be here to watch them."

"When's the hearing?"

"Next Thursday."

"Mama! I'm in school! Spring semester is just starting."

Carlene ignored this. "I've been trying to call you, but you never answer your phone. And I have to drive to town to call. Or use the phone at the Ropers."

Madison felt a rush of guilt, remembering how often she'd ignored the phone. She hadn't even listened to the messages.

"Listen. I'll come for the hearing, but it'll be Wednesday before I can get there."

"Thanks, honey. I know things'll be fine once you're here." In the space of a few minutes, Carlene's voice had gone from breathless panic to breezy confidence.

Madison clicked off and stood clutching the receiver. During the course of the conversation, a weight had descended. A yoke of responsibility, familiar from the time she was small. The burden of making sure everything turned out all right.

Seph was still there. He stood, a little shakily, using the back of the chair for support. "What happened?" he asked.

"I have to go home. Family crisis."

"Can I help?"

"No." She didn't really want to discuss her sad-assed family.

Seph reached for her, she took a step back, and he dropped his hands. "Look, I'll talk to my father. I think he's planning to stay through New Year's, anyway. If he can help with the boundary, I'll go with you."

Madison's heart lurched in gratitude. She could really use a friend. It had been so long since she'd had someone on her side. Then she thought of Seph in Coal Grove, meeting Carlene and the rest. Seph, who'd been born to money and raised in Toronto and gone to school in Switzerland and spoke French like a native.

No. Seph was her friend—more than a friend. Maybe they couldn't be together, but she still didn't want to look into his eyes and find embarrassment or pity.

Besides, he seemed to be in charge of saving everybody else.

"Thanks. I mean it, but I'd better handle this on my own."

Seph cleared his throat. "It might not be a good idea for you to leave the sanctuary by yourself."

Madison's mind was already racing, cataloging all the things she had to do. Now it stumbled. "What? Why not?"

"It's just a bad time. Everyone's trying to gain an advantage—D'Orsay, the Roses. Someone might have remembered what happened at Second Sister, and be looking for you."

So his concern for her had to do with wizards. Always wizards. Madison thrust her face into his. "Listen. I. Have. To. Go. I have no choice, understand?"

He raised his hands, capitulating. "When will you be back?"

"Not this semester, anyway. If I had to take a guess, I'd say I'll be lucky to be back in the fall."

Seph frowned down at her. "You're not serious. You've been working so hard to get to art school. And now you want to drop out of *high school*?"

She turned away, rounding her shoulders against his questions. "Don't worry. I'll think of something. I'll know more after I get down there."

"I wish you'd let me help."

She shivered, feeling sparks arcing over the chasm between them. Feeling totally alone. Maybe Seph couldn't leave. But she could. It would give her time to work this out. He wasn't the only one having a hard time.

"Maddie? Are you okay?" The dark brows came together in a frown. "You're shaking."

"Look, it's late," she said, backing away, putting her hands behind her back and nodding toward the door. "You'd better go. I need to pack."

He hesitated, as if he would say something else. Then he shook his head, turned, and was gone. She didn't even hear the front door open and close.

As soon as Seph was out of sight, Madison raced up three flights of stairs to the third floor, taking them two at a time. She shouldered open the door to her room and thumbed the light switch. The bulb in the overhead fixture fizzed, then exploded in a shower of glass.

Crossing to the window in the dark, she ripped open the curtains, her fingers leaving smoldering holes in the cloth. She flung open the wardrobe and snatched off the sheets draping the painting that stood inside.

Throwing back her head and closing her eyes, she extended her hands and sent power through her fingers like a breath long held and finally released. It streaked through the air and buried itself in the canvas, smelling like burnt coffee grounds. The paint blistered and ran into muddy swirls.

She backed away until the bed hit the backs of her knees. She slumped back onto the mattress, resting her feet on the bedframe, her elbows on her knees.

The painting reorganized itself, bleak, but recognizable and horribly animated. It was Second Sister all over again, Seph thrusting her behind him as Leicester and the alumni sent flame spiraling across the conference room. Only this time it struck Seph dead on, flinging him against the wall like a broken marionette.

It changed again—Seph laid out in St. Catherine's, pale and still, candles at his hands and feet, mourners filing past, pointing and whispering when Madison entered the church.

Buried in paint was the evidence of a dozen such attacks, an unrelenting series of scenes of Seph dying in every way imaginable.

Seph stirred the alien magic beneath her skin, woke it up like some monster of the deep. When she let it trickle out, Seph grew pale and tired, he developed raging headaches and his appetite dwindled. When she held it back, Seph visibly improved. But it built and built inside her until she had to release it or explode. There'd been several near misses until she'd discovered she could dissipate it into art—horrible art, but better than any other alternative. She'd tried to paint over it, to obliterate the sequence of awful images, but they continued to surface, like oil on polluted water.

It was a secret she had to keep from Seph—from everyone. There was no way Hastings or Linda or Nick Snowbeard would allow her to stay if they knew. They'd have no idea how to fix it, and Seph was too important to risk. She should have left long ago.

But she didn't. She couldn't give up her dreams of college and Seph McCauley both. She kept hoping the magic from Second Sister would eventually peter out.

Well, now she had no choice. Grimly, she began sorting through her belongings. There wasn't much to pack. She'd brought little from her life in Coal Grove. And she hadn't had the money to buy much since her arrival in Trinity.

After some thought, she pushed the hex painting back into the wardrobe and covered it over with a drop cloth. Two drop cloths. She closed the wardrobe and locked it. She wasn't going to take that thing to Coal Grove. She wouldn't need it once she got back home. Seph wouldn't be there to wake the monster.

While she worked, she sorted through her thoughts, as well.

She had no desire to crawl back to Coal Grove Consolidated High School for the last five months of the year. She was done with that. She'd met the curriculum requirements, and she'd taken all their arts courses. She'd hoped to get a year of college in before she had to pay for it herself. Now she'd probably lose the whole semester.

She knew how it would be once she went home. Her old life would wrap around her like a well-used quilt.

The whispering would begin again, stirred up by her presence. Bit by bit, they'd tear the flesh from the bones of her dreams.

She stared out the window at the hills and hollows of the lake.

Truth be told, she missed the hills and hollows of home, the texture of the timeworn land of her childhood. She missed the people, too, some of them. But not the limits they set for her and the assumptions they made, based on who her mama and daddy were. Not the notes that got left on her locker at school. Not the way people stuck crucifixes in her face like she was some kind of vampire—as if they knew exactly who she was and how she'd turn out.

Maybe she was just running from one kind of trouble to another, from the strange and magical trouble in Trinity to a more familiar kind. At home, they expected too little of her. And here, they expected too much.

Falling in love with Seph McCauley was the kind of bad move Carlene had made all her life. Her mother careened from crisis to crisis, thriving on calamity. She acted like love was something you caught, like cholera. Or a spell that took you unaware. So she couldn't possibly be blamed for screwing everything up.

Madison meant to be different. She meant to take hold of her life and get what she wanted and leave Coalton County behind for good.

"It'll happen," she promised herself. But not just yet.

The canopy bed with the pink satin coverlet and the leaping unicorns on the bedposts was reassuringly familiar. Aunt Millisandra had furnished the room and named it Leesha's Room when Leesha was only three. Until recently, Leesha had stayed there at least once or twice a year. It had always been a kind of confectionary cavelike retreat.

Only now she didn't feel safe.

She propped herself against the ruffled pillow shams and drew the coverlet up to her waist. Releasing a gusty sigh, she punched numbers into her cell phone.

Barber answered on the third ring. "Yes?"

"Well. I'm here."

Barber laughed. "Really? I always know right where you are, remember?"

Leesha fingered the gold circlet Barber had fused around her neck. Jason had said attack magic wouldn't work in the sanctuary. But maybe Barber could track her just the same.

"Look, this isn't working. It's like I said. Everybody hates me."

Barber tsked. "Haley doesn't hate you. You've never even met, right?"

"Well." Leesha hesitated. "I met him tonight. At a party."

"There you go. That's a start. I'm sure you made a good impression." Barber sounded hugely amused.

"The thing is, I just don't . . . I can't do this anymore. You'll have to think of something else."

Barber's voice was like velvet over stone. "That's where you're wrong. This is your problem. You made the deal with D'Orsay. You promised we'd deliver Haley and the Dragonheart. Those papers you gave me mean nothing if we can't consecrate the Covenant. You need to lure Haley out of the sanctuary and to a place where I can get at him. How you do it is up to you."

"I have money. I can pay you. Just take it off, okay?" Leesha struggled to control her voice. Begging didn't come easy.

"You think I have to come to *you* for money?" The velvet was gone. "I'm sick of you bluebloods treating me like a nobody. I know where you are and I know where your Aunt Milli lives. I better see some results or I'll squeeze the breath right out of the both of you." He hung up.

The phone fell from her nerveless fingers and plopped on the satin comforter. Wrapping her arms around her pillow, Leesha buried her face in the ticking and wept.

❦ Chapter Eight ❦
Transitions

The next morning Seph rolled out of bed late, his stomach knotted up, his head pounding. Then the events of the night before came back to him. It seemed like whenever he and Madison spent time together, it ended in a fight, resulting in him feeling beat up.

He'd never met a girl like Maddie Moss. She was like one of those untouchable plants that closed up their leaves when you brushed against them. It had been a totally frustrating six months. Other girls had made it clear they liked him, but Seph never reciprocated. Madison was like an intoxicating flower that pricked you till you bled, but it was somehow worth it to get close. She was at war with herself, she was at war with him, and yet there were moments . . .

And now she was going away.

He pulled on his jeans and a shirt and descended the winding staircase, catching glimpses of the frozen lake through the windows as he navigated his way to the bottom.

The sky was bluing up as the sun rose higher in the sky, kindling the icicles that hung from the gutters of Stone Cottage. It would be a beautiful winter day.

His parents were in the kitchen.

"Hey." Seph poured himself some orange juice and dropped an English muffin into the toaster. "Who's watching the boundary?"

"I am," Hastings replied. "As long as I'm here."

How does he do that? Seph wondered. He's not even breaking a sweat.

"You and I need to go over some ideas I have for monitoring magical traffic within the sanctuary," Hastings went on.

"We're talking to the sanctuary board later this afternoon," Linda added. "We're going to discuss contingency plans in the event of an attack. We'd like you to come." She focused in on him and frowned. "Are you all right, sweetheart? You look pale and you've got those dark circles under your eyes again."

"We were out pretty late," Seph said.

"Later, I'm meeting with Mercedes and Snowbeard at the church to go over the items Jason brought from the ghyll," Hastings said. "Your insights would be valuable."

Seph couldn't help feeling flattered. His father always treated him as if he were capable of great things. Which made him want to accomplish great things. Even if the pressure was hard to take sometimes.

This was quality time with his father.

Fishing his muffin out of the toaster, he slathered it with butter. He carried his plate to the table and Linda plunked one of her big milkshakes in front of him.

He rolled his eyes. "Milkshakes for breakfast? Again?"

"Drink up. You're skin and bones. You've been sick more often in the past six months than you've been in your whole life before that."

When Seph hesitated, Hastings added, "Listen to your mother. You're going to need all your strength today, I promise you."

Seph hated when they ganged up on him. He lifted his glass in a mock toast and took a long swallow. Peanut butter and chocolate. Kind of like a peanut butter cup in a glass.

Linda went upstairs to shower, leaving Seph alone with his father.

"How are things going in Britain?" Seph asked.

Hastings shrugged. "The Roses have laid siege to Raven's Ghyll, hoping to flush D'Orsay out of his hole. There's some question about the whereabouts of the Covenant. If D'Orsay were holding it, surely he would have acted by now to bring the guilds into line. But if he doesn't have it, who does?"

He paused, then, receiving no answer from Seph, changed the subject. "You're still going out with Madison Moss."

It wasn't really a question. "Yeah. Well, sort of. It's kind of off and on." He didn't really want to talk about girl trouble with his father.

"Snowbeard tells me she's ambivalent about our mission here."

Seph's defenses slammed into place. "That's right. She's not gifted. It's not her fight."

"She's not gifted in the traditional sense, true. But she has a talent that could be of great use to us, if . . ."

"She's not into it, okay? She's got classes and she's working a lot of hours because she has to pay for school next year."

"So you're saying she could be receptive to the right offer."

Seph thrust back his chair, leaving long scratches in the polished wood floor. "What I'm saying is, she's got her own problems. She's talented, but the talent she wants to work on is painting."

"Painting won't help us." Hastings leaned back in his chair. "We don't know a lot about elicitors, since they're not part of the guild system. Legend has it they are descendants of Aidan Ladhra's Dragonguard." Hastings snorted. "That's unlikely. But you know what happened at Second Sister."

Seph carried his plate and glass to the sink and dropped them in with a clatter. "I'm not listening to this."

"I want you to work with her, Seph."

He swung around to face his father. "Work *with* her or work *on* her?"

The wizard waved a hand. "I've seen the way she looks at you. Even if she is not vulnerable to wizardry, you can exert an . . . influence. I want you to find out everything you can about her capabilities."

"And then what?"

"Convince her to help us."

"Right. Just another sacrifice for the bloody cause." Seph splashed coffee into a mug, remembering Maia, who'd died in Toronto because of him.

"Do you have any idea how tenuous our position is? The presence of Trinity is an affront to the Roses. When they finish with Claude they'll come after us. Or, worse, they'll join forces with D'Orsay."

"No."

Hastings slammed his coffee mug down on the table and stood. "Given the powers arrayed against us, we cannot allow some ill-founded, unfathomable, *extravagant* set of principles to prevent us from seizing every advantage we can."

Seph stood, also, and suddenly they were standing toe to toe and face to face, energy crackling in the air between them. Seph was surprised to find that he was equal in height to his father. When had that happened?

"Sorry," Seph said, "but there are some things I just won't do."

Hastings stared at him as if he'd morphed into something unrecognizable. Then his lips twitched into a half smile. "Very well," he said. He sat back down at the table, and gestured at the other chair. "Please."

Seph didn't sit, but leaned forward, resting the heels of his hands on the table. "Madison's going away, anyway."

"What do you mean?"

"Family emergency. She's going home."

"For how long?"

Seph shrugged. "She doesn't know. Maybe even through the summer."

"That's bad for us and dangerous for her."

"I tried to talk her out of it. But she's going, unless we lock her in the crypt at St. Catherine's and slide food under the door. So how far are you willing to go?"

Not that far, apparently, because Hastings changed the subject. "The Roses have been in touch with you, have they not?" Hastings looked him in the eyes.

Seph hesitated, then nodded. "And D'Orsay." He felt guilty, even though he hadn't responded.

"If they can't lure you one way, they may try another," Hastings said. "They may use her to get to you." Hastings studied Seph, tapping the tips of his fingers together. "Well, I suppose there's no help for it now. Keep her departure quiet if you can. Don't tell anyone where she's gone."

"How long are you going to be here?" Seph asked.

"Not much longer, unfortunately." The wizard's hands moved restlessly over the table, the stone in his ring glittering in the morning sunlight. "I'm afraid you're going to have to take on even more responsibility in the near future."

When Hastings didn't go on, Seph prompted him. "Why? What's up?"

"Your mother and I are organizing an assault on Raven's Ghyll."

Seph blinked at him. "What? I thought you . . ."

"I don't think the Covenant is there. But given the fact that war is more and more of a certainty, the hoard may play a pivotal role. In fact, it already has."

Seph had heard of the legendary cache of weapons in Raven's Ghyll. "Has anyone actually seen it? I mean, I thought maybe the hoard was just one of those rumors that turn out to be nothing."

"Possible, but unlikely. The D'Orsays have taken advantage of their role as Masters of the Game to collect magical weapons for centuries. As far as we know, they're somewhere in the ghyll." He laughed. "The Roses are convinced, anyway. The hoard is what's keeping them from entering the ghyll. It might do the same for Trinity. At the very least, if we make it unavailable, the Roses may do our work for us and eliminate D'Orsay. And the last thing we want is for the hoard to fall into the hands of the Roses."

Seph felt a cold trickle of apprehension. "How are you going to do that? Break into the ghyll, I mean? How are you going to get past the Roses?" He had to ask, though he wasn't sure he really wanted to know.

Hastings smiled wolfishly. "There are lots of ways to get in. The challenge will be getting out."

That wasn't reassuring. "Jason wants to come with you."

"I know Jason wants to come. But he has a hard time following orders. I want him here, under Nick's supervision, and where he can help you. We're spread very thin, especially where wizards are concerned."

"You could cut him some slack," Seph said. "He saved my life, you know, at the Havens."

"I know that." Hastings rubbed his forehead with the heel of his hand like he had a headache of his own. "Jason will prove most useful to us if we can find a way to channel that passion of his, so he doesn't go up in flames and take the rest of us with him."

Madison found Sara Mignon in her studio on the third floor of Saddlewood Hall. Her art teacher was clad in a paint-spattered denim shirt and jeans, flinging exuberant splashes of acrylic onto a rough board the size of a small barn. Two graduate students toiled away at the bottom corners, laying in lines that Sara gleefully ignored.

When she saw Madison, Sara jumped down from her stepladder and set her paints on the bottom step. Using her sleeve, she wiped bright yellow from the tip of her nose. Her curly hair spiraled out every which way, a rich, blue-black color that came from a bottle. She looked like no teacher Madison had ever had before.

"Hey, Maddie. What do you think?"

"Well, it . . . it's fine. I like it." Madison was still startled when her professors asked her opinion. Not that she didn't have opinions, she just wasn't used to anybody wanting to hear them. She had gone to schools where you called the teachers sir and ma'am. As in, Yes, sir and Yes, ma'am.

Madison liked everything Sara did, though her teacher's work was really different from her own. Sara's art was tropical in its heat. Madison's painting was cool and smoky and subdued as dusk in the hollows.

Sara (as she insisted on being called) studied the painting critically, hands on hips. "That yellow draws the eye, doesn't it? It might be a little too assertive." She turned to Madison. "Are you here to talk about your capstone?"

"Well, ah . . ."

"Let's take a look at it, shall we?"

The capstone projects were displayed in a sunlit studio on the third floor of the art building. Moody oils, languid water-colors, pushy acrylics. Madison's painting was secluded in a corner, covered by a drape.

Sara swept the cloth away and they stood, side by side. Sara studied the work while Madison stared at her toes.

Why did I have to submit *that* one?

"I like the layering you've done, the flames laid over the stone, the blood splattered on the floor, the arrangement of the bodies, and the way the architecture of the piece carries the eye. There's a strong fantasy element here. Even horror."

Madison nodded mutely.

"This is really different from your other work," Sara said. "More abstract, more raw emotion, more hot shades. There's a violence here I haven't seen from you before. Can you tell me about it?"

No, actually. There was a lack of censure in Sara that invited confidences, but Madison knew better than to share this particular secret.

"It's . . . um . . . from a dream I had."

More like a nightmare.

"Well, it's interesting to see you getting away from landscapes and exploring new subjects and styles. At your age, I think that's important." Sara redraped the painting. "So. Will you be able to help me out next Friday?"

Madison stuffed her hands in her pockets. Saying it made it real. "I . . . ah . . . wanted to tell you I can't be here for your opening next week. I—I have to drop out. I have to go home. Family emergency. I'm really sorry." Tears welled up in her eyes and she turned away, mortified.

Sara put a hand on her shoulder. "Nothing serious, I hope."

"No," Madison said automatically. "Well, maybe. I think I can get it sorted out. But I'll probably have to stay home from now through summer."

"Going back to those dreamy mountains, are you?" Sara grinned. "I'd call that a gift for an artist."

Sara had a knack of making you feel good about yourself. She was as sunny as her paintings. "I guess so," Madison said, feeling a little better. "But I was hoping to get another eight credit hours this semester, what with the two courses I'm taking with you and the capstone. In the fall, I have to pay for it myself. And in the fall, you'll be going back to Chicago."

Sara frowned and tilted her head. "I don't know why we can't still work together. These aren't lecture courses. It's not like I'd be looking over your shoulder even if you were here. You can paint as well in—what is it—Coalville?—as you can here. Maybe we can meet once a month and I can look over your work and give you a grade at the end of the semester. Can you manage that?"

"I . . . well . . . it sounds great. But . . . would we still work through Trinity High School, or would we . . ."

"Don't worry," Sara said, reading her mind. "I'll handle Penworthy."

"I don't know what to say." Madison felt the burn in her face that said she was blushing.

Sara studied her appraisingly. "You know, Trinity's a good school, but fine art is not their specialty. Have you ever thought of coming to Chicago?"

"To the Art Institute? Oh, no. I . . . ah . . . I couldn't afford that." Madison swallowed down her hopes. It wouldn't do to let them get the best of her.

Sara gripped her shoulders and looked her in the eye. "Madison. Your landscapes are unique, totally refreshing, and you're not even a college student yet. Your voice is much older than your years. Your work is Appalachian, but it doesn't have a breath of folk art about it. You see the super-natural in common things. I would call it ethereal."

"Look, I really appreciate . . . everything. But I can't afford to live in Chicago, let alone pay tuition at AIC. The free ride is over after this year. I don't want to graduate a million dollars in debt when I don't know how I'm going to make a living."

Sara dropped her hands from her shoulders. "You let me worry about that. You just keep painting. I'd like to see more figure drawings and portraits, too. Not just landscapes. Then we'll put together a portfolio for you and see what happens. Deal?"

Madison could only nod.

Sara smiled. "Now, let's make sure you'll have everything you need. We'll just say it came out of course fees."

Madison left Sara's studio with a backpack full of books, paints, and other supplies. She wandered across Trinity Square, stopping in shops and galleries and using her tip money to buy little presents for J.R. and Grace and Carlene.

Without really meaning to, she found herself walking through the gate at St. Catherine's, crossing the snowy churchyard to the side door of the church. I'll just take one more look, she said to herself. I don't know when I'll be back here again.

It was a Tuesday morning, and the sanctuary echoed with her footsteps, empty of people save an elderly lady kneeling in the front pew, her head bent over her folded hands. Madison slipped quietly to the stairs in the front of the sanctuary that led down to the Mourner's Chapel, walking right through the wards and confusion charms Seph had built to distract anyone snooping around.

At the foot of the stairs, she turned to the left, entering the crypt itself. They'd left the Swift tomb open, trusting to Seph's barriers to keep the curious at bay.

The sorcerer Mercedes Foster and her small committee had obviously been at work. Magical artifacts were laid out in rows, sorted by probable function. Those that had been identified were labeled in Mercedes's neat hand. Symbols and diagrams had been sketched onto the walls, some sort of tally system.

The stone that Jason called the Dragonheart sat off by itself on its dragon stand, a jewel in an elaborate setting. The flames smoldering at its center sent shadows like haunts skulking along the walls.

What are you *doing* here? Madison asked herself, and got no answer.

She felt the tug of the stone from across the room, dragging her forward. As it had before, the Dragonheart seemed to react to her presence, brightening, colors sliding over each other like brilliant paints sloshing in a jar.

She stood over the stone. As she extended her hand, the light from the stone stained her skin. Her breathing slowed, her eyelids drooped. A rush of brilliant images coursed through her mind: a castle built of stone, a jewellike valley ringed by rugged mountains, a procession of courtiers bearing gifts. She heard the whisper of a half-remembered song, lines of poetry that broke her heart. She heard someone calling a name she wanted to answer to.

Within her, she felt the hex magic uncoil and quest forward like a serpent.

Without warning, flame rocketed between her and the Dragonheart, sizzling up her arms and into her collarbone. The magics collided inside her. She toppled backward, breaking the connection, landing on her back on the floor, striking her head hard on the stone threshold. She lay stunned for a moment, colors exploding in her head like fireworks in the night sky.

Voices whispered in her head, mingling and competing—

pretty promises, endearments, enticements, curses, and warnings. Like spirits battling inside a bell jar until finally they died away.

Gripping the edge of Thomas Swift's crypt, Madison dragged herself to her feet, remembering Min's words.

Do not mess with magic. That's not our business.

But it seemed like magic never tired of messing with her.

The Dragonheart kindled, sending long tongues of flame and shadow reaching toward her like clutching fingers. She had to fight the urge to rush into their embrace.

Madison backed away from the stone, stepped carefully over the threshold, turned, and fled up the stairs.

❧ CHAPTER NINE ❧
TERROR IN THE CRYPT

The next morning, Mercedes Foster sat back on her heels and studied the pentagrams she'd chalked onto the stone floor of the crypt. Scrubbing a smudge from her nose with the back of her hand, she looked up at Snowbeard. "What do you think, Nicodemus?"

The old wizard nodded. "It looks perfect to me, Mercedes."

The sorceress planted her fists on her bony hips and grinned at Jason. "Come on, then. Let's try again."

"I hope you know what you're doing." Jason reluctantly took his place within the inner pentagon of one of the pentagrams. The other two took refuge within diagrams of their own. The battered wooden box from Raven's Ghyll sat on the floor in the fourth pentacle.

Mercedes began to speak, a high, singsong chant. Pointing, Nick kindled a bright, hot flame where the four pentagrams came together. Careful not to lean out of the pentagram, Jason gripped the case with a pair of iron tongs and thrust it into the flames.

They waited. And waited. Flames licked across the surface of the box with no apparent effect. The wood was so impregnated with charms that it was impervious even to wizard flame.

They continued until Jason's arm trembled with the weight of the box and he had to support his elbow with his other hand. The tongs grew warm and then hotter and hotter so that he had to concentrate to keep his fingers from blistering.

Finally, Mercedes let her song trail away. "All right," she said, her long face settling into disappointed lines. "It's not working. I'm afraid we'll never get it open." She removed a silk scarf from her head and her wiry hair exploded free. She mopped sweat from her face with the scarf. "That's enough for today."

Gingerly, Jason set the box back on the floor, dropped the tongs, and wiped his seared hands on his jeans.

Rows of artifacts were lined up on one of the crypts, sorted by function and tagged with their magical names. There were heartstones of all kinds: pendants, scrying stones, amulets that strengthened the bearer, talismans of protection, lovestones that muddled the mind. Enchanted mirrors that displayed bewitching and confusing images of past, present, and future. Jeweled daggers that made wounds that would not heal. Belts and collars for holding magical captives. Recalling his escape from the ghyll, Jason was amazed that it had all fit in his backpack.

"We've done a lot already," he said, gesturing toward the catalogued items.

Mercedes nodded grudgingly. "Perhaps, but I can't help thinking that the most powerful *sefa*s are resisting us."

The remaining pieces were grouped forlornly in one corner: the small wooden box that could not be opened, a worn cloak carefully mended with glittering thread, a silver hammer inscribed with runes, faceted bottles filled with unknown potions, their stoppers larded with time-darkened wax. And, of course, the Dragonheart on its ornate metal stand.

Except for the opal, Jason couldn't remember why he'd chosen any of them. "Maybe this is just junk," he suggested. "Maybe I stumbled onto the magical landfill of Raven's Ghyll." Mercedes mashed her lips tight together, but he persisted. "There were tons of loose gemstones in the cave. I took a few, but I mostly focused on the magical pieces. Maybe the opal is just another gemstone in the pile."

As if to contradict him, the Dragonheart sent light spiraling around the crypt. It looked different from before, almost agitated. Power washed over him, warming the Weirstone under Jason's breastbone like a banked fire.

The three of them stood frozen, staring at it.

Snowbeard cleared his throat. "I think the stone is important," he said. "Else I wouldn't spend so much time on it."

Jason shrugged, struggling to hide his annoyance. "Whatever. Anyway, it's a waste of time to keep working on this. I'm thinking I should collect some of the most powerful pieces and take them back to Hastings in Britain. I hear he's planning a major attack on the ghyll. These could help."

"Has Hastings asked you to bring any of the items back to Raven's Ghyll?" Nick asked.

"No, but . . ."

"Didn't he say to keep them within the sanctuary?"

"They don't do us any good here!" Jason paced back and forth, making tight turns within the confines of the crypt. "I might as well have left them in the cave."

"I think the fact that they're not in our enemies' hands is a good thing," Nick said, his black eyes tunneling all the way to Jason's spine.

"When you think about it, this stuff belongs to me," Jason said. "I found it. I carried it out of the ghyll. I should be able to do what I want with it."

"Jason Haley!" The wizard's voice reverberated against the stone walls of the crypt, although he wasn't speaking particularly loudly. Snowbeard seemed to grow until his head nearly touched the ceiling. Flame flickered about his angular frame. "You know better than that. You are not a child who can demand your toys back. The future of the magical guilds may depend on how we use what's fallen into our hands. I will not allow you to recklessly endanger all of us with their ill-considered use."

Jason knew he should just shut up, but he couldn't help himself. "So you think we should just hole up here and wait to be attacked?"

"I think we don't know enough yet to see who our most dangerous adversary will be. If D'Orsay holds the Covenant, the hoard, and the ghyll, then why hasn't he acted? Why hasn't he consecrated the document and brought us all under his heel?"

"How would I know?" Jason stuffed his hands into his jeans pockets. "Hastings seems to think he's worth going after, now that I'm stuck back here."

Nick's voice softened. "Jason. This work we're doing is

important, even if you don't think so. I believe we've been given a rare gift, if we can just figure out how to use it."

Jason wasn't buying it. "You sound like Hastings."

"Indeed?" Nick lifted an eyebrow. "Perhaps there's a reason."

"I'll just take the opal, then," Jason said. "You can keep the rest." Impulsively, he reached for the Dragonheart.

And was slammed back against the wall with stunning force. He seemed to stick for a moment, then slid down the wall until his butt hit the floor.

"Jason!"

Mercedes and Nick leaned over him, both talking at once, checking him for missing parts. Once they figured out that he was okay, the interrogation began.

"Jason! What did you do?" Nick gripped his arm hard.

"I didn't *do* anything. Jeez. I just reached for it."

"Did you speak a charm of any kind?" Mercedes grabbed his hands, turning them palm up, as if to examine them for contraband. "Did you apply anything to the stone? Did you use a *sefa*?"

He shook his head, ripping his hands free. "I just went to pick it up." He felt humiliated and frustrated. Rejected by a *rock*.

Being a sorcerer healer, Mercedes was an empath, too. So she began to try and soothe him, which only irritated him more. "Don't worry. We've probably destabilized it with our poking and prodding," she suggested.

"I never had any trouble with it before," Jason said, remembering how he'd handled the stone in the ghyll, caressing its crystalline surface, the flames percolating gently under his fingers. He stood, rubbing his elbows where they'd hit the wall.

"We've been whacking at it for weeks," Mercedes said. "It might be time to give it a rest. *Sefa*s are temperamental, you know." She grabbed up the velvet bag. "I'll just put it back in the crypt."

"Mercedes—" Snowbeard began what sounded like a warning. But the sorcerer reached for the Dragonheart and the stone responded with an eruption of flame that sent her staggering back on her long bird legs. She would have gone down had Snowbeard not caught her arm.

"Well!" Mercedes gasped. "Well, well."

"*You* want to try?" Jason said to Snowbeard, feeling somewhat redeemed.

Snowbeard eyed the stone. Not being a fool, he snatched up his staff from where it leaned against the wall and extended the bear's-head tip gingerly toward the Dragonheart until they almost touched.

The stone seemed to explode, spinning the staff from Snowbeard's hands, shattering it into three pieces that clattered onto the stone floor.

They all looked from the broken staff to the Dragonheart and back again.

"Your staff!" Jason was shocked. Snowbeard had carried that staff for hundreds of years, probably. It was an extraordinarily powerful *sefa*. Or it had been. Jason collected the pieces, and laid them out on top of the crypt. "Man, I'm sorry. Can you fix it?"

"The head is intact," Mercedes said, fingering the broken shaft. "Maybe we can remount it."

"Hmmm? Perhaps, perhaps." Snowbeard seemed distracted. He poked at the broken staff, then turned and studied the Dragonheart, smoothed his beard, twisting the ends between his thumb and forefinger. "It's mounted a vigorous defense against us," he said. "What do you suppose accounts for that? What's changed?" He seemed more intrigued with the Dragonheart than concerned about his wizard staff.

"Who knows," Jason said. "But now we can't even touch it." So much for his plans to take it back to Raven's Ghyll. He eyed the stone, wondering if he could sneak up on it somehow.

"I wish we had the book you found," Snowbeard said. "That might tell us something."

"I can go back and get it," Jason suggested. When that proposal was met with silence, he added, "I'll tell you one thing. I'm not going to hide out here forever, sucking dust in a church basement."

He swung around to Mercedes. "See you around, Mercedes. I'm done for the day."

Hunching his shoulders against the disapproval emanating from behind, Jason clumped up the stairs to the side door of the church. He knew he should leave through the cold, miserable tunnel, but, just then, he didn't care.

When he emerged from the building, brilliant sunshine struck him like a club. It was a beautiful winter day, and he'd wasted it holed up in a cellar with old people.

"Hey, there."

The back of his neck prickled. He turned to see Leesha Middleton sitting on a stone bench in the courtyard that adjoined the church. Snow was melted in an arc around her.

Jason was amazingly glad to see her.

"You've been in there half the day," Leesha went on, crossing her legs and swinging her booted foot. "Choir practice, or what?"

Jason sat down next to her, taking advantage of the warm microclimate zone she'd created around the bench. He could think of no explanation to offer as to why he'd spent all morning in church. "Why? Have you been waiting for me?"

"Maybe." She put her hand on his arm. "It's Saturday. I'm bored. Want to do something?"

"Like what?"

She seemed surprised by the question. "Well. We could go for coffee. There are some places over by the campus."

"I don't like coffee."

"We could get something to eat."

"I'm not really hungry." Jason enjoyed saying no to somebody. He was still smarting from the verbal beating he'd taken in the crypt.

"Okay." She paused. "Well, we could go back to my house," she suggested, gazing out at the square. "My Aunt Milli's home, but she probably won't even know we're there."

Jason leaned his head back and looked up at the winter-pale blue sky. "What do you want from me? I can't help you with Jack, you know."

Leesha stood and faced him, her cheeks pink with indignation, her hands balled into fists. "I've never met a guy so full of questions. If you don't want to hang out, just say so."

Jason lifted a hand to stop the tirade. "I didn't say I didn't want to."

"You could've fooled me."

To be truthful, he *was* interested. It had been so long since he'd done anything for fun. And the frustration he was feeling made him want to spit in the eye of Hastings and Snowbeard and the rest. Going out with Leesha was one way to accomplish that.

He stood, taking hold of her hands and lifting her to her feet. "Let's go to the park."

"The *park*?" He might have said the city dump and got the same reaction. "It's *freezing* out."

He grinned and took her elbow, towing her along so she had to trot to keep up. "Perry Park is the absolute garden spot of Trinity, and I bet you've never been there." Perry Park was also the perfect marriage of public and private. Smack in the middle of the sanctuary, but they were still unlikely to be seen. And plenty of escape routes, if that became necessary, too.

❧ CHAPTER TEN ❧
COAL GROVE, ACT I

The hearing was like a play: everyone in costume, reading their lines, some better than others.

Ray McCartney was acting the part of the country lawyer, all cardigan sweater and khakis, collared shirt and holiday tie. He'd be representing Carlene for free, of course. He'd been in love with her for as long as Madison could remember.

Carlene wore a gray dress and jacket, pearls, and low-heeled pumps. She'd bought the outfit from Sears on credit, since she had nothing like that in her closet. Madison had coaxed her mother's blond curls into a French braid. That and her pink lipstick made her look very young.

Madison had her own costume: a long skirt and loose sweater, dark stockings and sober flats, her boisterous hair jammed into a clip at the back of her neck.

I look like somebody's nanny, she thought glumly.

They were gathered in a small hearing room on the second floor of the red brick courthouse. It was three days before

Christmas and the snow swirled past the windows. Madison didn't look forward to slip-sliding back up the mountain.

Aside from Madison and Carlene, there was Ed Ragland, the county's first African American judge, who always looked sleepy-eyed but was known to miss nothing. Bryson Roper, who owned Roper Coal Company and all the land around Booker Mountain. And his son, Brice, of course.

Mr. Roper was a roughneck turned coal company owner. His expensive suit hung uneasily from his broad shoulders, and his neck squeezed over his shirt collar. His eyes were the color of oak leaves after a long winter on the ground. Around Coal Grove, people said he was capable of almost anything, up to and including murder.

Brice splayed back in his seat, legs extended, collar turned up. He was air-brushed handsome, like someone in a department store ad. As if that wasn't enough, he emitted the faint glow of wizardry.

He was the kind of boy parents trusted. But shouldn't. He smiled over at Maddie, lifting his left hand to wave at her, and her gut twisted up in the same old way. She'd been away nearly a year, but nothing had changed.

Judge Ragland set the ground rules. "This is just an informal hearing, what I like to call a conversation with all the parties involved, so the court can find out the facts in the case and decide what to do about Grace and John Robert." He turned to Brice. "Young Mr. Roper?"

Brice could tell a story, Madison had to give him that. He explained that he'd been on his way home from school when he saw a plume of smoke rising from the old Booker place. He thought the house had caught fire, so he'd driven up there to find the shed ablaze.

"Where were the children at the time?" Judge Ragland asked.

"They were bringing water from the pump. I tried to put out the fire, but the shed was pretty much gone. I didn't know where Carlene—Mrs. Moss—was. So I brought the kids back to our house."

Ray McCartney leaned forward. "So for all you knew, Mrs. Moss was somewhere on the property."

"Well, no," Brice said, looking embarrassed he had to tell on Carlene. "The kids said she was at work."

"So did you take those frightened children to their mama?" Ray asked softly.

Mr. Roper Senior took over. "No, we turned them over to Child Welfare. Those children are left on their own up there all the time," he added. "It's time something was done about it. People around here pay more attention to their dogs than she does those kids."

Judge Ragland peered over his glasses, studying some papers on his desk. "Carlene, the report from Child Welfare says these children have been removed from your home twice before for cause. One time they were found wandering in downtown Coal Grove at two a.m."

"That was the sitter's fault," Carlene said. "I couldn't help it. I was in Las Vegas."

Ray gave Carlene a look. He'd told her to keep quiet during the hearing unless he asked her a direct question.

"I have to say, I'm troubled, Carlene," Judge Ragland said. "You've been in court several times on account of Grace and John Robert, but nothing seems to change. Why should I expect things to be any different from here on?"

Ray answered quickly, "Your Honor, this episode was just

a miscommunication. Ms. Moss's childcare provider didn't show. She wasn't aware . . ."

"I asked Carlene," Judge Ragland said.

"You know I have to work for a living," Carlene replied. "It's hard to find a babysitter who'll drive all the way up the mountain for what I can afford to pay."

"Which is why you ought to give up that place and move down into town," Mr. Roper muttered, looking up at the ceiling. "Those kids could have burned to death."

Judge Ragland glared his disapproval at Bryson Roper, and turned back to Carlene. "So what are you going to do about it? I can't return these children to an unsafe situation."

Carlene gripped her pink purse and leaned forward. "They're in school on weekdays. And Maddie'll watch them after school and on the weekend. That'll give me time to make arrangements."

"Is that so, Madison?"

All eyes were on Madison Moss. She'd anticipated this. She knew she had no choice. "That's right, sir."

"You're sure now?"

Madison nodded.

"What about your school? What are you, a senior?"

"That's all set up. I can still graduate."

Judge Ragland sighed and stacked the papers on the table in front of him. "Here's my ruling then. Child Welfare will retain oversight of the children, but we will release them into your custody, Carlene, with the stipulation that Madison is available to provide care for them while you are at work."

Madison felt the pressure of the judge's gaze, but she looked down at her lap.

"Madison, if the time comes that you can't do that, you

must notify the court. The court being me. In any event, I'll see you all back here at the end of August." He turned to his bailiff. "Will you show the children in?"

Grace marched in, back straight, chin raised high, like any ten-year-old queen, holding tight to John Robert's hand. But when seven-year-old John Robert saw Maddie, he ripped free and charged into her embrace.

"Maddie!" He wound his fingers into her hair, tearing it free of its clip.

Madison hugged him fiercely, pulling his solid little body onto her lap. Someone had glued down his blond curls with gel, plastering them over to the side. He was wearing a red-and-white-striped collared shirt and red pants. He looked like a cherubic used-car salesman.

Grace must've refused the fashion makeover, since she was wearing her own clothes, and her fine brown hair was pulled into its usual pony tail. She gave Brice Roper her patented look that would curdle sweet milk, and turned to Judge Ragland. "I want to charge this man with kidnapping." She jerked her head at Brice, who looked like he had something to say but thought better of it and shut his mouth.

"That's a serious charge, young lady," Judge Ragland began.

"An old shed caught fire on our property, and my brother and I were putting it out, when *he* showed up. We might've saved it if it wasn't for him. And then he drug us down the mountain and put us in jail."

"Is that so?" Judge Ragland looked over at Brice, who rolled his eyes and shrugged.

"Anyway, you ought to make him pay for the shed," Grace concluded, giving Brice the eye.

"I'll take that under advisement, Grace," Judge Ragland

said. "Meaning, I'll think about it. In the meantime, you go on home with your mama and mind her, hear me?"

He looked at Carlene, shaking his head. "Carlene, you're raising lawyers. Heaven help you."

With that, the hearing was over.

Ray McCartney patted Madison on the shoulder. "Good work, Maddie. Glad you're home."

But when Madison tried to give Grace a hug, her slender body was stiff and resistant.

She's mad at me for going away, Madison thought. She thinks it's my fault she ended up in kid jail.

Madison turned around and nearly ran into Brice Roper. "Hey, Madison, what's up?" he said. Running a hand through his artfully tousled brown hair, he grinned. That smile had charmed every girl in the Roaring Fork Valley, but it sent worms squirming down Madison's back. "We've missed you," he said. "Everyone says so," he added, apparently speaking for the entire Coalton County High School senior class. Of which he was president.

Madison folded her arms and tapped her foot on the weathered wood floor. "I'll bet they do." *They had to find somebody else to talk about and blame things on.*

Brice smiled down at her, and she took an involuntary step back. He always seemed to be crowding her, taking up more than his allotted space.

"So," he said, perfectly aware of the effect he was having. "When are you coming back to school?"

She shook her head. "I'm not. I'm . . . um . . . being home-schooled. It's a distance course." *So I can keep my distance from all of you.*

He stared at her a moment, a slight frown on his face, like

he didn't know whether to believe her or not. "That's too bad. Well, listen, I'll call you, then. We can hang out. I'll introduce you around," he added.

Un. Be. Lievable. After everything that had happened, Brice Roper was hitting on her. Again. For a minute she was speechless, the words seeming to stop up in her mouth. "Why . . . thanks so much, but I'm *from* here, I don't really need an introduction." In fact, there were people she'd like to be *un*introduced to. Guess who was top of the list?

"Besides, I'm going to be really busy, and, anyway, we don't have a phone right now."

"Right," he said. "Carlene's been using our phone a lot. Stop by and use it any time you want. I'm usually home in the afternoon unless there's something at school." He reached out and lightly brushed back her hair with his hand.

She slapped his hand away and he caught hold of her wrist, his face flushing to the color of old brick.

Bryson Senior spoke from the doorway. "Brice. What *the hell* are you doing? Come on. We're late already." He pointed at his watch, turned, and stalked out the door.

Madison looked back at Brice in time to see hatred pass across his face before he swept it clean. He let go of her wrist. "I'll be seeing you," he said, and turned away.

Not if I see you first, Madison thought.

"What did young Brice want?" Carlene asked as they descended the broad, shallow steps of the courthouse, Ray trailing hopefully behind.

"He wanted me to know everybody misses me."

"I believe he has a crush on you, Madison," Carlene said, reapplying her lipstick without breaking stride. "That boy has a hungry look."

"Mama. Just . . . don't."

"They say the Ropers have scads of money."

"They *say* a lot of things." Too much and too often. "Gramma Min told me to steer clear of him."

Carlene shrugged. "She never liked any of my boyfriends, either."

Ray followed them all the way to the car, buzzing around like a locust in summer. Carlene handed Ray the brush and he cleared snow off the car while she started the engine.

"I'll get the terms of the custody ruling in writing and get back to you on that," Ray was saying. "When's your birthday, Maddie?"

"Not till August."

"As long as you'll be here, we can arrange the paperwork so we're ready to transfer the deed to the house and all whenever you turn eighteen." Ray was the executor of Min's estate.

"I still don't know why Min would leave you the mountain," Carlene muttered. "I'm her daughter."

"Because if she'd left it to you, it'd be gone already."

Carlene shut up, then, fumbling for a cigarette, lower lip trembling.

There goes your wicked tongue again, Madison thought. Min always said you never could suffer a fool.

Carlene worked a shift that night, so after supper Madison helped John Robert with his bath, washing the foster-mom gel out of his hair and letting it dry into its natural ringlets.

While he brushed his teeth, Madison dug the Christmas presents out of her duffle and laid them under the artificial tree in the front room. She'd bartered for most of it with the

Trinity Square merchants. There was a CD player for J.R., a handwoven shawl for Grace, and a bracelet for Carlene.

Pulling on her coat, she walked out onto the porch. She rested her hands on the splintered porch railing, and breathed in the raw cold like a tonic. Lights glittered in the valley below. Off to the left, Booker Creek worried over stones and whispered secrets on its way down the mountain.

She explored the vacancy left by Seph's absence, like she might the space once occupied by a broken-off tooth. He was a constant presence in her peripheral vision, tall and silent and accusing, pale face framed in a tangle of curls. But he disappeared each time she turned her head.

There was something else, now, too. Ever since the encounter in the church basement, the Dragonheart seemed to be constantly on her mind, filling any unoccupied space, like images of fireworks seared into her retinas.

Navigating the crumbling stone steps, Madison crossed the side yard to where the charred remains of the shed huddled next to the greenhouse. Carlene had left the wooden bones to molder.

Her great-great-grandfather had shaped the timbers with a hand axe. Had laid the stones of the foundation higher at one end to account for the slope of the land.

Madison knelt and poked through the ashes with a stick, hoping not to find any witch signs.

A slight sound behind Madison alerted her to the fact that she was not alone. She stood and turned. It was Grace, who still couldn't decide if she was speaking to Madison or not.

Don't be like me, Madison thought. Raggedy mad all your life.

They stood side-by-side, staring at the ruins, their breath pluming into the crystalline air, stamping their feet to keep warm.

"So what happened to the shed?" Madison asked, after a bit.

"Some people set it on fire," Grace replied.

Madison turned and stared at her. "Who?"

Grace shrugged her narrow shoulders. "There were four or five of them, out here in the dark. It looked like they had torches or something," she said.

There was nobody better than Grace at keeping a secret. Which made Madison think she'd had too much practice. "And you and J.R. were all by yourselves?"

Grace shrugged her shoulders again. She picked up a stick and poked it under a charred beam, coming up with a scrap of cloth that dissolved into ash.

"Any idea who it was?" Madison asked.

"No. They were wearing hoods." She hesitated. "We tried to put it out, me and J.R. We poured water on it. But it wouldn't go out."

Madison shivered. "Did you . . . did you find any marks or signs or anything?"

Grace shook her head.

"Did you tell anyone?"

She wrinkled her nose. "Who would I tell? You were gone, and Mama, well . . ."

"You could've told the police."

"They'd probably say we made it up. Or blame it on us."

Madison nodded. "Probably." Grace was another old soul. She'd remember how little help the police had been over the past year, when Madison was the one accused.

"Must've been kids, I guess," Madison suggested. It could've been. Some people just liked to see things burn. And kids from the high school liked to drive up Booker Mountain Road when they needed to escape all the spying eyes in a small town.

It didn't have to mean the fires were starting up again.

Impulsively, Madison wrapped an arm around Grace's shoulders and pulled her in close. Grace resisted at first, then gave in, laying her head on Madison's shoulder. Grace had taken a shower as soon as she got home, and her hair smelled like the kind of shampoo you could get a quart of for ninety-nine cents.

It smelled like home.

"Are you going to stay with us all summer?" The words came out in a rush, like Grace had been dying to ask the question all night.

"I don't know about all summer. Till school's out, anyway."

"Will you have your truck? Can you take us places?"

"Well. I'll be working at home. Painting for school."

"Great." Grace scraped at the frozen dirt with the toe of her sneaker.

Madison thought of Grace, stuck on the mountain with no phone, no computer, and only John Robert to hang out with. Even the TV reception was chancy.

"Don't worry. We'll get out. We'll go down to town a couple times a week at least."

Grace rolled her eyes. "As if that's a thrill." But Madison could tell she was pleased.

❧ CHAPTER ELEVEN ❧
PAINTED POISON

Seph sprawled among the pillows on the wicker swing. The solarium at Stone Cottage was one of his favorite retreats in all seasons. His textbook was propped against his knees— *Problems in Democracy: A World View*—but it had been a long time since he'd turned a page. The text might as well have been written in Old English.

With another part of his mind, he monitored the sanctuary. Its energy hummed all around him, like a map splashed with an occasional spot of color where wizards and the other gifted moved through it. It was not the heavy-handed smooshing down of power like before. It was like navigating an elaborate video game grid, exerting subtle control over events. His father had taught him the technique.

Here and there a flareup indicated that magic was in play—the greens and browns of earth magic in Mercedes's garden, the silvers and golds of wizardry, the reds and purples that signified enchanters. Nowhere the angry orange that meant attack magic. In some essential way, he *became* the town of Trinity—its magical framework, at least. The day and its pleasures receded.

Something nibbled at the fringes of his consciousness. A voice.

"Seph."

All at once, the magical schematic disappeared from his frame of vision, and power flooded back into his body, heating him down to his fingers and toes. He opened his eyes to see Nick Snowbeard looking down at him, his expression severe.

"Seph. You extend yourself too much. I've warned you about this before. It makes you vulnerable." Nick was well into his scruffy old man persona, clad in canvas work pants, a flannel shirt, and work boots.

Seph licked his lips and turned his head slightly to look out toward the frosted lake. It had disappeared into the dark. It was late—later than he'd thought. Where had the time gone?

He managed to sit up on his second try. He felt stiff from long immobility. "What's up?"

"Your phone was ringing when I came in." Nick dropped a cell phone into Seph's lap. "It was Rachel Booker. She wants you to meet her at the inn."

Seph palmed the phone and squinted at Nick. "Rachel?" Rachel Booker was Madison's older cousin who owned the Legends Inn. He hadn't seen her since Madison left for Coalton County. As self-appointed protector of Madison's virtue, she'd always treated Seph with cool and cynical suspicion.

Not that he was any threat lately.

His heart accelerated. "Why? Did she hear from Madison?"

"I suggest we walk over to the Legends and find out."

Seph unfolded to his feet, grabbing the swing for support, still shaking off the effects of the mindquest.

"Are you all right?" Nick asked gruffly.

"I'm fine." And, really, it seemed like he was handling his magical assignments better, lately. The raging headaches had eased, he was less tired, less out of it, and he'd put on a little weight. Linda's milkshakes must be working, he thought.

He and the old wizard left Stone Cottage behind and headed west along Lake Road, an avenue lined with an eclectic mixture of old summer cottages and modern mansions. Streetlights bloomed under the skeletons of trees, and the wind off the lake was bitingly cold.

Nick navigated the uneven cobblestones without the help of his staff, as Mercedes had proclaimed it beyond repair. He seemed incomplete without it. Seph grabbed the old wizard's arm a couple of times to steady him on the icy street.

"You're not getting out among people enough," Nick said. "Madison's absence has not been good for you."

Seph rubbed his forehead irritably. "I feel like I'm out among people all day long."

"I don't mean in the virtual sense." Nick paused. "I think you should talk to Jason."

Seph rolled his eyes. "Why? Is he lonely, or something?"

"I'm worried about him. Hastings hoped I could involve him in the testing of the *sefa*s he brought back from the ghyll. Jason has considerable knowledge about magical objects, but archival work doesn't suit him, I'm afraid. He's taut as a crossbow."

"Jason's okay," Seph said, feeling guilty. It wasn't his fault things had worked out this way. In fact, he'd gladly hand off the boundary if he could. Even when he was healthy, it seemed like he just barely had it under control. The pressure was intense. Everyone was counting on him, and that was just what Jason craved. "It's just . . . I wish he could help with . . . something more important."

Nick snorted. "He *is* doing something important, he just doesn't see it that way. I'm afraid he may do something rash."

"Like?"

"He may go back to Britain on his own. He knows Hastings is planning something, and he's determined to be a part of it. And he wants to take some of the objects from the church back with him."

"I don't see how we can stop him."

"I can stop him, if I choose." Snowbeard was matter-of-fact. "I would prefer not to, however. I was hoping that, as a friend, you might be able to . . . redirect him."

"I can try," Seph said, again feeling guilty about talking behind Jason's back. "I don't feel like I should be telling him what to do."

"He may not be strong enough to handle the boundary, but there's more than enough other work to do. You need to delegate more," Snowbeard said.

Right, Seph thought. Delegate more. Fine. He had plans that would require more wizardry than ever.

"What do you hear from Madison?" Nick abruptly changed the subject again. The old wizard was on a mission, too, and Seph was somehow the vehicle.

"Not much. Their landline's disconnected, and cell phone reception isn't good down there. She e-mails me from the library sometimes. She's not coming back any time soon. Her brother and sister got released from foster care, since she's there to watch them."

Those e-mails were totally unsatisfactory: *I'm painting. I'm doing fine. The kids are a handful. It's been cold and rainy. Bright and sunny. Saw a wild turkey and a bald eagle yesterday.* She e-mailed photos of Booker Mountain and the paintings she made, landscapes seen through a smoky blue filter.

Seph hunched his shoulders in frustration. He did *not* want her to do fine in Coalton County; he wanted her to come home. It's just as well, he told himself. If we ever got to see each other, we'd just end up fighting.

But it might be worth it if he could just see her again.

They turned up the walkway, passing through the winter-scorched gardens that surrounded the inn, and mounted the steps to the porch. The receptionist at the desk in the foyer went to fetch Rachel. Seph ran his hand over the newel post of the elaborate oak staircase. Here he and Madison had planned their first date—the ill-fated picnic on the river.

Rachel appeared from the kitchen hallway, wiping her hands on her apron. Her hair was stick straight and black, unlike Madison's gilded waves, but she shared Madison's fair complexion, sprinkling of freckles, and slightly crooked nose.

"Thanks for coming," she said, nodding curtly to Seph and Nick. "I want to show you something." She turned and climbed the curved staircase, obviously intending them to follow. They wound up and up, crossing the landing at the second floor and continuing up the narrower staircase to the third, where Madison stayed.

"We were just talking about Madison," Seph said, easily

keeping pace up the steep stairs while Nick lagged behind. "Have you heard from her?"

"No," Rachel said, eying him with a peculiar expression. "Haven't heard a word." As they turned down the familiar hallway to Madison's tiny room tucked under the back staircase, Seph smelled wood smoke. Rachel stood aside at the entry to Madison's quarters.

The door was gone, or most of it, leaving a ragged hole. The wood around the doorframe was charred, and the floorboards dusted with a fine gray ash, smeared now with footprints.

Seph looked up at Rachel, who was glaring at him as if it were somehow his fault. And it probably was. "What . . . when did this happen?"

"Yesterday. That's when I noticed it, anyway. Go on in," she said.

Seph hesitated, unsure whether to open the ruined door or step through the gap. In the end, he did the latter, stepping carefully over the splintered threshold.

The room was totally trashed, the contents of drawers strewn on the floor, cupboards standing open, the mattress yanked from the bed and cut to ribbons, trunks rifled through, wastebaskets upended. The doors to the wardrobe had been broken open and hung slantwise on their hinges. Even her tiny refrigerator had been emptied onto the tile.

Though it had been a while since he'd been invited to Madison's room, it was a jarring contrast to what Seph was used to. Madison was a naturally tidy person.

He turned to Rachel, who had followed him in. "Who did this? What were they looking for?"

She folded her arms, tapping her foot in a familiar way. "I hoped maybe you could tell me."

"How would I know?" Seph said, knowing that the ruined door was wizard's work.

Nick stood framed in the doorway. "My word," he said. "What kind of devilry is this?"

"I can't make sense of it," Rachel said. "I mean, her room is way up here on the third floor, so it doesn't seem like a random break-in. A guest would be more likely to have valuables than a server."

"Depending on what you think is valuable," Seph muttered. "Did they take anything?"

"Not that I could tell. But it could've been. She didn't have a lot to begin with. She took her art supplies and her computer home with her. But she left her winter clothes and furniture and other school things."

Shrugging, Seph scanned the room—the Impressionist prints that lined the walls, the hat collection over the bed, the paint-splashed headboard. Her desk had been emptied, but there was no way to tell if anything was missing.

He hadn't noticed any unusual magical activity in the past two days. But it wouldn't take much to blow out a door.

What would a wizard be looking for? Magical objects? A home address? Phone records?

Apprehension flared under Seph's breastbone, but he managed to keep his voice steady. "Does she know?"

Rachel shook her head. "I e-mailed her, but she hasn't replied."

"Did you call the police?" Seph asked.

Rachel shook her head. "Maybe I did wrong, but I didn't. Didn't seem like your usual burglary. Like I said, why target a girl who's got nothing to begin with?" She gave Seph a narrow-eyed look. "You sure you don't know anything about this?"

He returned her gaze. "What would I know about it?"

"Well, all I know is there's something wrong between you and her. You were all lovey-dovey until about six months ago, and since then, well, you tell me."

Taken by surprise, Seph stammered, "We're okay. I mean, great."

"Really? Well, it occurred to me that maybe you came and tore this place up to—you know—get revenge. Because she left."

Seph was stung by the accusation. "I wouldn't do that," he whispered.

They stood glaring at each other. Then Seph said, "Did she leave any of her paintings here? If somebody wanted to wreck something that meant a lot to her, he'd start there."

"Well, there's just this one." Rachel reached behind the loveseat and pulled out a canvas. "It looked like someone drug this out of the wardrobe." She turned it so Seph could see it.

The paint seemed to swim on the canvas, nauseating swirls of brown and green. No. It was the figures in the painting itself. They were moving. He recognized the scene with a sickening jolt: it was the conference room at Second Sister. His father, Hastings, lay next to Gregory Leicester's altar, cradled by his weeping mother. Leicester was looking right at Seph, eyes glittering, his arm extended. Behind him the alumni stood, their power joined to his. Flame erupted from Leicester's hands, slamming into Seph's body. He screamed and stumbled backward, raising his hands to defend himself.

He awoke to find himself lying on Madison's bed with Nick sitting next to him, hands pressed to Seph's chest, muttering a healing charm under his breath. When Seph opened his eyes, Snowbeard released a sigh of relief and hissed, "Let me do the talking," in an odd, terse voice.

Seph struggled into a sitting position, and immediately vomited something black and nasty into a basin that Nick had at the ready. Nick wiped his face off with a washcloth.

"Nick," Seph whispered. "What did Rachel . . ."

"Stay down," Nick ordered, and went to dump the basin.

Rachel appeared in the doorway with a glass of water. "How's he doing?" Her usual cynical suspicion of Seph had been replaced with solicitous concern.

"Sorry for the trouble," Nick called from the lavatory. "He's had a touch of flu these past few days. When I gave him your message, he insisted on rising from his sickbed and coming over."

"I didn't know he was sick," Rachel said, twisting her hair between her fingers. "You should have said."

Snowbeard returned with the empty basin. Seph rinsed his mouth and spit into it. He felt awful, like the time he'd come down with mono at that prep school in Scotland and had ended up in the hospital. His entire body itched and burned like he was breaking out in hives. Hallucinations swam through his head.

"What did you do with the painting, Rachel?" the old man asked calmly.

"I put it down cellar," she said, shrugging, "but I still don't see why . . ."

"Better to be safe than sorry," Snowbeard said. "It's probably just the flu, but perhaps something in the painting triggered a synaptic shock to the brain, much like strobe lights trigger seizures in susceptible people."

Woozy as he was, Seph couldn't help thinking that Snowbeard was a remarkably good liar for one of the good guys.

"Would you like something to eat, honey?" Rachel asked. "I could whip you up an omelet, or some soup," she offered. "There's chocolate cake, and burnt-sugar custard."

Seph shuddered at the thought of confronting food. Snowbeard creakily rose to his feet and took Rachel's elbow. "Don't worry, my dear," he said. "I know how very busy you are. I'll stay here with Seph and we'll let him rest a bit, then I'll take him on home. You're sure there are no more of Maddie's paintings in the inn?"

"That's the only one I found. Either she took them all back with her, or the burglar stole them."

"Let's hope nothing was stolen." Effortlessly, Snowbeard ushered Rachel from the room. Moments later, Seph heard her descending the stairs. Snowbeard shut the door behind her and pulled a chair over to sit beside Seph.

"How are you feeling?" The old man's face was set in hard, angry lines.

"Terrible." And confused and embarrassed. "I don't know what I . . ."

"What did you see in the painting?" Snowbeard demanded, gripping his arm.

He's using Persuasion, Seph realized, feeling the hot flow of power. He immediately resisted, reverting to the habits of a lifetime. "The painting? I didn't get much of a look at it. I was kind of dizzy on the way over here, from the mindquest, I guess, and I just . . . why do you ask?"

Snowbeard studied him suspiciously. "You took one look at Madison's painting and collapsed. I want to know why."

"I don't even remember." Seph closed his eyes as if searching his brain, but mainly to avoid Snowbeard's keen gaze. What was the old man thinking, anyway? "What did it look like?"

"It was a painting of Trinity Harbor."

Not the painting I saw, Seph thought. He opened his eyes. "Er. Right. Now I remember."

Snowbeard's grip tightened. More Persuasion. "Don't lie to me. This is important for your own safety."

"How could a painting make me pass out, anyway?"

"There are a multitude of possibilities, my boy. Sorcerers can embed spells in objects. Certainly a curse could be embedded in a painting."

"So you think whoever broke in here cursed Madison's painting?" Seph asked carefully.

"Curses are generally embedded at the time the object is made. In this case, at the time the canvas was painted."

"Well, Madison painted it. So that's impossible." Seph looked Snowbeard in the eyes, daring the Old Bear to challenge him on it.

"Not only that," Snowbeard continued as if he hadn't heard, "the curse, if that's what it was, was directed specifically at you. It didn't affect Rachel or me, even though I removed the painting from the room and she carried it down into the cellar. Whatever it was, it was meant to kill. Had you been on your own, it might have succeeded."

"Curses and attack magic don't work in the sanctuary. We know that."

"Much is possible that is beyond our knowledge,"

Snowbeard said gravely. "You were the one maintaining the boundary. You might be vulnerable to a powerful curse directed at you or packaged in a different way."

Seph knew where this was going. He set his lips tightly together and waited for the punchline.

"Who knows what an elicitor is capable of? No one. Madison has declined to join this war on our side. Is it possible she has joined it on the other side?"

"No." Seph said it louder than he intended.

But why would she paint that particular scene? She'd seemed totally traumatized at the time, and it sure wasn't something he wanted to remember.

"She suddenly leaves town in the middle of the school term . . . ."

"She had to."

"It appears you are not getting along as you once did. . . ."

"Now, hold on." Seph propped himself on his elbows, fighting another wave of nausea. "Like I keep telling you, and my father, and my mother, and every other person—Madison wants nothing to do with this war. Nothing. She's not in this. Maybe she won't help us, but she wouldn't hurt us."

"Iris mentioned that Madison seems to be . . . in financial difficulties."

Seph blinked at Nick. "I know she's never had a lot of money, but . . . I could've helped her. All she had to do was ask."

"Maybe she preferred not to. She's proud. The Roses have deep pockets. Any of our enemies could make her rich."

"No. I don't believe it." Seph rubbed his forehead with the back of his hand. Madison wouldn't hurt him. He knew she wouldn't. "I passed out. That's all. Maybe I do have the flu. Try the simplest explanation for once. I'm sick of conspiracy theories."

Nick shook his head, agreeing to disagree. "Regardless of the source of the attack, I fear you are injured more grievously than you know. You lost hold of the boundary when you went down. Try to pick it up again."

"Right." Seph took a deep breath and extended himself into the sanctuary. Black spots swam before his eyes, coalescing into a smothering darkness that threatened to swallow him. He broke into a cold sweat, and let go, lying absolutely still until the dizziness eased. It had been hard enough before. Now it was impossible. "Sorry," he said, feeling a little panicked. *What if it didn't get better?* "I just need to rest a little."

"Maybe," Snowbeard said, sounding unconvinced. "I'll take it for now. But we need to determine exactly where Madison is and what she is up to. Perhaps that's something Jason can do."

✳ CHAPTER TWELVE ✳
A BABE IN THE WOODS

Snow sifted down from the treetops, glittering in the cold winter sunlight as Leesha stumbled down the icy trail. She kept a tight hold of unnoticeable Jason's hand, both to keep from falling and because he was the one with the *sefa*, after all.

"Where are we *going*?" she hissed. "And who are we sneaking up on?" Possibilities swirled through her mind. Assassins. Spies. Some kind of magical weapon being built in the sanctuary.

"You'll see," he whispered back mysteriously.

"This better be good," she muttered. As far as Leesha was concerned, winter was nature's way of telling you to stay indoors. All around, the snow was inscribed with animal tracks. Who knew what was out and about? "Are there bears around here?"

"Just little ones."

Would bears notice an unnoticeable person?

They clambered down into a half-frozen creek, up the other side, circled a ravine, and pushed into a thick stand of snowy pine trees. By then, she was gasping for breath. "Will you slow down? My legs aren't as long as yours."

"We're there. Wait till you see. This is really cool."

They paused under a pine tree whose boughs swept close to the ground. The air was filled with a clean, sharp scent, like room freshener. Stepping behind her, Jason gripped Leesha around the waist and lifted her up.

Right in front of her face was the teeniest owl she'd ever seen, no bigger than a robin. It was a brownish color with white streaks radiating from its eyes and white splotches. Its tiny feet were wrapped securely around a branch. It seemed to be sound asleep, but as she watched, it opened its yellow eyes and blinked sleepily at her, then closed them again.

Cautiously, she extended her finger and brushed the ruff around its feet, holding her breath. It opened its eyes, swiveled its head, then fluffed out its feathers and settled down again.

Jason lowered Leesha gently to the ground, then leaned in for a look himself. They took turns watching the owl for about ten minutes. Then Jason took Leesha's hand and led her out of the pine grove.

When they were a safe distance away, Jason disabled the unnoticeable charm and reappeared, grinning at her.

"What . . . what *was* that?" Leesha asked. "I never saw an owl that little!"

"It's called a Saw-whet owl," Jason said, looking pleased at her reaction. "I guess they winter around here. I saw it here the other day and looked it up online. Supposedly their call sounds like somebody sharpening a saw."

"Can't we take it home? It is *so* cute. I want to keep it!" Leesha said.

"Well. If you want. But these guys sleep during the day and eat mice, so you'd have to catch them."

Leesha shuddered. "Oh. So now you're the great hunter?"

"Pretty much." He knelt, scraping together a snowball. "I guess bow-hunting season is over. But snowball season is just beginning." He stood and came toward her, tossing the snowball in the air and catching it, eyeing her suggestively.

"Oh, no. Stay away from me!"

Jason lobbed the snowball. Leesha dodged behind a tree and the missile exploded against the bark. She knelt and patted together a snowball of her own, but when she stood up, Jason had disappeared.

"No fair! You are *not* allowed to go unnoticeable."

"No rules," Jason said from right behind her, stuffing a handful of snow down her back. She whipped around and he stole a kiss, then leapt back out of reach.

"No rules, you say? You'll be sorry." The fight began in earnest, then. Although Leesha had terrible aim, she found she could explode Jason's missiles with wizardry before they hit their mark, which evened things up a bit.

By the time they called a truce, they'd been racing through the woods for an hour, Leesha was actually sweating, and it was getting dark. They walked back to the park pavilion hand in hand. Leesha kindled a fire on the hearth to dry out their wet things, and Jason heated up some cider. They sat side by side on the hearth, their backs roasting, their fronts freezing.

Leesha was amazed at how much she'd enjoyed playing in the snow. Images came back to her from when she was little. She and Aunt Milli building snowmen in the yard. Cardinals and chickadees circling the bird feeder, coasting down to eat out of her hand. Consulting Aunt Milli's field guide to identify the rare birds.

"Come summer, we can move out here," Jason suggested, breaking into her reverie. "You know, sleep in hammocks in the trees, live off the land."

"You're totally insane, you know that?" she said, thinking she must be a little crazy herself.

"We can be urban guerrillas. Hold people for ransom. Trap squirrels and pigeons and steal picnic baskets."

"Listen, it takes a lot more than that to keep me comfortable," Leesha said. "Like hot showers and manicures."

Their conversations were often like this. They flirted, dancing around the hard issues that lay between them. But now Jason turned serious. He picked up her hand and examined it like he could read her fortune in it.

"It would be cool . . . if we could just . . . be together," he said. "You know, without having to worry about all this . . . political crap."

"We can be," Leesha said, forcing a lightness she didn't feel. "Who cares about politics? Let's run away. Where do you want to go?"

But the mood was broken. Jason set his cup of cider down and rose. "I'd better go. It's getting late."

She gripped his hand. "Stay a while?"

He shook his head. "Hunters need their sleep." He leaned down and kissed her. "See you."

Leesha followed Jason onto the porch and watched until his slender form dissolved into the trees of Perry Park. Unsettled, off-balance, she went back inside the pavilion, sat down next to the fire on the stone hearth, and wrapped herself in a comforter that stank of woodsmoke. She'd wait ten more minutes before she started walking back to town herself.

Who knew there were so many back-alley places in a small town—like the snack bar at the bowling alley and the study carrels at the public library and the beach in the middle of winter. Who knew she'd be willing to spend time in any of them? At first, she'd been focused on worming her way into Jason's confidence. But then one-on-one, they could be themselves. And, now . . .

It seemed like everybody she knew was either a hero like Jack Swift (not many) or a snake like Warren Barber (many). Jack was so virtuous he made her feel . . . contaminated. Jason was in between—wicked enough to be interesting, and yet . . . he believed in things. He lived by a personal code of honor. Not that she'd ever figure it out. Finally, Jason had a crooked, self-deprecating, sardonic way of looking at the world that made her laugh.

She could use a few laughs these days.

Poking at the fire with a stick, she thought, You're not falling for this guy, are you?

Leesha looked up, startled, when she heard a noise outside. She hoped it wasn't some kind of animal. They'd put up wards to keep snoops away, but whether they worked on animals, she just didn't know.

The door banged open and someone said, "Well, well. I don't believe it. A babe in the woods."

It was Warren Barber.

She was moving before he finished, and so was he. She tried to slam him with an immobilization charm, which, of course, didn't work, and he flung out a few attack charms himself. Those went nowhere. While he was processing that, she tried to circle round him and get out the door, but he blocked her path and tackled her, slamming her to the floor. He pinned her to the flagstones with his forearm, his face inches from hers. She found herself looking into his iced-over blue eyes, framed in bizarre white lashes.

"So, what's up, Leesha?" he asked. "You never call, you never answer your phone. I'm feeling just a bit . . . abandoned, know what I mean?"

"Get off of me, you perverted . . . pervert!" She shoved fruitlessly at his hands.

He brushed back her hair and touched the band around her neck. "And when I tried to apply a little *discipline*, nothing happened."

"I disabled the torc," Leesha lied breathlessly. "You might as well take it off."

"Did you now? And did you also disable my Weirstone, because I'm noticing some of my favorite charms don't work."

"I can't help it if you have a *performance problem*," she replied. "Can't you get something for that over the Internet?"

So, okay, that was a mistake.

The pale eyes narrowed to slits. He sat up and hit her, hard, in the face with his closed fist. Tears came to her eyes and blood poured from her nose. It felt like every bone in her face was broken.

You're going to pay for that, she thought. I just don't know how yet.

Barber examined his fist. "What do you know? This still works." He looked down at her, his face framed in shoulder-length, translucent hair. "I've heard that attack charms aren't allowed here in Trinity, but I never really believed they could make it stick. But now I'm thinking maybe the collar doesn't work so well in the sanctuary, either, know what I mean? And I'm feeling like you're getting kind of blasé about our agreement. That so?"

Agreement? Right. Leesha was drowning in blood. She blew her nose, spraying droplets all over Barber's shirt. "I told you. It's not easy. Everybody's always watching, and after what happened before, they don't really trust me."

"My patience is running out. I have the feeling you're not trying hard enough. You need to get Jason Haley out of the sanctuary and to someplace I can question him. You need to get me the Dragonheart. How hard can it be?"

Leesha bit back a response. There was enough damage to repair as it was.

"If you don't deliver, I'll tell your Dragon friends who you've been working for all this time. They'll kick you out on your butt, and then . . ." He circled her neck with his hands and applied pressure until she was suffocating, prying at his hands, squirming helplessly.

Finally, he let go, and she sucked in air desperately, her heart pounding.

Barber smiled. "I'll be around, even if they don't kick you out." He touched the collar. "I know where you are, every minute. Won't be hard to grab you in some back alley." His grin widened. "I'll stuff you in my car trunk and suddenly, you're *way* out of town."

"Wh—where are you staying, in case I need to find you?" she asked, wondering how he could possibly move around town without being spotted.

"Never mind where I'm staying." He stood, wiping his bloody hands on his jeans. "Someone set a nasty magical trap at my old place. I'm wondering how they knew where I lived. That better not happen again."

Damn, she thought. D'Orsay missed. He'd seemed so capable when they'd met at Raven's Ghyll.

Barber sat down on the bench of the picnic table, watching her as if she were the subject of some kind of violence experiment. "By the way, where's Madison Moss gone off to?"

That question took her totally by surprise. "M-Madison Moss? How should I know?"

"You're supposed to be the inside person, right?"

"You said to keep track of the gifted. She's not." Leesha paused. "Why do you care about her?"

"You weren't at Second Sister. When Leicester fired at McCauley, Madison Moss took the hit for him. Leicester went down, and all the alumni went with him. That's the kind of girlfriend to have." He looked at Leesha and raised a pale eyebrow like she should be taking notes. "Anyway, I paid her a visit, and her room's all emptied out."

"You paid her a visit?" Leesha shivered at the thought of Barber skulking around town. "Well, I heard she's gone, that she left town."

"Any idea where she went?"

'I have no clue. Maybe she and McCauley broke up. All I can tell you is, these Smallsville girls are ecstatic. They think they'll have a chance for a change."

Warren stood again. "Well, Leesha, as a spy, you've been totally useless. It's your job to make me happy. You have my number. You have three days to deliver Haley and the Dragonheart. Let me hear from you."

And then he was gone, and Leesha could hear nothing save her labored breathing and the wild beating of her heart.

❧ CHAPTER THIRTEEN ❧
UP MOUNTAIN

It was that time of day when the world holds its breath, awaiting the return of the light. To the east, beyond the mountains, it was already morning. The edge of the escarpment was iced with brilliance as the sun prepared to break overtop. Mist hung in the valley, like sheep's wool caught between the peaks. Each clump of grass, fern, and shrub was layered in ice, and Madison was wet to her knees before she'd crossed the home yard.

Her hands shook in the predawn chill as she squeezed paint onto the aluminum pie pan she used for a palette. She was lucky she hadn't broken her neck on the way up the mountain in the freezing dark. Any sane person would take a photograph and paint in the parlor, where it was warm and dry.

But then, everyone knows I'm crazy.

The moment arrived. The sun crested the east shoulder of Booker Mountain and splashed onto the slopes, setting each bejeweled twig and branch aflame. Madison loaded her brush and splashed paint onto the canvas she'd started the day before. Only two more days, she judged, and the sun would've changed position enough to ruin the effect. So she painted like one possessed.

By ten o'clock, she was on her way back down the mountain, following the ravine cut by Booker Creek, the cleanest stream in Coalton County. A half hour more, and the house came into sight.

It was two stories, with five big pillars in the front, and wide porches that wrapped nearly all the way around the house on both levels. There were red brick chimneys at either end, because it was built at a time when wood-burning fire-places provided the heat. It had always been painted white, though after five years in Carlene's care it could have done with a paint job. Though the house had good bones, it had the kind of beauty that needed constant care, or it began to look shabby.

It definitely looked shabby, now.

The house had been built by Madison's great-great-grandfather, Dredmont Booker, when he was courting her great-great-grandmother, Felicity Taylor. He was a prosperous farmer. She'd been a wild thing, a legendary blond beauty, who had no intention of staying in Coalton County and marrying a farmer, prosperous or not.

He swore he'd die if he couldn't have her. He built her the house, and a rose garden with a brick wall and gazebo and a path to nowhere. He bought her a black mare with four white stockings and a blaze on her forehead. He gave her the opal pendant that had belonged to his grandmother—blue and turquoise and green, with broad flashes of fire. It was the talk of the county because it was no proper gift from a man to a woman who was not his wife. Felicity Taylor had ignored the whispers and worn it whenever she liked.

Knowing what she knew now about inherited power, Madison wondered if Felicity had been an enchanter.

Word was, the view had finally won Felicity's heart. You could sit on the second floor porch and look right over the Ropers' place and see all the way to the river.

The pendant and Booker Mountain had been left to Min, who'd left them to Madison in turn, skipping right over Carlene. Min had left Carlene some money, which was long gone, and trust accounts for Grace and John Robert, to pay for their college.

The house and land would come to Madison later in the year. Ray McCartney had set it up. He might be in love with Carlene, but he was loyal to Min, too.

Madison would be land rich and money poor, once she gained control of Booker Mountain. Unless she sold it off, which everyone seemed to think she should do as soon as possible. If she sold out, she could attend the Art Institute of Chicago and shake the rocky soil of Coalton County right off of her shoes.

She reached under her sweatshirt and touched the opal, reassured by its solid presence. Maybe it was too fancy to be wearing around the house, but Madison wore it anyway. It was a tie to the past and it represented a possible future. It also felt like a link to the stone she'd left behind in Trinity.

The Dragonheart. She'd tried to put it out of her mind, but whenever she tried not to think of something, it seemed like she thought about it more. The only thing that could distract her from Seph McCauley was the Dragonheart. And vice versa. Some days her mind seemed to reverberate from one to the other, making her sick to her stomach. You'd think being far away from both of them would help, but not so much.

Once or twice a week, she went into town. She'd stop in at the library and find a clutch of e-mails from Seph. They were somewhat formal, polite, a little restrained, like old-fashioned love letters in digital text, where you had to read between the lines. It was as though he was afraid he'd scare her off, if he undammed his feelings.

Sometimes, she e-mailed him back, but these days she mostly wrote letters. She knew it was weird and archaic, but she didn't want to say just anything that came into her head. Instead, she'd sit up in bed and dwell over each word, as if she could infuse them with the power to untie the knots that plagued their relationship.

As for talking on the phone, that was totally out. She couldn't trust herself not to say something that would bring him flying down the interstate.

Nothing was stirring in the home yard, except Hamlet and Ophelia, the golden retrievers, who dutifully stood and swished their tails at Madison's appearance.

Lifting her canvas high out of danger, Madison squeezed between the dogs and went into the barn. It was a sturdy stone-and-wood building, once the home of Dredmont Booker's horses. During some prosperous period in the past, someone had put in water lines and servants' quarters. Now it was used as a sometime garage for Carlene's car. Madison had claimed the second floor as a studio and peopled it with dreams.

She should never have come home. Booker Mountain had a way of grabbing onto you, clouding your mind, and making you forget your intentions. Just like it had Felicity Taylor more than a hundred years ago.

Since she'd been away from Seph, her work had lost that lurid, dangerous quality and settled back into what Sara called ethereal exuberance. It could mean the hex magic had dissipated. She'd written to Seph, asking if he was feeling better, but he never responded.

A set of three small canvases glittered from the corner— each a view of the changeable Dragonheart stone against a matte black. The Dragonheart Series.

She cleaned her brushes in the sink and walked back to the house, skirting frozen puddles and patches of mud, followed by the dogs, their tails wagging hopefully.

She paused at the foot of the porch steps to look over the flower beds. New shoots were poking up from the prickly skeletons of the tea roses, and the climber on the trellis by the porch was leafing out bravely.

It was Saturday. Carlene had worked late the night before, and her door was closed. She'd still be in bed. There was breakfast debris on the table, signaling that Grace and John Robert were loose on the mountain. Rounding them up was like herding cats or butterflies. But they'd show up hungry any time now.

She'd take them to town for lunch, she decided. They could wander around Main Street and she'd buy some fertilizer for the garden.

Madison pulled the truck into the angle parking in front of the courthouse. The kids were out of the truck almost before it rolled to a stop.

She shoved two twenty-dollar bills into Grace's hand, taken from her dwindling supply of waitressing money. "Robertson's is having a sale," she said. "Why don't you look for clothes in there? Then take J.R. to to the five-and-dime. I'll meet you at the Bluebird in an hour, and we'll have lunch."

Grace studied the money as if it might be some kind of trick, then folded the bills and put them into her tiny purse.

"Stay together and don't wander off Main Street, so I can find you when I'm done." Madison turned away.

"Where are you going to be?" Grace had a tight hold of John Robert's hand. He was pulling away like a puppy on a leash.

"Hazelton's. I'm going to get some fertilizer for the flower beds."

Madison went into Hazelton's Implements. Josh Hazelton was behind the counter, as she knew he'd be. He'd been in Madison's class at school. Once they'd been friends and told each other secrets. He'd even kissed her under the stands at a football game. They'd awkwardly bumped lips like two goldfish meeting.

That was before he'd gotten in with Brice and them. Funny. Ordinarily, Brice wouldn't give Josh the time of day. So Josh was flattered to be invited into Brice's crowd.

Madison didn't have a crowd. Only Josh. And then not even him.

When Josh looked up and saw her, a guilty blush spread from his collar all the way to his ears. "Hey, Maddie!" he said, turning away from three other customers, all of whom Madison knew. "I heard you were back in town."

"For a while," Madison said, running her hand over a display of mailboxes painted with flowers in colors unknown to nature. "I need some fertilizer."

"Here, I'll show you," he said, eagerly pushing past the swinging gate at the end of the counter.

She raised her hand to stop him. "You've got customers. Just tell me where it is, all right?"

Josh pointed to the back right corner of the store. "Back there. Regular and organic. Five- and ten-pound bags."

She chose a bag of organic fertilizer and some gardening gloves, and brought them to the counter. By then the other customers had left. Josh rang them up for her.

"So how do you like it up north?" he asked, handing her the receipt.

"I like it."

"As well as here?"

"Better." She went to turn away.

"Uh, Maddie?" Josh hesitated, and then the words tumbled out like cats from a bag. "I thought maybe, you know, that you left because . . . because of all that crap last year." He waited, and when she didn't say anything, added, "Look, I'm sorry if . . . Some of us were just having some fun, you know?"

"I didn't realize we were having fun." She looked him in the eyes until he looked away, ears flaming.

"I never believed it. What they said about you," he mumbled.

"Really? I never heard you speak up."

"Well. Anyway. I'm glad you're back."

"Not for long," she said, pretending to look at purple-martin houses.

Josh still hovered. "Have you seen Brice since you've been back?" he asked.

"Yeah." She tried not to make a face. "You still hang around with him?"

He shook his head, coloring again. "Nah. I guess he's really busy."

"Right," she said.

"I hear he has some new friends who don't go to our school." He paused, then said, awkwardly, "You never liked him."

"No. Still don't." She didn't see any point in lying.

"He never could figure that out. Why you wouldn't go out with him."

Madison blinked at him. "He told you that?"

Josh shook his head. "Not exactly. But I knew. He thought you'd be . . . he thought you'd say yes."

Madison snorted. "Come on. I don't think having me as a . . . as a friend was ever high on his list."

Josh licked his lips. "You're wrong. I think it really bugged him. You always want what you can't have. And people—people *listen* to him, you know?"

First, she thought, Why are we talking about Brice Roper? And then it came to her, a revelation. "What are you trying to tell me? That he was behind the . . . people calling me a witch?"

"Well. It didn't take much to convince people. I mean, you're kind of *different*. You dress like a gypsy and always walk around with a frown on your face like you're mad at the world." He held up his hand. "I'm sorry, but it's true. And you were always painting all those pictures, and you lived up on the mountain in that spooky old house."

"It's not spooky," she retorted, then shut her mouth. Who cared what everybody thought?

Josh shrugged. "Your grandmother read the cards and hexed people, and your mom is . . . kind of wild."

"Shut up, Josh," Madison said, feeling the blood rush into her face. She turned away, staring out through the window at a boarded-up storefront across the street.

But Josh would not be silenced. "So one night a bunch of us guys were talking, and some of us had asked you out and been turned down. So Brice just started saying, what if, you know? And we were cracking up, we couldn't help it, he just has a way of putting things. So. I guess we . . . I guess we all kind of got it started. We put out notes and started texting people and then it sort of took on a life of its own, you know?"

Madison swung around and took a step forward and Josh flinched, like he thought she might hit him or spell him or something. "Why do you think I turned them down when they asked me out? Because some guys like to brag about things that *never happened.* All except you. I knew . . . you would never . . . I thought you . . ." She stopped, unwilling to trust herself to go on. It was really ironic that Brice Roper with his Persuasive hands and sleazy layer of wizardly charm would be accusing *her* of being a witch, when she didn't have a stitch of magic in her.

No magic of her own, anyway.

Josh cleared his throat, looking like somebody with his hand in a vise who can't wait to be released. "Anyway. I'm really sorry. I never believed you burnt anything down. I've been wanting to tell you."

She cleared her throat. "Well. Thanks. I guess."

"Want me to carry that out for you?" he asked, handing her the receipt for the fertilizer.

"I can manage." She rested the bag of fertilizer on her hip and turned toward the door.

"Um. Maddie? You know, prom's coming up."

She stiffened. "Josh, I . . ."

He rushed on. "Since I heard you were back, I've

been meaning to call you, but . . . well, you don't have a phone. I wondered if you might want to go with me. As friends, I mean. You could see everyone."

He thought he was offering her a gift, a chance to hold her head up and show everybody they didn't drive her off. But she realized she didn't care what they thought. Not anymore.

Madison shook her head. "I don't think so."

She left him standing behind the counter, hands hanging at his sides.

Grace and John Robert were ten minutes late for their rendezvous at the Bluebird. And when they showed up, Brice Roper was with them.

"Hello, Madison," he said, sliding right into a seat at her table. He was wearing jeans and a cotton sweater and a fleece-lined leather jacket that definitely didn't come from Robertson's. "I ran into Grace and John Robert at the five-and-dime."

Madison gripped the arms of her chair, her heart thumping. Josh Hazelton's revelations were fresh in her mind. But then, Josh hadn't told her anything about Brice that she didn't already know.

"I'm surprised you didn't hustle them off to Child Welfare," she said. "Being as I left them on their own in town and all."

Brice signaled the server. "Look, I said I was sorry."

"Actually, I don't think you did."

He shrugged. "Well, I meant to, anyway. So, to make up for it, I invited Grace and John Robert to come over next week and go riding."

"Let us go, Maddie, please?" John Robert was practically

bouncing in place, gripping her hand. The boy didn't know how to hold a proper grudge.

Grace was different. She wouldn't have forgiven Brice Roper for putting them in foster care. But she loved horses with the passion only a ten-year-old girl could muster. She'd mucked out stalls the summer before in trade for riding lessons. And the Ropers had the prettiest horses in the county. If there was a way to win Gracie over, this was it. She reverberated with indecision, vibrating like a plucked string.

Madison didn't want to be beholden in any way to the Ropers. And she didn't want Grace spending time with the wizard Brice Roper for reasons of her own.

"Absolutely not," Madison said, glaring at Brice. "I can't believe you'd even suggest that. Your horses are for experienced riders. They're not used to kids."

"But you know I can ride, Maddie," Grace protested. Like usual, if Maddie said no, Grace said yes. "I took lessons all last summer with Mr. Ragland. He said I was a natural born horsewoman."

"There's no better teacher around than George Ragland," Brice said. "And J.R.'ll be fine. We always have kids' horses around for the cousins."

"Pleeeeese," John Robert begged, hanging on Madison's arm.

"I said no, and I mean it," Madison said, dislodging John Robert. She looked up at Brice. "You turn the kids over to the county because Mama couldn't find a babysitter, and then you want me to let them risk life and limb . . ."

"No problem," Brice cut in, just as she was winding up. "I'll just ask Carlene."

And that shut Madison up, like he knew it would.

Carlene wouldn't hold grudges about court dates and child welfare. Carlene hadn't had to drop out of school and come back home to bail out the kids. If Brice asked Carlene, she'd let them go in a New York minute. She liked cozying up to the Ropers' money.

Madison sat frozen, cheeks flaming. Even Grace and J.R. knew she'd been outmaneuvered. Grace looked from Brice to Madison, her brow furrowed. "Don't worry, Maddie," she said softly. "We'll be real careful."

"I know you will, honey," Madison said through stiff lips.

"Great," Brice said. The server was hovering and he scanned the menu. "We'll start with a platter of wings and onion rings," he said. "Root beer for everyone. And then whatever else they want." He looked over at Madison as she opened her mouth to object. "My treat."

No, she thought. This was supposed to be *my* treat.

The server hurried off.

"We've got horses that you could ride, Maddie," Brice said, putting his hot hand over hers on the table. "Why don't you come?"

She ripped her hand free. "I'm busy all week."

"How about next week?"

"I'm busy every week." She stood. "Matter of fact, I forgot something at the hardware store." She nodded to the kids. "Go ahead and have lunch, if you want. I'll meet you over there."

But Brice just grinned at Grace and John Robert like they were co-conspirators. "We'll win your big sister over yet."

To Brice it was a game he was destined to win. But he had no idea the danger he was in. If Maddie'd had a gun, she would have shot him.

❧ Chapter Fourteen ❧
Gone South

"Alicia! Your young man—what's his name again?" Aunt Millisandra pointed her bejeweled hand at Jason, who tried hard not to duck.

"Jason," Leesha said, perched on the edge of her chair as if she were ready to spring. "His name's Jason, Aunt Milli."

They were sitting in a stuffy parlor decorated with highly flammable pine roping and a dried-out Christmas tree. The only light came from stubs of candles nestled dangerously in the greens.

"You're sure it's not Jasper? I used to know a Jasper. Jasper DeVilliers. He was French, a bit underpowered, if you know what I mean, but quite the ladies' man." Aunt Millisandra fixed Jason with her purple-shadowed eyes, as if expecting to extract a confession.

Jason shook his head. "Jason," he said.

"A peculiar name, Jason. Would you like another cookie, young man?" Millisandra extended a tray of charred and soggy shortbread. They'd started out okay, but then she'd set fire to them while trying to heat up the tea and had to extinguish them with lemonade.

"Um. That's okay. I've eaten lots already."

Leesha's Aunt Millisandra reminded Jason of one of those dried-up insect carcasses you sometimes found—fragile, like she might crack open if you touched her. She was about a million years old, the richest woman in town—and a wizard who'd lost some key cards from her mental deck. Spending time with her was about as chancy as sitting in the middle of a bonfire with a crate of cherry bombs on your lap.

"More tea, then?"

"No, thanks." He looked at his watch. Nine p.m. "Whoa, look at the time. I had no idea." He stood. 'Thanks for the tea and all."

"In for a penny, in for a pound," Aunt Milli said, waving her hand and shattering glasses all around the room.

"I'll walk you out," Leesha said, jumping to her feet.

In the foyer, she grabbed his hand. "Sorry. I thought she'd be asleep by now!" she hissed.

"Guess not."

"I think she likes you."

"If only my name was Jasper."

"Look, I know she's kind of—dangerous—now, but she's my favorite aunt. She used to take me all kinds of places. Whenever my parents didn't want me around, she'd always take me in."

"I could've used a relative like that," Jason said, forgetting the usual self-edit.

Leesha stood on tiptoes and brushed her lips across his cheek, nearly missing. "'Bye, Jason."

"Can't you come out? There must be someplace we can go."

Leesha glanced over her shoulder. "I'd better not." She'd seemed oddly jittery all evening, as if she'd had too much caffeine or something. It was almost like she was glad old Aunt Milli was there to serve as chaperone. As she turned back around, he noticed that her face seemed oddly misshapen.

Jason grasped Leesha's chin and turned her face up toward the porchlight. She flinched and pulled away.

"What happened to your face?" One side of it was swollen, and he could see bruises under the makeup. It hadn't been apparent in the candlelit parlor.

Leesha turned away from the light. "It was Aunt Milli. She took out a wall in the conservatory. I'm afraid we're going to have to put her in a home."

Were there homes for wizards with dementia? "Seems like you should slip some Weirsbane into her tea. She'd be easier to handle if she wasn't always setting things on fire."

"I've tried that. She can always tell." She paused. "Maybe tomorrow we could go to Cleveland or something. Someplace away."

Jason shrugged. "Maybe." There was nothing else to do but leave, so he left.

He walked home through dark streets. They'd been to the park twice that week already. In really cold weather, they hung out at matinees, where they were unlikely to be spotted, or went back to Leesha's house—er—mansion. Usually Aunt Millisandra went to bed early, but lately she'd had insomnia, or something.

He hadn't done so much sneaking around since he lived back at home with his dad and stepmother. That seemed like a lifetime ago. It was hard to keep a secret in a small town. He wasn't exactly answerable to Nick or Linda or anyone else, except maybe Hastings. He'd just prefer to avoid the lecture if he could. Jack, Will, Fitch, Seph, Ellen—they all hated and mistrusted Leesha Middleton.

So why didn't he? Not that he totally trusted her, but there was a reckless intensity to their relationship that appealed to him. She was the only spark in an otherwise dismal existence. Otherwise, he was going through the motions, marking time, contributing nothing.

Leesha'd had a hard life, in a way—she'd been an inconvenience to her aristocratic wizard parents until her escapades in the Trade made her an embarrassment. She was a survivor, but still somehow vulnerable, and she never did anything halfway.

He laughed. You are so out of your league, he thought. It was the story of his life.

When he arrived home, Linda Downey was in the kitchen, dishing ice cream into a blender.

"Jason! You're just in time. I'm making milkshakes." Linda gripped both his hands, warming him all the way to his toes.

"Milkshakes," he repeated stupidly. "I'm glad I came."

"You've got lipstick on your face," she said, reaching up and rubbing it off with her forefinger.

He liked that about Linda. She didn't ask hard questions. Then he noticed her suitcase sitting by the door. "You going someplace?"

She hesitated. "I'm meeting Leander in Britain."

"Right. Well. Great." His face burned, and the words seemed to stick in his throat. "Bon voyage, I guess."

He went to turn away, and she gripped his arm. "Seph's

in the solarium," she said, looking anxiously up into his eyes. "He's been waiting for you. He needs help with something." She nodded toward the back of the house.

Right. Probably wants me to shine his shoes. Feeling irritable and uncooperative, Jason went to find Seph.

Seph sat next to the windows reading in a puddle of light cast by a single table lamp. Past the patio there was a strip of snowy lawn, then a wall that marked the dropoff to the lake. In the background, the waves crashed in a northwest wind, claiming and relinquishing the beach.

Seph looked up and marked his place with a finger. "Jase! Where've you been?"

Jason shrugged. "Here and there. What's up?"

No answer. Seph sat motionless, staring into space, like he'd checked out completely. It was like talking to someone wearing headphones or reading his e-mail at the same time. Jason knew Seph must be monitoring the boundary.

"What are you reading?" Jason asked, trying to break in.

Seph looked up, a little startled. "AP Physics. We're having another practice test next week."

Jason dropped into a wrought-iron chair. "Can you really do both those things at the same time?" I couldn't do *one* of those things at the same time, he thought to himself.

In fact, Seph looked bad, kind of hollow-cheeked and twitchy, and his eyes glittered and burned. "You sound like Lin . . . my mom."

As if on cue, Linda appeared, carrying two tall milkshakes on a tray. And a big bowl of trail mix.

She clunked a milkshake down in front of Seph. "Here. See that you finish this. And you can let go of the boundary in a few minutes. Iris said she'd take over at ten."

"I'm okay." Seph sat up a little straighter. "I can keep it a while longer. Till I go to bed, anyway."

"We've already talked about pushing yourself, Seph. Don't argue." It was one of the few times Jason had seen Seph's mother exerting parental authority.

When she went back into the house, Jason said, "She acts like you're an invalid or something."

Seph shrugged and looked away. "Yeah. Well."

Seph obviously wasn't going to tell him what was going on. Jason tried again. "She seems kind of stressed."

Seph sucked down some milkshake and set the glass down. "It's the whole deal with being in charge while my father's away. She'd like to get some more wizards who could watch the perimeter, to give us a break, but Snowbeard is worried about trusting anyone new."

You could try me, Jason thought. He didn't bother to say it aloud.

"Nick's really fixated on that stuff you brought back from Britain," Seph went on. "Linda's good at managing the other guilds, but wizards always think they should be running everything. Some of them aren't used to taking orders from an enchanter."

Seph seemed to be avoiding mention of Linda's travel plans, so Jason said, "And now she's going to Britain."

Seph nodded while watching Jason, as if wary of his reaction. "So she's leaving, and she's worried about leaving me on my own." Seph leaned his head back. His mind seemed to drift again for a moment, then he said, "You still wear the *dyrne sefa*?"

In answer, Jason fished the pendant out from under his shirt.

Seph smiled. "Remember when we used to go out in the

woods and practice wizardry at the Havens?"

Jason didn't particularly want to remember his time at the Havens—especially what had happened to his father. Plus it just highlighted the magical performance gap that had grown between him and Seph. He found that contrast more and more oppressive.

"I taught you everything I knew. Which wasn't much. And now you've gone way beyond me. But Linda says you want to ask me something."

"I need to ask you a favor."

"Which is . . . ?"

"Someone broke into Maddie's room the other night."

Jason waited, and when Seph didn't go on, asked, "Did they take anything?"

"We don't know. I looked around, but I couldn't tell if anything was missing."

"What's she say?"

"I can't reach her. Their phone's disconnected and her cell phone doesn't work at her house. I e-mailed her, but I don't know when she'll get the message."

Where's this leading? Jason thought. "Maybe it was someone who knew she was gone and thought they'd take advantage."

"They used magic to blow a hole in her door." Seph paused long enough to let this sink in. "Hers was the only room they touched. And she's got nothing to steal." He looked out at the lake. "I didn't want her to leave in the first place. It's bad enough if they go after her because of me. But if they know what she can do . . ."

"What do you want me to do?"

"Go down there and bring her back. I'd go myself, but

Snowbeard wants me here. Besides, they'll be looking for me to go. You're less likely to lead them to her." Seph paused and cleared his throat. "There's something else. There was something left behind in her room, a painting with a hex in it, targeted at me. It hit me pretty hard."

"Whoa." Jason stared at him. That explained Seph's haggard appearance, then. But if he was handling the boundary, he couldn't be too bad off. "Are you okay? Did the . . ."

"I'm *fine*," Seph snapped. "But it was Madison's painting. So Snowbeard thinks Madison may be . . . may have turned." He muttered this last, as if he didn't want to honor it by saying it out loud.

Jason considered this. He'd known there was something off between Seph and Madison, but he still would've said they were crazy about each other.

Then again, you had to consider what Seph was competing against. A Claude D'Orsay or Jessamine Longbranch could make Madison rich beyond her wildest dreams. Rich enough to attend any art school in the country.

So he chose the safest response. "What do you think?"

"What do you mean, what do I think?" Seph leaned forward, practically shedding sparks. "It's impossible. She wouldn't do that."

"Okay, okay." Jason raised his hands to ward off harm. "I'm not disagreeing. But still, maybe it isn't a good idea to bring her back here if she may be . . ."

"Why would she have gone back home if she was plotting something? That makes no sense."

"Well. If she left you a spell-bomb, wouldn't she want to be as far away as possible when it went off?"

Seph stood, towering over Jason. Power bled from his skin and ran in rivulets to the floor, where it scorched a ring into the flagstones. He looked dragged-out tired, but hyper-juiced at the same time.

"Hey, man, will you chill?" Jason said. "I'm not disagree-ing with you, just asking questions. Or is that not allowed?"

Seph glared at him a moment, then subsided back into his chair, trembling.

Gotta tread easy here, Jason thought. He tried to think of something harmless to say. "So. Um. Does Snowbeard know you're asking me to do this?"

Seph massaged his forehead as if to pry loose a reluctant truth. "It was kind of Nick's idea. He wants you to go to Coalton County and spy on Madison and find out what the story is. Is she in danger, or is she working for the Roses or what? Is anyone else hanging around down there who might be behind the attack on me?" He looked up at Jason. "So you can do both. Check on those things and bring her back." He looked away. "Either way. If she's working against us, we can't . . . we can't risk letting it continue. If she's not, we can't risk leaving her out there on her own."

And what are *you* going to do if it turns out she *has* gone over to the dark side, Jason thought.

"I'm not exactly the go-to person when it comes to wiz-ardry." He shook his head when Seph made as if to disagree. "Just . . . don't. Why me?"

Seph shrugged, surrendering. "I can't leave, and neither can Nick. With Madison, it doesn't matter how pow-erful you are. It's almost a disadvantage to be juiced." He smiled apologetically.

"Why send a wizard, then?"

"Well. In . . . in case she's . . . in case there are wizards down there. That she's working with."

This was killing Seph, Jason knew. And if Jason brought back the news that Madison had turned, he just might kill the messenger. He tried a joke. "What if she won't come? My deadly charm won't work on her, you know."

Seph didn't look amused. "Convince her." He raked a hand through his hair. "I know you're back in school, but it should-n't take more than a couple of days to go down there and bring her back. Three or four days would give you time to scout around and ask questions, I guess."

He put his blistering hand on Jason's arm and looked him in the eyes. "Whatever happens, Jase, we need you back here when you're done. We've got some plans in the works that need wizardry, and that's what we're short on."

Jason considered this, taking his time. Seph wouldn't send Jason to Madison if he didn't think it was necessary. Otherwise the risk would outweigh the benefit. And, just as obviously, Jason was more expendable than either Seph or Nick.

Should he go? It would get him out of Trinity, though he guessed Coal Grove wouldn't be an improvement. But this might be the opening he needed to break away, to get out from under Nick's supervision and the obligation he felt to Seph. He could do him this one last favor, and then . . .

"How would I get down there?"

"I made Madison write out directions before she left. My mother says you can use her car, since she's leaving, anyway." Seph grinned, looking more like his old self. "Just make sure you bring it back in one piece."

Sweet. Linda drove a BMW Z4 roadster convertible.

Though Madison might have to drive her truck back if she wanted to bring more than a toothbrush.

The coil of tension inside Jason unwound a notch. It was a plan. He had some money saved up from working at the docks over the past year. He'd retrieve a few magical items from St. Catherine's that might help him in Britain. He'd accompany Madison back as far as Columbus, then send her on. By the time they realized he was gone, he could be back at Raven's Ghyll. He'd *make* Hastings take him on. If not, there were other places to go in the world, other battles to fight.

Right.

Of course this only worked if Madison was on their side.

"Okay. I'm on my way. Draw me a map while I pack my stuff."

It was just getting light when Jason parked the BMW in the lot at St. Catherine's.

The tiny trunk was already loaded with his clothes and music. Once on his way, he didn't plan on stopping. He hoped to leave town without dealing with Nick or Mercedes. With any luck, they'd slept late.

He felt bad about Leesha, but he'd text her to let her know he was gone, once he was on his way. He didn't feel like he could risk an in-person goodbye. When he was settled, he could get back in touch.

Using the key he'd copied from Seph's, he descended to the chilly darkness of the crypt and disabled the charms that had been laid over Thomas Swift's unused tomb. The magical pieces were sorted, labeled, and for the most part, put away.

The Dragonheart mocked him from its ornate stand in

the corner, awakening a hopeless longing as his Weirstone responded. He and Nick and Mercedes had tried everything they knew, but nobody had been able to touch the stone since that day he'd first gone out with Leesha right after Madison had left. He struggled to relate those different events, and gave up.

If the text from the cave could be believed, they had a weapon of unmatchable power, and they couldn't even get near it.

Maybe it'd be easier to accept if he was far away. Maybe he wouldn't feel so barren and empty.

He'd take only a few things that Nick and Mercedes might overlook. He ran through the possibilities. He had no need for lovestones; that had never been a problem. Nor collars for captives; he planned to take no prisoners. He wasn't about to carry around magic mirrors that weren't reliable anyway. But scrying stones were small and might lead him to what he was looking for. Amulets and talismans were always useful.

He lifted one of the magical daggers and weighed it in his hand. That might give him an edge against a more powerful adversary—D'Orsay or anybody else.

In the end, he chose a dagger, a scrying stone, a talisman for protection, and an amulet that was supposed to give strength to the bearer. He already had the *dyrne sefa* given to him by his mother—good for multiple purposes. He slid the chosen items into his backpack and left the rest where they were.

When he came out of the church, he skidded to a stop. Leesha was leaning against his car. He should've used the less accessible but more private water gate. Ordinarily, he'd be glad to see her, but he just wasn't in a position to be answering questions this morning.

"Back in church again?" She lifted an eyebrow and attempted a smile that didn't quite come off.

He shrugged, acutely conscious of the magical pieces in his backpack. How had she found him so quickly? It was early for her to be out. Had she followed him?

"Cool car," she said, resting her hand on the BMW, another question plain on her face. Where the night before she'd seemed antsy and distracted, today she seemed grim and determined. As if she knew he intended to split.

Damn. He should've left the car at home until he was ready to leave.

He stared at her, temporarily wordless, then said, "A friend let me borrow it."

"Take me for a ride?"

"I've got to return it, and I'm late already. I'll text you later, all right?" Jason tossed the backpack into the passenger seat and circled round to get in on the driver's side.

Leesha reached in and picked up the backpack by its strap. "What's in here?"

"Hey, leave that alone." Jason rounded the side of the car and grabbed the backpack out of her hands.

"What's in there, Jason? A present for me?" She lunged for the backpack and he caught her wrists to keep her from latching on again. For a moment they stood face-to-face, glaring at each other. With the whole town looking on if it cared to.

Jason released her hands and took a step back. "Please, Leesha. Just . . . Like I said, I'm kind of in a hurry. I'm sorry. I'll talk to you later, okay? I promise." He got in the car, putting the backpack on the floor at his feet.

"Right," she said, and stood, chewing her lip, watching as he drove away.

What was that all about? he wondered, as he navigated the tree-lined streets around the square. She'd seemed almost angry with him.

In the time it took to reach the interstate, he'd lost himself in the pleasure of driving the BMW. Interstate 71 sliced southwest, parting flat farm fields on either side. He cranked up the radio. There wasn't much traffic, so he cranked the speed up, too, reasoning he could always talk his way out of a ticket.

He knew he was taking stupid chances, with the invasion of Raven's Ghyll, and with Leesha, and with driving too fast, but somehow he couldn't help himself.

When he reached Columbus, he circled around, exited onto Route 23, then again onto another state route, heading southeast into the hills. He watched his mirrors intermittently, but could see no sign he was being followed. He passed through tiny towns: Glen Furnace, Floradale, Salt Creek. He planned to head straight down to Maddie's. These country roads would be easier to navigate by daylight.

His phone went off several times. Leesha calling. No message. He shut it off.

By the time he reached Coal Grove, it had clouded over and begun to sleet, a relentless needle-fine, bone-chilling rain that froze on contact. The cloud ceiling dropped until it nearly met the ground.

He drove east, out of town, Seph's directions beside him on the seat, his backpack on the floor on the passenger side. The landscape looked like it'd taken a beating and never quite recovered.

He had no idea how it would go at Maddie's. He knew from experience that Madison Moss couldn't be bullied. But maybe she'd be glad to see him, wanting news of Seph. And he could check out her reaction when he delivered it.

The road rapidly deteriorated from pavement to oiled gravel. It twisted and turned, but mostly it climbed. A thick, second-growth forest crowded in on either side, greening up for spring, punctuated now and then by a rural mailbox fronting a house trailer or a run-down farm. He passed a sign that said ROPER COAL: COALTON COUNTY WORKS, pointing down a more substantial side road. And, later, a prosperous-looking horse farm with brick gateway pillars and a sign, in a rope-like script, BRY-SON ARABIANS.

Somewhere along here was the turnoff to Booker Mountain. "Not well marked," Seph's directions said. By now, it was raining harder.

After traveling a mile farther, he began to realize he must have missed the turnoff. He did a quick U-turn and drove back the way he'd come. Jason leaned forward, peering through the rain-smeared windshield.

He rounded a curve and found the way blocked by a huge tree that lay at an angle across the road. He slammed on the brakes, skidding sideways in the wet gravel. The BMW came to a stop with its passenger door inches from the tree.

Jason rested his head on the wheel, his heart thumping in his chest. A tree on the slope above must have lost hold in the saturated earth. It must've just happened, since the way had been clear moments before.

Shoving the driver's side door open, he climbed out into the rain on rubbery legs. If he wanted to go forward, he'd have to get the tree off the road. Wizardry was good for making people do what you wanted or for moving the more fluid ethers like water, air, and flame. He wasn't sure he knew a charm for moving giant trees.

Jason yanked the backpack from under the seat. Maybe there was something there that would help. Kneeling on the soggy ground, he sorted through the magical pieces he'd taken from the church. He had a dagger that would inflict a mortal wound (on a man, not a tree), talismans of protection that he was unsure how to use, an amulet that gave strength to the weary (maybe he could lift the tree off the road), and a scrying stone that blazed up oddly between his hands. Like a warning.

There was something else, something unfamiliar, a small, flat metal object. He held it up to the light. There was a faint marking on it, like a stylized etching of a spider. How did that get there?

He looked up just as the car exploded into flames.

He rolled backward to keep from being engulfed. Propping up on his elbows, he stared in disbelief. The car was a blazing inferno, hissing and spitting in the pouring rain.

Oh, God, he thought. Linda's going to kill me. His next thought was, I'm out of here.

As he struggled to his feet, something struck him full in the chest, just beneath the collarbone, hard enough to spin him half around. He clutched at his shirtfront, but could find no wound or missile, only an awful spreading cold and numbness.

"Damn!" someone said behind him. "I hope that didn't hit too close to the heart. The idea is to immobilize you. Not kill you."

Jason swung around to face the speaker. It couldn't be.

The blond, almost translucent hair, the pale blue eyes and colorless lips. The lopsided, arrogant smile he hadn't seen since the ill-fated conference at Second Sister.

"Barber!"

The smile grew wider. "For a minute, I didn't think you remembered me. But, hey, the friendships we make at school are the ones that last."

"What are you doing here?"

"I followed you. Of course I didn't know you'd lead me to the crap hole of the universe." Barber flipped his hand, indicating their general surroundings.

"What did you shoot me with?"

"It's a wizard graffe. A virtual dagger with an effect very much like spider venom. Renders the victim immobile, but leaves the mind clear and able to perceive pain. Great for interrogations."

"What do you want?"

"To ask you some questions. But first we'll go someplace quiet where we won't be interrupted."

The paralysis was spreading. Jason's limbs were growing heavy. It was getting difficult to push air through his lungs. "Questions about what?" he mumbled. Even his lips and tongue weren't obeying his commands.

"Questions about what you're doing down here. About what you stole from Raven's Ghyll and hid in the church. About the Dragonheart. We can start with what's in your backpack." Barber extended his hand. "Hand it over."

Backpack. Jason's body might be sluggish, but his mind was clear. Barber knew Jason had left town. He knew about the church. He knew there was something in his backpack.

Leesha.

A cold anger seized Jason. "You want this?" he shouted hoarsely. As he raised the backpack, he thrust his hand inside, closing it around the amulet. *Gives strength to the bearer.* He muttered a charm calling forth its power and felt welcome strength flood back into his body. Slinging the pack over his shoulder, he reached up with the other hand and gripped the *dyrne sefa* that hung around his neck. Speaking the familiar unnoticeable charm he'd learned from his mother, he thrust himself sideways.

He landed rolling in the sodden leaves, but was immediately up and running, slipping and sliding down the hill, the backpack slamming against his shoulder. Barber was a powerful wizard, outclassing Jason on his best day. Unnoticeable or not, it wouldn't be healthy to stay around.

Barber was totally pissed. He sent flames roaring down the hillside in Jason's wake, then charged downhill after him, shouting and swearing. "Idiot! Where the hell do you think you're going? Give yourself up, or you're going to lie on your back in the mud until you're ripped apart and eaten alive by wild animals."

It was hard to understand with all the profanity mixed in, but it was something like that.

Jason staggered on. He had no intention of submitting to an interrogation of Warren Barber's devising. Being ripped apart by wild animals seemed appealing in comparison. Besides, he'd been played for a fool, and he would not, could not let them win.

Still, it was more than twenty miles back to town, and he had no idea how long the effects of the amulet would last. He knew Madison's house must be somewhere nearby, but he didn't want to lead Barber to her.

Realistically, he was dead.

At the bottom of the hill, Jason turned left and followed a wide creek through a ravine. Then he began climbing again. He climbed for a long time, following the stream, scrambling over rocks, splashing in and out of the water. Finally he left the creek and cut over a shoulder of the mountain. By then, he was stumbling, losing strength despite his tight grip on the amulet. He tried speaking the charm again, but this time there was no apparent effect.

He was completely disoriented. He had no idea which way it was to town, which way Madison's house might be. His only goal was to keep away from Barber.

That was easier said than done. Barber seemed to have an uncanny ability to stay with him. When Jason reached high ground and looked back, Barber was coming. Not following Jason's trail, exactly, but moving in the right direction, just the same. Sometimes cutting straight across ravines and stream-beds. It was almost as if Jason were sending off some kind of homing signal.

Idiot.

He shrugged the backpack off his shoulders and half-sat, half-fell to the ground. Digging through the pocket, he retrieved the mysterious spider stone.

It must be a lodestone, placed there on purpose, probably by Leesha outside the church. All Barber had needed to do was follow the stone to track Jason to Coalton County and through the woods in the rain.

Shivering, teeth chattering, resisting the urge to lie down where he was and sink into oblivion, Jason gripped the low branches of a tree, dragged himself to his feet, and looked around.

He'd been following a high ridge. On one side of the ridge the ground fell away into deep forest shrouding a series of smaller hills. On the other he could see the tracing of a road that followed the creek bed. Behind him, he could hear Barber crashing violently through the brush.

Drawing his arm back, Jason threw the stone as far as he could out into the valley. Then he descended the ridge on the opposite side, heading for the road. Hopefully, Barber would follow the stone.

There remained the problem of the graffe. Jason couldn't go much further.

He could try to attract the attention of someone in a passing car. A car probably came by every day or two.

As if that would even do any good. They wouldn't have a clue. All they could do was watch him die.

He worked his way down the ridge in a kind of stumbling trot. His legs were no longer working reliably. The rain had slowed to a sprinkle, but rivulets of muddy water still flowed down the slope, making the footing treacherous.

His breathing was growing labored again. He was conscious of a creeping cold, an inability to control his movements. He blinked away a double image of the hillside. Finally, he overshot a small overhang, tumbled twenty feet, and ended with his feet in the ditch and his head and shoulders on the berm of the road.

He hurt. Barber was right—his ability to perceive pain was functioning just fine. He'd slammed his elbow when he landed, and wondered if his arm was broken. But he lacked the strength to turn his head to check for certain.

He had no idea how long he lay there before he heard a rumble and felt a faint vibration beneath him. Thunder, he thought. Then he realized it must be a car coming.

Idiot. He was unnoticeable. No one would see him lying by the side of the road, not even when his unnoticeable sun-bleached bones mingled with the scattered remnants of roadkill skeletons. He gripped the *sefa* and disabled the unnoticeable charm with his last bit of strength. Then he lay on his back, staring up at the sky, unable even to blink against the relentless drizzle. He had to really focus to remember to breathe.

He heard the wet, sucking sound of tires as the car approached. Was he far enough off the road? Would the car run him over? Was he close enough to be seen?

He felt the air stir as the car neared, felt the freezing spray as it swept by. Bitter disappointment. He heard a squeal of brakes and caught a whiff of hot rubber. Wild elation. A car door slammed, then footsteps crunched on gravel, and then a voice.

"Hey, you okay? What happened? Someone run you over and drive off?" And then, moments later, *"Jason?"*

It was Madison Moss.

Seconds later, her worried face appeared in his field of vision. It was bronzed a bit—she'd been out in the sun—and her voluminous hair was pulled back in a ponytail. She wore jeans and a plain white T-shirt—different from her bohemian mode of dress in Trinity.

No, he thought dazedly. This girl is not hanging with the bad guys. I don't believe it.

"It *is* you! What are you doing here? What happened? Is Seph with you?" It was a cascade of questions, erupting too fast for his failing mind to follow.

"Madison," he tried to say, but his lips wouldn't form the syllables. He was struggling for breath, suffocating. Spots swam before his eyes. Barber hadn't meant to kill him, or at least not until after he'd tortured the truth out of him. He must've messed up.

Kneeling next to him, Madison touched his chest lightly where the graffe went in. "What the . . . ? It looks . . . it looks like your chest is on fire." Then she clapped her mouth shut, eyes wide, seeming to realize that he might not find that reassuring. Madison had the ability to spot magic in others— even Barber's deadly graffe, apparently.

"Don't worry, now. Let's just see." She pulled aside his jacket and lifted his sweatshirt to examine the wound.

"Gick," he managed. And, then, "Gick!" again, louder. Meaning, *We've got to get the hell out of here!*

She ran her cold hands up his chest until she found the wound and pushed her fingertips into it. He nearly screamed from the pain of it, but then he felt a kind of sucking, a reverse pressure, and immediately the hot burn over his heart eased. And again she pressed her hands against his skin, scrunching up her face as if it was as hard on her as on him. His body lost some of its creeping cold rigidity and he could swallow his saliva again. She was drawing the magical venom away.

Madison pulled her hands back, wiping them vigorously on the weeds at the roadside, shuddering. "Yuck. This is bad nasty, whatever it is. I'm going to have a devil of a time getting rid of this. At least it's not . . . Who did this? Where did you come from?" She didn't really seem to expect an answer.

Madison stood, hands on hips, and looked up the slope. She seemed very tall and angular from Jason's position on the ground. "I thought maybe you dropped out of the sky, but looks like you rolled down from up there."

He managed to croak, "Madison. Warren Barber's here.

We've got to go before he sees us." By now, Barber might have discovered his ruse and be heading back over the ridge in time to see what was happening at the side of the road.

"Warren Barber!" Madison had met Warren Barber before—at Second Sister—when she'd put him flat on his back in the inn garden.

At least she didn't ask a million questions. "Hang on, I'm going to put you in the truck. Nothing's broken, is it?"

Dumbly, he shook his head. His arm was killing him, but broken bones were small change against what Barber would do if he came over that hill.

Madison disappeared from his field of view. The truck door slammed, and she was back with a paint-spattered canvas tarp. Sliding her hands under his arms, she tugged him onto it. Then, gripping the edge of the canvas, she dragged him along the berm to her ancient red pickup. The tailgate was down, but the opening seemed a mile away. Jason couldn't fathom how she was going to get him up into the bed. She propped him against the truck. Then she climbed into the truckbed, leaned down, wrapped her arms around his chest, and hauled him backward into the bed. He landed flat on top of her, but she wriggled out from underneath him.

"Sorry," she muttered. She hurriedly arranged his extremities to her liking, then tossed the tarp over him, covering him completely. "Sorry," she said again.

The truck jounced on its failing springs as she jumped down from the bed, then climbed up into the cab. The door slammed and the engine came to life. Rain pattered on the canvas over his head. He didn't know where he was going, he didn't know where Warren Barber was, and he didn't know if he'd survive the day.

❧ CHAPTER FIFTEEN ❧
ALONG CAME A SPIDER

Jason didn't remember much about the next several days. He felt dry and hot one minute, and cold and sweaty the next. He wrestled with dreams like he hadn't had since the ones Gregory Leicester had inflicted on him at the Havens.

He dreamed he was back in the woods and Warren Barber spun out cords from his wrists like Spiderman, wrapping him into a giant cocoon. He injected poison into him with giant fangs and left him hanging helpless in his web, saying, "I'll be back, and then you'll talk."

He dreamed of Leesha and Barber, laughing together at Jason's stupidity and the deft way she'd played him. Jason had never been a magical powerhouse, but he'd always considered himself street-smart, at least. Right. Everyone had warned him about Leesha, and he'd ignored them. His only hope was that no one would ever find out what an idiot he'd been.

He burned with fever, embarrassment, and hot anger.

He'd wake, startled by the sound of his own voice reverberating in his ears, and he wondered what he'd said, how much he had revealed.

Madison was there, a lot of the time. She didn't suck out any more poison. Instead, she forced liquids and cups of soup into him.

He gripped her hands, in a rare moment of lucidity. "Maddie. Don't tell anyone about this. Not Seph. Not anybody. Please."

"You are crazy, you know that?" She pressed the back of her hand to his forehead, feeling for fever. "He needs to know what happened. I'm going to go to town and call him soon as I can leave you on your own."

He struggled to sit up, flailing wildly under the quilt. "You call him, I'm out of here. Right now."

She lifted an eyebrow. "You gonna hitchhike, or what? Now lay down before I club you for a fool. You need somebody who knows about magic to treat you."

"I'm much better. Really."

Madison snorted.

Jason groped for an argument. "Look, Maddie, if you call him, he'll blame me for messing up and putting you in danger. One little thing he asked me to do, and I blew it. He'll never trust me to do anything again. I'd rather you just shot me in the head." He pressed his fingertips against his forehead for emphasis.

She frowned. He could tell she was wavering.

"Besides, if you call him, nothing will keep him from coming down here. Meanwhile, everything falls apart up there."

"Well," she muttered, looking troubled, "we'll see. If you take a turn for the worse . . ."

He'd gotten to her. Jason smiled and closed his eyes and gave himself up to sleep.

The next time, he awoke to find two huge yellow dogs crowded in bed with him, one on either side. "Hey," he said weakly, shoving at the one with its head on the pillow breathing dog breath in his face. The dog opened its eyes and licked Jason's face with an impossibly long black-and-pink tongue, then went back to sleep.

Some time later, a solemn-faced little girl with straight brown hair set a tray on the floor next to him and sat down with a bump.

"Where's Madison?" he asked, drawing the sheet up over his bare, bandaged chest, squinting his eyes against the light that snuck between battered rafters overhead.

"She had to go meet with her art teacher," she said.

This didn't really process. What art teacher? "Who are you?"

"I'm Grace Minerva Moss," she said. "Maddie's sister. I made you lunch. Grilled cheese and tomato soup," she added, rather proudly. And, there, on the tray, was a paper plate with a slightly charred grilled cheese sandwich cut into two triangles, some saltine crackers, a mug of soup, a paper towel, and a can of root beer.

He was lying on a mattress on the floor, surrounded by paintings on easels, some unfinished. He recognized them as Madison's work. Heaving a pile of quilts aside, he tried to prop on his elbows but found his left arm was in a sling. So he rolled to his good side and sat up, raking his free hand through his hair. "Where am I?" he asked, when his head stopped spinning.

"You're in the barn. In the loft. Maddie's studio. *I* had to help Maddie carry you up here. You're real heavy, you know?" she added, accusingly.

He groped at his neck, and his hand closed on the *dyrne sefa*, still on its chain. "Where's my stuff? My clothes, I mean, and I had a backpack . . . ."

Grace Minerva Moss pointed. He twisted round. His backpack was hanging on a peg on the wall. His clothes were folded in a little pile underneath. It was clean and tidy, for a barn, he guessed. His eyes traveled over the ranks of paintings.

"Madison paints up here?"

"Some. Plus everywhere else."

Grace snatched up the paper towel and dropped it on his lap. A hint. He picked up the grilled cheese sandwich and bit into it. It was gritty with carbon, but had that deliciously greasy processed-cheese taste. He was suddenly ravenous. "This is great," he mumbled, his mouth full of bread and melted cheese. "Is anyone else home?"

"Just my brother, J.R. And my mother. She's still asleep." Grace leaned closer and whispered conspiratorially, "She doesn't know you're here."

Jason sucked down some soup, the comforting orange canned stuff familiar from when he was a kid. Grace studied him, then extended her hand toward him, stopping a few inches away. "You're all sparkly," she said, looking puzzled. "Like Brice Roper."

Before he could respond, there was a scuffling below, then the sound of wood creaking. Jason stiffened, once again reaching for the *dyrne sefa*. A blond head poked up, as if through the floor.

Grace tried to put herself between Jason and the intruder.

"John Robert Moss! I told you to stay in the sandbox."

It was a little boy—Jason wasn't good with kids' ages—apparently the brother, J.R. The boy hauled himself up through the floor and turned and sat with his legs dangling through the hole. His face was smudged and dirty, and he wore blue jeans rolled to fit. "What are you doing up here? Who's that man?" he asked, pointing at Jason.

"Nobody," she said furiously. "You shouldn't be in the barn at all. You know the hay gives you welts. Go away!" Jason thought for a moment she might poke him right back down the hole like a gopher in a cartoon.

"I want a grill-cheese sandwich," J.R. howled, seeing the last of Jason's disappear. J.R. did, indeed, seem to be breaking out in red blotches all over his face, whether from hay or rage, Jason didn't know.

"You already had lunch, and I . . ." Grace began, but stopped, frowning, head tilted. Then Jason heard it, too, the crunch of gravel as someone drove into the yard.

"Maybe Maddie's back," she said doubtfully. "But she said it wouldn't be until real late." She stood and carefully circled around the trapdoor to the window on the far end. She peered out, then looked back at Jason. "It's a blond-haired man, all sparkly, like you."

Jason didn't need to look to know it was Warren Barber. And he didn't need to think about it to know that a magical duel would be no contest at all, considering the shape he was in. He wished he had the Dragonheart. A machine gun. Something.

Bam! Bam! Bam!

Grace was still watching through the window. "He's on the porch, pounding on the door. He looks like he's mad."

Jason staggered to his feet and nearly fell. He gripped the wall for support, and wondered how he would manage the stairs. "Is there a back door? Can we get out of here without being seen from the house?"

Grace shook her head. "There's a ravine. It drops to Booker Creek behind here. The barn door faces the porch." She squinted through the glass. "Mama's come out on the porch. She won't be happy to be woke up." She watched a minute longer, then said, "They went in the house, him and Mama."

Just let him look around and leave, Jason prayed. Just let Mama keep her mouth shut and not mention Madison. Can't I be lucky, for once?

"You two go on, get out of here," Jason said to the kids. "Just run as far as you can out into the woods and stay there until someone comes to get you."

"Is that man after you?" Grace asked. "Is he the one that hurt you?"

"Yes. Now, go on." Jason slumped back down onto the mattress and put his head between his knees, trying hard not to barf the grilled cheese and soup. He was going nowhere. "I'll hide up here. It'll be easier if it's just me."

Grace folded her arms and tapped her foot in a familiar, stubborn way. Just like Maddie. "He'll look in here for sure."

"Will you go, already? If you stay here, you'll give me away," Jason said.

"I promised Madison I'd take care of you," Grace said. She looked out of the window again. "He's coming."

Jason swore under his breath. Even if he made himself unnoticeable, there was convalescent crap all over the place. It was very obviously a sick room, just what Warren Barber would be looking for. Barber'd be expecting an unnoticeable charm after what had happened in the woods. Maybe he'd even brought glitter powder along to ferret Jason out.

Jason slid himself back into a corner, gripping the *sefa*. "Come here," he said to Grace and J.R. "Squeeze in next to me. I can hide all of us with magic." He tried to sound confident, but who even knew if it would work, sick as he was?

"Magic?" Grace rolled her eyes. "There's no such thing. I'm not *stupid*." She looked from Jason to J.R., her brow furrowing in thought. "I know!" A smile broke, the first he'd seen on her. She turned to her brother. "J.R.! Get in that bed. Pretend you're asleep."

With two older sisters, it seemed J.R. was used to taking orders. He slid obediently under the quilts. By now his eyes were swollen to slits and he was scratching himself vigorously.

"Hide," Grace said to Jason.

Great. She thinks we're playing hide-and-seek. "Hand me that backpack," he whispered. "Then keep still and maybe he won't come up."

She handed him the backpack and sat down on the mattress next to J.R., waiting. Jason fumbled the zipper open and groped inside until he found the dagger he'd brought from Trinity, seemingly a century ago. Sliding the blade from its sheath, Jason gripped the knife in his good hand, crouched back in his corner, and murmured the unnoticeable charm. Maybe he'd be lucky, for once.

"Hey," J.R. said in a stage whisper, peeking out from under the blanket. "Where'd he go?"

Grace clapped her hand over his mouth. "Hush!"

Hinges screeched as the barn door opened beneath

them. He could hear Barber walking back and forth below, cursing violently, kicking stuff out of the way. Jason held his breath. Then he heard the stairs creak as they took Barber's weight.

No. He couldn't be lucky, not even once. He gathered his legs under him. Maybe the kids would distract Barber long enough to give him a chance. It was a magical dagger, after all. Maybe a scratch would do the trick.

Grace gestured frantically at Jason. "You have to hide better than that! He's going to *see* you."

Jason's overtaxed brain struggled to make sense of it. He was unnoticeable, he was sure of it. Unless, in his debilitated state . . .

Barber's head and shoulders appeared through the opening in the floor. He was trying to look everywhere at once, obviously anticipating an attack.

"Hi," Grace said promptly. "Are you Howie? I didn't think you were coming."

Startled, Barber raised his hands to throw a charm, almost losing his balance and falling backward down the steps. Which would've been great. But he caught himself and said, "What the . . . who the hell is Howie?"

"The new sitter. He was supposed to come today. I *told* Mama I could baby-sit my brother all by myself." She pointed at J.R. "He's sick. We're playing hospital. Want to play?"

"No, I don't want to play," Barber growled. His clothes were dirty and torn, and he was scratched and scraped up, like he'd been searching through the woods for several days. "I'm going to have a look around." He heaved himself to his feet. "You seen any strangers around here?"

"You mean, besides you?"

Jeez, Jason thought, don't antagonize him.

Barber glared at her for a minute, then kind of relaxed, as if he figured she was too young to be an actual smart-ass. "Yeah, besides me. I'm looking for a guy about my age, about my height, too, but thinner. Dark hair streaked blonde. He wears an earring." Barber touched his earlobe, in case she couldn't figure it out.

"Why are you looking for him?" Grace asked.

"I think he might be hurt. That's why I'm looking for him. To help him." Barber bared his teeth in his blood-curdling smile, pale eyes glittering with malice. He apparently took Grace Minerva for an idiot. He didn't seem to notice Jason in his corner.

"I haven't seen anybody. We haven't been allowed to go anywhere since my brother got sick, 'cause it's catching." Grace pretended to spoon soup into the pretending-to-sleep John Robert. Her hand shook a little.

Barber stomped around the room, peering into the rafters, shoving aside farm equipment, and inspecting spaces too small for Jason to fit in. He reached into his pocket, pulled out a pouch, and dumped something into his palm. Glitter powder.

Barber suddenly flung the powder into the wrong corner, and it floated down, shimmering in the shafts of sunlight. Revealing no one.

"Hey," Grace said uncertainly, glancing at the corner Jason was hiding in. "What's that stuff?"

Barber ignored her, continuing to stalk around the room, flinging powder. Just a little closer, Jason thought, and I'll have you before you have me. Maybe.

Barber paused before one of the paintings, studying it,

rubbing his jaw thoughtfully. Uh-oh, Jason thought. It was the inn at Second Sister, silhouetted against the dying sun, perched on the rocks overlooking Lake Erie. Site of the ill-fated conference. Barber frowned, as if trying to remember where he'd seen it before. "Who's the painter?" he asked.

"Me. Be careful that glitter stuff doesn't get in the wet paint," Grace said. "Now sit up, Johnny, so I can give you your medicine."

John Robert obediently sat up, and Barber got a good look at his swollen eyes and red welts.

"What's wrong with him?" Barber demanded, taking three steps back.

"It's real catching," Grace said, pretending to daub John Robert with a rag.

Barber looked horrified. "Why? What's he got?"

"Chicken pox." Grace shrugged. "He was vaccinated and everything. I guess it itches like crazy. Mama says I'll probably get it, too."

As if on cue, J.R. sneezed wetly.

Barber retreated hastily to the steps, then took one last narrow-eyed look around the studio. "You sure you haven't seen anyone?"

"Mama won't let anyone in, since we're contagious," Grace said importantly. "I'm real surprised she let you in."

Ha, Jason thought. He'd be glad to visit the chicken pox or any other plague on Barber after what he'd done to him. Maybe Leesha'd catch it from him.

Barber couldn't leave fast enough. Jason heard him descending the steps, banging out through the barn door, then his car starting up. Jason waited until the sound of the engine had died away before he slumped back against the wall, trying to gather enough strength to make it back to his makeshift bed.

"That was lucky he didn't see you," Grace said, glaring at Jason. "Why didn't you hide?"

"Well, I . . ."

"Who are you talking to, Grace?" John Robert erupted out of the quilt. "Where did that man go?"

Jason looked from Grace to John Robert, back to Grace. He disabled the unnoticeable charm. John Robert flinched back, but Grace didn't react.

Ah, Jason thought. Elicitors may be rare, but they come in bunches.

❦ CHAPTER SIXTEEN ❧
ARRIVALS AND DEPARTURES

After the trauma of lunchtime, Jason slept most of the afternoon. He half awoke twice to the sound of car engines—Madison's mother leaving for work, and Madison arriving back home. He woke up a third time when she switched on the light.

"Hey," she said softly, sitting on the edge of the mattress. "How're you doing?"

"I've been better," he said. He managed to sit up. One of the yellow dogs was sprawled across his feet. His chest wound had been seeping and his T-shirt was stuck to it. He pulled it away from his body, gritting his teeth at the pain. "You?"

"I'm good," she said, fussing with the bedclothes, smoothing them down. She wore faded blue jeans and an embroidered white cotton shirt and multiple necklaces looped around her neck. Her hair was pulled back into a loose braid, exposing long, dangly earrings.

"So, Barber was here." She had this way of getting right to the point.

He nodded. "Grace saved the day. She was amazing. She's not afraid of anything."

Madison nodded. "She's fearless, all right. It's scary sometimes."

"You never said she was an elicitor, too."

Madison froze in mid-fuss, her eyes fixed on the quilt. "What are you talking about? She is not."

"Madison. Hello. It's me."

"She's *not*," she repeated, louder.

"Have you told her?" When Madison said nothing, he shrugged. "Guess not. She doesn't seem to know anything about magic."

She finally looked up at him, her eyes darkening to a deep-water blue. "She's not in this."

"Yet."

"Never." Madison was like a person who presses her thumb over the hole in the dike while the water gushes through all around her. "You can't tell anyone."

"Maddie, it was just dumb luck that Barber didn't figure it out when he was here."

"That's why I have to stay out of this thing. To protect her."

Then, all of a sudden, she was crying. Tears streaked down her face and Jason cast about for something, anything to say. "Um, hey, listen, Madison, I . . ."

"It's been hell around here, you know that?" Her voice rose and the dog stirred and opened his eyes. "Last year, somebody was setting fires all over the county, and everybody blamed it on us, saying we're witches. Kids were teasing Grace at school. Her best friend's mother told her to stay away from her. It got vicious. When I left, that finally died down."

She sniffled a little and dabbed at her eyes. "I was happy in Trinity. Then Second Sister happened. I can't get involved with this. If they find out about Grace . . . My family—they're all I've got."

"And now I've brought Barber down here," Jason said, thinking of Leesha. "I'm really sorry."

"Do you think he'll be back?"

Jason shrugged. "He's probably just checking everywhere close. I doubt he'll be back, unless he finds out you live here. That would be too much of a clue."

"It still says Booker on the mailbox," Madison said. "Everybody knows who lives here, though." She paused. "So. What does Barber want? What are *you* doing here?"

I came to find out if you're working for the Roses, Jason thought of saying. Or, I came to spy on you. Or, I came to drag you back to Trinity, willing or not. Not that he was in any condition now to do that.

So of course he said none of those things. "Barber's looking for the Dragonheart. I guess he thinks I have it."

"But you don't." She slid a sideways glance at him, trying to act casual. "Is it . . . is it still in the church?"

"Yeah," he said. She still wants it, he thought.

"Any luck using it? Figuring it out?"

He shook his head. He thought of saying, No, the thing bites me every time I try and lay a hand on it. But he didn't say that, either. He still had hopes. "We've got the rest of the stuff pretty much sorted."

They both fell silent, checking each other out like candidates for the same job.

"So," he said finally. "You met with your art teacher?"

She nodded distractedly. "My teacher from Trinity College. I met her in Columbus so she could look over what I'd done so far. She was there for an opening."

"So what'd she say?"

She stared at him a moment, then reached forward and grabbed the front of his T-shirt and pulled his face perilously close to hers. "Jason Haley! You did not drive all the way down here to ask about my homework!" And she gave him a little shake.

"Easy! I'm an invalid, you know," he said, and she let go of him. "I came because someone broke into your room at the Legends and tore it all up." He watched carefully for her reaction, and got basic bewilderment.

"Why would anyone do that? There's nothing there to steal."

"It was a wizard," Jason went on. "Seph thought it might have been the Roses."

"The Roses! Why would they break into *my* room?"

"They might be trying to find you," Jason suggested. "You sure there wasn't anything there worth stealing?" And then, on impulse, asked, "Did you leave any of your paintings behind?"

Madison turned a kind of skim-milk color, revealing freckles Jason hadn't even known were there. "*Paintings?* Well, I didn't . . . I mean, I . . ."

Jason stared at her. "It's not a hard question."

"No, but . . ." She swallowed hard. "I don't think I left . . . anything. Why do you ask?"

"Well, Seph took a look around, but he couldn't tell if anything was missing."

Now Madison looked positively panic-stricken. "Seph was in my *room*?"

"Well, yeah, he and Nick . . ."

"Seph *and* Nick? What were they doing? How did they get *in* there?" Madison leaned forward.

"Um. I guess Rachel asked Seph to come over. Actually, she thought maybe you two had a fight, and he trashed your room for revenge."

Madison laced her long fingers together. "Did they . . . did they mention seeing any paintings?"

Damn, Jason thought. I don't believe it. She's totally guilty. She *knows* that painting was bad news.

But if she meant for Seph to find it, why is she acting so freaky? Was she going to give the thing to somebody—some coconspirator? Did she have a plan for it and now it's messed up? If it's messed up, do I want her to *know* it's messed up?

"Jason?" Madison was staring at him, biting her lip, waiting for some kind of response.

Acting on instinct, he shook his head. "No, he didn't say anything about a painting. Why? Is one missing?"

"Um, no," Madison said. "Just wondered."

She was absolutely hopeless as a liar. There was something wrong with this whole picture of Madison as secret agent or assassin. Like maybe he'd put the puzzle together by forcing the pieces in a way they were not meant to go.

They avoided looking at each other.

Finally, Madison spoke. "So. You came all the way down here to tell me about . . . about a burglary?"

"Well, ah . . . pretty much." Jason cleared his throat. "Seph wants you to come back to Trinity. He'd . . . like to keep a better eye on you." Well. That was true enough.

"What?" She sat down on the floor next to the mattress, wrapping her arms around her knees. "Did anyone think of asking me about it?"

"He doesn't think it's safe for you to be down here on your own."

"I'm sorry, Jason, but I really don't think anyone's out to get me."

Well, no, not if they're coconspirators. Another puzzle piece jammed into place.

"I'm safer here than there, anyway," Madison went on. "If someone could break into my room with Rachel on guard, they could do anything else they wanted, too. If a stranger showed up in Coal Grove, he'd be noticed in a hot second. The only wizards I know of in the whole county are you, Warren Barber, and Brice Roper. And Barber followed *you* down here."

Jason blinked. Grace had mentioned that name. "Who's Brice Roper?"

"A jerk and a liar. He lives at the base of the mountain. He has horses." She seemed to think that was word enough on Brice Roper because she clamped her mouth shut, and Jason felt sort of sorry for Brice Roper, whoever he was.

Jason turned and dug in his backpack, pulled out a pack of cigarettes and a lighter. He looked up to find Madison glaring at him. "What?"

"You think I'm going to let you light up in a *barn*?"

"Oh. Sorry."

She snatched the cigarettes away from him. "Matter of fact, this entire mountain is smoke free where you're concerned."

"Huh?" But Madison had that mulish look on her face

again. "Look, I'll smoke in the yard. I'll smoke in the woods. I'll smoke in the fricking outhouse. Whatever you want." He extended his hand.

She stuck the cigarettes in her jeans pocket. "If you think I'm going to let you poison yourself after all the yick I went through to save your life, you are a crazy man." She made a face and wiped her hands on her shirt.

"Fine," he said. "I'll smoke twice as much after I leave." He paused. "So. Are you coming back with me?"

Madison stood and began to pace, flinging her hands out as she talked. "I can't just pack up and leave. Judge Ragland released Grace and J.R. on condition that I'm here to watch them. If I leave, the county will take custody again."

Jason sighed. He'd known this wouldn't be easy. And if Madison was conspiring with someone, it was a tough call whether it was better to bring her back into the sanctuary where they could watch her, or to keep her at a distance. The ban on attack magic didn't seem to work in her case. But he still didn't understand how she could put a hex in a painting, if she wasn't gifted.

If she was working for the Roses, though, wouldn't she be hot to come back to Trinity so she could get her hands on the Dragonheart?

Realizing she was waiting for a response, he said, "So what are you going to do?" It was no use to try and force Madison into anything. Wizardry would do no good on her, and in his present condition he couldn't very well carry her kicking and screaming to the car.

If he had a car.

"Look," Madison said, "If I don't get this portfolio done, I'll lose the whole semester. And the kids are depending on me. I can't go tearing back to Trinity because of a break-in. Seems like I'd be heading for trouble instead of away from it." Madison waited, twisting a lock of hair between her thumb and forefinger. When Jason didn't respond, she said, "How is Seph doing?"

"Cranky as hell. He misses you."

"I thought he'd be feeling better . . . with me out of the way."

Jason stared at her. He'd decided a long time ago that girls had this totally warped world view. This just confirmed it. "He's crazy about you, Madison. Why would he be feeling better?"

"I told him he should get out of Trinity. I warned him. I told him it was going to end up bad."

By now Jason's paranoia was in overdrive. Did she know it was going to end up bad because she had inside information?

"He won't leave, Maddie. They don't *have* anyone else."

She stared down at her hands. "I am coming back. When I get things settled here. In the meantime, I'll lay low."

Right. Like she could lose herself in the teeming crowds of Coal Grove, Jason thought.

"Seph won't be happy." The argument was wearing him out. The cold pain in his chest had returned. Was he ever going to be back to normal?

"When you get back, you tell Seph to stop worrying about me and take better care of himself," Madison said.

"I'm not going back to Trinity," Jason said, without thinking. Damn! He was an idiot, trying to play this complicated game with his head still swimming from the effects of the poison.

"Where are you going?"

"Back to England." He paused, then brandished the only weapon he had. The one he would never use. "So. No one needs to know about Grace. And no one needs to know I'm here." He met Madison's blue eyes straight on. He needed time to recover, and he didn't want them sending someone down to interrogate him in the meantime.

Her eyes narrowed and her mouth tightened into an angry line. "Fine! It's your funeral."

"Exactly," he said, smiling a little, trying to defuse the tension.

"What am I supposed to tell Seph? He's expecting to hear from you."

"If he asks, tell him I never showed."

Madison's eyes went wide with shock. "*If* he asks? Jason! He'll think you either ran off or something happened to you."

Jason beat back a wave of guilt, knowing Seph deserved to know about Barber, at least. But Jason would be staying a while, in case Barber came back.

Right. Last time, a ten-year-old saved your butt.

"Trinity would be safer for you, you know," Madison said, as if reading his mind.

"Safer for me, but not for you?" He paused, and when she couldn't come up with an answer, added, "Anyway, I'm not looking for a hideout."

She stood. "Still. You better lay low. In case Barber's looking for you."

"He'd better worry about me looking for him!" he called after her.

When the door closed behind her, he settled gratefully

back against the pillows. He wasn't afraid of Warren Barber. He just needed to rest a bit and get back in shape.

If Madison were involved in some kind of conspiracy, he couldn't very well leave Seph at her mercy. But Seph would never believe anything bad about Madison without evidence. Since he had to hang around Coal Grove for a while, maybe he could find out for sure whose side Madison Moss was on, and who she was hanging with, and who this Brice Roper was.

Perhaps if he just closed his eyes . . .

Madison threaded the pickup between the twin brick pillars that marked the entrance to Bry-Son Farms. Pristine white fencing marched away in both directions, marking the boundary of the Roper property. She navigated the long drive, past the Greek Revival mansion and around back to the horse barn.

A body would never know this whole thing was built on the backs of coal miners.

The horse barn was freshly painted red. Four dapple-gray Arabians with velvety black noses poked their heads over the paddock gate. In the pasture beyond, crocus and snowdrops poked up between patches of snow.

This is a farm out of a romance novel, she thought. I'll bet the horses don't even crap in their stalls.

As she turned toward the house, she saw three riders emerge from the woods at the far end of the pasture. Grace rode a high-stepping, fine-boned bay mare. Brice came along behind on a big-boned black gelding and John Robert on a small dapple gray. When Grace saw Madison, she applied her heels to the horse's sides and came flying across the pasture, her hair streaming out like a banner, reining to a hard stop just in front of Madison.

"Grace!" Madison said, waving away the dust that boiled up around the horse's feet. "Don't be a show-off."

Grace's cheeks were flushed with excitement. "Maddie! This is Abby. Well, that's her barn name, anyway. Her registered name is Barbary's Abby Ann. She's so sweet. Brice says he's never seen her take to anyone the way she . . ."

"Where have you been?"

Grace blinked at her. "Why, we rode up to the old furnace."

"That's on our property. You had no business taking *him* up on the mountain." She tilted her head toward Brice.

Brice reined in next to Grace. He'd been setting his pace to John Robert's. "It's my fault. I asked her to show me the waterfall."

"Like you haven't snuck up there on your own before now."

"Why do you always have to be so mean?" Grace stage whispered to Madison.

Brice just rolled his eyes and swung gracefully down to the ground.

Grace dismounted, too, then stood uncertainly, clutching the reins.

"You can go on up to the house," Brice said. "Mike'll look after the horses."

Grace didn't move. "Mr. Ragland always said you should take care of your own horse."

"I won't tell anybody." Brice lifted John Robert out of his saddle and set him on the ground.

"I could've got down myself!" John Robert protested.

Brice patted him on the shoulder. "You and Grace go ask Sylvia for some lemonade and cake. Madison and I will be up in a little while."

"No," Madison said quickly. "We can't stay. I have a lot to do, and I've *wasted* most of the day already."

"Oh, come *on*," Brice said impatiently, gripping her arm. "Don't rush off. Sylvia made a seven-layer chocolate cake. It'll break her heart if there's only me to eat it. Besides, I want to show you something."

"Let go of me!" Madison ripped her arm free. "When are you going to learn to keep your hands to yourself?"

Brice shook his head in disbelief. "What's *with* you, any-way?" he demanded, as if she were being totally unreasonable. Meanwhile, Grace and J.R. stood there awk-wardly.

"Chocolate cake, Maddie?" J.R. said wistfully.

"This won't take long," Brice said. "I promise, okay?"

"Fine," Madison said. "Let's get this over with." Why couldn't she make Brice Roper sick, instead of Seph? It was only fair. After all, Brice made *her* sick.

Brice led her along the fence line on the far side of the pasture. Someone had laid a cobblestone path and planted lemon thyme between the stones. The path angled into the woods, into the chill of the shade. They followed a small stream, some minor tributary of Booker Creek.

They finally broke out of the woods and into a small clearing overlooking the river below. It was centered by a small cedar-and-stone cottage. Though it appeared to be fairly new, it had an abandoned look. The surrounding meadow was thigh-high in winter-charred thistle, black-berry, and tree seedlings.

The view was breathtaking. Far below, the river wound between steep banks. The hills rolled away to the south and east, smoky blue and green and gray where the snow had worn away.

"What *is* this?" Madison whispered, knowing there must be a story.

"This was my mother's studio." Brice led her around the building. The whole front was glass, embracing the crinkled land beyond.

Brice opened the front door with a key. The front room was a soaring space, with thick beams bracing the roof far above, skylights between. There was a kitchen and dining area at the rear of the house and a spiral staircase to what must be sleeping quarters above.

Like the meadow, it had a neglected look. The furniture was covered with canvas drop cloths, and dust glittered in the sunlight that poured through the skylights.

"You know my mother's an artist, too," Brice said. "After my parents divorced, she moved to New York City."

Naturally, he assumed Madison knew the story about the nasty divorce, the new young wife. Which naturally, she did. The Ropers were the royalty of Coalton County.

"My stepmother doesn't come up here." He was cool, matter-of-fact, with no element of judgment in his voice or expression.

Unlike Madison. She'd spent her whole life judging people against her personal set of standards. She was great at holding grudges. She should get a prize.

She stood at the window, looking down over the valley. "Very pretty," she admitted. "But why'd you bring me here?"

"I thought maybe you'd want to use it."

She swung around. "For what?"

"For painting. Grace says you've been painting like a fiend."

"Why would I want to come here? I can paint at home." Why was Grace telling Brice Roper *anything*?

He shrugged. "It's a great space, and it's going to waste."

"Just because you've got something doesn't mean I want it."

He stepped closer and stood, looking down at her. She tried to step back but came up against the window. "We could deed it over to you."

"I have a house. What do I need with two?"

"You don't *need* a rundown ruin on top of Booker Mountain," Brice said. "Mr. McCartney says you'll own the mountain in a few months. You know my father wants to buy it. He'll give you a good price for it. A great price, in fact. You'll be rich."

"Wow. Sounds like a dream come true," Madison said.

Encouraged, Brice pressed on. "So you can stay. Or you can get out of this dump of a town entirely. You can go to art school. Wherever you want. And after you graduate, we could help set you up. My mother knows people. She has gallery connections in New York and Chicago."

"So. How would you get the coal out of Booker Mountain?"

He blinked up at her, surprised at the change of subject. "Carlene let my father drill some test holes. The seams are close to the surface, so he'd probably take the top of the mountain off."

Mountain topping, they called it. "And drop it into Booker Creek?"

He nodded. "Most likely. Then they'd follow up with some augur mining to get at the lower seams. They really won't know until they get in there."

"You sound like an expert."

"Yeah, right," he said, with surprising bitterness.

"And your dad and Carlene worked this all out together?"

"Well, I guess they talked about it." A hint of uncertainty crept in. "Just preliminary, you know."

"And then they handed you the job of talking me into it?"

Brice cleared his throat. "Well, it seemed like a win-win for everybody."

"A win-win." Madison stuck her hands into her jeans pockets and rocked back on her heels. "Answer me this," she said. "Did Carlene know you were going to set the shed on fire?"

She'd surprised him. He'd underestimated her. And so, for a moment, the truth showed plain on his face.

"I don't believe this," she whispered, shaking her head as if she could somehow say no to betrayal.

Brice recovered, regained his smile. "I don't know what you're talking about."

"Your daddy wanted to buy Booker Mountain, and Carlene wanted to sell. Only problem was, she didn't own it. So they figured that if it looked like the kids were in danger, the county would take custody. And if the county took custody, then I'd have to come home. And if I came home, then you could work on me and persuade me to sell. I bet you can be very persuasive. I bet no one ever says no."

"Maddie."

"So Daddy offered Carlene some kind of cut. And you set fire to the shed and hung out until Grace and John Robert tried to put it out and then took them down to town. Now tell me. What would you have done if one of the kids had been hurt?"

"Maddie, listen . . ."

"Don't you call me Maddie. My friends call me Maddie. Your problem is, you think everyone else is an idiot. Don't you think I had plans for this summer? You sit down here with your fake farm and your 'Sylvia will be heartbroken' when Sylvia probably wouldn't care if you took her seven-layer cake and nailed it to the barn door."

Brice looked like he'd just taken a severe blow to the head. "What? What's Sylvia got to . . ."

"Because Sylvia has a life, aside from being your house-keeper. And I have a life that doesn't involve sucking up to you. So if you think you're ever going to get your hands on Booker Mountain, you better think again."

That got his attention.

"You're *nobody*." He looked at her as if she was something he'd scraped off his shoe. "Fifth generation inbred trash. But when I ask you out, you have the nerve to say no. Like *you're* too good for *me*, when you've been with every other guy at the high school." He snorted.

Correction: she'd been *asked out* by practically every other guy at the high school. And said no. But that didn't stop them from talking.

"The only reason you still have that mountain is because nobody ever wanted it before," he went on. "Carlene's total-ly pathetic, but at least she understands the way things work."

"You leave my mother out of this," Madison said, which was pretty stupid when you thought about it. "I'd rather be who I am than who you are, ripping the tops off of mountains, poisoning streams, crapping all over the land and never cleaning up your own mess, bowing and scraping to your daddy, who'd run over a kitten on his way to the bank."

"You'd better watch your mouth. I'm warning you." Brice swelled up with power like a kind of magical toad disguised as a male model.

Her mouth *had* gotten away from her again. Not that Brice didn't deserve it, but the last thing she wanted was to have him try wizardry on her and raise more questions. She stared out the window, fighting for control.

"Are we done here?" She turned toward the door. "We'd better get back to the house."

Brice was on her in three quick strides. He grabbed hold of her upper arms, stinging fingers biting into her flesh. "We're *not* done here. We're going to settle this."

He clumsily slammed power into her. It was meant to cause pain—meant to be a quick, convincing jab, but it was a far cry from the elegant delivery she was used to. Then his smile slid away, his eyes widened, and he reared back, struggling to free himself. Finally, drained dry, he crumpled to the floor and lay, face up, arms flung out in front of him like he was trying to grab onto something he couldn't reach.

Madison leaned over him. "There's something else you don't know about me. I'm not afraid of wizards." She turned and walked out of the studio, leaving him lying on the floor.

So much for hiding out, she thought as she made her way back down the path. So much for laying low. It would be nice if, for once, you could think something and not say it out loud. Who else did Brice know and who might he be talk-ing to?

When she arrived at the house, Grace and John Robert were sitting at the dining room table, stuffing down big slabs of chocolate layer cake and tall glasses of lemonade garnished with mint sprigs, lemon slices, and with lemon sugar on the rims. Like poor folk invited up to the big house.

John Robert's face was smeared with frosting and enthu-siasm. "Try this cake, Maddie. It's awesome!"

"I'm sure it is." Madison avoided looking at Sylvia, who was hovering nearby. "But, you know, I can't eat chocolate cake and lemonade together. Makes the lemonade taste sour and the cake too sweet. Finish up now, J.R. We have to go."

"Where's Mr. Roper?" Grace asked.

"He's up at his mother's old studio," Madison said. "He decided to stay a while."

"Mr. Roper says I can come back and ride Abby when-ever I want," Grace announced, daintily blotting her lips with her napkin.

"I think Mr. Roper's changed his mind," Madison said.

Grace dropped her fork onto her plate with a clatter, thunderclouds gathering on her face. "Why, what did you say to him?"

Madison hesitated, then decided to go with the truth. "Mr. Roper's daddy wants Booker Mountain. I said no. He's kind of mad about it."

"Where would we live if he took the mountain?" J.R. asked around his last bite of cake.

"That's one of the problems," Madison said. "That's why I said no."

"We could move someplace else," Grace suggested.

"I don't think that's going to happen," Madison said.

On the way up the mountain, Grace commented that Brice Roper was kind of a jerk, but he had nice horses. Madison told her that there was no such thing as a free ride.

❧ CHAPTER SEVENTEEN ❧
STRONG-ARM TACTICS

Leesha felt like the outside man in a crime-scene stakeout. She'd sat in her car in the far corner of St. Catherine's parking lot all morning, watching the custodians patch a hole in the asphalt. The new blacktop steamed and reeked in the noon sun. There was little traffic in and out of the church at midday on a Monday.

She'd been in the church a half-dozen times herself. Had spoken to the frumpy woman in the church office, to the priest, and the nerdy altar boy after Mass. Had enticed them to the garden, where at least she could use Persuasion. They'd shared all their pathetic secrets, but it was clear they knew nothing about magical artifacts. She'd searched the sanctuary, but turned up nothing. If the Dragonheart was there, it was hidden securely behind magical wards.

Churches were like saunas. They made you sweat and flooded all your magical pores. It was a relief to be outside.

Leesha's new plan was admittedly sketchy. She'd wait

until one of the Weir showed up, then follow them into the church and see where that led her. If the church surveillance turned up nothing, she'd have to contemplate more direct action to find the location of the Dragonheart.

Maybe she was wasting her time. Jason could have taken the Dragonheart with him when he left. Maybe Jason was dead, and Barber already had what he wanted.

Jason.

She'd had no choice, she told herself. Barber wasn't playing around. The beating he'd given her was just an introductory offer. D'Orsay had tried to kill Barber and failed. She couldn't run away because Barber would use the torc to kill her, if she left the sanctuary. As long as she wore the torc, Barber knew just where to find her. And only he could take it off.

No choice. She'd be dead by now if she hadn't given Jason up. She stared glumly out at a world that seemed gray and colorless without him in it. She wished Barber would contact her, just so she'd know.

A battered old Jeep pulled into the lot and a familiar figure vaulted out, not bothering with the door. It was that awful Ellen Stephenson, who'd hooked up with Jack after Leesha broke up with him. Who'd slimed her with hot fudge at Corcoran's that one time. Who'd turned out to be the Red Rose Warrior and conspired with Jack to destroy the Covenant at Raven's Ghyll.

Definitely a person of interest.

But Ellen didn't go into the church. Instead, she cut across the parking lot and headed into the woods between the churchyard and the lake. Strange.

Leesha slid out of the car and crossed the lot, trailing after Ellen.

Ellen followed a wood-chip path that snaked north, toward the lakeshore. The warrior walked fast, and what with her long legs, Leesha had to move at a trot to keep up. The path was narrow, and briars caught at her clothing and tore at her hair while Ellen put more and more distance between them. Leesha crashed along behind, giving up on trying to move silently through the forest. If she'd planned on hiking, she'd have worn flats. As it was, she'd probably catch poison ivy.

Eventually the path emerged into a small clearing, studded with stickers and small bushes. No sign of Ellen. Leesha pivoted to scan the meadow, then froze as something cold touched the back of her neck.

"You looking for me?"

Leesha turned to see Ellen on the other end of a very long sword that pressed into the base of Leesha's collarbone.

"Hey!" she said, taking a step back. "Careful. Do you know how hard it is to get blood out of silk?"

"Won't be a problem if you're dead," Ellen replied, then looked up, over Leesha's head, and smiled. Not reassuring. Leesha carefully turned, and there was Jack, packing his own big sword and wearing a nasty expression.

"Oh!" Leesha said. "Well. Excuse me. I didn't mean to intrude on your woodland rendezvous."

"You're not intruding," Jack said. "In fact, you're the guest of honor."

Leesha felt the first pricklings of panic, but tried to keep it off her face.

"I was thinking of hunting renegade wizards." Ellen shrugged. "You up for it, Jack?"

"I'm game." Leesha couldn't help noticing that he had a surprisingly wicked smile. And he used to be so nice.

"We want to know what happened to Jason," Ellen said. "And what part you played in it."

"I have no idea what you're talking about. I haven't seen Jason for days."

"Jason's disappeared," Jack said.

"Well, that's a shame. But why ask me about it?"

Jack glared at her. "You two have been hanging out."

"Have not."

Ellen's blade pressed into her throat again.

"OK, fine. I hang out with a lot of people." She conjured up her most patronizing expression. "I mean, it's nice of you warriors to be worried about Jason and all, but I think he can take care of himself."

"Jason's our friend," Ellen said. "And we're wondering who you're working for."

"What makes you think I'm working for someone?"

"You're a trader. Traders are always in it for the cash." Ellen looked down her long nose at Leesha. "Still, it's hard to believe anyone our age would be such a *mercenary*."

That's what she was. A mercenary. She'd sold Jason out. No matter how many times she told herself she'd had no choice. Still. It wouldn't do Jason any good if she got kicked out of the sanctuary, and Barber ended her pathetic life.

Leesha drew herself up to her full height, which, to be honest, wasn't that impressive. The warriors still towered over her. "I don't answer to you. Now, why don't you run along and hone your weapons or rattle your swords or whatever warriors do in their spare time."

"Whoa," Ellen said. "Good thing we're here in the sanctuary, where attack magic doesn't work. Otherwise, I'd be wetting myself." Sliding her giant sword into its case, she reached for Leesha.

From force of habit, Leesha spoke her immobilization charm, knowing as she did so it was useless. And it was. *Crap*.

Ellen gripped her wrists, bending her arms painfully behind her back. Jack lifted the tip of his sword so it rested at the base of her throat.

Jack smiled. "One thing you can say for magical swords. Even in the absence of magic, they retain a certain *functionality*."

Which couldn't be argued with, really.

"So what's up, Leesha?" Jack said. "Why are you still here?"

"You wouldn't hurt me," Leesha said. Which ordinarily would be true. Jack was so the heroic type. Unless he was angry. Angry warriors could lose control. Who knew Jack and Jason were so tight?

Then there was Ellen, who was twisting her arms, practically yanking them out of their sockets. Ellen wouldn't hesitate to hurt her. She still held a grudge about Leesha and Jack.

No attack magic. It was unfair.

She couldn't help Jason. Wherever he was, he was beyond reach. And if Jack and Ellen knew she'd played a role in his betrayal . . . But she could give up Warren Barber. She hated Warren Barber's guts. And all his other parts.

Besides, traders were not known for giving their lives for their employers.

"Okay," she said. "Ease up. What would you like to know?"

In answer, Ellen pushed Leesha down to her knees in the

tall weeds, still keeping hold of her wrists. "Tell us about Jason," she said.

"I'm not sure what happened to him, but I can tell you that Warren Barber was involved." That was perfectly true.

"Warren Barber?" Jack looked totally blindsided. "I thought he was dead or something."

Leesha shook her head. "Nope. Unfortunately."

"Why would he go after Jason?" Ellen asked from behind.

Leesha knew she should choose her words carefully, but it was hard to think. "Barber knew that Jason stole some things from Raven's Ghyll. He wanted to get them back."

"How did he . . . What gave him that idea?" Ellen demanded, releasing Leesha and circling around in front.

Because Leesha had told him, of course. "D'Orsay must've told him," Leesha said, rubbing her arms and rotating her shoulders.

Jack squatted in front of Leesha. "Why does D'Orsay think it was Jason that snuck into the ghyll?"

"I guess Jason ran into D'Orsay's son on his way out," Leesha said.

Jack and Ellen looked at each other, then back at Leesha. "What was it that Jason supposedly stole?" Ellen asked.

"Magical stuff."

"So Barber's working for D'Orsay?"

"He's working for himself." She took a breath. "He has the Covenant, you know. The one that makes D'Orsay king for life."

"What?" Jack swore under his breath. "*Barber* has it?"

Ellen sat back on her heels. "How'd he get it?"

"He took it from Second Sister in all the confusion."

Jack squinted at her suspiciously. "What good does it

do him? Does he really want to answer to Claude D'Orsay?"

"I think he sees himself as more of an equal partner."

"So why haven't they consecrated the agreement, then?" Ellen asked.

Leesha shrugged. "I don't know. But Barber wanted to find Jason."

"How do you know all this?" Jack asked.

"He wanted me to help, but I refused, of course."

"Right." Ellen swept her hair off her forehead.

"He might've found out Jason was leaving the sanctuary and intercepted him. So if Jason was carrying the stuff, Barber has it. If not, he probably knows where it is by now. He can be very persuasive." Leesha resisted the temptation to touch her collar.

"Any idea where Barber is?" Ellen asked.

"Nope." Leesha stood, brushing at her clothes. "Don't say thanks or anything."

Jack seized her by one arm, and Ellen by the other. "Where are you staying, Leesha?" Ellen asked.

"You know where. With my Aunt Milli. At Shrewsbury Commons. Why?"

"Let's go get your stuff."

"Why? What do you mean?" Jack and Ellen said nothing, but began manhandling her back toward the parking lot. "Oh, no. I'm not leaving the sanctuary. I can't, not after what I've already told you. Barber will kill me."

"Just make sure you're far away from here when he does it," Jack suggested.

"Look, you can't kick me out of the sanctuary. It's open to everybody."

"We're changing the rules," Ellen said. "Too much riffraff

coming in and ruining the small-town ambience."

Leesha tried to dig her heels in, but the two warriors simply picked her up and carried her. It was humiliating. Leesha kicked and squirmed and swore. "I won't forget this. You'll be sorry." She tried releasing Persuasion into them, but they dropped her to the ground, then picked her up again when she was done.

In no time they were back at the parking lot and maneuvering her toward the Jeep.

"Okay, *fine*!! You *win*!" Leesha said, in a voice that made heads turn across the street. She wrenched free of their grip and slumped against the side of the Jeep, breathing hard and scared to death. If she betrayed Barber, she'd be dead in a heartbeat. But she had no choice. Again.

"All *right*," she said. "You let me stay in the sanctuary and I promise I'll give you Barber."

✧ Chapter Eighteen ✧
Mind-Burner

Dystrophe turned his collar up against the raw breath of the lake, knowing he must be getting close. He had no need to consult the scrap of paper in his pocket—he'd memorized the address and the description of the house.

Stone Cottage, it was called. He'd been told that the boy was likely to be alone. His natural wariness had been aroused, however, by the fact that Longbranch was offering an astoundingly generous stipend for a supposedly easy target.

The job had its challenges, of course. It was said that attack magic was forbidden within the sanctuary. But then, murder was likely forbidden, also.

He fingered the blades in his sleeves, and smiled. A scratch from any one of them would suffice to cut the thread of life that was often so strong in the young.

He turned up Lake Street. It was paved in brick, its wrought-iron gas lamps casting pallid pools of light into the darkness. As an assassin, he was fond of dim historical districts.

The houses to the right were waterfront, and some of them had little signposts labeled Land's End and Sunset House, Sailor's Rest, Dry Dock, and Snug Harbor. Excruciatingly cute. Dystrophe disapproved.

That must be it, up ahead. An actual *stone cottage* set amid a rather unkempt garden, overlooking the lake. The porch light was on.

Dystrophe walked around the house, securing the perimeter with magical barriers to prevent escape. Then he turned up the walk, negotiating the uneven pavement. Perhaps the boy would actually let him in.

But there was no answer when he rapped on the door. Ah, well. No need to delay their meeting. It was a thick oak door, but a precisely targeted charm slammed it off its hinges.

Would the boy be asleep? He thought not. Boys of that age liked to stay up late, didn't they, playing video games and what not? He secured the doors behind him, then began to search the rooms downstairs. The boy was not in the kitchen, the parlor, the dining room, the pantry, or the study.

Just then he heard movement in the back of the house, and a banging noise, like someone trying to force open a window.

Ah, Dystrophe thought. He followed the sound.

At the back of the house was a solarium, probably a lovely room in daylight. The wall overlooking the lake was entirely of glass. Waves pounded against the rocks below. And there in the dark, silhouetted against the rising moon, was the boy.

He turned when Dystrophe entered the room and stood facing him. Dystrophe gathered light into his hands and tossed it down on the floor between them. It flared up, illu-minating the boy's angular features, shadowed eyes, and tangle of dark hair. He was dressed in a T-shirt and blue jeans, and still wore the big-boned, coltish look of adolescence.

It was him, Dystrophe was sure of it. "Joseph McCauley?" he inquired.

"Who are you?"

"Relax, Joseph," Dystrophe said soothingly. "I'm not here to hurt you." *I'm here to kill you.* It was an important distinction, but most people didn't seem to find it reassuring. Sometimes, at this point, they tried to run, but McCauley didn't, which Dystrophe appreciated. Chasing down prey was not his style.

"Who sent you? The Roses?" McCauley's voice rose a little. He was a boy, after all.

"Is it important?"

"To me it is."

"Then, yes. The White Rose. Dr. Longbranch."

The boy nodded, filing the information away as if he had a future. It was unusual for one so young to have so many enemies. But these were turbulent times.

Palming one of the knives, Dystrophe glided forward, considering possible targets: the pale column of the boy's throat, the arms that poked out of his short-sleeved T-shirt. "I assure you, you won't feel a thing. I'm very good at what I do."

"Don't do this," McCauley said, his hands still at his sides. "I'm warning you." Not begging. Warning. Ah, the arrogance of the young.

"Please. I'm not impressed by threats and theatrics. It's just business, you know. Nothing personal."

The boy adjusted his stance, preparing. The green eyes darkened to the color of deep water in shade. Flame coalesced about his spare figure and splattered onto the tile floor.

Dystrophe forced back a trickle of doubt, then came on. When only a few feet divided them, the assassin struck like a snake, seizing the boy's left wrist, meaning to drag the poisoned blade across McCauley's exposed forearm.

Dystrophe gasped and nearly let go when the heat from the boy's skin seared his fingers.

The boy grabbed his other wrist, his blade hand. Dystrophe was stronger, but McCauley made no attempt to shake free the knife or turn it toward his attacker. Instead, he poured in Persuasion, a hot river of magic that filled the tributaries of Dystrophe's mind, driving memory and will before it.

"How peculiar," Dystrophe thought, and then there was nothing else but the boy's voice, and he didn't think anything more.

Jack and Ellen found Seph in the garden, on a bench that overlooked the water. He sat rod-straight, his hands on his knees, gazing out toward the lake. He looked whipped and dangerous, like a frayed electrical wire, sending off sparks. Lately, they often found him in the garden, despite the cold, as if he used this setting to clear his mind for magical activity. Besides, he was probably hot enough to heat the whole lakeshore.

He turned his head and watched as they descended the path toward him. His face seemed unnaturally pale, and he looked like he'd slept in his clothes.

"Hey, cuz," Jack said, lifting his hand in a kind of salute. He had the sense that Seph was not at all surprised to see them. It was a little unsettling.

Something crunched under Jack's foot. "Hey," he said, scanning the ground. "There's broken glass everywhere."

"Yeah," Seph said. "Guess I need to clean that up."

Jack looked around. "Where'd it all—jeez, what happened?" He pointed to the solarium window at the top of the cliff. The glass had been smashed out as if by a massive fist, leaving the room open to the elements.

Seph glanced up at the ragged hole, then back at Jack. "Somebody jumped," he said, shivering a little, his eyes wide and haunted-looking.

"Who jumped? What are you talking about?" Ellen sat next to Seph and put her hand on his shoulder, then yanked it back, sucking on her fingers. "Ouch! You're really juiced, you know?"

"The Roses sent another assassin last night," Seph said. He rubbed his eyes with his thumb and forefinger. "He had knives. I told him to leave and he . . . went through the window. He's in the lake."

Jack dropped onto a stone bench, unsure what to say. "How many is that, now?"

Seph shrugged. "Three. No. Four."

"This has got to stop," Ellen muttered. "One of these days they're going to get lucky."

"Maybe you need a bodyguard," Jack said.

Seph's head came up. "And who's going to do that? We're spread thin enough as it is." The lake wind stirred the trees overhead and the light played across his face. There was something about his eyes . . .

"Have you heard from your mom?" Jack asked. "She and Hastings need to know about this."

"No," Seph said. "Haven't heard anything from her or

Hastings. Don't know how to reach them." He paused. "Nick knows what happened. He came over last night, after." His voice trailed off.

This is crazy, Jack thought. Some sanctuary. If you want to kill someone badly enough, you'll manage eventually.

"How'd it go with Leesha?" Seph asked abruptly, obviously wanting to change the subject.

"It was great," Ellen said, pulling off her gloves. "We were bad cop and bad cop."

"We put on a lot of pressure, and she caved. We think," Jack added. You could never tell with Leesha.

"Does she know where Jason is?"

"She says she doesn't. But it turns out everybody who's anybody knows Jason was at Raven's Ghyll. D'Orsay. Warren Barber. God knows who else. She says if Jason's missing, Warren Barber's behind it. Barber said he was going to get the stuff back from Jason."

"Warren Barber?" Seph squinted at Jack. "What's Barber got to do with any of this? I haven't seen him since Second Sister. And how does he know Jason was at Raven's Ghyll?"

"Jason was spotted. And Barber and D'Orsay are partners now," Jack said.

"*Partners?*" Seph shed his distracted look. "What are you talking about?"

"But wait," Ellen murmured. "There's more."

"Barber has the Covenant," Jack said. "Leesha thinks he took it from Second Sister."

Seph looked from Jack to Ellen. "If he's working with D'Orsay, and he has the Covenant, why haven't they consecrated it?"

Ellen shrugged. "Leesha doesn't know. But everybody's

trying to get back what Jason took out of the ghyll."

They looked at each other wordlessly. "Why do you suppose that is?" Jack said finally.

"Well, Jason said the Dragonheart was supposedly a weapon that could control the guilds or destroy them," Ellen pointed out. "That'd be a good reason."

"How do they know that?" Jack persisted. "Jason said he dropped the book in the ghyll, but . . ."

"So," Seph broke in. "Leesha *is* working for Barber?"

Ellen shrugged. "She was. But now she says Barber will kill her if she leaves the sanctuary."

"Leesha's been hanging around the church," Seph said. "Do you think she suspects where the stuff is?"

"If she does, you know she's been in and out of there already," Ellen said. "I hope your wards did the job."

Seph stared at her a moment, then stood and crossed the terrace, snatching up a metal goblet from a tray on the garden wall. Raising it to his lips, he drained it, then set it down. He closed his eyes and concentrated, body rigid, lips moving silently.

After a long pause, Seph opened his eyes. "There are fifteen wizards within the boundary, including Leesha. Barber's not here. The crypt at St. Catherine's is secure." His eyes glittered green and gold, his pupils pinpricks of light. "Except for a few things Jason took a week ago, before he left for Coalton County. That makes me think he was planning something."

Jack blinked at him. "You're on duty? You can tell all that from here?" Always before, Seph had been semifunctional when monitoring the magical barrier.

"I'm not just maintaining the boundary. I'm watching the whole sanctuary. Hastings taught me how to do it." And then, as if Jack had asked the unspoken question, Seph added, "I found a way to deal with it."

Ellen picked up the goblet and raised it to her nose, sniffing. Then glared across at Seph. "This," she said, waggling the cup, "is a bad idea."

"What is it?" Jack took the cup from Ellen and passed it beneath his nose. A prickly heat ran up his neck and exploded through the top of his head. It was like sticking a finger into an electrical outlet. Or chugging brandy.

"What is it?" he repeated, a little breathlessly.

Seph remained silent, so Ellen answered for him. "*Aelf-aeling.* Roughly translated from the Anglo-Saxon, it means, burning mind. The common name is wizard flame. Where did you get it?"

"Mercedes had some," Seph said, shoving back his sleeves as if overheated.

"She *gave* this to you?" Ellen asked, lifting an eyebrow.

"Not exactly. I used to help her out with her extractions, you know. I know where she keeps her stuff."

"You're not going to keep using it."

Seph twitched irritably, his hands opening and closing at his sides. "I don't use it all the time. Only when I'm on duty. It lets me watch a hundred things at once. I can see a leaf fall in the park and keep tabs on Leesha Middleton and track an assassin when he's stalking me. I'd be dead by now, otherwise. Plus I'll know if anyone messes with the stuff in the church."

"What's wrong with it?" Jack asked Ellen.

"The name is fairly literal," Ellen replied. "Mind-Burner. Wizards get addicted to it to the point that they can't function without it. Use it long enough, and you go insane."

"How do you know so much about it?" Jack asked.

"Paige and Wylie were into performance enhancers. They used to dope me a lot when I was in training." Simon Paige was warriormaster for the Red Rose, and Ellen's old trainer.

"It's just till the war is over," Seph said, leaning against the wall.

"When exactly will that be?" Ellen demanded. "It's been going on for centuries."

"Does Hastings know about this? Or Linda?" Jack asked.

"No. And they'd better not hear it from you. They're counting on me to handle this, and I will. Whatever it takes." Seph never raised his voice, but it was clear from the set of his shoulders that this issue was nonnegotiable.

Usually wizard power, when it was noticeable at all, was a subtle thing. Seph was so hot, the air around him shimmered and his arms trailed flame, like iridescent wings.

Ellen shook her head. "Doping will ruin your body, you know that? That's one of the reasons the Weirlind died off."

"Look. I'm not an idiot. I won't use it unless it's absolutely necessary," Seph said. "It's just that . . . I haven't been entirely . . . myself . . . ever since that thing with the painting."

"Painting? What are you talking about?" Jack asked.

Seph looked like he wished he hadn't opened his mouth. "I ran into a hex. In a painting. That's all."

As if he thought that would shut off the questions.

"What painting? Where?" Jack asked.

"What kind of hex?" Ellen wanted to know.

Seph sighed. "I thought Nick would've told you. It was in one of Madison's paintings. It kind of knocked me out. Made me really sick. But I'm getting better. I just need . . . a little help right now."

"How would a hex get into one of Madison's paintings?" Ellen sat down on the swing, kicking off with her feet. "I never heard of that."

"Who knows?" Seph said.

"How could a hex work here in the sanctuary?" Jack asked.

Seph shrugged. "Nick thinks it might be some kind of elicitor thing."

Ellen planted her feet, bringing the swing to an abrupt stop. "Hold on. He thinks *Madison* did it?"

"He's just throwing out possibilities. We don't know."

"Madison wouldn't hurt you," Ellen said with conviction.

I hope you're right, Jack thought. In wizard politics you always have to watch your back.

Seph rose and began pacing. "I still don't get it. Madison says Jason never showed. Something must've happened to him on the way down there. But we're the only ones who knew he was going."

"Well," Jack said reluctantly. "He has Linda's car. Is it possible he might have just . . . taken off?"

Seph swung around. "What?"

"It's no secret he's been wanting to go back to England, you know, and . . ."

"Jason wouldn't do that," Seph said dismissively.

Okaaay, Jack thought. If Madison had hexed Seph, was it possible *she* had something to do with Jason's disappearance?

Jack knew better than to voice that theory aloud.

"What about Maddie?" Ellen asked. "Is she coming back?"

Seph shook his head. "She says she can't. Not now, anyway."

Jack thought it best to change the subject. "So what do you think we should do? About the assassins, I mean?"

"Everybody seems to know about the Dragonheart," Seph said. "I can watch for magical activity, and do something if I see it, but anybody can walk into my house and try and kill me. Or walk into St. Catherine's and walk out with the Dragonheart. There's always the chance they'll get away with it."

"That'd be a trick," Jack said. "None of us can get near the stone without getting slammed. Plus isn't the crypt totally warded?"

"Too many things I didn't think *could* happen *are* happening," Seph said. "Like the hex."

"Not that it's done us any good so far," Jack pointed out. "The Dragonheart, I mean."

"And the sanctuary is open to everybody, technically speaking," Ellen said.

"That's going to have to change."

They both turned to look at Seph.

"We need to change the way we handle security in the sanctuary."

"How do you mean?" Jack asked.

Seph released a long breath. "Wizards are collecting like vultures. The White Rose, the Red Rose, the unaffiliated. The Dragonheart must be drawing them here. It's like something woke it up—and now it's sending out a beacon. Wizards are constantly in and out of town, like they're looking for something. I'm using mind magic to keep them away from the church. Like when Leesha was poking around in there today.

"It's delicate, though. If I'm too heavy-handed, it'll draw their notice. If I lose focus, they'll be into the church in no time. Meanwhile, I always have to watch my back. Nobody wants to close the perimeter, but I don't think we have a choice." He ran his tongue over his cracked lips. "I just . . . I just can't do this much longer, and there are other things that need attention. As long as there was hope that no one knew about the loot from Raven's Ghyll, fortifying the boundary would've only tipped them off. I think we're past that."

"But how can we do that?" Jack asked. "It's a *town*. Not a fortress. I mean, people commute to Cleveland and everything."

"We still let the Anaweir come and go. It's risky, but we can't help that. We build a Weirwall that will keep the gifted out. We'll get the sorcerers involved. Mercedes can be in charge, she's good with materials. We establish a gate, with gatekeepers." He looked up at Jack and Ellen. "That would probably be the warriors, living and dead."

"Isn't Mercedes tied up with the artifacts at the church?" Ellen asked.

"We've catalogued everything we've been able to classify. There are still a few mysteries, but we've kind of run into a dead end."

Jack eyed Seph. "I still don't see how that would work."

"I'm responsible for security within the sanctuary," Seph snapped. "And I'm going to do whatever I have to."

Jack spoke into a dead silence. "*You're* in charge of security? Says who?"

"Hastings. He handed the responsibility to me, and I'm going to do my best to see it through."

"Why you?" Jack raised his hands in preemptive

surrender. "Not that I'm disputing his choice, or anything."

"He's been working with me all summer," Seph said. "Well, when he's been here. Him and Nick. Teaching me how to monitor magical activity within the sanctuary. And now that Linda's gone . . . "

"No offense, but why not Nick?" Jack asked.

"He and Hastings talked about it and decided it should be me. Nick's got other things to worry about, I guess. He's acting chair of the sanctuary board since my mother left, and he's still working on the things in the church." Seph glanced up at Jack and down at his hands. "I . . . I don't really want it," he whispered. "I . . . feel like it's an impossible job, but if I mess up . . ." He shuddered.

Jack shifted in his chair, remembering how Aunt Linda had handed him the knowledge of his warrior destiny, then left him to sort it out on his own. "What does Nick say?"

"We talked about the wall, if that's what you mean, and he's on board with that. Especially after last night." He hesitated. "You know, Nick doesn't look so good. I'm wondering if his age is catching up with him. Or if his staff breaking had some kind of effect on him."

"Nick's okay," Jack said, too quickly. "He's just working too hard, lately."

"It'll be way easier once we get the wall up. I won't have to do so much scanning. And we can boot out and keep out violators." Seph flexed his hands. "I just wish we had more wizards to help. We could really use Jason back again. If . . ." Seph's voice trailed off, as if he didn't want to make their worries come true by speaking them aloud.

No wonder Seph's so stressed, Jack thought. "I know Madison's been writing to you and all. But maybe we should send somebody else to Coalton County. You know, to see what's going on," he said. "Except it's kind of like one of those horror movies, where they keep sending people to check on the missing guy, and they keep disappearing."

"Can't we wait on the wall until Hastings comes back?" Ellen suggested. "By then we'll be out of school."

Why are we talking about high school? Jack wondered. At this point, it's pretty far down on the list.

"We can't wait any longer," Seph said. "Like I said. There are fifteen wizards in Trinity at the moment. Any of them could be spies or assassins. And only three are on our side."

✺ CHAPTER NINETEEN ✺
BOUNDARIES

The doors and windows of Trinity College's McAlister Chapel shimmered with magical wards designed to exclude the uninvited. The portraits of James and Mallory McAlister frowned down from the walls, as if disapproving of the proceedings.

There were probably three hundred people spread among the pews—disappointingly few, Seph thought. And they were mostly Anawizard Weir: sorcerers, seers, enchanters, and warriors. The elected board sat down front— the wizard Iris Bolingame, the seer Blaise Highbourne, and the sorcerer Mercedes Foster, of course. Plus the enchanter Akana Moon, who'd been with them at Second Sister. After her experience there, Seph was impressed that she was willing to sit as representative again.

Nick had insisted on bringing Leesha Middleton, who sat off to one side. A small group of unfamiliar wizards sat together at the back.

Conversations in a dozen languages reverberated around the room. Shimmering ghost warriors in period dress slouched up the side aisles and peered down from the balconies.

Well, we have the votes at this point, Seph thought. What we need are sorcerers to sign onto this project. He glanced down at the notes on the scrap of paper in his hand.

"Let's begin," Nick murmured, touching Seph on the shoulder. The old wizard shuffled to the podium and gripped it with both hands. "Guildfriends!"

Conversations died away.

"Thank you for coming," Nick continued. "Most of you know me. I am Nicodemus Snowbeard, acting chair of the board of governors of the sanctuary in Linda Downey's absence. We've met as a board to discuss matters such as the development of emergency housing and language programs, to mediate disputes, and so on. But tonight we are here for a different purpose—to discuss a change in security procedures for the sanctuary."

He paused, scanning the room for questions, then continued. "Recently, we have seen an unusual influx of wizards into Trinity. They may be innocent tourists, they may be spies, or they may intend to make off with our arsenal of magical weapons. We don't know. But redirecting them requires constant vigilance."

"What magical weapons?" demanded a twitchy-looking wizard in the back. "Where are they? Why weren't we told?"

"Wizards? Innocent tourists? Bah!" a young French seer in the front row said. A rumble of assent followed. "We should expel them all before they knife us in the back."

Ellen stood. "I've got more reason to hate wizards than

most people," she said. "But we need wizards to fight wizards, and they've got a plan. I think you should listen to it." She glared at the crowd until the grumbling subsided, then sat down quickly.

"All right," Nick said, taking advantage of the lull. "Seph McCauley has agreed to coordinate security matters for the sanctuary. He'll answer any questions you have."

Seph mounted the steps to the stage and sat down in a folding chair onstage. Conversations rose on all sides, beating against his flame-sensitized ears.

"He's just a boy," said one of the wizards in the back, looking down his long nose at Seph. "Why is he handling security? Are things that desperate?"

"He's Hastings's son," the twitchy wizard muttered. "He's bound to be juiced."

"Juice is one thing." The first wizard snorted. "Experience and common sense quite another."

A third wizard, a youngish woman with Asian features, shushed the other two. "Didn't you hear what he did at Second Sister?" she hissed. "Dueled twelve wizards at once and killed them all."

"Like I said, Felicia, no common sense," the first wizard said.

"He's a wizard," Seph heard one sorcerer say to another. "And he's going to be protecting the Anaweir?"

Great, Seph thought. Everybody already has an opinion. He looked out over the crowd, making eye contact with several people he knew. Mercedes winked at him, and he relaxed a fraction.

"So," Seph said. "As most of you know, some of us have been—um—standing guard since then, to make sure the rules written at Raven's Ghyll hold here in the sanctuary. But it's been harder, lately, because of all the intrusions."

"They aren't intrusions," the long-nosed wizard said. "The sanctuary is open to all."

"We have to change that," Seph said from his chair on the stage. "Lately wizards have been swarming in. If we leave the sanctuary open, there's a chance the balance of power will be tipped in favor of the Roses. With things as unstable as they are, we could be overwhelmed before we can mount a defense."

"What do *you* have in mind?" the Asian wizard asked.

Seph straightened and met the wizard's eyes. "We're going to put up a Weirwall."

There was an instant uproar. He'd expected it. Weirwalls were controversial. They were first used during the Wars of the Roses, to ensnare wizards. They were mostly the work of sorcerers, but some wizards (like Barber) had the skill as well. Many wizards considered them foul play.

"What kind of Weirwall?" one of the sorcerers finally asked, shouting above the hubbub. "And who's going to design and build it?"

"Great question," Seph said, relieved it was a question he could give to someone else. "Mercedes?"

Mercedes Foster strode up to the podium and glared out at the Weir. "Give the boy a chance!" she shouted. "He didn't ask for this job. He deserves your thanks, not your criticism. He's trying to save your sorry butts."

The noise diminished somewhat.

"Where's Hastings?" Long Nose demanded. "And Linda Downey? Seems like they created this mess, they should be here to handle it."

"Looking back to the good old days, are you,

Randolph?" Mercedes said acidly. "When wizards ruled the guilds?"

"It was certainly . . . a lot more efficient," Randolph retorted.

"If you don't like it here, leave." Mercedes turned away from him, waving a sheaf of papers in the air. "I've agreed to coordinate the building project, but I'd welcome input from anyone experienced with this sort of thing. I've made a map and some preliminary sketches. It's a traditional curtain wall that selects for Weir. Nobody'll get stuck in it, if that's what you're worried about. You can come and go through the gate. Anaweir can pass freely."

"So the Anaweir can pass, and not us?" Randolph said, vainly looking around for allies. "Who's going to staff the gate?"

Jack stood. "The Warrior Guild has agreed to stand watch at the gate," he said. "Unless you have a better idea?"

Randolph settled back, still fuming. He had nothing.

"Just so you know, Jack," Iris said. "Some of the merchants around the square have been complaining about ghost warriors bivouacking on the green. Well, actually, the Anaweir think it's some kind of reenactment group. They've been hanging out in campus bars, playing cards, flirting with patrons, and getting into fights."

"Well, they *are* soldiers," Jack said, shrugging. "I'll check into it. I guess I can move them off the green and up into one of the more remote parks."

"The building of the wall will require considerable magical labor," Mercedes said, firmly turning the topic back to the matter at hand. "The board has already voted to proceed. But we need volunteers to help. Sorcerers and wizards primarily."

"When are you planning to start this?" one of the sorcerers asked.

"Tomorrow morning," Mercedes replied. "I have a sign-up sheet here. Anyone willing to help should see me." She glanced at Nick, and he nodded. "That's it. The meeting's adjourned."

Wizards and sorcerers lined up to volunteer for wall-work. Seph was surprised to see Leesha among them. When she was finished, she walked over to where Jack, Seph, and Ellen were waiting for Nick. She looked almost cheerful.

"This is cool," she said. "I like the idea of a wall. We don't want just anybody coming in here."

"If you're talking about Barber, you promised you'd help us find him," Jack reminded her. "Otherwise *you* might be the one on the outside."

Leesha immediately looked less cheerful. "I know. Only, I'm still trying to figure out how to get him to come into the sanctuary."

"He's not going to come in here," Seph said. "Especially with the wall going up. Whatever we think about him, he's not stupid. We're going to have to go after him on the outside."

"Well," Leesha said, fussing with her hair. "Um . . . how about this? I could set up a meeting with him, and you could be waiting with a dozen wizards."

"We don't *have* a dozen wizards," Seph said. "If I went after Barber, Nick would have to stay here."

"Besides, I think we want you right there with us," Ellen said. "You know. Just in case there's a double cross or something."

Leesha clasped her hands together, looking a little

panicked. "But, I really . . . I'd really rather not leave the sanctuary," she said in a small voice.

"If you try and back out of this, you'll be leaving the sanctuary in a hurry," Jack said. "You said Barber knows something about Jason, and we want to know what he knows."

"*Okay*," Leesha snapped. "I *said* I'd do it. I'll figure something out."

❧ CHAPTER TWENTY ❧
THE TRADER

Warren stood in the second-floor window of the warehouse and scanned the empty street. He checked his watch for the fourth time. You'd think she'd learn.

Well, she'd pay, one way or another, for being late.

Leaning against the window frame, he lit another cigarette, careful where he flicked his ashes. The place was a firetrap, for sure. Many of the old buildings in Cleveland's Warehouse District had been rehabbed into studios, restaurants, and bars. Not this one. It was decrepit, still littered with trash, abandoned industrial equipment, and barrels of God knows what. He could hear rats scurrying around when he lay down at night, and he made sure he put out wards to keep them away.

There was no sanctuary for Warren Barber. He felt twitchy, uneasy. The stench of betrayal was all around him, stinging his nostrils and crawling over his skin. Assassins had come after him, twice now. Both times, he'd escaped, but his luck couldn't hold out forever. They were sent either by Claude D'Orsay or by the servant guilds in Trinity. Either way, Leesha had talked.

So Warren had left his apartment and moved into this place three nights ago. After he met with Leesha, he'd move again, though if Leesha came through as promised, maybe he wouldn't need to.

The day before, Leesha had called to say she'd finally found where they'd hidden the Dragonheart, along with the rest of the things stolen from the ghyll. She'd wanted him to meet her in the sanctuary, but he wasn't fool enough to fall for that. She'd tried to make a deal over the phone, but Warren demanded that she meet him here to talk terms. And from this vantage point, he could see if she brought anyone with her.

Traders. He snorted. They always thought they were in a position to negotiate.

If she was telling the truth, things might work out after all. It had been stupid bad luck that Jason got away before Warren had a chance to interrogate him. Warren had sweated it, worrying he'd never get the information he needed. But now things were back on track. Once he had the Dragonheart, he'd have no need of D'Orsay. With the covenant and the Dragonheart, wizards would flow to his banner. He'd make the rules. There'd be no more skulking in back alleys, watching for death over his shoulder.

If Leesha showed, she'd bring the goods. Otherwise, she wouldn't dare leave the sanctuary. She'd want the collar removed. As if that would ever happen. Hunted as he was, he needed someone to do his bidding. Slave Leesha. He wasn't ready to give her up.

Something was moving on the street below. Warren focused, feeling the proximity of the collar. He leaned into the opening, careful of the broken glass on either side.

It was Leesha. She passed under a mercury vapor light on the side of a building, her shadow stretching out in front of her, a backpack slung over her shoulder. He looked up and down the street. She seemed to be alone.

It was funny when you thought about it, a teenage girl walking alone in this neighborhood at 2 a.m. Any mugger who thought he saw an easy target was in for a surprise.

She reached the warehouse and turned aside, passing under him to the entrance. Warren slid through the window and descended the fire escape into an alley. Once again, he looked up and down the street, alert for betrayal. There was nobody.

As he entered through the side door, Leesha was spinning around, flame spattering out in all directions. He flung himself backward, throwing his shields up, then realized he was not the target. Blueblood Leesha was frying rats.

"Hey! Be careful with that. You'll burn the place down."

She swung toward him. "As if that would be a loss. I can't believe you asked me to meet you in this dump," she said.

He relaxed a little. It was Leesha, all right.

"Funny," he said. "People keep trying to kill me. This place seemed safer than my apartment."

"Really? Darn. Well, I don't want to be here any longer than I have to in case somebody tries again." She unslung the backpack, setting it on top of a barrel like it was made of glass. "OK. I brought it all. The Dragonheart. And some other stuff. Only—be careful. It's really powerful and hard to handle. They've been having trouble controlling it, I guess."

"Where'd you find it?"

"They had it hidden under McCauley's porch."

"How'd you find out it was there?"

"I bribed someone."

"Good work, Leesha. I'm proud of you."

She shifted from one foot to the other. "I was wondering. What happened with J . . . with Haley? Did you . . . did you find him?"

Good, Warren thought, crossing one problem off his list. Haley is history. Never called. Never wrote. Never came back and snuffed Leesha Middleton for ratting him out. He must be dead after all.

"Yeah, I did find him, as a matter of fact," Warren said, smiling. "Why do you ask?"

Leesha bit her lip. "Just . . . wondered, is all," she whispered.

Don't tell me Leesha Middleton is growing a conscience, he thought. That would be inconvenient.

But she pulled herself together and checked her watch. "Look," she said coldly. "You asked for the Dragonheart and I delivered. Now take this thing off and I'm out of here." She slid her forefinger into her neckline and lifted her chin, exposing the glittering torc.

Warren laid his hand on the bag. "You expect me to take your word for it?"

"See for yourself. The Dragonheart's in the velvet bag on top. I'd rather you not mess with it until after I leave. In case you set it off."

"Nuh-uh." He shoved the backpack toward her. "Show me."

Hissing with irritation, Leesha unzipped the backpack

and pulled out a velvet bag with a drawstring. She worked free the knotted ties.

Then she flung the pouch at him.

He leaped to the side and hit the floor rolling. When the pouch landed, it exploded into a shower of carbon-black powder. Like coal dust.

Gemynd bana. Mind-Slayer. Meant to knock him out in an instant.

Leesha was more agile than he'd given her credit for. She backflipped out of range of the powder explosion, and scrambled madly for the door. He could have used the collar; he could've used an immobilization charm, but some things are best done directly. He charged after her, three long strides, and then tackled her, bringing her down on the floor under him. Her head bounced, hard, on the battered wooden floor.

He threw up a shield in time to turn an immobilization charm and a gout of flame. Pinned her hands to keep her from scratching his eyes out, then sent a little disciplinary flame through the collar. She screamed and thrashed around, trying to rip her hands free.

"You scheming little double-crossing trader," Warren muttered. "What did you hope to accomplish?" And then, understanding flooded in. "Who are you working for now? D'Orsay? Longbranch? McCauley?" He could've gone down a whole long list, but just then the front door shattered, spraying them both with wood splinters and hardware.

Two tall figures stood in the empty doorframe. One had a wicked sword in his hand. The other didn't need one. A warrior and a wizard side by side.

It was Jack Swift, looking like a muscle-bound action

hero. Except for the Trinity Soccer T-shirt and blue jeans.

And Seph McCauley. Leesha was right when she said he was scary. He was scarcely recognizable as the naive blueblood who'd arrived at the Havens. He was taller than Warren remembered, thin and angular and intense, as if he'd outgrown his weight. He wore a black hoodie and jeans, and his pale face and green eyes were framed in a tangle of curls. You could see Hastings's blood in him—distilled down and concentrated. Leicester had been an idiot not to spot it at the Havens.

Warren rolled to his feet. He reached down and grabbed Leesha by the arm and hauled her up in front of him, pressing his fingers into her carotid, where a whisper of power could stop the flow of blood.

"They *made* me!" Leesha said, flinching at the sting of his fingers.

"Sure they did," he muttered. He followed that with the classic, "Back off or the girl dies!" Wondering if they'd care.

Swift scanned the room for other enemies, then focused back on Warren. "I guessed that we'd run into each other again, sooner or later. I should've killed you the last time I saw you."

Right. He should've. But Jack Swift had been too noble to cut the throat of a helpless enemy. Which was why Barber was totally going to win.

McCauley extended a hand and muttered a charm, and Leesha went limp in Warren's arms. Immobilized.

Clever. Warren could still choose to kill her, but he'd have to drag her body around with him if he wanted to keep using her as a shield and hostage.

He tried the countercharm but it went nowhere. McCauley's magic was wicked strong. Warren was getting sick of it. How many times was he going to have to face off with him?

"Put her down, Barber, and let's talk," McCauley said. "We want the Covenant, and we want to know what happened to Jason."

The Covenant. Jason Haley. You couldn't trust a trader with any kind of secret if someone else made a better offer. "I don't know what you're talking about. Leesha asked me to meet her here. Said she had a proposition. Then she attacked me."

"Right." Swift feinted with the sword, and Warren turned, keeping Leesha between himself and the warrior's blade. But it was an exhausting business, and Warren wasn't exactly fast on his feet.

"Don't be stupid," Warren said. "She's a trader, remember? She'll say anything if she thinks she can turn a profit."

"Lucky you're here to set us straight." McCauley fired an immobilization charm, and Warren lunged sideways to avoid it. Swift rolled fireballs off the tip of his sword, spinning them past Warren's ears. Leesha just wasn't big enough to provide good cover. Warren countered with a wizard graffe that barely missed nailing McCauley, but then the boy wonder whipped off three charms in answer, and Warren knew this was a battle he couldn't win.

His only advantage was that they probably wanted him healthy enough to interrogate.

Lifting Leesha's limp body, Warren pitched her into Swift and McCauley. He spun a razorwire net, gathering it up and sending it spiraling over them. Limp Leesha, Swift, and

McCauley ended up tangled together on the floor in a kind of giant bleeding cocoon, the wire cutting into their flesh. Swift struggled to maneuver his massive sword into position so he could cut through the net without decapitating anyone. Warren sent cascades of wizard flame boiling into their midst until McCauley put up a makeshift shield.

Warren didn't wait to see the outcome. Swiveling, he sprayed the perimeter of the room with flame. It went up with a *whoosh*.

What do you know? he thought. This warehouse *is* a fire-trap.

Wizard fire was notoriously hard to extinguish. The place was history, and three of his major problems would go up with it.

Though in Leesha's case, there was no need to trust to luck. Regretfully, he dismissed thoughts of Slave Leesha and muttered a charm that activated the torc. Would she burn to death, or strangle first?

He sprinted toward the rear door, pausing in the back hallway long enough to weave a web over the doorway. Even if they freed themselves from the net, the web would slow them down long enough to allow the flame and smoke to do their work.

As he turned to make his exit, he heard a sound behind him and instinctively dodged aside. Something crashed down on his head. If it hadn't caught him off center, he would've been done for sure.

He stumbled, almost went down. Blood streamed into his eyes. He staggered backward, spewing flames in all directions. There followed a massive blow to his shoulder, and he screamed in pain, his left arm rendered almost useless.

He turned, mopping blood from his eyes to clear his vision.

A girl, with a mother of a big sword. Familiar, somehow. The girl, not the sword. Then he remembered. Ellen Stephenson, the warrior he'd encountered the first time he'd gone to Trinity in search of Seph McCauley.

If she'd wanted to kill him, she could have taken his head off with that blade. She'd hit him with the flat of it, so she was trying to take him alive. That was good to know.

He flung out a charm, but before he could finish he had to pitch himself backward as the blade slashed past his midsection, slicing through his shirt and the top layer of skin. Damn, she was good. He didn't even know he'd been cut until the blood came.

Smoke boiled into the corridor, stinging his eyes. He drew a breath, coughing, spinning out flame like an out-of-control firework to keep Stephenson at a distance. She easily parried his scattered attack with her sword, then advanced toward him.

"Your friends are burning to death in there!" Warren gasped, nodding toward the main storeroom. "Make a choice!" He turned and zigzagged down the hallway. Bursting through the exit door, he stopped long enough to barricade it with another web.

Warren ran down the alley, then cut between several rows of warehouses and descended into the Flats along the river. He tried to support his injured arm, gritting his teeth when he jostled it. He threaded his way around the great concrete feet of a lift bridge, then slowed to a brisk walk, following the river, trying to blend in with the late nighters headed to the bars. Those that were still sober cut a wide circle around him, furtively checking out his blood-matted hair and clothing. It was all he could do to resist the urge to pitch them over the side into the water. He was several blocks from the warehouse before he heard sirens.

Good luck, he thought.

Warren was pissed. His arm hurt like hell. Apparently, everyone in Trinity knew he held the Covenant. Just a few more thousand people to jump into the hunt.

Worse, Leesha had been his go-between. Killing her might bring him some small satisfaction, but now he needed someone else to serve as his proxy. But who?

The only thing that cheered him was the notion that he'd left Jack Swift, Joseph McCauley, and Leesha Middleton in the burning building. With any luck, Stephenson would go down, too.

In the end, it wasn't a difficult choice, just a frustrating one. Ellen gave up on Barber and groped her way back through the smoke. The door into the other room was scorching hot. She stood to one side, extended Waymaker, and cut through the door, releasing a blast of heat and smoke.

The doorway was woven over with a labyrinth of translucent cords. Barber's work. The interior of the room was an inferno. Ellen's entire front was immediately roasted. The skin tightened on her face and hands. No, she thought. Oh, no.

"Seph! Jack!"

A faint answering call came from somewhere beyond the web.

Ellen swung her blade and slashed through the cords. It took four strong strokes to hack out an opening she could get through. She bulled her way forward, pushing through a wall of smoke and flame.

"Where are you?" she shouted, and flinched when the reply came almost from under her feet. She nearly stumbled over a pile of bleeding bodies. The razorweb had done its work. Jack, Seph, and Leesha were cut in dozens of places, coughing and choking as they breathed in smoke. Leesha flailed about, struggling to get free, which only increased the damage done by the web to all three prisoners.

"Lay still, Leesha, or I'll leave you here to fry," Ellen said.

Leesh blinked up at her in surprise, and then, to Ellen's amazement, obeyed.

Ellen tried to ignore the heat and flames rushing toward them. She gripped Waymaker's hilt with both hands and slid the tip into the razorweb, delicately slicing through the strands without pulling on the net. She focused on freeing Jack, who practically reverberated with impatience.

Finally, Jack shook free of the last tendrils of razorwire and erupted to his feet. Seizing Shadowslayer, he helped Ellen cut Seph and Leesha loose. Seph pushed himself upright and extended his bleeding hands, pushing back the wall of flame that threatened to engulf them. It grew increasingly difficult to breathe. Leesha, especially, kept coughing and choking and ripping at her throat.

When Seph and Leesha were free, Jack hauled them to their feet. Leesha fell again when he released her, so he slid his arms under her and slung her over his shoulder.

That girl will do anything to get next to Jack, Ellen thought crossly.

Holding hands to keep from losing each other in the oily smoke, they groped their way to the back of the room, out the door, and into the fresh air.

Seph looked back at the burning warehouse. By now, flames had broken through the roof and were shooting into the air. Usually so calm in times of crisis, he seemed jumpy and agitated. "Go on," Seph said, pulling his hood over his head. "Get as far away as you can. I'll be right behind you."

"Seph! Wait!" Ellen made a grab for him, but he side-stepped her and disappeared into the burning building.

Shaking her head, Ellen drew in lungfuls of cool air, but Leesha was still choking. Jack carried her to the far side of the parking lot and laid her down on the asphalt. "Take it easy, will you?" he said. "Relax. We're out."

Leesha gasped something that sounded like, "Barber!" and "Get it off!" She tore open her neckline to expose a gold collar biting into her flesh. The skin around it was mottled purple and red, covered with angry blisters.

"What the . . . ?" Jack tried to take hold of the collar with his hands, but yanked them back, swearing. "It's blazing hot!"

"Barber did this?" Ellen asked.

Leesha nodded. Tears ran down her face and her entire body shook with silent sobs. Ellen and Jack gripped her arms and pulled her upright, hoping to find a clasp, an opening, something, but no luck. It was solid and seamless all the way around.

Ellen pulled out her belt dagger and tried to slide the point under the collar, but it was already too tight.

Jack tried some countercharms from his repertoire, but they had no apparent effect.

"Remember when Leicester used a torc on Leander Hastings?" Ellen muttered. "The collar could only be removed by the wizard who placed it."

And that would be Warren Barber.

By now Leesha's face was blue and her struggles were growing weaker, less organized. She's going to die, Ellen thought, feeling totally helpless.

"Hey! What do you kids think you're doing?" A burly firefighter confronted them in full regalia, his features scrunched down with suspicion. "Nobody's supposed to be back here." Beyond him, a half dozen firefighters poured from the alley, dragging giant hoses and equipment into the lot.

Ellen slid Waymaker back into its baldric, smothering the flames that ran along the blade. Shadowslayer was slung over Jack's back, but the hilt stuck up over his shoulder. That'd be tough to explain if the firefighter noticed it. She moved in closer to Jack. He had some wizardry. Maybe he could . . .

"You can't stay back here," the firefighter growled. "What with the onshore breeze and all these old warehouses, there's a good chance the fire will spread to the whole block." He pointed them toward the cross street. "Get back behind the police line."

Then he squinted at them suspiciously. "What happened to you? You're all cut up and covered in soot. Were you kids in the building?"

"We saw the smoke," Ellen said. "And, um, we came to see the fire." She was a terrible liar.

But the firefighter was distracted by Leesha. "What's wrong with her?"

Jack knelt next to her, furiously tearing off pieces of his shirt. He wrapped the cloth around his hands and tried again to get a grip on the collar. Leesha didn't seem to be breathing any more.

"Our friend got hurt," Ellen said, not knowing what else to say. "She's not breathing."

Jack drew his belt dagger and leaned over Leesha, eyes squinted, mouth tight with determination. Oh, God, Ellen thought. He's going to try to do a tracheotomy. Like on TV. Two years ago this boy couldn't splint his own broken leg on the battlefield, and now he's doing surgery.

"Hey!" the fireman said when he saw the blade. "What are you doing?"

"What's up?" Seph materialized out of the smoke like a wraith, blood and sweat streaking through the soot on his face.

Jack looked up, a little wild-eyed. "Barber put a torc on Leesha. It's strangling her."

Strangled, more like, Ellen thought. Past tense. It was weird that she had time to think all that. It was like events had slowed down to a crawl. The firefighter was yelling something in the background, calling for police backup, maybe.

Seph dropped to his knees next to Leesha, wrapped his hands around the torc as if oblivious to the heat, and shut his eyes. Jack stepped between Seph and Leesha and the fire-fighter to prevent interference.

It's no good, Seph, Ellen thought. Only the wizard who placed it can remove it.

Power rippled around Seph. He tilted his head back, con-centrating, muttering charms. Sweat rolled down his face, though the night was growing chilly. He swallowed once, twice, the long column of his throat jumping. Then the metal dissolved from under his hands and Leesha was free.

A second passed. Leesha took a rasping breath.

"What the hell?" the firefighter said, leaning sideways to peer around Jack.

Seph remained on his knees, his hands resting on his thighs, trembling like he'd caught a chill. Then he looked up at the firefighter. "She's breathing again, but maybe she should have some oxygen?"

Firefighters swarmed around Leesha, unpacking equipment.

The battalion leader stepped around Jack and clutched Seph's sweatshirt in his fist, dragging him to his feet. "I want to know what happened to her and what you just did."

Seph put his hand on the firefighter's shoulder and the Commander flinched. "Nothing happened, Commander," Seph said softly, looking him in the eye. "Her necklace melted from the heat and burned her neck. That's all."

The commander blinked at him and nodded, slowly. "Right. Well. We'll want to get your names. As witnesses."

"You won't need that," Seph said, his hand still on the man's arm. "It'll be fine."

"Okay," the commander said.

"Commander!" Another firefighter loped up the alley. "I think we can cancel the third hook and ladder." He hesitated. "I . . . I can't explain it, but it looks like the fire is out."

"What?"

The other man shrugged. "There's still lots of smoke and a few hot spots, but the fire is basically . . . out."

The fire was contained within the skin of the building, so they couldn't see for themselves, but the heat seemed to be diminishing rather than growing.

"Come on," the battalion leader said. "Let's go take a closer look." He turned back to Ellen and the others.

"You three—get out of here. We'll transport the girl to the burn unit at Metro Hospital."

But Leesha was already fighting off the oxygen and struggling to sit up. "I'm *fine*," she hissed. "What are you all making such a *fuss* about?" She put several firefighters down on their butts and struggled to her feet. "Leave me alone, will you?"

Wizards were resilient, Ellen had to admit. And stubborn.

The paramedic tried to reason with his uncooperative patient. "Uh, miss, you have second and third degree burns that need treatment," he said.

"They'll be okay. I'll just use a concealer for a while." She also declined pain medication and a tranquilizer. "I'm leaving with my friends, understand? I'll sign any form you want." She looked up at Ellen and the rest. "Let's go."

Despite her bravado, Ellen could tell that Leesha was shaken. She staggered along beside them until Jack and Ellen ignored her protests and each took an arm, supporting her. She kept touching her neck as if to convince herself the torc was gone, then peered over at Seph like he was some newly discovered wonder of the world.

"Why didn't you tell us about the torc?" Ellen asked, catching Leesha for about the fourteenth time when she stumbled.

Leesha's voice was low and raspy, and it sounded like it hurt to speak. "I knew . . . there was nothing you could do . . . to take it off." She took a deep breath, as if she were still short on air. "As long as I was in the sanctuary, he couldn't use it against me. But I knew once you knew about it, I'd be too high risk. You'd kick me out."

"How did he ever get it on you, anyway?" Ellen asked.

Leesha rolled her eyes. "Don't ask."

"What did you think was going to happen tonight?" Jack asked. "Why did you agree to meet him outside the sanctuary? He almost killed you."

"I just hoped somebody would kill him," Leesha said, brushing her fingertips over the ring of blistered flesh where the torc had been. "Me or you, it didn't matter. I couldn't stand it anymore."

"Well, the torc is off, but he's still out there somewhere," Jack said. "Unfortunately, we don't know any more than we did before about what happened to Jason and where the Covenant is."

Leesha shrugged and stared at the ground, her lower lip trembling. Ellen found herself actually feeling sorry for her.

Seph spoke for the first time. "I don't think you should go back to your aunt's." He left it at that, but everyone knew what he meant. Barber was still at large and the wall wasn't up yet.

Leesha swallowed, wincing. "But, if I can't stay at Aunt Milli's . . ."

"We'll ask Nick," Jack said. "He'll find a place. And somebody should look at your neck, anyway."

Seph said nothing more. He just strode along, head down, hands thrust into the front pocket of his sweatshirt, lost in his own thoughts. But Ellen had her own questions that needed answering.

"So what'd you do?" she asked Seph as they threaded their way past emergency vehicles on their way back to the car.

"What do you mean?"

"With the fire. Wizard fire is impossible to put out."

He shrugged slightly, still looking straight ahead.

"How'd you get the torc off?" she persisted.

Still he said nothing. Refused to look at her.

"Seph."

When he finally spoke, his voice was low and ragged. "I didn't want the whole neighborhood to burn because of us, okay? I didn't want anyone else . . . anyone to be caught in it." His voice broke and he swiped at his eyes with the back of his hand.

Ellen put her hand on his arm, and almost yanked it away. He was still totally hot with power. "Seph. Look at me."

Seph finally looked up and met her stare. "What?" he demanded. When she said nothing, Seph added, "Look, there was a fire—in Toronto. A friend of mine died." His green eyes were unnaturally bright, his pupils pinpricks, his face deathly pale. He looked away.

He's using flame again, Ellen thought, even though he'd promised he wouldn't—except in extraordinary circumstances. She couldn't fault him—he'd put out the fire and saved Leesha's life.

But it seemed those extraordinary circumstances were coming along more and more often.

CHAPTER TWENTY-ONE

LIFE AS ART

Two weeks went by, and Grace and J.R. didn't go riding at the Ropers again. Madison ran into Brice once or twice in town, and he pretended not to see her. She tried to look at the bright side: at least he wasn't trying to romance her any more.

Grace was hopeful of being invited back at first, and then angry, and that kind of petered down to being disappointed—her usual state. Madison took Grace and J.R. fishing at the reservoir. She helped them bake dog biscuits for Hamlet and Ophelia and played long games of Monopoly that slid over from one day to the next. But it was hard to compete with Arabian horses and miles of trails. And Madison hesitated to take them to town for fear she might run into Warren Barber. Was he still hanging around, looking for Jason, or had he climbed back into whatever hole he'd come from?

Jason was surprisingly patient with Grace and J.R. He

taught them how to play blackjack and 5-card stud and Texas hold 'em. As he got to feeling better, he went down to Booker Creek with them to look for salamanders and tadpoles. He found an old fish tank in the cellar, set it up, and got the pump working. They populated it with striped shiners, rainbow darters, silverjaw minnows, and ones Madison didn't know that Jason made up names for, like slack-jawed sidewinders and malaclusive bottom feeders.

John Robert thought everything Jason said was hilarious and smart, and even Grace made excuses to go out to the barn to show him something or see if he needed a snack or a book to read.

Jason didn't risk going into town, either, but he walked all over the mountain with Maddie, hauling canvases and easels and supplies and taking photographs with the camera Madison had borrowed from Sara.

Madison knew it was wrong to keep his presence a secret from Carlene, but she was so in the habit of working around her mother that secrecy came naturally to her. She couldn't quite figure out why Jason was still there—whether he hoped he'd eventually convince her to come north, or if he was there as bodyguard or spy.

She'd expect him to be totally antsy, stuck up on the mountain with nothing to do, but he actually seemed content, more relaxed than she'd ever seen him. It was as if he'd managed to set down the armloads of pain he carried around all the time—temporarily, at least.

The Booker Mountain effect at work, no doubt.

Jason was a constant reminder of everything and everyone Madison had left behind in Trinity. She thought of going down into town and calling Seph, just to get the news and hear his voice. But then he'd ask about Jason and she didn't think she could pull it off, lying to him. Besides, she'd moved beyond the razor edge of grief into long-term mourning, and she was afraid any conversation between them would reopen those wounds. So she wrote long letters and sent e-mails and kept Jason's secret.

One afternoon, Madison came in from the barn to find Carlene sitting at the kitchen table, smoking a cigarette and tapping the ashes into an empty Pepsi can. Her mother had on her waitress uniform, a shirtwaist dress with CARLENE embroidered over the pocket that looked like one of those retro uniforms, but wasn't.

Madison hadn't said a word about Brice Roper or the shed. What good would it do? It wouldn't turn either one of them into different people, people who agreed on anything. Madison would own Booker Mountain in three months. It would be up to somebody else to make the next move.

Brice had told Carlene some of what had happened at the Ropers—Madison was sure of that. Carlene would sneak rabbity looks at her from the corners of her eyes as if expecting some kind of confrontation. Not that they saw much of each other, what with Carlene's work and sleep schedules and Madison's habit of spending her afternoons secluded in the barn. That kind of kept their encounters to a minimum.

Madison opened the refrigerator, scanning the meager offerings, wondering what to fix for supper.

And then Carlene asked, "Who's that boy you got stashed in the barn?"

Madison yanked her head out of the refrigerator and swung around, banging her elbow. "Ow! What?"

"He your boyfriend?"

"Ah . . . well, no," Madison stuttered. "He's just a friend who needed a place to stay."

"Well, tell your friend he can stay in the house if he wants. There's plenty of room. That's rude, making him stay out there." Carlene gestured toward the other chair with her cigarette. "Sit down a minute, honey."

Madison shut the refrigerator, came and sat down at the table. "Okay. I'll tell him, but I think he's leaving pretty soon." She hesitated. "Please, Mama, don't tell anybody he's here."

Naturally, Carlene didn't commit to anything. "You don't even have a crush on him?"

Madison tore the paper towel that stood in for a napkin into careful strips. "No, I don't. What makes you say that?"

"I'm trying to figure out why you don't like Brice."

"Mama, there are a hundred reasons why I don't like Brice, beginning with the fact that he's a self-centered, arrogant . . . jerk."

"But good-looking. And rich." Carlene waved away *self-centered* and *arrogant* like his other stellar qualities canceled them out.

"Maybe *you* should marry him, then."

Carlene considered this, then shook her head. "He likes you."

"He *likes* Booker Mountain. If you owned it, he'd like *you*." Careful, Madison, she thought. Just calm down.

"If I did own it, I'd sure consider selling it to him."

"Where would you live, then?"

Carlene looked around the kitchen, with its battered linoleum floors and tired flowered wallpaper, everything glazed over with years of propane residue. "Anywhere. Anywhere but here." She paused. "Think what it would mean to Grace and John Robert if they could move someplace with good schools, where they'd have friends close by to play with."

She stubbed out her cigarette. "They're talking serious money, Maddie, enough to pay for college, for a new house, for . . . for everything. We'd be millionaires. We could move wherever we wanted and make a fresh start, where people don't have . . . attitudes."

Booker Mountain is mine, Madison wanted to say, though she felt like it belonged to Grace and John Robert, too. But it wouldn't belong to any of them if they sold it away. If Min hadn't been so stubborn, it would be gone already.

Madison imagined the bulldozers coming in, the draglines scraping the top off her mountain, all of Coalton County dusted black from the blasting.

"Mama, you know what they're planning to do to the mountain," Madison said. "Brice told you about it. How could you ever let that happen?"

"Now, baby," Carlene coaxed. "Don't exaggerate. They'll fix it up, after. Besides, there's other mountains. We could move out west somewhere, like Las Vegas. There's mountains all over out there."

Madison thought of the little graveyard upslope in the hollow, the crazily tilted headstones like crooked teeth where the frost had pushed them out of the ground. There was the cave by the waterfall where she'd found Native American petroglyphs and never told anyone because she was afraid somebody would sneak in and wreck it, the way people always did. The old iron furnace by the creek, built by her great-grandfather, one of his crazy, money-making schemes.

She felt like she was under siege, between Brice Roper and Carlene and Children's Services and Seph and the onrushing wizard war and the Dragonheart pulling at her asleep and awake.

"Do we have to talk about this now?" she asked wearily.

"Madison." Carlene looked her in the eyes. "Do you want to wait until Grace and John Robert are growed up? We're not the kind of people who can afford to be romantic about things. We have to be practical."

Practical. Coming from Carlene. "Did Mr. Roper ask you to talk to me?" Madison demanded.

Carlene nodded. She snapped and unsnapped her cigarette case. "I told him I would. It don't make sense, the way you're treating him and Brice."

"Well, If I have to decide now, the answer is no."

"Don't decide now, then." Carlene stood and picked up her pocketbook, fished inside and pulled out a twenty. "I have to go to work. Here. Go on and take the kids to the movies in town tonight. And don't be stubborn. Sometimes you have to think of someone besides yourself."

Torches guttered in sconces along the walls, painting the great stone hall in reds and yellows. Prisoners processed up the aisle to the altar at the front, chains clanking, clad in rough-spun hooded robes that bore the insignia of their Houses. The Red Rose. The White Rose. The Silver Bear. The Dragon. In an endless line.

The executioner stood beside the altar, holding a great staff with the Dragonheart mounted at the tip. A clerk stood alongside, reading from a parchment, calling names, confirming the sentences. Many of the names were familiar: Leander Hastings. Linda

Downey. Claude D'Orsay. Jessamine Longbranch. Jackson Swift. Jason Haley. Joseph McCauley. The charge: Anarchy. Rebellion. Murder. Each of the condemned knelt at the altar and mutely laid his head upon the stone. The executioner raised the great staff, pointed it at the prisoner. Flames erupted from the Dragonheart, incinerating the condemned in an instant. The stench of burned flesh filled the hall.

The executioner's hood fell back, revealing her own face.

"Maddie, wake up! Maddie, you're dreaming." Someone pulled at her arm, practically yanking it out of its socket.

Maddie opened her eyes and Grace's worried face came into view—solemn gray eyes and a sprinkling of freckles, straight brown hair pulled back in a ponytail. "You're scaring me, yelling like that."

"Oh." Maddie propped on her elbows and tried to swallow away the bad taste in her mouth. She went to sleep thinking of Seph. She woke up thinking of the Dragonheart. Now they were invading her dreams. "Sorry. What time is it, anyway?"

"I don't know; it's late," Grace said, switching on the lamp. "You must've fell asleep on the couch after supper. Did you ever take Jason anything to eat?"

Madison shook her head. "No, I . . . drat!" She focused on the kitchen clock. "It's after eight o'clock. I was going to take you and J.R. to the movies tonight."

"Can't we still go?" Grace begged.

"It's too late tonight, there's just an eight o'clock showing. We'll go tomorrow, to a matinee, and then we'll have enough money for popcorn, too. Okay?"

"Okay. I guess." Grace sat on the edge of the couch. "What'd you dream about, anyway?"

The Dragonheart, Madison almost said. She massaged her

forehead with the heels of her hands. Even when she didn't focus on it, it shimmered in the periphery of her mind, stirring up the kind of longing she associated with art. And Seph McCauley.

When she didn't answer, Grace said, "You never used to have nightmares."

"Maybe I was just less noisy about it." Madison shook her head, trying to rattle loose the images that remained. "Thanks for waking me up, Gracie," she said, forgetting that Grace now officially hated to be called Gracie. "I'd better take Jason something to eat."

Madison poured iced tea into a metal Thermos—the one her father used to carry to the mine. She slathered leftover biscuits with butter and honey and rolled them in a napkin, wrapped leftover fried chicken in waxed paper. She supposed she should ask Jason to come up and eat at the house, but it didn't matter now, anyway. He'd have to leave. Carlene couldn't keep a secret as well as Grace and J.R. The whole town would know about Jason inside of a week.

Surely Warren Barber must've gone back to wherever he came from. Nobody in town had mentioned seeing him. He would stick out wherever he was, but especially in Coal Grove.

The security light created a little oasis in the black woods. The outbuildings threw long shadows across the grass as she crossed the yard, past the flowerbeds where Min's peonies and bearded irises were pushing their way out of the ground. Bats fluttered like black handkerchiefs among the trees at the edge of the clearing.

Hamlet rose and dog-stretched in greeting, nudging his food bowl with his nose.

"This isn't for you," Madison said, scratching him behind

the ears with her free hand. "You already had your dinner, remember?"

Hamlet stiffened and pointed his graying muzzle toward the woods, the hair around his collar ruffing out. He growled and drew his lips back from his teeth, which was a surprise, because he was stone deaf and half blind.

"Hey, Hamlet," Maddie said, shivering a little, peering into the trees. "What'd you spot? A ghost? A raccoon?"

She saw several shapes moving in the trees, and for a moment, she thought it really *might* be ghosts, since they had a spooky glow about them. And then she realized what they must be, and dropped Jason's supper in the dirt.

Four wizards stopped just inside the cover of the trees and stood, looking toward the house. They hadn't seen her yet, hidden as she was in the shadow of the barn.

That they were there for mischief, she had no doubt. The fact that they were all wearing black hoods with eyeholes cut out confirmed it. They must have left their car down the road a way.

Her truck was parked inside the barn, but Grace and J.R. were watching TV in the house and there was no way she could collect them and get back to the barn and out of there without being intercepted. She could wave the shotgun at the intruders, but that was in the house, too.

She stood frozen, thoughts spiraling. It might be the Roses coming after her. Seph had warned her that might happen. Or it could be the Roses, or Barber, or practically anybody at all, coming after Jason.

The wizards left the trees and moved silently toward the house, walking purposefully. They were dressed all in black, framed in light.

"I thought you said nobody'd be home," one of the wizards said. "The house is all lit up." To her surprise, his voice said he was local.

Madison hadn't realized she was holding her breath, until she let it out. Okay, she thought. At least this problem is homegrown.

"Don't worry," the tallest wizard said. "They probably just left the lights on." His voice sounded familiar, but it was hard to tell, muffled through the hood.

"You're sure there's no kids in there," the first wizard persisted.

"Will you shut *up*!" the tallest wizard hissed. Madison thought he must be the leader. "We came all the way up here, let's do it and go." They continued moving toward the house.

Then Madison remembered Grace's story about the burning of the shed. *There were four or five of them, out here in the dark. They had torches. . . .*

No. I will not let this happen, she thought. Not on my mountain.

"What *the hell* do you think you're doing on my property?" She shouted it out really loud, hoping to warn Grace and J.R. in the house and Jason in the barn.

The wizards jumped at the sound of her voice and milled around in confusion, peering into the darkness, trying to figure out where she was.

With any luck, Grace would be levelheaded enough to grab J.R. and leave out the back door. She'd know better than to come out and get mixed up in this.

"I *knew* it. I *knew* somebody was home," the first wizard said.

"Look, she can't stop us. What's she going to do?" The

tall wizard continued walking toward the house, trailed by his accomplices, who kept looking back over their shoulders.

"What are you doing?" Madison called. When he didn't answer, she screamed, "There are kids in that house!"

"Well, then you'd better get them out now," the wizard said coldly. "Because we're going to burn this dump to the ground." He extended his hands, and fire coalesced around his fingertips.

And then she knew for sure. "Brice Roper! You come away from there or I'll have the sheriff all over you!"

That brought him up short. He stood frozen for a moment, then shrugged and swung around, yanking off his hood and raking a hand through his mashed hair. "Hello, Madison."

"Brice," one of the other wizards whined. "This isn't what we . . ."

"*Shut up*, I said," Brice muttered. "I should have just handled this on my own. Don't make me sorry I brought you along."

"I'm warning you," Madison said. "You'll never get away with it."

Brice laughed. "Who's going to believe *you*? This place is a firetrap. It'll be your word against mine, and I'll be sure and have an alibi and ten witnesses to put me someplace else. If anyone does believe you, I'll *persuade* them they don't."

"People know me around here," Madison said, trying to sound more confident than she felt. "They'll believe me."

Right. When have they ever believed you about anything?

"Really? You think so? I say the word, and you're a witch. I say the word, and you burned your house down yourself.

The people in this town are sheep, Madison, and I can drive them wherever I want."

"You're the ones who set all the fires last year," Madison breathed.

Brice bowed mockingly. "Proves my point, wouldn't you say? Here we were, burning up the whole valley, and these idiots are blaming you. If the whole town turned against me, I'd sell out and move away. But you didn't. Oh, no. Instead, you pull a shotgun on them. You're stubborn as a rock. And about as smart."

In that moment, the gut-clenching sensation went away and she was just really, really angry. She strode toward them, into the light. "People know what you are. Some of them, anyway."

"I'll tell you one thing they know," Brice said. "My father provides jobs for half the county—anybody who's making a decent living. What's going to happen when we close up the mine? This place'll just dry up and blow away. Booker Mountain will keep Roper Coal going another ten years or more."

"And then what?"

"Well, then they'll have a nice flat place to park something on, won't they? It'll be the only level piece of land in the whole county."

"I won't sell," Madison said. "Not to you, I won't."

"Where are Carlene and the kids going to live, then, after I burn this place down?" Brice snorted. "You can't even afford a phone. I bet you can't scrape up the first month's rent. You going to pitch a tent, or what?"

Madison clenched her fists and took a step forward. "How can you live with yourself?"

"It's your fault. You should've agreed to sell. That's the way the world works. Everybody knows that. But not you. You walk around like you're royalty in rags or something. Like you're better than me. *Me!*" he repeated, his voice rising.

"Brice," one of the other wizards said. A girl, from her voice. "Let's do it or go."

Brice collected himself. "All right, Madison. You have five minutes to get those kids out of the house, and anything else you want to keep. There can't be much worth saving." He smiled. "Don't worry. We'll still give you a good price. The house doesn't add any value, if you know what I mean. We'd just tear it down." He paused, and when Madison didn't say anything, added, "You'll thank me in a year."

Madison caught a flicker of movement out of the corner of her eye, and then someone screeched in pain. One of the wizards—the whiny one—went down on the ground, clutching at his head. He lay there, groaning, pressing his hands into his bleeding scalp.

Then Madison saw Jason, backpack slung over his shoulder, J.R.'s baseball bat in his hand, backing away from the downed wizard. A baseball bat against wizardry? She opened her mouth, meaning to shout, to say something. Jason shook his head, raising his hand to shush her.

And then she realized—he was unnoticeable to the other wizards in the yard. Noticeable only to her, the elicitor.

"Hey! Carl? What's up?" Brice called. "You trip over your feet or something?"

Carl only moaned some more.

Jason pulled a knife from his backpack and headed directly for another of the wizards, a stocky boy in low-slung camouflage pants and those giant high-tops. Jason came in close, thrust in and up with the knife, four quick strokes, and the wizard screeched and clutched at his midsection. He ripped open his shirt, revealing a crude *M* scratched into his chest and belly. "Wh-wh-what's going on?" he mumbled. "I'm bleeding! Something stuck me. It—it looks like a . . ." He looked up at Madison, eyes widening. "Did . . . did *you* do that?"

Thinking quickly, Madison drew herself up, tossed back her hair, and smiled at him. "What do *you* think?"

The three wizards still on their feet bunched up, facing Madison. She advanced, hands extended, and they retreated. All of the anger, fear, and humiliation of the past year bubbled up inside her. She found herself wishing she *did* have magic, that she could incinerate them with a gesture.

Jason kept moving. He pulled a metal can from his backpack, one that Madison recognized from the barn.

What is he doing?

He unscrewed the cap and upended it over the girl wizard. The girl shrieked and covered her head with her arms, fighting off her invisible opponent.

"What *is* this?" She sniffed, then screamed and ripped off the hood, flinging it away, revealing a pale, horrified face. "That's kerosene!" She backed away from Madison, shaking her head slowly from side to side. "If you think I'm going to set fire to a house while I'm drenched in kerosene, you're crazy." She turned and fled into the woods.

Madison walked toward Brice, forcing a smile onto her face. She was afraid her heart might burst right out of her chest, it was beating so hard. "So, Brice," she said, "I hear you like to play with magic."

"What th-the hell?" The usually articulate Brice looked

like he was in the middle of a very bad dream and hoped he'd wake up soon. "How are you doing that? You're not a wizard. I . . . didn't feel anything . . . when I touched you."

"You say the word, and I'm a witch," Madison said, low in her throat. "Isn't that right?"

Brice backed away as Madison advanced, raising his hands to fend her off. "Stay away from me." Meanwhile, Jason came at him from the side.

"Spell me, why don't you?" she taunted. "See if you can. I dare you." Her shadow extended before her, tall and angular.

He stretched out his hands, but then pulled them back, no doubt remembering what had happened in the studio. "Madison. Come on. Let's talk about this."

She extended her hand toward Brice, mimicking a hex sign Min had used. Unnoticeable Jason swung the bat, smashing Brice in the face. Brice jerked backward, yelling, pressing his sleeve to his face to stem the flow of blood from a perfect nose that was now smashed off-center.

"Ouch!" Madison said, shaking her head. "You're really not all that good at this, are you? I guess you need a little more practice. Want to play again?"

Brice spat out blood and a broken tooth. "I don't get it," he mumbled through his damaged mouth.

"No. You don't. But I'll tell you what. I'll make the same deal you offered me. I'll give you five minutes to gather up anything you want to keep." She glanced around—at Carl, who had sat up, blotting blood from his face with his shirt; at the other wizard who was still contemplating the wound in his midsection, looking like he might pass out. "Can't be much worth saving," she added.

Brice slid his hands under Carl's arms and hauled him to his feet, both of them beat up and bloody.

"One more thing," Madison said. "You better hope my life runs real smooth from here on. Anything happens to this place—fire, explosions, earthquakes, the well goes dry, bridge goes out, the apple trees get blossom-rot—I'll know who to blame. And I'll come after you. You ever set foot on my property again, I'll *incinerate* you."

For once, Brice had nothing to say. He and Carl hustled off into the woods, heading for the road.

Madison waited until the wizards had been out of sight for a good five minutes. Then she crouched next to the old chicken coop and vomited, heaving until she had nothing left. Jason squatted next to her, gathering her hair in his hands and pulling it back out of danger. Then he fetched her a mason jar of water from the spigot so she could rinse her mouth. He helped her back to the house, and they sat down on the porch steps. Madison was trembling, her teeth chattering. Jason put his arm around her and pulled her close, patting her back.

"God, you're good," he said, shaking his head. He seemed stunned by her performance. "I couldn't believe it. You're so brave. You scared the hell out of them."

"Me?" Madison said, shuddering. "You." Tears pooled in Madison's eyes, escaped, and ran down her cheeks. "I've been . . . so stupid. I should have seen it coming. I *know* him. I know what he is. What would have happened if you hadn't been here?"

"You could've taken them," Jason said, taking her hand in his and squeezing it. "No problem. You're like a . . . a lioness, defending your den. I mean, juice ain't all it's cracked up to be, compared with that." He rolled his eyes and she laughed, but there was something in his expression, like he'd had an epiphany.

"I better go find the kids," she said, wiping her tears away. "They must be scared to death." She stood and turned toward the house, but just then she heard Grace's voice from the woods back of the barn.

"Madison? What's happening? Can we come out?"

"Come on," Madison said, and Grace and J.R. emerged from the woods, Grace with a vicelike hold on her brother's hand. Madison sent up a silent prayer of thanks. Grace had done just the right thing. She'd taken J.R. and hidden in the woods.

Her little sister was growing up.

"Where'd those men go?" Grace asked, glancing around the barnyard. "Those were the same ones who set fire to the shed."

"How much did you see?" Madison asked, exchanging glances with Jason.

"We didn't get to see *anything*!" J.R. complained. "Grace made me go in the woods."

"Don't worry. Jason and I ran them off," Madison said. "I don't think they'll come back."

After the kids had gone to bed, Madison invited Jason into the house for his belated dinner. They sat at the kitchen table, and the dogs laid practically on their feet.

Things had changed, though Jason couldn't quite say why. For one thing, he'd stake his life—and Seph's, too—on the fact that Madison Moss was not in league with Warren Barber. Or the Roses. Jason didn't know how to explain the painting, and he knew it would freak her out if he asked about it. But, somehow, he no longer needed to.

"So. What are you going to do?" Madison asked Jason. So she, too, sensed they'd reached a turning point.

"Maybe I better stick around in case Brice and his friends come back," Jason suggested.

"You don't have to," she said. "I'm guessing Brice won't want to tangle with me any time soon."

Okay, Jason thought, I'm expendible again. But this time he felt it was more like he had options. "Well. I'd wanted to go back to England. Hastings is planning an attack on the ghyll, and I wanted to get in on it." He shrugged "It's probably already happened, by now."

"So you've changed your mind?"

He nodded. "I could go back to Trinity, I guess. But, I never felt that useful when I was there. I felt like, next to Seph, I was . . ." His voice trailed off. He couldn't quite believe he was confessing all this to anybody. "I couldn't stand that, doing nothing. When I left to come here, Seph told me he needed me to come back, that he could use my help. But I figured he was just saying that, because we're friends."

Madison put her hand on his arm. "Since you're friends, I think you ought to believe him." She hesitated, then rushed ahead. "Me—I'm a mess. I miss Seph so much. I want to be with him, but I can't. And the Dragonheart—it's like an itch I can't scratch. I can't seem to get it out of my mind."

Jason stared at her. That was it exactly. They both lusted after the stone, but it couldn't be for the same reason. Jason looked on it as some kind of tonic. He could feel the flow of power to his Weirstone, every minute of the day. But Madison didn't have a Weirstone.

Just then Ophelia raised her head and looked toward the door. A car rattled into the yard and stopped.

What now? Jason thought. I mean, this is getting kind of relentless. He held up a finger, signaling for Madison to stay put, and crossed to the door, peering through the screen.

Two people were climbing out of an old Jeep that he instantly recognized. Breathing a long sigh of relief, he walked out onto the porch.

"Jason!" Harmon Fitch crowed, a smile spreading across his face. He turned to Will Childers and slapped hands. "The dude's alive! That's the first good news we've had in a while."

They sat around the kitchen table. Jason seemed nervous and distracted, like he was trying to think up answers to the questions he knew were coming. Madison delayed the interrogation as long as she could, making small talk, rooting in the refrigerator for drinks, pounding ice cube trays on the counter, and dumping chips into a basket.

Finally, twitchy Fitch could stand it no longer. "In case you're wondering why we're here," he said, "everybody's been worried because we haven't heard from you."

"What have you guys been doing?" Will asked. "Why didn't you call?"

Well, Madison thought, because Jason begged me not to tell, and threatened to tell about Grace being an elicitor, if I did. She looked at Jason pointedly, waiting for him to speak, while he looked like he kind of hoped she'd handle it.

"I *did* e-mail Seph," she said finally. "And wrote a lot of letters."

"But *you* said Jason never showed," Will said.

"Well. Um. I guess so," Madison stammered. "But . . ."

"It was my fault," Jason broke in. "I was an idiot. I wouldn't let her call. I didn't want anyone to know I was here."

Will lifted an eyebrow. "You wouldn't *let* her? Did you tie her hand-and-foot or what?"

"Something like that." Color stained Jason's cheeks.

He's actually *blushing*, Madison thought. That's a first.

"That's messed up," Fitch said. "What's the matter with you? Everybody was going crazy. Some people said you took off." Fitch removed his glasses and polished them on his shirttail. "But Seph wouldn't believe it. He was convinced something happened to you."

"Well." Jason looked at Madison, then back at Fitch. "Something did."

So they told Will and Fitch about Barber, and Jason's injury, and Brice Roper.

"You should've *told* us," Will said, a betrayed look on his face. "Nick or Mercedes or somebody could have helped you."

"I *was* going to run off, *okay*?" Jason's voice rose. "And I would've if I hadn't been hurt. I wanted to get away from the whole Trinity scene. And then, after, I was . . . um . . . out of my head." He stared down at the table. "I'm better now."

Fitch eyed him, then nodded grudgingly. "Well," he said, "seems like things are almost as dangerous down here as at home."

Madison's mouth went dry as cotton. "Why? What's going on in Trinity?"

"Well, for one thing, Barber's been sighted up our way," Will said. "Jack and Ellen and Seph got into this big battle with him in some old warehouse in Cleveland and practically burned the place down."

"What?" Madison looked from Will to Fitch. "How did that happen? Are they all right?"

"They're okay," Will said, rearing back under the onslaught of questions. "Just some scrapes and burns," he said. "Routine for them."

"And?" Jason demanded. "What about Barber?"

"He got away." Will hesitated. "Leesha Middleton told us that he was after you."

Jason's face seemed to drain of its usual animation, and his blue eyes went narrow and hard. "Did she?" he said, in a cold, disinterested voice.

"She was the one that led them to Barber," Fitch added, frowning at Jason.

"That was Barber's mistake," Jason said lightly. "Trusting Leesha." Hamlet nudged him, whining, and he scratched the dog behind the ears.

What's going on? Madison wondered. Did Jason think Leesha had something to do with . . .

"Anyway," Fitch persisted. "Leesha's really helped out, and I wanted you to know. I know some of us haven't exactly . . . welcomed her back, but . . ."

"So what else is going on?" Jason broke in, still focusing on the dog.

Will shrugged. "Mercedes is building a magical wall around Trinity. Well, with a lot of help, I guess. Not that we've actually *seen* it, or anything."

"They're building a *wall*?" Jason looked from Will to Fitch. "Are you talking about the boundary?"

Will shrugged his shoulders in a *how should I know* way. "Guess it's different. Like a real wall. Real for the Weir, anyway."

"See, the thing is, Jason, they could really use your help," Fitch said. "I don't know much about it, but seems there's a real shortage of wizards. Mr. Hastings is still gone, and it's just Seph and Nick and Iris, and a few other wizards, doing it all. Jack's helping some, but once the warriors start manning the gate, he won't be around much. It takes a lot of magic, I guess, to prop up the wall."

"You need to come back with us," Fitch said. He smiled crookedly. "I'll tell you one thing—I don't want to be the one to tell Aunt Linda about her car."

Jason hesitated. Madison touched his hand and smiled at him encouragingly. "Seems like Barber's left, anyway," she said. "It's your call, but I think you should go."

He nodded. "Yeah. I think so, too." He actually looked relieved, like he'd been carrying around something heavy and just set it down.

"Seph wants you to come back, too, Madison," Fitch said.

Madison shook her head, feeling even lonelier than before Jason came. She was going to have to settle things once and for all with Brice Roper. And her mother. Somehow. "I can't leave. If Brice finds out I'm gone, he might have another go at the house. But tell Seph . . . I really miss him."

It was so lame. So inadequate. But it was all she had.

❧ CHAPTER TWENTY-TWO ❧
STRANGE BEDFELLOWS

Spring was usually a golden time at Raven's Ghyll. The bitter winter winds that roared down out of Scotland departed in favor of soft, spring breezes laden with the scent of high country flowers. Clear streams fed by melting snow tumbled out of the heights. Best of all, the tourists who plagued the rest of the Lake District in fine weather came nowhere near.

But this was a barren season. The tall grass that rippled across the ghyll withered and turned brown, beaten down by cold and unrelenting rains. Buds shriveled on the trees, reneging on their promise of flowers. Birds and wildlife disappeared. Most nights, the furnace in the cellar rattled into life, and the servants kindled the fire on the hearth in a vain effort to warm the sitting room. D'Orsay was forced to spell his servants to keep them from running off to friendlier climes. It would be risky to bring in new, who might be assassins working for the Roses. Wizard lights glittered on the surrounding hills, evidence that the Roses hadn't lifted their siege.

They'd heard nothing from Alicia Middleton and had consequently lost track of Warren Barber. Which might mean they were dead, the new Covenant taken or lost. As for the Dragonheart, D'Orsay had to assume it was still in the sanctuary. Unless the Roses held that also.

He and Dev rattled around Raven's Ghyll Castle, snapping at each other—they who had always got on so famously.

Then, finally, they had a message from the Roses. Not a demand for surrender, as D'Orsay expected, but a request for a meeting.

It took days to negotiate the terms. Would it be safer to hold it in Raven's Ghyll, or would that open the ghyll to invasion? Could the D'Orsays feel secure in a meeting outside of the ghyll? Would it be necessary to hold the meeting in the nude in order to prevent the smuggling in of _sefa_s?

Finally, the terms were nailed down, mostly because both sides were eager to meet and resolve the impasse. They met in a high meadow that overlooked the ghyll, a site scoured clean by both sides prior to the event.

It was usually a lovely spot in spring, starred with bluebells and buttercups. But now it was sere and silent, like the site of some horrible industrial accident.

It was an intimate gathering—D'Orsay and Devereaux, Jessamine Longbranch of the White Rose, and Geoffrey Wylie of the Red Rose. The last time they'd all been together had been at Second Sister—when D'Orsay and Leicester's coup against the Roses had nearly succeeded.

It was a spare meeting, without ceremony or hospitality, since neither side trusted the other enough to break bread together. They met in a tentlike pavilion with a planked wood floor covered in wool rugs.

"Jessamine. Pleasure." D'Orsay gripped her gloved hands and kissed her cheek. He nodded curtly to Wylie. "Geoffrey. This is my son, Devereaux."

Poor Dev hunched his shoulders and stuck his hands in his pockets. As usual, he was awkward and tongue-tied in company.

They settled into a circle of chairs. A grate at the center spilled welcome warmth into the chill.

"I don't ever remember it being this nasty up here in April," Jessamine said, shivering, despite her layers of leather and fur. "Can't you do something about it?" As if the weather were a failure of his hospitality.

"The weather is unusually cold," D'Orsay admitted. "But then, as the poet says, 'April is the cruelest month.' I assume you didn't come up here to discuss the weather. Except as it relates to other events."

Jess jumped on that like a trout on a mayfly. "What do you mean by that?"

"You first, my dear," D'Orsay said graciously.

"We know you have the Covenant," Jessamine said bluntly. "But you're unable to consecrate it."

D'Orsay tilted his head. "What makes you think that?"

"Because you would have already done so, if you could."

"All right," D'Orsay said, with the air of a man who is humoring difficult guests. "So why are you here? Why not just let us dwindle away into obscurity?"

"Because you hold the ghyll. The ghyll houses the Weirstone. And something's gone wrong."

"Wrong?" D'Orsay felt ludicrous, like the captain of a sinking ship, still manipulating the wheel as the deck sloshed under the waves.

Wylie lifted both hands, indicating their surroundings.

"Please. You are presiding over a wasteland, Claude. When I think of what it used to be . . ."

"Don't be overdramatic, Geoffrey," D'Orsay said. "This is merely the consequence of unusually foul weather and incompetent gardeners."

Longbranch pressed her fingers into her chest. "The Weirstone is dark. I can usually feel its presence, anywhere in Cumbria. And, now? Nothing." She shivered. "It's as if the source of our power has moved, as if it's at a great distance."

In point of fact, D'Orsay had already made his decision. Politics made strange bedfellows, and he was definitely running out of options. He needed to get out of the ghyll, or he and Dev might just slit each other's throats.

"I've noticed it, too," D'Orsay conceded. "It feels like true north has shifted, doesn't it?"

"The question is, why?" Wylie settled back in his seat

"Perhaps it's the effect of the siege," D'Orsay suggested. "What's it been, six months?"

"You could surrender," Longbranch suggested. "Just a thought."

D'Orsay looked up at the surrounding hills, at the wizard fires blazing there. "You could withdraw your forces."

"It's not because of the siege," Wylie said impatiently. "The shift in power was rather sudden. Back in midwinter, I believe."

"Do you really want to know who's responsible?" D'Orsay asked, emitting a bit of power to warm his feet.

"Who?" Longbranch leaned forward.

"Jason Haley."

"Jason Haley?" Wylie frowned. "The one from Second Sister?"

"The same."

"What about him?" Longbranch demanded.

"He stole the Dragonheart."

Longbranch and Wylie looked at each other. "What's that?" Wylie asked. "I never heard of it."

"The magical heart of the ghyll. A weapon of infinite capability. The source of power for all the Weirguilds."

"I never heard of it," Wylie repeated. "Don't tell me you believe those old stories about mythical beasts spitting flames. And even if you do, that was a long time ago."

"Whether I believe in dragons or not is irrelevant. The point is, the Dragonheart is a powerful *sefa* that sat under the Weirstone on my ancestral lands for centuries. Somehow, it fueled the Weirstone. The Weirstone is still there, but it's gone dark."

"So you knew this stone was there, all along?" Longbranch asked.

It was easier just to lie. "Yes," D'Orsay said. "But I've only recently become aware of its full power."

"Why *are* you telling them this, Father?" Devereaux demanded.

"It's all right, Dev," D'Orsay said, patting Dev on the shoulder. Dev flinched away.

"Why are you telling us?" Wylie asked suspiciously.

"Because the time has come for us to work together," D'Orsay said. "I'm trapped, as you know, in the ghyll. I need your cooperation in order to go after the stone."

"Do you have any idea where it is?" Wylie asked.

"In the sanctuary, I presume," D'Orsay said. "Unless they've moved it. For a time, I had an operative in Trinity. I know Haley returned there after looting the ghyll, and I did receive reports that magical items were hidden there."

"All right," Longbranch said. "Now that you've told us, why do we need your involvement? We can go and get the piece ourselves."

D'Orsay had anticipated this, also. "Two reasons," he said. "I hold the journal kept by the person who hid the stone in the ghyll, which provides details about its use. Powerful as it is, one doesn't want to make an error, does one?" Perhaps he was exaggerating the value of the journal a bit, but such was the nature of negotiation.

"And the second reason?"

"The Dragonheart is only one piece. Perhaps you've heard of the Raven's Ghyll hoard?"

"Another legend?" Wylie stuffed his hands into his pockets, shrugging his shoulders against the cold.

"Not at all. The hoard includes a treasure trove of magical artifacts and *sefa*s accumulated since the founding of the guilds."

"And we would need these because . . . ?" Longbranch feigned indifference, but her eyes glittered greedily.

"The Dragonheart is said to be the most powerful *sefa* known, capable of destroying us all. We don't know if the servant guilds realize how powerful it is, or how to use it. Still, it would seem prudent to go armed to any confrontation with them."

"If Hastings is involved, we can assume he has it sorted out," Wylie said, his mouth twisting in distaste.

"My operatives in Trinity tell me he's not there," Jessamine said. "Nor is Linda Downey."

"One wonders who is in charge," D'Orsay murmured.

"Snowbeard's there," Jessamine said. "Otherwise . . ." She

hesitated, then ticked them off on her gloved fingers. "It's the boy, McCauley, basically. And Iris Bolingame. Jason Haley seems to have disappeared. Perhaps there are other wizards. Jack Swift and Ellen Stephenson have organized an army of ghosts." She rolled her eyes.

"Eliminate McCauley, and the whole thing falls apart," Wylie said. "He would seem to be the strongest link."

How hard could it be? D'Orsay thought. "Don't you have anyone inside the sanctuary?" he asked delicately. "An all-out assault may not be the way to go."

"We've sent in assassins," Wylie said bluntly. "They never returned, never reported back. They must have been identified and eliminated immediately."

"McCauley seems to be well-protected," Longbranch mused. "He *is* just a boy, after all."

"You *sure* it's not Hastings?" D'Orsay asked, suppressing a shudder.

Wylie shook his head. "As far as we know, Hastings and Downey are somewhere in Europe."

They all glanced over their shoulders, as if the pair might at that moment be sneaking up on them.

"Well," Jessamine said, smiling, "perhaps we can just walk in and take it, then."

Now there were smiles all around.

The wind howled over the Ravenshead and the pavilion shuddered under its force. Fat droplets of rain splattered against the canvas. D'Orsay gestured, and the flames in the grate burned hotter.

"Father." Devereaux spoke up again. "Why should we give them anything? They've got nothing to trade."

Clever boy, D'Orsay thought fondly.

"We offer you the freedom to come and go," Jessamine said. "As your father no doubt realizes. If we secure the Dragonheart on our own, your Covenant is worthless. Join us, and we'll negotiate an amended Covenant that distributes power among us. It seems the stone has been the source of power all along, while we've been slaves to old myths and legends about dragons. There'll be no need to adhere to the old restrictions, to share power outside our circle." She fingered the emerald that hung around her neck. "The possibilities are limitless."

Claude D'Orsay smiled. It was a familiar playing field, at least. Another proposed wizard agreement involving terms to be negotiated later. With assassination and bloodshed, no doubt. And, given the fact that he held no cards at all, not even the Covenant, it was attractive.

"Surely we can work something out," D'Orsay said, looking at each of the players in turn.

"Father," Devereaux protested. "We can't just let . . ."

"Later, Dev," D'Orsay said, raising his hand.

Dev subsided, his hands twitching with irritation.

D'Orsay turned to the others. "My son and I will inventory the hoard and arrange for an in-person survey."

Following discussion of a few more logistics, the meeting broke up. The D'Orsays sent the Roses on their way, and set the servants to dismantling the pavilion. D'Orsay and Dev descended into the ghyll, eager to retire to the fireside in the castle.

"So," D'Orsay said, when they'd reached the valley floor, "You don't like the idea of sharing the hoard with the Roses."

"Why should we? It belongs to us. *Our* family."

"We have to get out of this bloody ghyll, Dev. Whatever

the Dragonheart is, whatever it does, we have to get it back. Then, we're players. We've not heard from Alicia in weeks. So it's not likely we can succeed without the Roses."

"What do you think happened to that girl? Alicia?"

"Hard to say. It's risky out there, Dev. That's why I've kept you close."

"*She* goes wherever she likes. *She* does whatever she pleases," Devereaux said enviously.

"And *she* may very well be dead," D'Orsay replied testily. What had gotten into Dev lately?

Dev paused at the foot of the gardens leading up to the castle. "That's weird," he said. "The drawbridge is up and the gate is shut."

D'Orsay blinked away rain and peered up at the castle. The drawbridge had been little more than a decorative piece since the signing of the Covenant centuries ago.

In fact, he'd last closed the drawbridge the night Jason Haley broke into the ghyll. After all, he had wards and sentries to warn him of danger.

The drawbridge was closed now.

"What the devil?" D'Orsay muttered. "Perhaps Stephen is being overzealous tonight, given our visitors."

"Well, he should be looking out for us," Dev said. "He should have noticed we were coming, and opened the gate." Dev was intolerant of poor service from the staff. He began speed-walking up the road, probably meaning to give Stephen a piece of his mind.

"Devereaux! Wait!" D'Orsay hissed, but the boy was already way out ahead of him. D'Orsay was puffing by the time he reached the garden shed near the top of the garden. He leaned on the wall of the shed, glancing inside as he did so, and noticed, tucked beneath one of the benches, a body, stripped to its undergarments. And, further in, another.

D'Orsay peered into the dim interior, disbelieving his eyes. "Stephen?" he muttered. Then he turned and sprinted after his son, who was out of sight by now. When he topped the hill, he saw Dev standing on the near side of the moat, shouting up to the gatehouse.

"Stephen! Open up, you pathetic imbecile, or I'll . . ."

"Devereaux!" D'Orsay bellowed. "Come away!" He slammed his son aside just as a blast of wizard fire erupted from the gatehouse and scorched the ground where Dev had been standing.

D'Orsay thew up a shield in time to turn three more attacks from his own hold. Had the Roses taken advantage of their absence from the hold to sneak unobserved into the ghyll? Had his guard turned on him?

Wards were crystallizing all about the fortifications, powerful barriers to any magic that might be used to bring down the walls. Not that D'Orsay intended to knock down his house if he could help it.

They retreated to a safe distance. Dev was shaken but unhurt. He quickly added his strength to D'Orsay's shielding. "What's happened, Father? Has that idiot Stephen gone berserk?"

"Stephen is dead, Dev. I found him in the garden."

"Stephen? Dead?" Dev's eyes widened. "That's horrid. I can't believe it."

Just then a dozen guardsmen in D'Orsay livery trotted up. "What's going on, sir?" the officer gasped. "We saw flames from down below."

"I would expect that *you* could have told *me*, if you'd

been at your posts where you belonged," D'Orsay said dryly. "Where have you been?"

"We . . . um . . ." They looked at each other and shuffled their feet. Obviously no one wanted to be the one to confess. Finally the captain spoke up.

"My lord, we heard a woman singing, and went to check it out."

"You heard a woman singing." D'Orsay paused, just in case he'd misunderstood, and the captain nodded. "And you—*all* of you—went to investigate."

"Well." The captain fussed with his sleeve. "Yes. It was . . . well, you'd have to hear it for yourself."

"Bewitched, were you? And did you find this woman?"

He shook his head. "We found this." He held out his hand, and a small crystal bird sparkled in the center of his calloused palm.

D'Orsay struck it out of his hand. "An enchanter's trick. And you fell for it. And now *someone* has locked me out of my own home."

And then it came to him, a suspicion of who that some-one might be.

D'Orsay turned back toward the castle, cupped his hands, and shouted, "Hastings!" He waited, and then repeated, "Hastings! I know it's you, so you may as well show yourself!"

A moment later, he heard a woman's amused voice from the parapet. "Leander, why is it you always get the credit for everything?"

They stepped out onto the wall walk, side-by-side, iced in magic—the tall wizard and the small enchanter, looking like a Romeo and Juliet in climbing gear.

Or the new lord and lady of the manor.

Linda Downey. *And* Leander Hastings. And Claude D'Orsay had them trapped in the ghyll.

That was one way to look at it.

D'Orsay turned to his guard. "Surround the hold," he snapped. "They mustn't be allowed to escape."

"Oh, we have no intention of escaping," Hastings said. "We like it here."

"There is no way the two of you can hold the keep against an army," D'Orsay said, trying to sound convincing.

"Who says there are just two of us?" Downey replied. "And it seems amazingly well-built. Are there any weaknesses we should know about?"

D'Orsay very nearly told her before he caught himself. Her voice was like a song that insinuates itself into your mind until you find yourself humming along.

Damn her! The Master of the Games generally preferred to keep his distance from violence by delegating it. But just then he would have welcomed the opportunity to rend the pair of them into little bits. Personally. By hand.

The worst of it was that, with the exception of a few caches of choice pieces that D'Orsay kept elsewhere in the ghyll, the lion's share of the hoard of magical weapons was in the inner keep of Raven's Ghyll Castle—now in Downey and Hasting's possession, and no longer accessible to D'Orsay and his new allies. There was the risk that the Roses would be unimpressed with what little he would be able to deliver—his contribution to the cause.

"We'll starve you out!" he blustered, though he was not one to make empty threats.

"It appears that will take some time," Hastings said. "My

compliments on your wine cellar, Claude." He paused. "In fact, I'm finding your cellar very . . . intriguing."

He'd found the hoard, then. It was heavily warded, but, still . . . it *was* Leander Hastings. Soon enough, he'd be using the *sefa*s against them.

"Where will you be staying in the meantime?" Downey asked sweetly. "In case someone calls?"

Dev pressed forward, and D'Orsay grabbed his arm, hauling him back. "No, Dev, they are trying to make you do something foolish."

"Make them leave!" Dev's face was white with fury. "That is *our home*!"

"Never mind, Dev." He turned to his captain. "I want a twenty-four-hour guard on this castle. No one enters or leaves without my permission. Anyone left alive inside, stays there." He paused. "And, damn it, next time you hear someone singing, stop up your ears."

"Where will we live, Father?" Dev asked, shoulders slumped dejectedly. "All my *things* are in there."

D'Orsay patted his son on the back. "You've wanted to leave here, anyway. So, we'll gather up the weapons we can salvage, and go on to Trinity. I think it best that we're there to keep an eye on our new allies.

"You see, I believe Hastings and Downey have made a tactical error in coming here. Possession of the hoard is unimportant next to possession of the Dragonheart. With Hastings and Downey in the hold, the rebels have lost two of their most effective agents. We'll see how the children do on their own, hmmm?"

⊗ CHAPTER TWENTY-THREE ⊗
AN ULTIMATUM

"Jack."

Jack Swift paused with his hand on the latch of the back door and looked back up the stairs. His mother stood on the landing, gazing down at him.

"Where are you off to?" she asked.

That was a difficult question to answer, since he was off to pull guard duty at the Weirgate, where his job was to prevent the unfettered coming and going of spies, assassins, and would-be magical thieves. He blessed the fact that Shadowslayer was hidden in the duffle bag slung over his back.

"I'm . . . going hiking. At Perry Park." The Weirgate was within Perry Park, the largest tract of unbroken forest in the sanctuary.

Becka descended the steps until she was at a level where she could look him in the eyes. "Okay if I come along? It's been a long time since we've been hiking together."

"Well. That would be . . ." *A disaster.* "That'd be great, except we're going rock climbing. At the gorge. It's a technical climb. You wouldn't like it."

She crossed her arms. "Okay. I'll be more direct. What's going on?"

"Going on?"

Becka hesitated. Nagging didn't come naturally to her. "Harold's complaining that you haven't been around to prep the boats for the season. He's had to hire another full-time captain to keep both boats in service. Seph's quit working at the docks altogether. Jason, too."

She sighed, an exasperated sound. "You'll be graduating in a few weeks. I'd think you'd want to earn money this summer. Or get a head start on your classes. Or do you want to go to Boston and work with your father?"

"No," Jack said quickly. "I want to stay here."

"And do what?" She paused, and when Jack didn't answer, said, "I feel responsible for all three of you with Linda out of town." A hint of judgement crept in. "Even though *she* seems to think Seph and Jason are fine on their own. I haven't seen Jason for weeks. And he hasn't been at school, either, from what I understand."

Official-looking notices from the attendance office at the high school had been arriving regularly at Aunt Linda's, addressed to *Parent or Guardian of Jason Haley.*

Here was one piece of good news he could give her. "Jason's back, Mom. He got back two days ago. He . . . uh . . . was visiting Madison in Coalton County."

"In the middle of the semester?" She lifted an eyebrow.

"Yeah, well, then he came down with something."

"You know how important attendance is. Mr. Penworthy will be all over him."

"He was. All over him, I mean. Jason was in the attendance office all morning." Jack couldn't help thinking there was a reason why the classical heroes didn't have lawyers for mothers.

"It's not like you're lying around at home playing video games. In fact, you're never home." She reached out and put her hands on his shoulders. "On the plus side, it's obvious you're getting your exercise. And I haven't heard any reports of all-night parties on the beach."

Ironically enough, that would be harder to get away with in a small town than building a magical fortress. Linda and Hastings weren't the only ones with an intelligence network centered in Trinity. Information flowed to Becka Downey from all over town.

As if she'd read his thoughts, Becka leaned against the banister and said, "Bill Childers says he's afraid you and Will had a falling out." Will's father, the newly elected mayor of Trinity, was one of Becka's regular contacts and closest friends.

"What? No, we're fine," Jack said. "It's just been kind of crazy with Will's work schedule. Plus he's on the soccer team and there's practice and . . . everything."

"That's another thing. You didn't even go out for the team this year." She paused, and when he didn't speak, continued. "Why not? You love soccer, or you used to."

"I just . . . I just didn't think I had the time, with my classes."

"Bill asked if Ellen had been spending time over here. I guess she's among the missing, too." Ellen lived with Will's family.

"Yeah. We've . . . um . . . been spending a lot of time together. Hiking." Jack snuck a glance at his watch. He and Ellen were sharing the next shift on the wall, and she'd be on his butt if he was late. She was totally into military discipline when it came to the security of the sanctuary.

"Has Ellen decided what she's going to do next fall?"

"Hmmm? Oh. She's still thinking about it."

"I'm worried about her. She's so bright, and has so much *potential*. But she doesn't seem to be considering her future at all." Becka brushed dust off the newel post with the hem of her T-shirt. "If money's an issue, let me make a few calls. I'll see to it that she has the funds she needs to go to college."

And she would, too. All his life, his mother had been taking in strays.

She was also a pacifist. So he didn't know how to tell her that, absent the impending crisis in Trinity, Ellen's obvious vocational outlet was a post in a magical mercenary army.

"You know visit day at Trinity College is tomorrow."

Oops.

"Do I really need to go? I feel like I've spent my life on that campus. I could probably lead the tour and give the dirty lowdown about most of the faculty."

Becka laughed. "I'm sure you could. But this time you'll be there in a different role." She paused. "I hate to admit it, but your father might be right. About going away for school, I mean, Ivy League or not."

"Mom, I . . ."

Becka plowed on. "You've lived here all your life. You've never known anything else. To be honest, I'm surprised you want to go to Trinity. I know living in a small town gets on your nerves. Sometimes you have to go somewhere else to appreciate what we have here."

"I do appreciate what we have here," Jack said desperately. "I don't want to go away to school. Trinity's fine."

"Listen to yourself. 'Trinity's fine.' When I was your age, I couldn't wait to go away to school. I wanted to be as far away from my parents as possible. I wanted to live in awful student housing and immerse myself in the English poets and stay out all night." She frowned and bit her lip. "All right. Forget that last part."

He did his best to avoid the explicit lie. "I feel like this year is like—you know—a turning point. Like nothing is ever going to be the same. Fitch is going to Stanford. Will's going to Ohio State. I know they'll be home for holidays and stuff, but still."

He looked down at the floor, avoiding her eyes. "Seph and Ellen and Jason and I—we're just trying to find our way. I want to get through the summer before I make plans for the rest of my life. I hope you can just—you know—trust me."

He looked at her. "Believe me. I don't think my future will hinge on whether I get into Harvard Law School."

She studied his face, then nodded. "All right. I'll give you some space. But I do want you to go down to the registrar's office tomorrow and sign up for classes. You can always drop, but deciding you want to go in September won't get you into a closed section."

"Okay." He shifted from one foot to the other, conscious of Shadowslayer's weight across his back. "Thanks, Mom. See you later."

Moving at a trot, trying to make up for lost time, Jack

cut across campus on his way to Perry Park. Ivy-covered buildings clustered around grassy quads. Tall trees shaded the stone walkways that quilted the greens. It was a place to be sequestered from the outside world. But, the outside world had a way of intruding into Jack's life.

Despite his rapid pace, he was intercepted before he made it into the margin of the trees. Will Childers appeared on one side of him and Harmon Fitch on the other. They were wearing athletic shorts and soccer jerseys, carrying duffles, and he knew they'd just come from soccer practice. He felt a twinge of envy.

"Hey, there, Jack," Fitch said, keeping step with him, despite Jack's longer stride. "What's up?"

"Long time no see," Will added.

"That's not true," Jack said. Must be "catch up with Jack" day, he thought.

"Fitch, do you think he knows we're going away in another three months or so?"

"Couldn't possibly, Will. Otherwise he'd be more attentive to old friends. Nostalgic about old times. Anticipating the big good-bye."

"So where you off to, Jack?" Will asked, tugging at Jack's duffle bag. "War games in the woods?"

"How can we help?" Fitch asked. "We fetched Jason back. Now what else can we do?"

"This isn't . . ."

"I know," Will said, holding up his hand to stop the speech. "This isn't our fight. It's only taking place in our town and involves all our friends. Let's pretend we argued about this and finally agreed that it *is* our fight."

"Well," Jack said, giving in. "Come on. I'll show you what

Ellen and I have been up to." Not that there'd be much for them to see.

Perry Park straddled the city limits of Trinity. Mercedes had located the Weirgate deep in the woods in the hopes the traffic would be less noticeable to the nonmagical citizens. Nick Snowbeard had built a barrier around the gate meant to turn the average Anaweir hiker away. It was a confusion charm with a bit of structure to it. Jack had to create an opening for Will and Fitch. Still, passage through the barrier was not particularly pleasant for them.

"This reminds me of Raven's Ghyll," Will said, shivering.

Fitch turned so pale the freckles stood out on his face. "Why does it have to be so nasty?"

"It's just ahead here," Jack said, pointing Will and Fitch in the right direction.

"What?" Fitch peered ahead, into the trees. "Where?"

"It's right there," Jack said, gesturing. "It's finally finished. It's—oh—about forty feet tall and fifteen feet wide. We're going to the gate." Jack unzipped his duffel and pulled out Shadowslayer.

Will looked back at him suspiciously, as if he might be the butt of a joke. "We're supposed to believe there's a wall there."

Jack nodded, swinging his sword experimentally, feeling the usual thrill of connection with Shadowslayer. The blade glittered in the light that filtered down through the trees.

"I saw the other barrier wall thingy. At Raven's Ghyll," Fitch said. "But I don't see this one."

"That's because this one is just for the gifted. They're the only ones who can see it. You can pass right through." He strapped on his baldric and slid his sword into its scabbard.

"Remember when Seph first came to Trinity, and those wizards put up a barrier to keep him out? Same kind of thing."

But it was not the same kind of thing, not at all. Warren Barber had built a monster spiderweb around Trinity meant to catch Seph McCauley. It was utilitarian—woven of snake-like tendrils that would grab you when you tried to cut through.

But Mercedes couldn't bear to create anything that didn't add beauty to the world. So this wall was an elegant structure—like the crystalline rampart of some fairy castle, iced with crenelations, finials, towers, and turrets. Banners bearing the Silver Dragon flew from the towers.

The gate was in an impressive barbican that jutted from the wall. Jack could hear Ellen before she came into view.

"Come ahead and try me," she shouted. "Who wants to be first?"

Jack heard the music of her blade as she swung it.

This was followed by a garbled hiss of wizard voices.

Jack slid Shadowslayer free and barged through the arch-way to find Ellen, Waymaker in her hand, confronting four pissed wizards.

Ellen looked pale, stubborn, and more than a little shaken. For good reason. Lined up against her were Ellen's former warriormaster, Geoffrey Wylie of the Red Rose, and Jack's old surgeon and would-be warriormaster, Jessamine Longbranch of the White Rose. His fingers crept to the spot on his chest where she'd made her incision, saving his life and changing it forever.

Unbelievably, there was also Claude D'Orsay, Gregory

Leicester's co-conspirator who'd made his play at Second Sister to wrest control of the guilds from the Roses. What was he doing hanging out with them now?

With D'Orsay was a fair-haired boy, maybe fourteen, who was taking everything in with avid interest. Now and then D'Orsay leaned down and said something to the kid, as if explaining.

Some kind of apprentice monster? Jack wondered.

It was like one of those scenes where you confront the demons from your past. He never thought he'd see leaders from both Wizard Houses working together. Let alone come to reconciliation with Claude D'Orsay. It gave Jack chills.

"So glad you could make it," Ellen muttered through gritted teeth as Jack took his place next to her. The wizards shuffled themselves, each trying to move to the back. None seemed eager to go up against Shadowslayer.

"Where were you?" Ellen demanded.

"I got hung up at home. My mom wants to know where we're spending all our time and if you're going to college."

"Oh. What'd you tell her?"

The wizards edged forward. Jack blasted flame through the tip of his blade, driving them back. "I said we were trying to find our way."

Ellen nodded, grudgingly. "That was good."

Actually, Jack thought as a group the wizards looked kind of sick and beaten down. But they seemed jazzed, too, like they'd just seen the cure coming over the hill. They kept looking toward the center of town, like filings lined up against a powerful magnet, though Claude D'Orsay kept himself somewhat aloof.

Jessamine Longbranch finally shouldered her way to the front.

"Jackson. I'm glad you're here," she said, flinging back her mane of black hair. "This warrior refuses to admit us into the sanctuary. Tell her to step aside before I do something irreversible."

"Losing your head," Ellen snapped back. "*That's* irreversible." Waymaker sang in a broad arc, showering sparks over the wizard party. Longbranch jumped back, nearly falling.

"New rules, Dr. Longbranch," Jack said. "The sanctuary's closed until further notice."

"By whose order?" Wylie demanded. The wizard's voice had a dry, hissing quality, like air escaping from a tire, and his scarred face was twisted up in a scowl.

"The sanctuary board," Jack replied.

"Rubbish," Wylie said. "Wizards are slaughtering each other all over the world. We haven't time to deal with the servant guilds." He made as if to brush past. Jack thrust the wizard back with a concussion of air, landing him flat on his back.

Jack extended Shadowslayer, pressing the point into Wylie's neck until blood trickled down. The other wizards stirred disapprovingly, muttering among themselves. Wylie stared at the blade, his eyes wide and kind of crossed.

"Next time I go deeper," Jack said, lifting Shadowslayer away from Wylie and stepping back. He shivered. What was happening to him? He remembered a time when the notion of drawing blood seemed unthinkable.

Longbranch glanced down at Wylie as if she didn't mind seeing him butt-down on the turf, then looked up at Jack.

"You've always been so delightfully physical, Jack." She said this like he was some kind of volatile barbarian curiosity. "Now. We demand to speak with the *wizard* in charge about this new policy."

A new voice said, "That would be me."

Heads turned.

Seph McCauley hadn't dressed the part (he wore a black T-shirt and jeans), but Jack had to admit he had a certain presence about him that made you take him seriously. More and more, he reminded Jack of Hastings. It went beyond his looks—it was the aura of power he had, or maybe the intensity that seemed barely contained within his skin.

"*You're* in charge?" Longbranch studied Seph with narrowed eyes.

"Well." Seph shrugged modestly. "Of security, anyway."

"So it's true. This place is actually being run by upstart adolescents."

Seph half smiled. "If it was a matter of age, they'd have picked the oldest person."

Wylie struggled to his feet, brushing at his clothes, giving Jack a poisonous look that said he'd be sorry some day.

But not today. Jack had received so many of those looks from wizards he'd just have to put it on account.

Nick Snowbeard was there. Just like that. He'd always had the amazing ability to appear out of thin air. It wasn't that he moved quicker than light. It was like you just hadn't noticed him up until then.

"Jessamine. Geoffrey. Please," the old wizard said. "Stop wasting our time and tell us what the devil you want."

Longbranch looked toward the center of town, where the bell tower of St. Catherine's poked up above the trees. Then back at Nick. "These young warriors are denying us entrance."

Nick nodded. "That's their job. Per orders of the board and Seph as master of security."

"You can't do that," Wylie snarled. "We have as much right to enter as anyone."

"What's up?" Heads swiveled again. Jason Haley walked out of the trees.

"So," D'Orsay said softly, but loud enough for Jack to hear. "You *are* here." The blond boy next to him tapped D'Orsay on the arm and pointed at Jason, whispering something to the Master of Games.

"Well, well. Jason Haley," Wylie said, looking Jason over like you might an old girlfriend you maybe shouldn't have broken up with. "I haven't seen you since Second Sister."

"Right," Jason said. "When Seph and I saved your butts." He turned, and stumbled back a step, pretending to spot D'Orsay for the first time. "D'Orsay! And little D'Orsay! So far from home? What gives?" He smiled, crocodilelike.

D'Orsay inclined his head and said, "Mr. Haley," eyes glittering, looking just as predatory.

Jason looked from Longbranch and Wylie to D'Orsay and back again. "Whoa, this can't be right. You're with them?" He pressed the back of his hand to his forehead, as if checking for fever. "Hold on, is this a dream?"

"If you will not admit us, we will require a meeting," Longbranch said, trying her best to ignore Jason.

"We-ell, forgive and forget, right?" Jason grinned.

". . . with *whomever* is in a position to negotiate," Longbranch continued doggedly.

"Hey, D'Orsays, I'd watch my back, if I was you," Jason

went on. "Lock my doors, change the password, hire a taster, all that. That's the great thing about wizards, you never know from day to day who's with you or what."

"All *right*, Jess," Nick said. He seemed to be fighting off a smile. "We'll admit you for a meeting." He looked at Seph. "What do you suggest?"

"No more than three wizards," Seph said, looking over the players. "No *sefa*s."

"Surely Devereaux can come along," D'Orsay said. "He's just a boy, after all, and I hate to leave him on his own."

Seph hesitated, then nodded. "All right. Jack, Ellen, maybe we should bring up a few more warriors to fortify the gate."

Jason noticed that Longbranch and Wylie kept sneaking looks at him all the way to the pavilion. You could almost see the wheels turning, which was weird, because most wizards had no difficulty smiling to your face while they reached around and stabbed you in the back.

D'Orsay kept Devereaux close by his side, as if Jason might attack him, given the slightest opening. Jason smiled at the two of them in his most non-reassuring way.

They arranged themselves around a redwood picnic table.

"So," Nick said, steepling his gnarled fingers on the table-top. "What's this all about?"

Longbranch brushed a redwood splinter from her palm. "The wizard world is in chaos. Assassinations, robberies, pitched battles. Some of the hoards have been broken into and weapons stolen. It's every wizard for herself. The rule of law has been forgotten. Yet when we come to the sanctuary, we find it closed to us."

Seph cleared his throat, the corners of his mouth

twitching. "Um. Are you saying you're here as . . . refugees?"

"We're saying we all need to work together to restore order to the guilds," Wylie put in smoothly.

"The need to restore peace has already brought former enemies together," D'Orsay said virtuously, gesturing toward Wylie and Longbranch. "We are hoping that you will agree to join with us, also."

Next thing you know, they'll break into a chorus of "Kumbaya," Jason thought, drumming his fingers on the table.

"And then what happens?" Jason asked.

Wylie straightened his sleeves, playing for time. "What do you mean?"

"Who's in charge?"

"I'm sure we can come to a . . . satisfactory shared governance arrangement," Longbranch said, arching her dark brows.

"Did you have something specific in mind when you say we should work together?" Nick asked.

The three wizards looked at each other. Of course they did.

D'Orsay spoke for the first time. "We know that Haley broke into Raven's Ghyll and stole some important magical artifacts—*sefa*s that have been in our family for generations." D'Orsay looked at Jason as if he might break down and confess.

"Artifacts that by rights belong to all of us," Wylie put in. "We have reason to believe that they are here in the sanctuary."

"So what's the point?" Nick asked, his legendary patience dwindling. "What do you want?"

"We want what was taken from the ghyll," Longbranch said. "We want the Dragonheart."

It was like she'd dropped a bomb in the middle of the table. Everyone sat frozen, studying each other.

"The Dragonheart," Seph said, slowly and deliberately. "And that is . . ."

"It's the weapon of the age," Wylie snapped. "Incredibly powerful."

"Really?" Jason leaned forward. "Who told you that?"

"We have the book that you dropped in the ghyll when you attacked my son," D'Orsay said, patting little Devereaux on the shoulder.

"It was more like he jumped me," Jason said.

"While you were *trespassing*." Devereaux half rose from his seat. "You're a *thief*, is what you are."

"Devereaux, now is not the time," D'Orsay murmured, pulling his son down into his chair. Devereaux jerked his arm free, scowling.

D'Orsay pretended not to notice. "The journal very clearly says that anyone who controls the Dragonheart will rule the guilds. Or destroy them."

"We'll use it to restore order," Longbranch said. "And ensure a lasting peace."

"Restore order," Nick said thoughtfully. "A tricky business, to be sure."

"Don't try to deny that it's here," Longbranch said, cheeks flushed, as if she were overheated. "We can feel its presence. Surely you realize that things can't go on as they have. And, once things are stabilized, everyone at this table will have a role to play." Her gaze swept over them all.

Yeah, Jason thought. I'll be playing the cadaver. One among many.

"If we had a weapon," Seph said, "why would we share it with you?"

Wylie smiled. "Powerful *sefa*s must be handled with delicacy and skill. Otherwise it is riskier to use them than to let them be. We're willing to take that risk for you."

"Generous," Nick murmured. "Do you have any idea how to use the Dragonheart? Or will it be a stab in the dark?"

"Not a worry," D'Orsay said, with breezy confidence. "The text provided detailed and explicit instructions."

"I don't remember seeing that," Jason said. He'd had just a quick look, but the Dragonheart hadn't even been mentioned until the last page, when the dragon was dead and her servant dying.

"You must have overlooked it," D'Orsay said, while Longbranch and Wylie eyed him suspiciously.

"So," Wylie said. "I think you can see that it's in your best interest to cooperate. Otherwise, we can make life most uncomfortable."

"If we were to hand you an incredibly powerful weapon," Nick said, "it seems to me you could go way beyond uncomfortable."

Longbranch's eyes glittered with irritation. "Let me be plain. Give us the Dragonheart, and you will rule the guilds alongside us. Refuse, and we will destroy this town and everything and everyone in it. Down to the smallest child and family pet."

So much for "Kumbaya," Jason thought.

Nick stood abruptly, a signal that the meeting was at an end. "We let you come in and speak your piece. Now I'll speak mine." He paused, looking around the table. "Be careful who you threaten, or you may find yourself on the receiving end of a power you cannot even imagine."

"What are you saying?" Wylie blustered. "You don't even . . ."

Seph unfolded to his full height, a deadly snake uncoiling. "What we're saying is: if you attack the sanctuary, *we will use the Dragonheart*. It'll be the last mistake you'll ever make."

Longbranch rose and signaled to Wylie. "If it comes to war, nobody within the walls survives." She shot a venomous look at Will and Fitch, standing at the periphery. "And that includes your family and your Anaweir friends."

Nick raised his hand impatiently to stop the flow of ultimatums. "Jason. Could you show our visitors to the gate?"

Jason nodded and stood. "Be my pleasure."

They walked back toward the gate, Jason and Longbranch side by side and Wylie, D'Orsay, and Devereaux out ahead. Longbranch slowed her pace to put more distance between them.

They were scarcely out of earshot of the others when Longbranch turned on Jason. "You seem like a rather clever young man," she said. "And yet, you were sent to do the risky job at Raven's Ghyll while McCauley and Snowbeard and Hastings give the orders."

Jason looked straight ahead. "I . . . um . . . volunteered."

"Why?"

"I have my reasons."

She put her hand on his arm and he felt the bite of power. He swung around and they stood, facing each other, shrouded in a circle of trees.

"The stone belongs to you, by rights," Longbranch said.

"*You* brought it out of the ghyll. *You* should be the one who benefits from it."

Jason said nothing. The stone was never far from his thoughts, and it was even more intoxicating now that it was within reach.

Encouraged by his silence, Longbranch pressed on. "What do you want? You could rise in the hierarchy, if that suits you. Or, you could avoid politics and live like a king with a retinue of enchanters, sorcerers, and Anaweir to serve you. We can offer you unlimited access to whatever makes you happy."

"Whatever makes me happy?"

"Yes," Longbranch whispered, leaning close. "What is it you want?"

"D'Orsay."

Longbranch blinked at him, momentarily speechless. "What?"

"I want D'Orsay. That's why I volunteered to go to the ghyll." Jason smiled crookedly. "But, then, you've been trying to get at him for months without success. I got closer than you ever did, and I got out alive. So I've got no reason to think you can deliver."

Longbranch glanced at Wylie and D'Orsay, then looked back at Jason and smiled. This time it was sincere. "Don't worry about that. You get me the Dragonheart, and I can deliver D'Orsay."

⤜ CHAPTER TWENTY-FOUR ⤛
FOOL

Leesha knew the footprint of the apartment by heart. She'd paced it out a thousand times, from the door that led to the outside and freedom, through the efficient kitchen, past the sitting area, and into the tiny bedroom beyond. Every room lined with bookcases. Every bookcase full of books.

She slept on a futon on the third floor, in the workroom with its racks of scrolls and bins of mysterious gunk and bottles of stinky potions. The worktables were piled with manuscripts, blueprints, unidentified magical objects, and odd machines.

The old man had told her what was off-limits, and, after two weeks, she knew better than to touch any of it. She sucked her blistered fingers absently, picked up nonforbidden objects and set them down again. The high point of the day was when Jack's mother, Becka, came out of the house, got into her car, and drove away.

She even missed Aunt Milli. Although living with her

could be terrifying in its own way, her aunt had always given Leesha the gift of time and attention she'd had from no one else.

Still, she knew in her heart that there were far worse things than being hidden away in Nick Snowbeard's thoroughly warded apartment over the garage.

Barber was out there somewhere. At least, now, with the wall up, he couldn't pass freely in and out of town. Hopefully, he thought she was dead. Even here, in the heart of the sanctuary, she found herself flinching at small noises and waking in the middle of the night in a cold sweat.

Every time she thought of Jason, it made her sick to her stomach, which meant she felt nauseous nearly all the time. A memory came back to her—the sun glittering down through snowy pine trees, the tiny ruffled owl, Jason's brilliant blue eyes and his eagerness to show her something new.

"It would be cool if we could just be together," he'd said, in a way that didn't try to claim anything more from her than her company.

How could she have given him to Barber? Why couldn't there be do-overs in life?

She wasn't used to guilt. She was used to being a player. She was used to having options, always planning her next move. She could look for other allies—Longbranch and Wylie, for instance. She could go back to D'Orsay. The Dragonheart could be her ticket into their good graces.

She could feel its constant pull, night and day, a tether to her Weirstone. It was like the stone had woken up, and its burgeoning power pulsed throughout the sanctuary.

Finding it wasn't the problem, even though it was no

doubt heavily warded. *Her* problem was, she was immobilized, weighed down by loss. She didn't care to be a player any more.

As if her thoughts had called the devil, she heard a noise in the garage. Then the slow, measured sound of feet on the stairs. A key rattled in the lock and the door flew back.

It was Snowbeard. The old man stood in the doorway, parcels in his hands, his smile turning to puzzlement. "Are you well, Alicia?"

She swallowed down her fear. "How do you think I am?" she whispered.

"Ah." He shuffled forward, dropping the keys into a dish by the door and setting a bakery bag and a tin of tea on the table. "Were you not able to amuse yourself?"

Which made her feel like it was her fault she was bored. "Amuse myself? How?"

Snowbeard put the kettle on, reached a plate down from the cupboard over the sink, and arranged some sinful-looking brownies on it. "Did you try any of the books I left you?"

She shook her head, her eyes on the brownies. "I couldn't concentrate."

"A shame. They are some of my favorites. I was hoping we could discuss them this evening." He gestured toward the table. "Please. Sit. We'll have supper in a little while, but I believe we should eat dessert first. Would you like tea, coffee, soda?"

Somehow she said, "Tea," and moved to the table and sat.

She bit into a brownie. She was glad she had a wizard's metabolism. The old man brought killer sweets home every day.

When the kettle shrilled, he brought it to the table and poured, then sat down himself.

Leesha blew on her tea and reached for another brownie. "I can't stand it," she said. "Not knowing what's going on, I mean."

"Well, let's see. We met with Wylie, Longbranch, and D'Orsay today," Snowbeard said.

Leesha choked on her tea, splattering it on the table.

Snowbeard pretended not to notice.

Leesha dabbed at the tablecloth with her napkin. "All of them together?"

The old man nodded. "It seems they've found common ground."

They all hated Alicia Middleton, for one. "What did they . . . what did they say?"

"They requested permission to enter the sanctuary."

Leesha gripped her teacup. "And you said . . . ?"

"We declined."

"Did they say why they wanted in?"

"They want the Dragonheart."

"The Dra . . . what's that?"

Snowbeard shook his head, looking disappointed. "Please."

She bristled. "I don't care what anyone says, I never . . ." Her voice trailed off as the old man's eyes nailed her to the chair. She swallowed hard. "So now what?"

He shrugged and rested his wrinkled hands on the table. "They've threatened to destroy us all."

"What'd you say?" Leesha asked, fascinated in spite of herself.

"Basically, we told them to come and try." Snowbeard

grinned, and actually looked kind of boyish.

"Wow, you're . . . um . . . confident."

Snowbeard rubbed the side of his nose. "We have weapons they've never dreamed of."

"What are you going to do about me?" Leesha watched the old man, hoping he'd give away his intentions. They would kill her. She knew they would. She had no idea why she was alive, even now, unless they were waiting for Hastings. She'd helped with the wall, but that wouldn't matter when you weighed things out. She'd kidnapped Will and Fitch, betrayed Jason, and failed to deliver Barber.

Of course, they didn't exactly know about Jason.

"The existence of the Dragonheart and its presence in the sanctuary is common knowledge, it seems. Therefore, you have no information that can harm us. So. You have a choice, my dear. You can leave the sanctuary and go where you will."

"You'd let me go?" Leesha burst out.

Snowbeard smiled blandly. "With the stipulation that you never return."

Leesha turned this over like she might a precious stone, looking for flaws. "My enemies will murder me," she said. "Barber and Dr. Longbranch."

"I think you may find that they are . . . otherwise occupied . . . in the short term, at least. It might be a good time to disappear."

Leesha nodded. "Okay. You said I had a choice. What's my other option?"

"You can stay here, as you have been."

She indicated the tiny apartment with a sweep of her arm. "I'll die of boredom if I stay here any longer." Die of guilt, more like. She needed something to do, something to distract her from thinking about Jason.

Snowbeard's mouth twitched. "Don't worry. If you stay we *will* find something for you to do."

"Why would you let me stay?" Leesha was genuinely curious.

"Well," Snowbeard said, "given your history, there's something to be said for having you where we can see you. And wizards, especially, are in short supply." He paused. "Before you make your decision, there's something you should know. Jason came back two nights ago."

For a moment, Leesha thought she was going to faint for real (she'd faked fainting dozens of times.) All the blood left her head and traveled wherever blood goes when you've had a shock.

If she hadn't been sitting down, she would have collapsed. "J-J-Jason's *back*? He's *alive*? He's *okay*?" She practically screamed it.

"Well, yes, to all three."

"I can't believe it!" Impulsively, Leesha hugged the old man (not the kind of thing she normally did), then drew back and eyed him suspiciously. "You wouldn't lie to me, would you?"

"No. I wouldn't." Snowbeard studied her shrewdly. "Though Jason did have a rather nasty encounter with Warren Barber."

There was a long pause. He *knows*, Leesha thought. The geezer knows. But she was too happy to care. "Well. Did Jason . . . say anything about me?"

"I think you two will need to talk between yourselves," Snowbeard said.

Even that prospect failed to dampen her spirits. In the

end, it might do her little good that Jason was still alive, yet it totally cheered her.

In the back of her mind, a voice crowed, *Do-over*.

Maybe.

"Should you decide to stay, I should point out that you can't change your mind later," Snowbeard said. "Once they lay siege to the city, it will be difficult to get out."

It was ludicrous, the notion that they'd soon be under siege. She felt the gathering presence of hundreds of wizards, like a noose tightening around the town. Yet, she was strangely reluctant to leave, like those idiots who elect to ride out the hurricane in a trailer park.

There was a power in this town, like some great thrumming heart that drew you into its rhythm until you matched it, beat for beat. To turn away from it was like walking away from the hearth and out into a winter's cold.

It was the Dragonheart. It must be. But maybe there was more to it than that. And if she stayed, maybe she could find a way to win Jason back.

"What are you going to do about the Anaweir?" she found herself asking.

"God knows," Snowbeard said, rolling his eyes. "Do you have any suggestions?"

Well, she thought, at least the Anaweir were malleable. Perhaps they could all be sent to Cedar Point for a few weeks on holiday. Or loaded onto boats and ferried across the lake. Good thing the college wasn't . . .

She looked up abruptly. "What are you doing to me?" she demanded.

"Doing to you? What do you mean?"

She and Snowbeard both reached for the last brownie

and their hands collided. The old man broke it in two, and gave her half.

"You're spelling me or something. Using Persuasion. You've got me worrying about the fricking Anaweir when I should be thinking about saving my own skin."

"My dear, I assure you, if you are worrying about the Anaweir, you are doing it on your own." He rose and carried the plate to the sink, then turned and leaned back against the drainboard. "I am a very old man, Alicia, and have made many mistakes over a very long life, some of them unforgiveable. I have to believe that people can change. That people deserve a second chance."

"I could really stay here?" Leesha asked humbly.

"So I said. Would you like to?" There was all knowledge, yet no hint of judgment, in the old man's face.

"I would like to," she said simply. And said to herself, "Fool."

❧ CHAPTER TWENTY-FIVE ❧
SIGHTINGS

Warren Barber was hungry for news, stuck on the periphery, and running out of options. After lying low for a while, he'd returned to Trinity, hoping he could get word on the outcome of the fire at the waterfront tavern. To his surprise, the town was surrounded by a forty-foot Weirwall much more elaborate than anything he'd ever built. And who was guarding the gate? Jack Swift and Ellen Stephenson, who'd somehow escaped the trap he'd put them in.

Leesha was certainly dead. No one but him could've taken off that collar. But Leesha dead was not necessarily a good thing. Because there was no way he'd get past the guards at the gate on his own.

He felt like a kid locked out of the circus—convinced it was all happening inside. He wandered back to the perimeter, again and again. Ripples of power emanated from the town—like someone had thrown a rock into the center of a magical pool. The whole town was juiced and he just wanted to soak in it.

Well, he never claimed to be a poet.

Warren wasn't the only one killing time on the wrong side of the wall. There was a virtual encampment of wizards in the countryside and lake resorts surrounding the town. He'd had to duck out of sight when he spotted his erstwhile ally Claude D'Orsay with Geoffrey Wylie of the Red Rose. They were inspecting the wall, testing it with cautious bits of magic. Looking for weaknesses, no doubt.

What was up with that? Since when were they all chummy? D'Orsay was supposed to be working with him, *against* the Roses. Of course, there'd been no communication between them except through Leesha, and D'Orsay wasn't supposed to know who her partner was. Like Leesha hadn't betrayed him immediately.

Warren was beginning to feel irrelevant. It had been weeks since anyone had even tried to kill him. As long as someone was trying to kill you, you knew you were important.

He had the Covenant, but it was seeming more and more like a worthless piece of paper, since he didn't have the means to consecrate it. It hadn't drawn anyone useful to him.

It was a class thing. Warren might be a wizard, ruler over the Anaweir and the servant guilds, but the aristocrats who lorded over the Houses would never give him a seat at the table.

After a few days, he grew tired of basking in reflected rays. What he needed was a new partner. Or, preferably, a servant. He could have his pick of the Anaweir, but he wanted someone who could contribute more.

Someone like Madison Moss.

As far as he knew, Madison had left Trinity. He'd found

no clues as to where she'd gone when he searched her room. But if she wasn't in Trinity, she was somewhere.

It was pathetically easy. He grabbed a car from a nearby parking lot and drove into Cleveland, found a public library branch and got online. His search on Madison Moss turned up a number of hits from art shows in Coalton County, Ohio.

Coalton County. He'd followed Jason Haley south to Coalton County. Warren had never been able to find out why he was down there.

Now he knew. And now that he had a name and a place, it shouldn't be hard to find her.

Brice Roper was beginning to think that being a wizard was overrated. Yes, he could have *almost* any girl, get *almost* anything, burn up *almost* anything he wanted.

But it had been that way all his life. He was rich, he was spoiled, and ever since he could remember, he'd focused on what he didn't have. And what he didn't have was the ability to get what he wanted from Madison Moss. That was linked to a lot of other things, like impressing his father, which was important because he couldn't recall that ever happening. Those were his goals—impressing his old man and then getting out of Coalton County for good.

It gnawed at him, even though he knew he should just leave and forget about Roper Coal and his father and being humiliated on Booker Mountain.

It was on his mind when he woke up, and it was on his mind when he went to bed, and it contaminated his dreams. He brooded on it in class, and snapped at those brave enough to sit down at his lunch table. All the charms of being king to a court of high-school seniors were wearing thin.

It didn't help that his father became more and more of a pain as he traveled further down the road to financial ruin. Bryson Roper, Sr. had formally approached Madison Moss about selling Booker Mountain, and she'd formally refused. The only good thing was, Bryson, Sr. was out of town a lot, trying to line up financing, cut some deals, find a partner, something.

Carlene was no help. She claimed she'd talked to Madison until she was blue in the face, and it made no difference.

Brice still couldn't figure out where Madison fit into the magical scheme of things. He'd asked around, and nobody had heard of a Witch Guild. Nobody but wizards ever displayed that kind of power.

What he wouldn't admit was that his insides turned to water at the thought of confronting her again.

So he spent his days sleepwalking through classes, avoiding his father, and dreaming of revenge.

One Saturday he'd just finished a long ride and handed his horse off to Mike. He was walking up to the house to take a much-needed shower when someone rattled up the drive in a Jeep and pulled up in front of the barn.

They didn't get many unannounced visitors, so Brice waited, leaning against the split-rail fence that enclosed the paddock.

It was a boy, a stranger of medium height, maybe a little older than Brice, with shaggy white-blond hair and pale blue eyes that were somehow startling. He walked with a smooth gait, flowing across the ground like a predator. Brice felt both intense interest and prickling unease. He glanced back to see whether Mike was still in sight, but he had led Annie into the barn.

"Can I help you?" Brice asked, aiming for a nonchalance he didn't feel.

"Maybe," the boy said, smiling. "I guess I'm lost. I'm looking for Madison Moss." His voice was soft, but, like his gait, it got your attention. "I heard she lived up this road. Is this the place?"

No, Brice wanted to say. It's not. Now get the hell out of here.

But he didn't. This guy was looking for Madison. Could he be a witch, too? Was that why he was so intimidating?

"You *are* lost," Brice said, forcing a smile. "What do you want with Madison?"

"We met last summer and I've been looking for her ever since," the stranger said. "I wanted to surprise her."

It was an odd thing to say—kind of stalkerish—but Brice had the sense this guy didn't care what Brice made of it. Like what he thought didn't matter.

"Maybe she's mentioned you," Brice said, again looking over his shoulder for Mike, who had not reappeared. "What's your name?"

"That's not important," the pale-haired boy said. "How do I get to her house?"

"Well," Brice said, aiming for dismissive. "I don't want to send you up there if I don't know who you are."

The stranger struck quick as a snake, shoving Brice back against the fence. He gripped Brice by the shoulders and sent a flood of Persuasion into him. Brice's reflexive magical defense was feeble by comparison, but it got the other boy's attention.

"You're a wizard!" he said, letting go of Brice. He sounded surprised and looked a little wary, but not particularly impressed.

"Y-you, too?" Brice stammered.

The wizard kept his hands raised to waist level, as if ready to defend himself. "Well, well," the boy said. "Who knew?" He studied Brice, then looked around, as if other, more powerful wizards might come out of the woodwork. "What House are you with?"

"Um," Brice said, feeling an unaccustomed social inferiority, "I'm . . . um . . . unaffiliated at present."

"What do you know? Me, too," the other boy said. "What's your name?"

"Brice Roper."

"You a friend of Madison's or what?"

"Not really," Brice said, assuming that was the safest answer. The other wizard still hadn't supplied his own name. It was more like an interrogation than a conversation. "I know her, is all. I went to school with her."

"You're not going out, then, or anything?" The boy's tone was faintly mocking.

"Not hardly!" Brice couldn't keep the bitterness out of his voice.

The boy smiled. "Then you won't mind if I pay her a visit, will you?"

Brice felt flattered. It was a kind of wizard-to-wizard thing, like the boy was seeking his permission to come into his territory.

"Well, I guess I'd like to know what you want with her." Not that Brice was worried about Madison, but by now his curiosity was aroused.

"Don't worry," the boy said. "I don't mean her any harm." He smiled, eyes glittering. "Not if she cooperates."

Brice stared at the other wizard. Hope crowded out

surprise. Maybe he'd found the solution to his problem. A way to get back at Madison.

But then he thought of the episode on Booker Mountain. Did this arrogant wizard know what she could do?

"Well," Brice said. "She's . . . um . . . not been that cooperative in the past," he said. "I'd be careful, if I were you."

"Really?" the boy said, appraising him with sudden intensity. "Tell me more."

"Why don't we go on up to the house," Brice suggested. "And I'll tell you all about her." He turned toward the house, then paused, recovering a little confidence. "What did you say your name was?"

Annoyance flashed across the boy's face, and Brice thought he'd made a mistake. Then the wizard smiled and extended his hand. "Actually, I didn't. I'm Warren Barber."

❧ CHAPTER TWENTY-SIX ❧
NO-MAN'S-LAND

Jason spoke the unnoticeable charm and slipped through the Weirgate, hearing the whisper of magical locks as one of the ghost warriors, Mick, pulled it shut behind him. It was after midnight, but the moon had not risen. Beyond the wall, the dark pressed down, and a steady rain swallowed the light. But Jason walked this path nearly every night in his role as spy. He'd had plenty of practice, slipping around unnoticed back at the Havens. Now he slid between the trees like a vapor.

He was well-suited to the role of spy, since it required little in the way of magical power. Still, the perimeter was difficult to navigate these days. You could hardly move without tripping over wizards. Everywhere he looked, wizard fire sparkled in the darkness like stars fallen to earth. Wizard voices in multiple languages collided under the canopy of trees.

They'd come from all over, more and more every day.

The Red Rose. The White Rose. Traders. The unaffiliated. Drawn to Trinity by the thrum of power within its walls.

Wizards fricking *camping*. Roughing it in the forest. Like a Wizard Woodstock. It was almost funny.

But not quite.

And all the while, the Anaweir came and went, oblivious to the gathering horde, unaware of the growing tension on either side of Mercedes's wall.

Dodging around several warded campsites, Jason crossed a rocky streambed and climbed the ridge beyond. From there he could monitor the comings and goings from the wizard camps and take a rough count of the Weir on the perimeter. But this time, as he crested the rise, he saw that the view had changed dramatically. The landscape was obscured by an ominous shadow that extended as far as he could see in both directions. It took him a moment to fathom what it was. And when he did, he swore and pounded his fist into his open palm.

The Roses were building their own wall, a few hundred yards from Mercedes's fortification. It was tall and slick and menacing, iced with razorwire, lacking the grace and style of Mercedes's barrier. A poisonous green light reflected back from it, like an oil slick on black water.

It was a nightmarish kind of wall—the kind the witch builds to keep the prince out. Or in. The kind that surrounds the dark lord's castle. It was a wall that would trap both Weir and Anaweir. And from the looks of things, it was nearly finished.

They must've used glamours to hide their progress. Even if they'd waited to begin construction until after dark, they would have had more hands to share in the work than

Mercedes and her crews. Not to mention unlimited magical firepower. It was a testament to the forces arrayed against them.

Jason descended the ridge on the far side, slipping and sliding on the loose shale. He knew who to credit for this latest play.

Wylie and Longbranch and D'Orsay's elaborate, heavily warded pavilions now stood just outside the half-built wall. There they hatched schemes and fought with each other, from what Jason had gleaned over the previous days.

As he approached the pavilions, Jason moved with exquisite caution, alert for traps and alarms. He'd be way better off dead than to be caught out here on his own. Ahead he could see the glowing silk walls of the tents, enchanted to turn the rain. Above the peaks flew the banners of the Red and White Rose, and a black raven on white that was D'Orsay's new signia.

Geoffrey Wylie stood outside the tents, issuing orders to a huge crowd of eager young wizards clad in damp camouflage. Among them was Bruce Hays, an alumnus of the Havens, holding Gregory Leicester's glass and metal wizard staff, and looking damn proud of it.

With Wylie were Jessamine Longbranch, dressed in couture camoflage. And Claude D'Orsay.

D'Orsay's patrician features were clearly revealed in the light that leaked from the pavilion. The tall wizard stood in the midst of his enemies, seemingly at ease, expending bits of power to keep the rain off him. He wore rings on both hands—powerful *sefa*s, if Jason was any judge. So D'Orsay had come well armed to this meeting.

Devereaux stood next to his father, eyes wide, taking it all in.

"We'll begin immediately," Wylie said. "The Anaweir are . . . er . . . unaware of the rebels' Weirwall, since they can pass freely through it. However, anyone leaving the sanctuary will be trapped inside *our* wall. You'll capture them—Weir and Anaweir—and bring them to the retention area for processing and identification. As word gets out, panicked townspeople will no doubt come flooding through the inner wall. We'll have hundreds of hostages, some of them with strong ties to the rebels."

"What are we going to do with them?" Hays asked.

"When we go to breach the inner wall, we'll pack the area between with immobilized hostages. That way, the rebels won't be able to use their arsenal against us."

This was, apparently, Wylie's plan, because Longbranch rolled her eyes. "Do you really think wizards will negotiate for Anaweir hostages?"

Wylie shrugged. "Who knows? They've seemed unaccountably attached to them in the past."

"Strange." Longbranch turned back to the soldiers. "You must immobilize the prisoners as quickly as possible, so there's no outcry. Particularly the Weir." She distributed leather pouches to the soldiers. "This is *Gemynd bana*. Mind-Slayer. It will knock them out without being detectable by those inside the walls. Just be careful with it, or you'll end up flat on your back yourselves."

Jason stood frozen. Panic constricted his throat, making it difficult to breathe.

Crap, he thought. It's beginning. It's really happening. When you're scared, why is it that your mouth goes dry while your hands get sweaty?

"If there's any question," Longbranch went on, "use

an immobilization charm. Try not to muck things up. Now, go."

The wizard soldiers dispersed, leaving the three wizards and the boy alone.

"It would help if we knew more about the weapons you've supplied us, Claude," Longbranch said.

"Hmmm?" D'Orsay seemed distracted, gazing wistfully past Longbranch and Wylie to the sanctuary walls.

Forget it, Jason thought. You'll never get your hands on the Dragonheart.

D'Orsay wrenched himself away from his study of the Sanctuary, turning to Longbranch. "You know as much as I do, Jessamine. We'll have to take a bit of a chance."

"It appears to me that *we're* taking the chance, since it's *our* wizards who'll be involved in the attack."

"I'd be more than happy to contribute," D'Orsay replied, "but I'm afraid I'm a bit short on armies at the moment. I had to leave my guard behind to secure the ghyll."

"I can fight, Father," Devereaux said eagerly. "I'm only one person, but . . ."

"No, Dev," D'Orsay said, scowling. "Not this time." He turned to the Roses. "How do you propose to find the Dragonheart once we're inside?"

Longbranch and Wylie glanced at each other, then looked toward the sanctuary. "Do you really think it will be hard to find?" Wylie said.

Jason studied the odds, considered and discarded several options. He might hear more if he stayed, but wizards already lay waiting for anyone who passed beyond the barrier. There was no time to lose.

He backed away from the wizard pavilions, placing his

feet carefully so as not to betray himself, though he felt like his heart was pounding loud enough to be heard on its own.

As soon as he was away, Jason turned and ran back the way he'd come.

As he neared the inner wall, his pace slowed. The moon had risen, and shafts of light penetrated the canopy of trees and bathed the trail in silvery light. The way seemed clear ahead.

Jason left the path and cut through the trees, approaching the gate from the east. He scanned the smudged border of forest across the clearing and saw movement in the shadows there. Then, startlingly close at hand, someone slapped a mosquito. It was all Jason could do not to flail backward into the underbrush.

The trap was already laid for the residents of Trinity. Jason was determined not to fall into it. Unnoticeable or not, Mick would still need to open the gate to let him in.

Half-holding his breath, Jason crossed the open meadow toward the gate. The back of his neck prickled. At any moment, he expected to be slammed with an immobilization charm.

When he reached the wall, he pressed his palm against the gate. "Mick," he muttered. "Open up."

There was no response.

"Mick," Jason repeated, a little louder. "It's Jase. Let me in. Get a move on." He glanced over his shoulder and saw three wizards step out of the trees, peering toward the gate. Jason recognized Bruce Hays, packing his fancy staff.

Jason pounded on the gate with the heel of his hand. "Come on, Mick. Open the fricking gate!"

Finally, he heard movement within, the unfortunately

loud rumble of Mick's voice spewing Irish profanity from another age. "Can't a man take a bluidy leak in the middle of the bluidy night athout you getting your bollocks in a bluidy . . ."

Jason looked back at the wizards. Hays raised his staff and pointed it directly at Jason.

"Aetywan!" Hays shouted. Mist spewed from the tip of the staff and enveloped Jason in a cloud of vapor.

Unable to respond in his unnoticeable state, Jason held his breath to avoid breathing in the fumes, crouched to make a small target, and struggled to remember his sparse Anglo-Saxon.

Aetywan. That would mean . . . *reveal?*

"It's Haley!" Shouts reverberated across the clearing.

Jason looked down at himself. The formerly unnoticeable Jason was indeed revealed. It was like being stripped naked in the middle of Main Street during a block party thrown by your worst enemies.

"Get him!" Hays shouted. "Grab him! Take him alive!" They charged toward him, baying like hounds on a scent. More wizards poured out of the woods.

"Mick!" Jason threw up a pathetic shield, braced his feet against the wall, gripped the edge of the gate, and yanked. "Open up now or you might as well forget it!"

He was surrounded by wizards, a kaleidoscope of excited faces, many flinging mind-slayer at him. Lame as it was, his shield repelled the powder. A wizard staggered and went down, a victim of friendly fire.

The gate was moving now, excruciatingly slowly, with Mick's litany of oaths continuing on the other side, though now with a certain sense of urgency. Jason heard running feet inside the double-gated barbican, a thud of bodies against the gate, and it slammed open, spilling Jason and a handful of warriors into the no-man's-land between the barriers.

Jason scrambled to his feet as Mick bolted past him, gleefully swinging his axe, bellowing a Gaelic battle cry. Jack and Ellen and Jeremiah followed, weapons blazing, driving the wizards back toward the outer wall. Wizard fire spewed into the air, setting the treetops ablaze.

How long before the fireworks and sounds of battle drew Anaweir past the inner barrier and into the hands of the Roses?

Weaponless, Jason sprinted after the warriors as two wizards closed in on them from behind. Jason tackled one of the wizards and disabled him by wizard's grip, thrusting his fingers under his chin and applying power directly to that vulnerable place. Ellen leveled the other one with the flat of her blade.

"What is going on?" Jack demanded, smashing back a bolt from Hays's fancy staff. "It looks like all hell's broken loose."

"Big trouble," Jason gasped "There's an army waiting out there. They've put up their own wall. They're planning to trap people and take hostages. We've got to go back."

Reluctantly, the warriors left off chasing wizards and retreated, spraying flame in their wake to discourage pursuit. Once inside the gate, Jason helped slam the locks into place while the walls shuddered under the wizards' assault.

"Where's Seph?" Jason gasped. "We can't wait any longer. We've got to do something about the Anaweir. Right now."

❧ CHAPTER TWENTY-SEVEN ❧
A DEAL WITH THE DEVIL

The radio in Min's old pickup only got three stations. You could listen to whatever you wanted as long as it was country and western or classic rock and roll. Madison turned up the volume and sang along, making up the words she didn't know.

She rolled down the windows, and her hair whipped around her shoulders. Now spring peepers and the low growl of thunder competed with the radio. The taste of the air said it would rain before morning.

As the hills crowded in on both sides, even the most powerful stations began to break up. So she switched off the radio and practiced her lines.

"I'm Madison Moss. I go to the Art Institute of Chicago." And then her stomach did that little flip again—half fear, half joy.

Sara had found the money through a scholarship program for disadvantaged students. Who would've thought that living on nothing but dreams all her life would pay off? But Sara said it wasn't just based on need.

"The scholarship committee loved your work, Maddie," Sara had said. "They said you had a unique perspective that appeals to those who like both primitive and high-concept art. They can't wait to meet you."

That part made her nervous. What if they saw her wild mane of hair and thrift-shop clothes, and heard the way she talked and decided they'd made a mistake? What if they treated her like some kind of awkward, backwoodsy charity case?

Never mind. The work was what was important. She'd find a way to survive the committee. And attend the Chicago Art Institute in the fall on scholarship.

Her portfolio rode alongside her in the passenger seat. Sara had been a bit bewildered by some of the more exotic images. But she thought they would play well in Chicago.

Chicago. Madison had never been there. There would be libraries and museums and theaters. She could sit in cafés and talk about books and art and music. Things nobody ever talked about in Coal Grove. Every day she'd see thousands of people who knew nothing about her. Who hadn't already made up their minds about Madison Moss.

She could hardly wait.

She was scared to death.

One dream could lead to another. Maybe she could still convince Seph to attend Northwestern. If it was too late for fall, he could come as a transfer student in the spring. It could work. He was at home anywhere. Plus he was comfortable in cities. He had a way of organizing the world around him so it fit him like a skin. Knowing that she had one friend would make all the difference. Knowing it was Seph . . .

She was ambushed by the image of his face: his gray-green eyes, like smoke layered on still water, hiding secrets. His rangy frame filling a doorway. His smile: so worldly-wise, yet not full of himself. The way he switched into French when English just wouldn't do.

His kisses.

She had to stomp on the brake and wrench the wheel around to make the turn-off to Booker Mountain.

You're hopeless. Just like Carlene. Seph will never come to Chicago. Not on your account. Not while the fate of the world hangs in the balance. And who knew what would happen if he did? She let go of the wheel and examined her hands. Since the day she'd touched the Dragonheart, there had been no sign of the hex magic she'd absorbed at Second Sister. Was it really and truly gone, or was it just that she'd been away from Seph?

Falling in love was like falling off a cliff. It felt pretty much like flying until you hit the ground.

The road plunged back into dense forest and rippled through several hairpin turns, crossing Booker Creek on the stone bridges her great-grandfather had built.

The first big splats of rain hit the roof of the pickup as she pulled into the yard. It was pitch dark by now and Carlene hadn't even turned on the porch light.

Madison pushed open the driver's door and slid to the ground. She grabbed a bag of groceries from the seat, slung her backpack over her shoulder, and shoved her portfolio under her arm, meaning to make one trip to the house before the deluge.

By the time she made it up the steps, it was pouring. She hesitated under the imperfect shelter of the porch roof, thinking Hamlet and Ophelia might come to greet her. But no enthusiastic wet dogs came splashing onto the porch. No Grace or John Robert, either.

Guess they know enough to stay in out of the rain.

As soon as she shouldered open the front door, she could hear the television going in the front room. She set her portfolio and backpack down next to the door.

"Mama?" she said. "Grace? J.R.? I have the best news. Just wait till you hear."

"Hi, honey," Carlene said from the other room. "I'm watching my shows."

Madison put the eggs, milk, juice, lunchmeat, and cheese into the refrigerator to join a jar of Miracle Whip, moldy bacon, four bottles of beer, and a pitcher of Kool-Aid.

She threw out the bacon.

It was dark in the living room, too. Carlene was slumped in a corner of the couch, her face illuminated by the changing images on the television screen.

Madison switched on the table lamp. "You sitting here in the dark, Mama?"

"Hmmm?" Carlene blinked up at her. "I guess so." She looked kind of sleepy and out of it.

"Where are the kids?"

Carlene shrugged and looked around, as if she hadn't missed them. "Oh. Right. They went to the Ropers."

"To the Ropers!" Dreams of Chicago evaporated. Madison stared at Carlene. "What for?"

"I guess they went riding."

Madison looked out through the streaming windows. "Well, they're not riding now. It's pouring down rain. When did they go?"

"This morning." A crease appeared between Carlene's penciled brows. "I think."

Madison was tempted to grab her mother's shoulders and shake her. But something stopped her. Carlene seemed almost . . . spelled.

"Mama." She sat down next to Carlene and took her hands. "How did they happen to go riding at the Ropers?"

"Brice Roper come by. With another boy. Never saw him before." Her mind seemed to drift.

"What did the other boy look like?"

"He had long hair paler'n John Robert's."

Min's words came back to her from long ago.

I see four pretty men coming. Two will claim your heart in different ways. Two are deceivers. Two will come to your door, one dark, one fair. All of these men have magic. . . .

But they have no power that you don't give away.

Madison stood, put her shoulders back, and took a deep breath. Crossing to the hearth, she dug her father's gun out of the wood box and stuffed it into her backpack. Snatching up her keys, she returned to the living room.

"You stay here, Mama," she said, though Carlene wasn't making any move to go anywhere.

Carlene nodded absently, already lost in the flickering screen.

Maddie's truck with its nearly bald tires slipped and slid on the rain-slick road. It seemed to take forever to get to the turn-off. She swung into the Ropers' drive between the fancy brick pillars, and the house and barn came into sight through the smeared windshield. Brice's fancy sports car was parked in the middle of the drive in front of the house. She pulled next to Brice's car, banged open the truck door, and jumped to the ground. Turning, she thrust her hand into the backpack and closed it on Jordan Moss's pistol.

She climbed the broad steps onto the porch and would have pounded on the massive walnut door, but it swung open under her fist.

The house yawned empty before her, seeming to echo with her footsteps. She walked across shining hardwood, through the foyer and into the hall, looking into richly furnished rooms on either side. At the back of the house, a fire blazed on the hearth in the two-story family room, providing the only light. To the right, a doorway led into what must be the dining room.

A body lay in the doorway, booted feet sticking out into the kitchen. The boots were familiar—expensive black leather.

Stifling a scream, Madison stumbled toward Brice Roper's body.

"I wouldn't get too close," a voice said behind her. "It's kind of messy. Not my best work."

She swung around. Her keys clattered as they hit the stone-tile floor.

He stood between her and the hall like a candle in the dark, glittery bright with power, steaming as he drove the rain from his clothing. He was dressed all in black, but his hair was so pale as to seem translucent.

It was Warren Barber.

He smiled. "You're not easy to find."

Though her heart was pounding, she managed to speak in a clear, steady voice. "Where are they?"

"What? No tears for poor Brice?"

"I want to know what you've done with my brother and sister."

"You know, Madison, you really had him going. What'd you tell him—that you were a witch?"

Madison said nothing.

"But you're not a witch, are you? You're something else entirely." He paused, inviting her to speak, but she still said nothing. "Anyway, he was sure convinced. Poor Brice was so happy to have a little more firepower on his side. He hated your guts, you know. You should thank me."

Thoughts stumbled through her mind. How had he found her? How much did he know? Could she make him try and spell her?

"What do you want?" she asked.

"I need your help, Madison." He seemed to like saying her name, as if he owned it. "I need you to do something for me."

"You're out of your mind."

Barber laughed. "We'll see. I think you're going to do whatever I ask."

Maybe he knew less than she thought. He seemed almost too confident. Maybe if she charged him, he'd send power into her.

His pale eyes glittered with malice. "I haven't forgotten what you did on Second Sister." He took a step toward her. "Big mistake. No one comes after me with a knife. I should teach you a lesson." He raised his hands, raising Madison's hopes, then dropped them again, smiling. "But I'm willing to forgive and forget."

He knows. He's just toying with me.

She pulled the gun free, gripped it with both hands like her father had taught her, and pointed it at Warren Barber.

Barber stopped smiling when he saw the gun.

"I *said*—tell me where my brother and sister are."

Barber went very still for a long moment, then said, "I'm losing patience, Madison. Now put that down before someone gets hurt." He took a step toward her.

"I'm warning you," Madison said. "I'm a deadeye shot." Which was true. Her daddy had taught her to shoot. Only she was a failure as a hunter because she'd never been able to shoot anything living. Barber might be the first.

Barber's eyes, with their pale centers and fringe of white lashes, were cold and unblinking as any snake's. "All right. You're all business, huh? I have something to show you." He patted his jacket pocket. "May I?"

Grudgingly, Madison nodded.

He thrust his fingers into his pocket, came up with something glittering. He extended it toward Madison.

She gestured with the gun. "Toss it on the table," she said.

Barber tossed, underhand. Two objects clunked onto the battered formica. Madison put the table between her and the wizard and looked down.

It was like somebody had reached into her chest, grabbed hold of her heart, and squeezed.

One of the objects was a beat-up Swiss Army knife with the initials *JR* carved crudely into the cover. The other was a gold locket engraved with roses on a lightweight gold chain.

The knife had belonged to their father. John Robert carried it with him everywhere and slept with it under his pillow. Min had left the locket to Grace. Madison had fastened the clasp a thousand times when Grace couldn't manage, had carefully removed it and set it on the dresser when Grace fell asleep with a book. She wore it every day of her life.

Madison looked up at Barber. It took a couple of tries to get her voice going.

"Where are they?" This time, she couldn't keep the quaver out of her voice.

"No one will ever find them if you shoot me."

She braced herself, aimed lower. "I don't need to shoot you in the head," she said.

"And if I bleed to death?" He raised an eyebrow. "Come on, Madison, you're not a killer. Besides, I can probably block the shot. Put down the gun, and we'll talk."

"If you've hurt them, I'll . . ."

"You're the only one who can prevent that. Cooperate, and I'll let them go. If not . . ." He shrugged. "That'd be a shame."

"How do I know they're still alive?"

Barber waved away her question impatiently. "They're my leverage. It'd be stupid to kill them. Unless you disappoint me. When our business is done, I'll let them go. See? Nobody gets hurt. Now put down the gun before I lose patience."

Grace and John Robert. Defiant, strong-willed Grace and innocent John Robert in the hands of this monster. What did he want from her that he'd gone after them?

Carefully, she set the gun on the table, took a step back, and stood, arms at her side, staring daggers at Warren Barber.

"Good," Barber said. He nodded toward the kitchen table. "Please. Sit down."

Madison walked woodenly to the table and sat. She tried to look everywhere but at Brice's body and the blood splattered over the floor. Barber was right. She wasn't a killer.

Barber crossed to the refrigerator and rummaged inside. "You hungry?"

"No." Madison's stomach lurched, threatening to reject what little it had inside it.

Barber pulled out two bottles of pop and a plate of cold pizza and carried them back to the table.

"Conflict always makes me hungry, know what I mean?" He set a bottle of pop in front of her.

"Do . . . do J.R. and Grace have anything to eat?" she whispered.

"You worry too much. Doesn't do any good, and takes years off your life." He sat down across from her, rolling the other bottle between his wizard hands. Spiderweb tattoos crawled over his forearms.

She pushed the pop back toward him. "I don't . . ."

"Drink it," he said.

She looked into his iced-over eyes, grabbed up the bottle, took a long swig, and somehow forced it down her throat.

"That's better," he said, smiling. "Get used to doing what I say, and we'll get along. Now. Here's what you need to do. You go get the Dragonheart. Then we'll do a trade—the Dragonheart for Grace and J.R. Fair enough?"

"Wh . . . what do you want with that?" she asked, seeing no use in denying she'd heard of it. "What are you planning to do?"

"You just focus on getting hold of it," Warren said, taking a bite of pizza. "Let me worry about the rest."

Thoughts and images tumbled though her mind like rocks down a slope, crashing into each other. The Dragonheart still pulsed within her like a second heart. If it was as powerful as they said, could she put that kind of power in the hands of someone like Barber?

Seph and Jason and Jack and Ellen and Nick—all were fighting against impossible odds for something they believed in. It was bad enough that she hadn't helped them. Now Warren Barber wanted her to march into the middle of the sanctuary and betray the people who meant the most to her.

Except Grace and J.R. were in this mess because of her. Seph had warned her she couldn't escape by running away, and she hadn't listened. And if Barber found out that Grace was an elicitor, too . . .

All my life, I've been paying for Carlene's mistakes, she thought. Grace and J.R. aren't going to pay for mine.

"It might not be easy," she said. "It might take a little time."

Barber crammed the last of the pizza into his mouth and wiped his fingers on the tablecloth. "Just remember, the longer it takes, the longer Grace and J.R. stay locked up."

✇ CHAPTER TWENTY-EIGHT ✇
TO THE SALT MINES

One thing Jack had always appreciated about his mother, Becka, was her ability to make things happen, even when awakened from a sound sleep in the middle of the night. Looking back on it, he couldn't even remember what he'd said to her. Or maybe it was his appearance—all muddy and bloody from the fight outside the perimeter. Anyway, it was enough to roust her from bed and send her to the phone. When she found it dead, she sent out runners and the result was this meeting around the kitchen table at Stone Cottage a scant hour later.

The wind raked over the house, and hail clattered against the windows. Thunder growled out over the lake. It seemed like it was always storming, these days.

It was a disparate group. Ellen prowled the room, flushed and restless, still pumped from the unfinished business outside the perimeter. Sweat glistened on her sinewed arms, and she mopped at her face with her shirt, despite the chilly breeze coming through the terrace doors. Her gray eyes were as turbulent as the surface of the lake.

Jack understood—the blood still pounded through his veins, his rebellious body in endless preparation for battle.

Nicodemus Snowbeard looked like he'd aged several hundred years, yet his black eyes still shone with the same old intensity. Nick had insisted that Leesha Middleton be included, though most everyone else would've voted against it. But the old man was a majority of one.

For once, Leesha had little to say. She sat on the edge of the hearth, arms clasped around her knees. She kept looking over at Jason, as if trying to catch his eye, and Jason was looking everywhere *but* at her.

Jason was his usual twitchy self, shifting his weight, checking the time on his cell phone. Nothing ever moved fast enough for him.

Seph, brooding and dangerous, practically smoked with power.

Mercedes Foster resembled a Manga construction worker in her coveralls, kasuri robe, and Japanese slippers. Iris Bolingame slumped in the corner, exhausted. She'd just come off the wall.

Will and Fitch hung close to Jack and Ellen, as if determined not to be left out of whatever was to happen.

Will's father, Bill Childers, mayor of Trinity, and his uncle, Ross Childers, now chief of police, looked as awkward as two Baptists at a Hindu temple.

"I think we're all here," Becka said to Jack. "Now suppose you tell us what's going on."

"This had better be good," Ross added gruffly, yawning behind his forearm and glaring at Will. "*Real* good."

Nick levered himself to his feet, using his staff. "Ross. Bill. Becka. These young people are about to tell you an extraordinary story. But I can assure you that it's absolutely true. I hope you will listen to what they have to say with an open mind." He nodded at Jack.

"So," Jack said, clearing his throat. "That is, we . . . ah . . ." He'd been keeping secrets so long that it was hard to let go of them. In desperation, he reached over his shoulder and drew Shadowslayer from his baldric, laying the great sword across the kitchen table. Ellen followed suit, pulling Waymaker from its scabbard and resting it next to Shadowslayer.

Everyone stared at the two brilliant swords on the table, as if the weapons might speak.

Becka found her own voice. "Jack. Where did these swords come from? They look like museum pieces."

Ellen rested her hand on the hilt of her sword and spoke, rather formally. "Waymaker was taken from a hoard of weapons in Raven's Ghyll, in Cumbria, U.K. Near where you stayed with Mr. Hastings that time. It is one of the seven great blades, made by sorcerers under the rule of the dragon Aidan Ladhra. Jason . . . ah . . . found it and . . . um . . ."

Her voice trailed away. Becka and Ross and Bill Childers stared at her like she'd grown another head. She looked down at the floor, the color coming up in her cheeks. Ellen hated speaking in front of people under the best of circumstances.

Jack rested his right hand at the base of Ellen's spine and touched the hilt of his sword with the other. "Mom. This is Shadowslayer. It's another one of the seven. It belonged to Great-Great-Grandmother Susannah. We—Will and Fitch and I—dug it up from her grave, down in Coalton County."

"Susannah owned a sword?" Becka frowned suspiciously at Jack, then turned to look at Will and Fitch for the punchline.

"Susannah was a magical warrior," Fitch said into the skeptical silence. "Like Ellen and Jack."

"They've been fighting off an army of wizards, Ms. Downey," Will added. "Remember when we went down to Coal Grove with Aunt Linda to do genealogy? We found the sword, but then wizards attacked us, trying to steal it, and we had to hide in a church. Aunt Linda pulled up in the parking lot, and Jack, he flamed . . ."

"Linda? What about Linda?" Becka interrupted. "You're saying she's a warrior too?"

"Well." Will cleared his throat. "Ah, no. She's an enchanter."

"An enchanter," Ross Childers said, grinding the heel of his hand into his forehead. "Right." He'd asked Linda out—several times—before her relationship with Hastings became public knowledge.

"We made it back to Trinity, but then wizards came after Jack here," Fitch said. "Remember when those dudes tried to snatch him from the high school and Mr. Hastings chased them off?"

Becka's head came up and she wore that familiar lawyer expression that said she was about to drill an unreliable witness. Though she hadn't totally bought the story they'd told at the time, she wasn't buying this one either.

"They were traders," Will explained. "There was this huge price on Jack's head, and they were going to sell him at auction. You see, wizards play warriors in these big magical tournaments. Called the Game."

"You're telling me those men were *wizards*. And Leander Hastings chased them off?" Becka lifted her eyebrow.

"Well, actually, they're sort of buried under the school parking lot," Jack admitted. "He had to do something with the bodies before the police came." He shot an apologetic look at Ross, who'd been the commanding officer on the scene.

"Mr. Hastings is a wizard, too," Will said. "So is Nick."

Everyone turned and stared at Nick, who inclined his head slightly. "Indeed," he said. "I'm afraid so."

Bill Childers looked from Nick to Will, then conjured up an explanation of his own. "You got us all out of our beds to talk about . . . about some kind of role-playing game?"

"No," Jason said from his spot against the wall. "It's real. And there's going to be a massacre if we don't . . . if we don't do something."

"Now hold on," Bill glared at Jason, who never looked particularly reliable. "A *massacre*?"

"Wizards have this town surrounded," Mercedes said in her clipped fashion. "We put up a Weirwall, a magical barricade. That's the only thing that's keeping them out at the moment. Now the wizards have put up their own wall—a wizard wall. They mean to capture or kill everyone who tries to leave."

"Look," Ross said, shedding his jacket and tossing it over a chair. His shirt had big sweat spots under the arms. "I've been in and out of town a dozen times over the past two weeks. I haven't seen any one wall, let alone two."

"You can't see the Weirwall," Mercedes said. "It's invisible to the Anaweir. The non-gifted. Those without Weirstones. Like you."

"The other wall went up tonight," Jason said. "That one, you can see. I can show you, but we'll have to be careful. They're already out there waiting."

"You expect us to believe that someone built a wall all the way around the town since sunset." Ross rolled up his sleeves, exposing his beefy arms.

Mercedes sniffed. "Well. It *is* an ugly thing. Slipshod. But we have to assume it's effective."

"You've seen this wall?" Bill asked.

"I have," Jason said. "When they start grabbing the townies, there'll be mass panic. We have to find a place to stash the Ana—the non-gifted—until this war is over. One way or another."

"We're wasting time." Seph spoke for the first time. "The morning commute begins in two hours. We've got sentries posted to turn people back, but anyone who slips through will be trapped inside the outer wall and taken. I'm not going to let that happen. I'll immobilize them all if I have to."

Becka blinked at him. "Seph?"

"Look," Ross growled, exasperated. "I've known most of you kids all your lives, but I have to say, you're scaring me. I'm thinking we should all get back to bed and see if those wizards have disappeared by morning."

"Listen with an open mind," Nick repeated softly.

"Hey." Jason stared out the terrace doors toward the lake. "Come look at this."

They crowded onto the terrace, lining up against the wall, hunching their shoulders against the ice pellets drilled into them by the wind. Jason extended his hands. Light spilled from his fingers, gilding the tops of the waves across a gray expanse of water until it struck a thick black barrier a

hundred yards from shore that stretched from horizon to
horizon. It resembled storm clouds come to earth, or a layer
of thick, roiling smoke with greenish lightning playing
around its edges.

"What the hell?" Ross stared out at the lake, scrubbing
his palm across his bristled face. "Is that some kind of water-
spout or squall line or . . ."

"It's part of the wizard wall," Jason said flatly, "And it
wouldn't be a good idea to try and take your boat through
that. It means there's no escape by water."

"How'd you do that?" Bill demanded. "That thing with
your hands?"

"Magic," Jason said matter-of-factly. "Get used to it,
because you're going to see a lot more of it, whether you like
it or not."

Jack recalled his own experience, two years before, when
Aunt Linda had told him that she was an enchanter, that Jack
was a warrior, that wizards were hunting him down.

There was just no way to ease into it.

Jack ducked inside, retrieved Shadowslayer from the
table, and strode back onto the terrace.

"Stand back," he said.

Gripping the hilt with both hands, he swung the great
sword in a wide, hissing arc, sending bolts of flame screaming
across the dark waters to smash into the wall, feeling the
familiar exhilarating release as he did so. Smoke and flame
fountained into the night sky and smaller explosions reverberated along the rocky lakeshore. And again. Flame ripped into
the night, exploded against the barrier, painting the waves in
gaudy colors of red and orange. When the smoke dissipated,
the wall remained, though a bit more ragged than before.

"God almighty," Bill said, after a moment of stunned silence.

An acrid, burnt scent came back to them, carried by the onshore breeze. Dogs barked furiously, all along the shoreline.

Becka slumped against the wall, bracing herself with her hands. Emotions tracked across her face. Astonishment. Fear. Regret. Guilt. "This has got to be a dream," she said.

"It's okay, Mom," Jack said, embarrassed, sitting down next to her and leaning Shadowslayer against the wall.

Ellen took one look at the two of them, then firmly herded the rest of the group inside. "Take ten, Jack. We'll bring the townies up to date." She pulled the doors shut.

"There's not much time," Jack said. "I'm sorry it had to come out like this."

"I must've been blind," Becka said. She looked up at Jack. "When did you know?"

"Not till my sophomore year. Warriors don't manifest until they're old enough to . . . um . . . fight."

"But what about after that? Why didn't you tell me?" She caught his chin with her hand, and forced his face around so she could look him in the eyes. "I should have asked more questions. You've had to deal with this all on your own."

"Mom. You asked," Jack said desperately. "About a hundred times you asked what was up. I just couldn't tell you. I didn't know how." He looked down at his lean, muscular body. Designed for one purpose.

"How was I supposed to tell you I'm a warrior? A hard-wired killer? This is so totally opposed to everything you believe in—that I've believed in, all my life." He leaned his arms on the wall, his chin on his arms, staring out at the lake. "I mean, I wasn't totally on my own. Linda knew, all along.

And Nick was here, to keep an eye on me, I guess. He taught me some wizardry. And Hastings taught me how to fight."

"Hastings." She let out a long breath. "What about Ellen?"

"Ellen's had the life I might've had if . . . things were different." He paused, collected his thoughts. "They sent her here to kill me. And she could've. But she didn't."

Seph stuck his head through the doorway. "Jack."

Jack stood, looking down at his mother. "All year you and Dad have been trying to get me to focus on my future, I don't know if I have a future, if I'm even going to get through the year. I know we need to talk. And we will. But for now I want to say I love you. And I'm sorry."

Becka stood, reached her hands up, pulled his face down, and kissed him on his forehead. "I love *you*, Jack," she said fiercely. "And I believe in you. Wizard, warrior, whatever." And led the way back into the house.

The others were gathered around the kitchen table, slugging down coffee in lieu of sleep. Something had happened in the interim. Wizardly Persuasion, perhaps. The mayor and the chief of police had moved from dogged skepticism to foot-dragging belief.

"I still don't get it," Ross was saying. "Why would they attack a little college town in Ohio? What do they want?"

Nick and Seph exchanged glances. "We have something they want," Nick said gently. "A magical object that is said to be extraordinarily powerful. A small group of wizards hope to use it to seize control of the magical guilds. In effect, to rule the world."

"Can't we use it against them?" Bill asked.

Seph shook his head. "We don't know how."

"Could we . . . couldn't we give it to them?" Ross asked. "I mean, if it's no good, anyway."

"That's not an option," Nick said. "You'll have to trust me on that."

What does he know that he's not telling us? Jack wondered.

"We're just a small-town police force," Ross said. "We don't have the manpower or equipment to handle major trouble. We need help. I could call the governor's office. Bring in the National Guard."

"It wouldn't do any good," Seph said. "They might kill a few wizards with conventional weapons, if they took them by surprise. Then the Roses would immobilize and slaughter them. There'd be just that many more bodies on the ground."

Ross nodded, looking almost relieved, as if he didn't want to contemplate that conversation with the governor. "Okay. What if the—ah—underguilds left? Wouldn't the—wizards leave Trinity alone?" The police chief was doing the best he could to master the jargon, to grapple with the monsters who'd come out from under the bed.

"It's too late for that now," Jason said. "There are hundreds of wizards out there. There's no way we can get through without being captured or killed."

"These are children, too, remember." Becka leaned her hips against the kitchen counter. "Whatever powers they have, you can't expect them to . . . fall on their swords."

"It doesn't matter, Mom," Jack put in. "We'd try to bust out if we thought it would do any good. We'd surrender if we thought it would save the town. But . . . they know we're intertwined with the people here. And wizards are vindictive. The Anaweir are throwaways to them. Those they think they can use as hostages, they'll take captive. The rest, well . . ." He found he couldn't quite put it into words.

But Jason could. "They'll kill everyone: men, women, children, down to the dogs and cats. There won't be a building left standing. They'll burn everything to the dirt. Then poison the ground so nothing grows here again. It'll be like someone nuked the commons."

"Isn't there anyone who can help?" Becka asked. "Where are Linda and Hastings?"

"We don't know, Becka," Nick said softly. "They went to England, to secure a hoard of magical weapons, to keep them out of our enemies' hands. So we'll have to do the best we can on our own." He patted her shoulder. "All is not lost. We have some principled wizards on our side. Seph may be young, but he's quite powerful. And there's Jason. Iris. And me," he added, as if it were an afterthought.

"And me," Leesha said. She was still sitting on the hearth, but her chin came up stubbornly, like she was ready to pick a fight.

"All right, Seph, Jason, Iris, me, and Leesha," Nick said. "And a few others."

Dread coalesced in the pit of Jack's stomach. A handful against hundreds. If they could even trust Leesha.

"We have warriors," Nick went on. "There's Jack and Ellen, of course, and we also have a formidable army of ghost warriors. We have hundreds of sorcerers, enchanters, and seers. We hold a large collection of magical weapons, and we actually know how to use most of them." Nick grinned, and Jack felt a little better.

"All right, then," Becka said, straightening, regaining her familiar focus. "Think. What can we do about the . . . people?

We could put them in the Convocation Center, but that would just become an easy target."

"We need to hide them somewhere," Ellen suggested. "Tell them some kind of story to make them stay put. How many basements would it take to hide ten thousand people?"

"You know, I can't picture telling citizens of Trinity we're under attack by wizards," Bill said. "Being drummed out of office is the least of it. I wish we could find a way to get them out of here."

And how, exactly, are we supposed to do that? Jack thought. Dig a tunnel under the wall? And how long would *that* take?

That gave him a glimmer of an idea.

"We have to come up with a place to put them until this is over," Seph said. "Like . . . like a bomb shelter, or something."

"Well," Jack said thoughtfully, "There's the salt mines."

"Come on, Jack," Jason snapped. "We don't have time for . . ."

"I'm *serious*," Jack said. "There's plenty of room, and they're well-ventilated and . . ."

Jason's bleak expression reorganized into interest. "What are you talking about?"

"They mine salt under the lake," Ross Childers explained, eyeing Jack speculatively. "Have for years. The mines are like huge, man-made caverns that go halfway to Canada."

Jack grinned. "Halfway to Canada, but all the way to the Sisters."

Bill Childers nodded grudgingly at Jack. "You know.

That's an idea."

"I never heard of any salt mines," Jason said. "Where are they?"

"The entrance is in the industrial park on the lakefront," Ross explained. "Within the—ah—perimeter. Some students and faculty from the college got arrested for picketing there back in the spring. Seems there was a proposal to close the mines and use them as a nuclear waste reservoir." Ross rubbed the bridge of his nose with his forefinger, looking over at Becka.

Jack rolled his eyes. Naturally, his mother had been the ringleader of the protest.

Becka waved her arrest away, not the least bit apologetic. "After we killed the nuclear waste idea, the owners gave us a private tour of the works. It's like an underground palace, what they call room-and-pillar construction. The mines run as far north as the Sisters, and there are ventilation shafts that come up through some of the smaller islands."

"So we could bring people out through the mines and up on the Sisters," Ross concluded.

"It'll be like the Mines of Moria," Fitch said. "Hopefully without the orcs."

Jack nodded. "It's not perfect. I mean, you'd still have to work out the food, and there'd be long lines for the Porta-Johns."

"We have tons of bottled water and MREs in the basement of City Hall," Ross said. "In case of terrorist attack."

"Well, I'd say this qualifies," Ellen muttered.

"The food bank is full," Becka said. "We just finished the annual drive. But how are we going to get people to go into the mine?"

"Imminent nuclear accident," Fitch proposed. "At Ohio Power. All of northwestern Ohio could be contaminated. It'd be better than a chemical spill, since radiation is nondetectable. So we go door-to-door and tell people they have an hour to pack . . ."

"Half an hour," Seph put in.

"Half an hour, and then they have to go down into the mines for their own protection until the all clear."

Seph leaned against the mantel. "Nobody's allowed to leave. We can't let word leak out about what we're doing. The Anaweir will be vulnerable once they leave the sanctuary."

Jack shuddered. It was his idea, and if it all went bad . . .

Ross's thick fingers twitched, beating a tattoo on the table. "Once they reach the Sisters, we could fly them out then, or send boats from the mainland, and . . ."

"No." Seph shook his head. "No way. If the Roses get wind of it, they'd be even more vulnerable out on the water.

"I'll take care of the phone service on the islands, too," he added. "We can't let anyone know they're there. Which means we have to finish this thing before the food runs out," he said, half to himself.

"Don't worry," Jason said, smiling crookedly. "Once this starts, it'll be over in no time."

"Will and I'll go door-to-door," Fitch said. He was dressed in his urban-pirate garb, khakis and camouflage and military-surplus boots, heavy chains around his neck, a bandana tied rakishly around his head. Next to him, Will looked like a member of the Jaycees.

"You'll need help," Seph said, inspecting him skeptically.

Jack knew what he was thinking. Some people in town would likely slam the door if Fitch appeared on their stoop in the middle of the night. "We have to reach everyone before people begin leaving for work."

"Fitch, why don't you and Will handle college housing?" Becka suggested. "When you finish the dorms, start in on the streets south of campus. I'll work the north end."

"I'll help, too," Leesha announced.

Everyone swung around to look at her. Jack had forgotten she was there.

"You?" Jack blurted.

"You *can* use my help, you know," she said defensively. "I can be very persuasive."

"We can use every willing hand," Nick said.

"Deal," Fitch said. "You come with us. Let's go." He tossed Leesha a bandana like the one he wore. "Tie that on your head or arm or something."

Leesha glanced at Jason, who was gazing into the fireplace, pretending not to be listening, then followed Fitch out the door.

Oh, well, Jack thought. If Fitch can forgive being kidnapped and dragged to the ghyll as a hostage, I can go with it.

"Ellen and I will work the perimeter, to make sure no one sneaks out," Jack said to Ross.

"I'll go back to the station and brief first shift," Ross said. "I'll send along some black and whites to help clear the houses, escort people to the mine, and keep them from slipping away. We'll stick with the story about a nuclear accident."

He banged through the door.

The others left in twos and threes until it was just Seph, Jack, Ellen, and Jason.

"Well," Ellen said, sliding Waymaker into its baldric. "We'd better get going, too." Ellen looked from Seph to Jason. "What do we do when the Anaweir go? Do we go with them or what?"

Jason shook his head. "If we go, the wizards will know we've escaped somehow. It won't take them long to find the entrance to the mine. And if we take the Dragonheart with us, they'll track us down for sure. I don't think we want to be out on a rock in the middle of the lake when that happens. We have to make a stand, and here is as good a place as any."

But they'll level the town, Jack thought. He felt his childhood spiraling away from him, like rope uncoiling from a spool. "It seems weird. Everybody knowing, I mean," he said. "Even if we get through this, it's never going to be the same."

"I don't think that's going to be a problem," Jason said. "We'll all be dead."

When Seph opened his mouth to speak, Jason raised his hand to stop him. "I know we have weapons. I know we have talent and smarts and right's on our side and all that. But I've seen what's out there. Wall or no wall, they're coming in. If this were any kind of a fair fight, we'd win. As it is, we lose. No matter how much flame you take."

Seph stiffened. "I'm not . . ."

"Come on," Jason muttered. "Do you think we're stupid? As if you're not juiced enough on your own."

"Seph." Ellen stood and got in Seph's face, coming up on the balls of her feet, her hands fisted at her sides. "You promised."

"I promised not to use it unnecessarily. And I don't."

"It'd be nice if he'd share with some of the rest of us," Jason said.

"Come on, Ellen," Jack said, suddenly eager to leave the stifling room behind and commit mayhem on someone. "Let's go help round up the stragglers."

"So," Jason said, when Jack and Ellen had gone, "you haven't heard from your parents?"

Seph looked at him warily, as if worried they were still on the topic of flame. Then he shook his head. "Wish I could've asked D'Orsay if he'd seen them, but I didn't want to give anything away. I don't even know if they made it to the ghyll."

"Well," Jason said, "if they're in Raven's Ghyll Castle, that would explain why they haven't called."

"Yeah." Seph knuckled his forehead, as if it hurt. He looked bad, Jason thought. There were dark shadows under his eyes, the bones in his face stuck out even more than usual, and his hands trembled a little. When he noticed Jason looking, he shoved them into his pockets and glared at him, tight-lipped, as if daring him to raise the subject.

Whatever, Jason thought. Nick and Linda and Hastings had dumped on Seph, for sure. And they were dancing all around the possibility that Linda and Hastings might be dead.

Maudlin. You're getting totally maudlin.

"So it's as bad as all that?" Seph asked.

Jason looked up, startled, thinking Seph had somehow seen into his mind. But then Jason realized he was talking about the situation in the sanctuary.

Jason recalled the ranks of pavilions that encircled the walls, the flicker of wizard lights through the trees. "Yeah.

Worse." He paused, wondering how to frame his next words. "I've been thinking. There's some kind of connection between Madison and the Dragonheart. We should bring her back."

"No." Seph answered so quickly that Jason knew he'd been thinking the same thing.

"But she can help," Jason persisted. "The Dragonheart is the key, and we need to give her a shot at it. It's not just us. It's everybody else, too. There's going to be a slaughter. It could be the end of the underguilds."

"She's not one of us. She has her family to think about." Jason got the impression Seph was trying to convince himself. "Besides, she may not be vulnerable to magic, but she can be killed just the same. I don't want to be responsible for that."

"She'll do it if you ask."

"You sound like my father." Seph raked his hair back impatiently. "Of course she'd say yes if I went to her and told her we'd all be killed if she didn't."

Jason shrugged. "I don't like it either, but . . ."

"Don't you *get* it? I've done nothing but put her in danger from the time we met. If we knew anything for sure, it'd be one thing. But it's all hunches and speculation. We have no proof Madison could help us at all. If it's as bad as you say and we bring her here, she'll be killed with the rest of us. At least, this way, *somebody* stays alive."

Looks like there's no easy way out of this, Jason thought. Maybe not even a hard way. And if they lost, well . . . He shivered. Wizards had a talent for torture and something to prove. He hadn't forgotten his experiences at Leicester's hands.

Note to self: don't be taken alive.

He'd talk to Mercedes. Maybe she wouldn't give him flame, but she'd have something—some kind of poison pill that could put him out of reach if need be.

❧ Chapter Twenty-nine ❧
Exodus

Jason had never seen so much activity on the streets of Trinity, Ohio, at five in the morning. Police with hooded flashlights walked house-to-house, pounding on doors and rousting the occupants—smashing windows and clearing houses by force when necessary. Families poured out of their homes, towing suitcases and sleepy children, carrying duffle bags and pets in cages shrouded against the wind. Squad cars and ambulances hauled the aged and infirm.

Jack and Ellen had pulled on their leather gauntlets and light chain mail. Their great swords poked up over their shoulders, but under the circumstances, no one paid them much mind. Getting away with stuff depends a lot on attitude, Jason thought.

The evacuees had scrounged what protection they could. One entire family down to a babe in arms wore helmets fashioned out of aluminum foil to protect against radiation.

The Cosmic Shop next to campus had opened its doors and was doing a brisk business in healing crystals.

Will and Fitch and Leesha had done their work in the dormitories and student apartments. Students cruised by on skateboards, bikes, and rollerblades, wearing backpacks, headphones, and earbuds, wrapped in fleece blankets, carrying stuffed animals and cradling laptops. Many were still dressed in nightclothes under their coats: T-shirts and sweatpants, flip-flops or clogs. They looked like refugees from a country that favored audio technology, impractical footwear, and personal transportation.

At street corners, marshals clad in bright yellow storm coats labeled TRINITY POLICE directed the flow of people toward the lake.

"Hey, man!" A student shoved his radio toward Fitch and tapped his headphones. "How come I can't get any stations?"

"Must be radiation," Fitch replied.

Despite the crowds, and maybe because of the early hour, the exodus was relatively quiet. People shuffled along silently, clutching their belongings, fear and apprehension on their faces.

Good, Jason thought. Maybe we can actually pull this thing off without attracting the attention of the wizards outside.

Jason left the flow of traffic toward the salt mine and veered west along the lakeshore. Lightning strobed almost continuously, and thunder rattled the windows of the beachside cottages. Waves thrashed against the breakwater, drenching him in freezing spray. The wind howled off the lake and ice pellets stung his exposed flesh.

Wizards making a point.

He worked his way down the row of cottages, perfecting his evacuation system. If there was no answer when he knocked, he'd blow a hole in the door, reach in, and unlock it. He'd rouse the family, apply Persuasion to the head of household to get immediate cooperation (no one would agree to venture out in that weather otherwise), and hustle them out. He had it down to fifteen minutes per, after a few.

Just inside the Weirwall was Shrewsbury Place, looking like a wad of pink stucco bubblegum stuck onto the lakefront. He'd visited there when Leesha was staying with Aunt Millisandra. Before he went to Coalton County. Now Leesha was staying at Snowbeard's. But what about Aunt Milli?

He checked out the compound, which was embroidered with an elaborate wrought-iron fence. Leesha would've already come and picked up her aunt. She must've.

But she was working the south end, by campus.

No one answered when he knocked, so he let himself in the usual way.

People tended to wake up when he blew out the door, but no one responded, and he hoped that meant Aunt Milli was gone already.

He ended up surprising the old woman in her bed. Aunt Millisandra screamed when she opened her eyes and found him looming over her. She winged a lamp at him, followed by a blast of fire. He threw himself face down on the Persian rug, flames singeing the back of his head.

She hopped out of bed with amazing agility for one so old and locked herself in the bathroom. He could hear her just on the other side of the door, whimpering and talking to herself.

He was afraid to blow out the door with her so close. "Hey, I'm not going to hurt you. It's Jason, remember? Everybody has to leave. I came to get you. Please. Move away from the door."

She didn't reply, but kept muttering to herself. He could hear glass shattering, fixtures exploding. Water gushed out from under the door. Aunt Milli was creating her usual magical disaster area.

Damn. He didn't have time for this. "Come on, Aunt Milli. Just calm down and move away from the door."

Nothing. He was going to have to blow down the door, whether he liked it or not.

He heard a sound at the front of the house, a door slamming.

It was Leesha. Her cheeks were rosy from the cold and she had Fitch's bandana tied around her curls. She'd taken him by surprise, and it struck him how much he missed her.

"She's in there," he said, swallowing hard, nodding toward the bathroom.

"Aunt Milli?" Leesha knocked on the door. "It's Alicia. Open up." There was no answer, and she repeated herself, louder. "She's kind of deaf, remember?" she muttered aside to Jason.

A tremulous voice came from the other side of the door. "I don't believe you. Go away."

"Aunt Milli, I'm sorry Jason scared you. Remember Jason? He came for tea."

"I don't remember any Jason."

How about Jasper? Jason thought. Remember him?

Leesha looked down at the ankle-deep water. "You have to let us in, Aunt Milli. It looks like there's a flood."

"It's the middle of the night," Millisandra quavered.

"No, it's early yet," Leesha said. She paused, then said,

"There's a dance at the pavilion by the lake, and I thought you might like to come."

There was a pause, then, "Really? It's not too cold?"

"It's a lovely night," Leesha coaxed. "The moon's out, shining on the water, and I bet you can hear the band all the way to Canada."

"Oh, my, well, it's been a long time. Perhaps I *could* come for a little while."

Jason heard fumbling at the lock, and then the door eased open, revealing a shyly smiling Millisandra.

Leesha brought up her hand and fluffed a powder puff in her aunt's face. *Gemyn bana*. Mind-Slayer. Aunt Milli collapsed, and Jason caught her smoothly before she hit the tiles. He lifted her in his arms. She weighed nothing.

They joined the streams of humanity flowing along the lakefront toward the mines.

"Thanks for fetching Aunt Milli," Leesha said, touching his arm. "I don't think I could've carried her."

Jason said nothing.

They took a half dozen more steps, then Leesha said, "Jason, look. I'm sorry. About Barber."

"Seph and Jack told me about the collar." Jason looked straight ahead.

Leesha seemed determined to say her piece, as if she thought she wouldn't have another chance. "Barber beat me up. He told me he'd out me to all of you if I didn't help him. You'd throw me out of the sanctuary, and then he'd kill me."

Jason remembered the tea with Aunt Milli, the night before he left for Coalton County. Leesha's face had been bruised and swollen.

"So you had no choice," he said. "Understandable."

"After I put the lodestone in your pack, I knew I'd made a mistake. I tried to call you, to warn you, but you didn't answer."

Jason remembered the missed calls on his cell. "Guess it's my fault, then." Every time he opened his mouth, cold, hard words kept coming out.

"Jason." She put her hand on his arm again, and he shook it off. "I . . . I didn't mean that, I just wanted you to know that . . . I didn't want to."

He was afraid to look at her, afraid he'd give in. "Okay," Jason said, kicking fallen branches out of the way. They were coming up on the police checkpoint at the entrance to the mines. "I believe that you're sorry you gave me to Barber."

"I guess . . . he hurt you?" She shook ice from her curls, blinked it from her eyelashes.

Not as much as you did, Jason thought. It was his own fault. It wasn't like he'd walked into it blind. "I'm okay."

Two EMS corpsmen brought up a stretcher, and he carefully laid Aunt Millisandra on it. "Better stick with her, make sure she stays out," he said to Leesha, imagining what kind of chaos she'd create in the mines. "I'll go do another sweep."

But Leesha wasn't going to let it go. She sidestepped into his path. "If you believe I had no choice, what is it, then?" When he didn't say anything, she persisted. "What?"

"I thought you actually liked me. I didn't realize it was all a setup." Pathetic.

She grabbed his hand, gripped it tight in both of hers, like she never meant to let go. "I *do* like you. Jason, please, you've got to believe me. I . . ."

"I don't have to do anything. And I don't believe you. Not anymore." Gently, he extricated his hand from hers.

And walked away.

❧ CHAPTER THIRTY ❧
AGREEING TO DISAGREE

Jessamine Longbranch was tired of the privations of war.

She missed her palace on the banks of the Thames: the gardens layered in white roses, the servants who waited on her hand and foot, the more civilized intrigue that went on under the guise of wizard politics.

Shivering, she pulled her jacket close around her shoulders and pushed away her plate of shrimp. She was alone in her pavilion at three in the morning.

The problem with laying siege to a fortress was that the besiegers were as trapped as the besieged. It might be amusing to play army for a day or two, but this was excessive.

She couldn't shake the nagging sense that they'd been cheated. Where were the Anaweir citizens of Trinity? Why weren't they bursting through the Weirwall to be snatched up by the waiting wizards? Where was the panic in the streets? Just what this siege needed to end the impasse. Though it was Wylie's idea, she'd thought it would work.

Leaning forward in her chair, she poured herself another glass of wine. Then nearly spilled it when someone said, "Hey."

She whipped around, knowing it was already too late to defend herself.

"Relax," Jason Haley said, raising his hands to show that he was as unarmed as a wizard can be. "If I'd come to kill you, you'd already be dead."

"Then why are you here?" Jess demanded, still rattled. "And how did you get in?"

He ignored her question and dropped into the chair opposite her. "I need safe passage out of the sanctuary."

Jess blinked at him in surprise. "What? Why?"

"McCauley's insane," Haley said bluntly. "He's going to get us all killed."

"Ah." Jess settled more deeply into her chair. Intrigue and dissension. Perhaps she wouldn't call the guards just yet. "So this weapon he's talking about isn't so powerful after all?"

Haley shook his head impatiently. "Wrong. It's incredibly powerful. That's the problem."

"What do you mean?" Jess asked, growing impatient with the trickling pace of the story. The boy seemed jittery. He flinched at every sound and drummed his fingers on his thigh, tapping out an erratic rhythm.

"They're all dead," he said finally, looking up at her, then away. "The Anaweir."

"What?" Jess stared at him, thinking she must have misunderstood. From the look on his face, she hadn't. "How did that happen?"

"It was an accident." Haley stared off into space, a muscle in his jaw working. "He was experimenting with the Dragonheart."

"You're saying McCauley killed off the entire Anaweir population of the town?"

Haley nodded, taking a deep breath. "There are a few in the hands of the healers, but even if they survive, I don't think . . . anyway. It was a disaster." He scrubbed a hand through his ragged hair.

Jessamine scanned his face. Either the boy was a damned good liar, or he was telling the truth. "Becka Swift? Those boys who came to Raven's Ghyll?"

He nodded, looking down at the ground.

Jess couldn't help admiring the strategy, even while it made her task more difficult. "How convenient. Now McCauley doesn't have to deal with them."

From Haley's lack of response, Jess assumed he'd been thinking the same thing, even if he wouldn't say it.

"Well," she said. "Poor Jackson must feel a bit betrayed."

"I don't know what he thinks. People are afraid to say much. Now McCauley sorta kinda knows how to use it, but that's not good enough when it could destroy all of northern Ohio and Indiana. But he doesn't care. Ever since—well—what happened, he's determined to make it work. You know, to make the sacrifice worth it."

McCauley *had* seemed arrogant and self-important last time she'd seen him.

"And you don't want to be a martyr?" Of course he didn't. Whatever she thought about Jason Haley, he wasn't a fool.

"I don't want to throw my life away for nothing. I'm going to try and end this."

Jess raised an eyebrow. "You're going up against McCauley? Isn't that a bit of a . . . mismatch?"

Haley's head snapped up and Jess smiled into her wine.

The boy was jealous, naturally. McCauley was getting all the attention. He was the star of the rebel show.

"We'll see," Haley said. "I don't dare touch the Dragonheart. It's that unstable. But I'm going to bring back somebody who can handle it without getting killed."

Longbranch rubbed her chin. "Someone more powerful than McCauley?"

"In a way."

"Who?"

"Madison Moss."

Longbranch leaned in close. "The girl from Second Sister? Is she really gifted, then?"

"Not exactly. She can't use the stone like a wizard would. But she won't set it off."

She studied him. "You know this for sure?"

Haley nodded.

"Where is she?" Longbranch asked.

Haley snorted. "Right. Like I'm an idiot."

Jess sighed. "What are you proposing?"

"I'm thinking we could—you know—make a trade. If I bring you the Dragonheart, McCauley will surrender. He won't have a choice."

"Why would you do that?" Jess asked. "Why would you hand us the one weapon you have?" She wanted to believe it.

Haley jerked his head toward the town. "There are people in there I'd like to save. Plus, you give me D'Orsay. Like you promised."

Hmmm. She wouldn't mind losing D'Orsay now that his usefulness was over. They had the *sefa*s from the hoard, disappointing as they'd turned out to be.

"How do we know you're not going to fetch Hastings?"

"You control the outer wall," Haley pointed out. "How would he get in without your knowing? I'm betting you'd love to catch him on his own out there."

Ah. Yes. Indeed. "Why would Madeline . . . Madison Moss help *you*?" she asked delicately. "Isn't she going out with McCauley?"

"*Was*," Haley said. "They broke up. Let's just say she's open to new . . . possibilities." He looked at her dead on, delightfully shameless.

Haley had an edgy kind of charisma. Teenage girls always went for the bad boys. This was looking better and better. But Jess was suspicious when things looked too good to be true.

Haley smiled, as if reading her thoughts. "Look. Whether you believe me or not, you're not risking much. My presence or absence won't make much difference in the end result. If I'm telling the truth and we do a deal, you'll be saving all your skins. Trust me. Everybody dies if McCauley uses the Dragonheart."

"You'd betray your friends?" she asked, thinking, Why not? It was, after all, the wizardly thing to do.

"Better betrayed than dead," Haley said. "We can negotiate amnesties once this is over."

"Of course," Jess said smoothly. "When do you plan to go?"

"Tonight," Haley said. "I'll come through the outer gate just after midnight. Make sure you have my get-out-of-jail-free card ready."

Stone Cottage was deserted, as was usual these days. It took Jason less than an hour to gather his things and stuff them into a duffle. He wouldn't need much.

It was a long, spooky walk through near-deserted streets to the park. Jason kept to the shadows, hoping to avoid running into anyone he knew. The Trinity safety forces had entered the mines along with the citizens, maintaining the fiction that they were evacuating because of "radiation contamination."

A few ghost warriors patrolled the streets to prevent looting. It seemed a waste of effort to Jason. The town would be toast before long, given the Roses' proclaimed scorched-earth policy.

The hands on the clock tower scissored together as he cut across the vacant commons. The bells pealed out twelve times.

The usual motley of warriors stood guard at the Weirgate. Jason nodded briskly as he walked past, hoping to discourage conversation, but Jeremiah Brooks stepped out from their midst. "Mr. Haley, i'nt it?"

Jason raised his hand in a kind of salute. "Brooks." He kept moving, which he hoped would convey the message that he was on an urgent mission. But the warrior left his comrades and kept pace with him.

The night breeze carried the warrior's scent to Jason: a faint miasma of sweat, leather, old blood, and tobacco. He'd painted his face and stuck a few feathers into his hair, giving him a fierce, primitive look.

"So where you off to, then?" Brooks asked, a lilt in his voice betraying his eighteenth century Brit origins.

"Thought I'd have a look around outside," Jason said vaguely. "See if there's any movement along the boundary."

"Right," Brooks said. "Well, then." He rubbed a finger alongside his nose. "You take care out there. The Roses—they're right tricky."

"Right," Jason said. "See you." He passed through the gate and into no-man's-land. The skin on the back of his neck prickled. He couldn't help wondering if Longbranch would really play, and if the plan had been communicated to the wizards on guard. Otherwise this might be a very short journey. He resisted the temptation to recheck the location of all the *sefa*s hidden on his person.

As he approached the outer wall, he saw a half-dozen White Rose wizards collected around the wizard-wall gate. Longbranch's house. No sign of the Red Rose.

The sentries barred his way. "Name?"

"Haley."

Silently, they parted to allow him through.

The gateway yawned before him. Jason took a step forward, then another, expecting at any moment to be incinerated by some trap they'd forgotten to disarm. Five more steps, and he was through. He looked back. The White Rose wizards stood watching. He turned and kept walking, through the maze of wizard pavilions, past the camps of the Roses. Fifty more paces and he was well hidden in the woods. He paused a moment to brush away all the magical spyware and tethers that had been attached to him at the gate.

He moved ahead at a trot. Amazing how much stamina he had now that he'd quit smoking. He'd have to find a house, appropriate a car. He didn't have much time.

He looked back only once more, as he topped a small rise. Trinity swam uneasily in a sea of wizard mist like a fairy castle, the turrets of Mercedes's wall punching into the sky. Dark clouds rolled in from the lake, casting deep shadow over the town and thickening the night.

He turned, and ran faster.

☙ CHAPTER THIRTY-ONE ❧
ARMAGEDDON ON THE LAKE

Maybe we should've met at Jack's house, Seph thought. Just now it seemed perilous to be perched on an outcropping of rock at the edge of the lake.

The wind howled, flinging foam-speckled waves against the breakwater, ripping slate shingles from the roof and sending them spiraling away into the darkness. The trees in the garden bent double under glittering skins of ice. Sleet clattered against the leaded windows of Stone Cottage, the witchy wind screamed down the chimneys, and thunder and lightning clamored over the lake. They had to speak loudly to be heard over the din.

It was worse for Seph than for anyone else. The *aelf-aeling* made him hypersensitive—to the conjured storm, to the lowering cloud overhead, to the legions of wizards that drew close around the walls, like darkness around a shuttered lamp. It was as if his nerves had been sandpapered to exquisite tenderness. The magical activity at the boundary was a constant flickering, just out of his field of vision. He could see all of the possibilities, and they all looked bad.

He thought of the refugees out on the Sisters, and wondered how they were faring. They must think the world was truly coming to an end.

"Wonder what the weather people are saying about this one," he muttered.

"One can only imagine," Nick observed dryly, from his place by the fire. "Given that it is their habit to make a run-of-the-mill thunderstorm sound like Armageddon."

The old wizard had drawn a wool blanket around his shoulders. He and Leesha sat, a chessboard between them. Either she was really good or Nick was letting her win. He seemed to be working really hard at cheering her up, for some reason.

Jack and Ellen came banging in, shaking off the sleet and rain like dogs. And after them came Will and Fitch.

Seph looked from Will and Fitch to Jack and raised an eyebrow. "Aren't these two supposed to be on the Sisters?"

"They were hiding out," Jack explained. "But it's not like they haven't been busy."

"They've been mining the no-mans-land between the walls," Ellen said, grinning, slapping Will on the back, sending ice flying in all directions. "We've been providing cover."

Will and Fitch resembled high-concept members of the French Resistance, clad in black jeans and hoodies and black knit caps, faces smudged black so as not to shine out in the dark.

"The Roses are looking for hostages, you know," Seph said. "Not a good idea to be out there."

"Been hostages, done that," Fitch said, poking in the refrigerator and coming up with a bottle of juice.

Seph turned to Jack for help. "Aren't you afraid of blowing up our own warriors? I mean, we're out there patrolling that area."

"The motion sensors will tell us someone's out there," Fitch said. "But nothing blows up until I say so." He produced an electronic device, small as an MP3 player, and dangled it in front of Seph.

"Anyway. We're not going into the salt mines," Will said, thrusting his chin out belligerently, as if anxious to put the issue to bed. "So forget it."

"You don't have a chance against wizardry," Seph said.

Will's response was something like "Hmpf."

"All right," Seph said. "Thanks. But don't get killed, okay?" He made a mental note to try and put them out of harm's way when the bad stuff happened. One more thing to think about.

Mercedes had come in while they were talking. So they were all there except . . .

"Anyone seen Jason?" Jack asked, looking around in an exaggerated fashion.

"Jason?" Seph shrugged. "He'll be here. Probably got hung up. Why?"

"He was supposed to meet us two hours ago," Ellen said. "To go over the layout of the camp outside the walls. He didn't show."

There was a long, charged pause, full of throat clearings and significant looks. "What are you suggesting?" Seph said testily.

"I just think it's strange, that's all." Jack thrust the tip of the poker into the flames on the hearth. Sparks spiraled up. "I mean, he's been a loose cannon all along. Crazy to leave."

Seph waited for someone to disagree. No one did.

"Jason's been frustrated, yeah, but that was because he thought he could do more good in Britain than here. He can't still believe that."

"So where is he?" Jack asked.

"Hey." Ellen frowned at Jack. "Ease up."

Silence crackled among them.

"Brooks saw him outside the perimeter just before midnight," Jack said, propping the poker against the hearth. "He was headed for the Wizard Gate. No one's seen him since."

"What are you saying?" Seph asked. "That he ran out on us?"

Jack shrugged.

"He wouldn't just leave," Seph said flatly, feeling some of the old friction with Jack.

Without meaning to, Seph reached out with his mind, looking for the angry spark that was Jason. And did not find him anywhere within the perimeter. Could he have gone out to the Sisters? Was he somehow incapacitated so he couldn't be detected?

If not, how would he have breached the outer perimeter and navigated the wizard lines outside?

"He wouldn't run out on you," Leesha said suddenly. They all turned to look at her. "He *wouldn't*," she insisted, shoving the chess board away so the pieces toppled onto the floor.

Jack gave her a look and rolled his eyes, as if to say, *Consider the source.*

"Nobody said that," Seph said, looking around at the others, daring them to disagree. Jack fixed him with his blue-eyed gaze, but said nothing. Seph remembered what Ellen had told him, more than a year ago. *Jack's more wary than he used to be. Before Raven's Ghyll.*

"Perhaps we should discuss what will happen tomorrow," Nick suggested softly.

Jack was conscious of overwhelming thirst. Fatigue dragged at his legs and arms like millstones. Or maybe it was the armor he wore. Whenever he closed his eyes, he saw the images of the men he'd killed, as if they were painted on his eyelids. So he struggled to keep his eyes open, blinking against the dust and sweat and blood caked on his face.

He was looking for his comrades. He'd somehow lost them during his last one-on-one with a wizard who wouldn't go down. By the time he'd finished him, and yanked his sword free, he was alone among the trees, in a wood littered with bodies and watered with blood.

And so he moved silently through the woods, listening for the telltale clash of metal and magic that would direct him to the ongoing fight. But nothing. Even the birds had left that desolate place hours ago, understanding that it was no place for living things. It's a peculiarity of man—this lining up and marching toward death. The only other creatures who don't flee a killing field are the scavengers who come after the fact.

On all sides lay the detritus of terrible endings. Or heroic endings. The results looked the same.

Finally, he broke from the forest and onto a field pegged with ancient trees, many of them charred and splintered and broken, as yet unaware they were doomed, thrusting fistfuls of leaves into a brilliant blue sky. Stone buildings ringed the green on all sides.

The commons. And, everywhere he looked, bodies.

"Jack!" Ellen gently tugged at Jack's arm. He responded by swinging his fist at her, and she captured it between her two hands, forcing it down onto the pillow. "Jack, you're dreaming, cut it out!"

His body bucked and twisted as he tried to free himself. His red-gold hair was sluiced across the pillow, damp with sweat, and he muttered something unintelligible.

"Come on, Jack, you're waking up the whole house!" Man, he's strong, she thought, unable to resist a little professional envy.

Another near miss with that big fist, and she picked up a glass from the bedside table and sloshed the contents into his face.

He surged into a sitting position, spluttering, groping for his belt dagger. Good thing he didn't have it, or she might have been skewered before he came awake. She avoided his grasp, slid to the floor, and retreated a few yards away, watching him.

Finally, his bleary blue eyes cleared and focused on her. "What the . . . ?"

"You were dreaming," Ellen repeated. "You've been screaming and yelling half the night. Nobody can sleep."

He stared at her as if she were a ghost. It was unnerving.

"I was elected to come in and put a stop to it. You sure wake up grouchy. Don't take a weapon to bed, is my advice."

"Ellen," he whispered hoarsely, "I killed them. I killed them all." He gazed down at his hands, turning them palms up, as if they were covered in blood.

"You killed who?" Ellen asked, but Jack didn't seem to hear her.

She came and sat on the edge of the bed. "Come on. It was just a dream."

With that he threw back the covers and erupted from the

bed, oblivious of his state of dress. Yanking his duffle bag from the closet, he emptied it onto the floor. He groped through the debris of clothes and came up with a chamois-wrapped package.

He sat down next to Ellen on the bed and ripped away the leather with trembling fingers. It was a mirror, its silver frame engraved with dragons and other fantastical images. He stared into the glass with a desperate intensity.

"Wow, that's cool," Ellen said, combing her fingers through Jack's hair, which stuck out in all directions. "What does it do?" She leaned close so she could see. "Is it magic?"

What she saw was not Jack's face, but an image that looked like a battlefield. Only familiar.

"Is that no-man's-land?" she asked.

A lone warrior stood at the center of the field, the sunlight striking his red-gold hair, head bowed, cradling a comrade in his arms. And all around him lay the fallen—warriors from five centuries, surrounded by the gear and weapons appropriate to their time.

"That's you," Ellen said. "What's it mean?"

Jack snatched the mirror away and flung it across the room. It smashed against the wall, and dropped behind the dresser.

❧ CHAPTER THIRTY-TWO ❧
DON'T LOOK BACK

Madison Moss had long ago mastered the gift of looking forward—of achieving that narrow focus on goals. Not that there wasn't a price. Sometimes she wondered if she was doomed to repeat the mistakes of the past, since she'd trained herself not to look back at it.

But Maddie was, first and foremost, a survivor. Beyond that, she'd protect the ones she loved. Whatever it took. That, at least, gave her direction.

So, for now, she could set aside wondering what had happened at Bryson Farms. Set aside the Chicago Institute of Art and Seph McCauley.

Set aside Warren Barber's threats.

It didn't take her long to pack. She stuffed two changes of clothes into a duffle. After some thought, she returned her father's gun to the wood box, made two sandwiches from the groceries she'd bought, and piled them in a six-pack cooler with a couple of cans of pop. She didn't mean to stop.

Finally, she pulled on blue jeans and a sweatshirt and boots over heavy socks. Clothes that said she meant business. She set the duffel by the door and laid her silver-studded denim jacket on top, then tied her hair back with a bandana.

Her plan was simple—she'd drive back to Trinity and go directly to St. Catherine's. Seph's barriers and wards wouldn't give her any trouble. With any luck, she'd take the Dragonheart and be gone before anyone knew she was there.

That was it. What would she do if she ran into Seph? She'd make something up.

She tried to think of what came after that, but drew a complete blank. She didn't trust Barber, but she had no clue how to get around him.

She heard the clatter of gravel against metal as a car pulled into the yard, followed by a door slamming.

Had Barber come back for some reason? The police? County child welfare? None of the possibilities were good. She thought about running out the back, but she'd still have to get past whoever it was to get down the mountain. So she knelt on the floor beside the wood box like a cornered animal, one hand gripping the loaded pistol.

She heard footsteps cross the creaky porch, but still jumped when someone banged on the door.

"Come!" she said, aiming the pistol through the wood box at the front door.

The visitor stood silhouetted against a rectangle of sunlight, squinting into the darkened room, then took a few hesitant steps forward.

"Madison?"

"Jason?" She let go of the pistol and sat back on her heels, her breath whooshing out in relief.

The light struck his face as he moved out of the doorway. He looked better than when she'd last seen him, when he'd left for Trinity. His coloring was restored, though he looked like he'd not slept for days. His hair had grown out in a haphazard way.

She wanted to grab hold of him, to somehow hand off her load of problems. But he might not be an ally. She had only one agenda—could have only one agenda. His might be different.

She stood, a little shakily, thinking furiously. "So. Not to be rude, but what are you doing back here?" she asked.

The question seemed to take him by surprise, as if he hadn't planned anything further than getting to Booker Mountain. "Well, we—um—that is, I wondered if you'd heard what was going on in Trinity."

Barber had told her there was trouble, but she wasn't sure what kind, and besides, it wouldn't do to say she'd been chatting with Warren Barber. So she shook her head. "What's going on in Trinity?"

Jason's eyes lit on her duffle bag, sitting by the door. "Were you going somewhere?"

"Well." She thought a moment, decided, and answered in a rush. "Actually, I was just getting ready to leave. To come back north. My . . ." She gulped, lost for a moment, then went on. "Someone else has the kids for awhile. So I thought . . ."

"Great," Jason said. "That's great." They stood in awkward silence for a moment, then he glanced toward the kitchen. "I drove straight through. Could I get something to drink?"

"Well. Sure." She motioned him to the kitchen table and fetched him a cold pop from the refrigerator. All the while itching to be gone.

She set it on the table in front of him and leaned back against the kitchen counter. "You look better," she said.

He grimaced. "Yeah. Well. I'm close to a hundred per cent. But a hundred per cent ain't that great." He didn't say it like he was fishing for a compliment. "Damn Warren Barber, wherever he is."

Yeah, she thought. Damn Warren Barber.

"So. How is Seph?" She couldn't help herself.

Jason's words came out in a rush, as if some internal dam had broken. "Bad. Look, Maddie. We need your help, but he won't ask for it. Trinity is under siege. The place is surrounded, and they say they'll attack tomorrow if we don't surrender."

She blinked, momentarily diverted from her urge to be gone. "What do you mean, the town is surrounded? By who?"

"The Roses. And D'Orsay. They've put up this mammoth wizard wall all around the town that keeps everybody inside—Weir and Anaweir. Well, first, Mercedes put up a wall. Remember? Will and Fitch told us about it when they came. But that one just worked on the Weir."

Seconds passed while she processed this. "Okay. You're saying there's two walls, one inside the other. And the outside one catches the Anaweir. So nobody can get in or out of Trinity? How can that be? It's not like no one would notice. What about the . . . the police?"

Jason dismissed the police with a wave of his hand. "What do the Roses care? The Anaweir authorities can't do anything. Trinity is sort of isolated to begin with. They've clothed the wall in confusion charms, so no one can find us. Phones, TV, radio don't work inside the wall. We might as well be in the Middle Ages."

An image came to her—Trinity as a fifteenth-century university town under siege, in perpetual twilight, shadowed by menacing black walls. "But . . . isn't everyone going crazy inside? What about the kids at the high school? And people . . . people have jobs. . . ."

Jason hesitated, as if debating the wisdom of sharing a secret. "The Anaweir are gone. Seph snuck them out of town."

"And Seph is . . ."

"He's using wizard flame," Jason said brutally. "It makes him incredibly powerful, but it's dangerous, I guess. He's going to save the town and everybody in it or die trying."

No. Focus forward. Don't look back. There's nothing back there but monsters. "But. Why are they doing this? What do they want?"

"They want the Dragonheart."

Madison turned and stared out the kitchen window, over the sensuous hips and shoulders of mountains that rolled into the distance. She hoped the view would soothe her so she wouldn't vomit into the sink. "What do they want with it?"

She felt the hot pressure of Jason's gaze on the back of her neck. "They think it's a weapon—like, the mother of all weapons."

"A weapon?" So that's why Barber wanted it. Madison had never thought of it as something *dangerous*. But what did she know? "Well. If it's a weapon, can't you use it against them?"

"We don't know how. We're not even sure what it does." He took a breath. "And . . . we can't get near it."

She swung round to face him. "What? Since when?"

"Ever since you left. It's like it's got some kind of force

field around it. If we try to touch it, it erupts in flame or slams us down on our butts."

"You're saying four wizards can't pick up a stone?" He nodded, and she said, "Why didn't you tell me?"

He shrugged unhappily. "I kept thinking it would settle. I . . . I wanted to try and use it."

Could things get any worse? "But you handled it before, didn't you? The Dragonheart. Did you have any trouble then?"

"No." Jason rubbed his stubbled chin. "Nick and Mercedes and I fooled with it for weeks, trying to figure out what it did. But it's like something woke it up. Power just rolls off the thing. It's like this big antenna that's drawing wizards and Weir from all over." He looked up at her, fixing her with his blue eyes. "It seemed to respond to you before. I thought maybe . . . your leaving . . . set it off. Somehow."

She'd last touched the Dragonheart the day she left for Coalton County. It had blazed up, so bright it hurt her eyes. Magic had poured into her until she ripped her hands away.

Maybe she'd had something to do with the change in the stone. Maybe she'd been the one to mess it up. Either that or the hex magic it had driven out of her.

Jason was still watching her, waiting for a response.

"What do you think I can do?" she asked.

He studied her, as if assessing his chances of success. "Two things. I want to see if you can do something with the Dragonheart. You're not vulnerable to magic, so you ought to be able to handle it, at least."

"But . . . I'm not gifted," Madison protested. "I don't know how to do magic." She was torn so many different ways, she didn't even know how to strategize.

Jason gripped her hands and played his best card. "Look. Seph and Nick saw the painting you did. The hex painting. It put Seph down for days. He still hasn't fully recovered. That's why he's using flame. They thought maybe you were . . . maybe you'd sold out. That's why I came down here before. I was supposed to find out for sure."

Madison flailed for an answer. "I would . . . I would never hurt Seph," she stammered, feeling like the worst kind of liar. "He should know that."

"He does. He never bought the idea that you'd turned. But he needs your help now. The Dragonheart aside, you can help us when the Roses attack. Maybe you can disarm them like you did at Second Sister, if we handle it right."

I can't.

But, maybe, after she gave the Dragonheart to Barber, she could somehow help them. She could make up for what she'd done. If they weren't already dead. If they'd even accept her help.

Her plan was in a shambles now. There was no way she'd get in without Jason's help.

She swallowed hard. "The town is surrounded, you said. Can you get me in?"

He hesitated for a fraction of a second, then said, "Yes."

"Guess we'd better go along, then," Madison said. "Time's a-wasting."

A relieved smile broke onto Jason's face. "Great," he said. "Great. Um, could we take your truck? I kind of borrowed a car without asking. I'd rather not be driving around in it."

Madison had planned to propose that she follow him in the truck so she could leave when she'd finished in Trinity.

But there was a wired intensity in Jason's movements that told her this was nonnegotiable.

"Oh. Okay." She scooped up her keys from the table and slung the duffle bag over her shoulder.

But he gripped her wrist and took the keys from her hand. "I'll drive," he said.

✂ CHAPTER THIRTY-THREE ✂
WEIRSTORM

Before dawn, the Roses woke the remaining residents of Trinity with a fusillade of magical projectiles—cannisters of *ligfyr*—launched from atop the wizard barrier. They burst against the rebels' elaborate inner wall with bone-rattling force, drenching the territory between with wizard fire. Toxic smoke boiled up from the fires between the walls, bloodying the underbelly of the lowering clouds. Defenders toppled from the inner wall like rotten fruit, clutching their throats.

The rebels answered with withering fire of their own, raking over the top of the outer wall, clearing it of wizards and weapons. Jessamine leaned forward, squinting into the murk, gripping the parapet. A tall, spare figure strode to the battlement at the front of the barbican over the rebel gate, ignoring the shells exploding all around him. McCauley. Again. He raised both arms, and the smoke roiled back, away from the rebels, enveloping the Rose fortifications in a cloud of poison.

Jess charged out of her bastion and attempted to drive the smoke back where it belonged, then dove for cover as a blast of fire slammed into the wall just beneath her.

Peering over the edge, she surveyed the damage: a huge bite had been taken out of the smooth surface of the wizard wall, and great chunks of stone lay scattered on the ground beneath. Much more of that, and the wall would be porous as a sieve.

How did he do it? Their barrier was built to withstand magical assault—that was the whole point. She stormed back along the wall, sweeping past the wizards flinging flaming *ligfyr* stones against the rebels from heavy cover.

"Send a patrol down to repair the wall immediately," she ordered. "And kill McCauley," she added, as an after-thought.

Outside the gate, the army of the Roses sprawled across farm fields and littered the wooded groves. Wizards, mostly, with a few sullen sorcerers stirring cauldrons of magically enhanced *ligfyr*. Others beat out throwing stars of glowing metal, infused with deadly enchantments.

D'Orsay's famous hoard had been disappointing to say the least. Jess couldn't help wondering if he was holding back—if he had a secret stash someplace. They'd been forced to use the weapons sparingly—more to inspire panic among the defenders than anything else. Some were delightfully horrible—like the glass spheres that broke open on impact, releasing hundred of deadly *naedercynn* vipers within the sanctuary. Or the *gliwdream* pipes whose high-pitched music drove the defenders insane.

Jessamine stopped to question her operatives at the gate. Still no sign of Haley.

Out on the drilling field, Geoffrey Wylie struggled to

bludgeon hordes of wizards into order. Wizards were not terribly good at teamwork. It hadn't been considered a virtue up to now. When he saw Jess, he broke off his harangue and turned the command over to a handsome young wizard in Red Rose garb. Hays was his name, if she remembered right.

"I don't like this dual-wall system," Wylie said, brushing ice from his shoulders (the latest Weirstorm had overshot its mark a bit). "We could be trapped in between and annihilated. We'd better take the outer wall down when the time comes to attack."

Jessamine brushed away the suggestion. "And have them scatter like quail and regroup somewhere else? I think not. We need to teach them a lesson. Besides, we can't risk the possibility of losing the Dragonheart."

"You're not the one who has to lead the charge through the gate against an unknown weapon."

Jessamine twitched with irritation. Wylie had been chosen as commander because he'd attended West Point a century ago. And he looked the part, certainly, being tall and commanding.

But Wylie belonged to the wrong house. The second worse thing to losing the Dragonheart to the rebels would be to have it fall into the hands of the Red Rose.

"They're as good as they're going to be," Wylie persisted. "If we're going to breach the walls, we should do it soon." Wylie tilted his head toward his magical army. "If we keep this many wizards together much longer, they'll be killing each other."

"Why don't you assign troublemakers to repairing the wall? McCauley is ripping holes in it, God knows how."

Jess preferred to wait for Haley for a number of reasons. Anything could happen during a melee inside the fortress walls. Anyone could come up with the Dragonheart. Wylie, for instance. That would be a disaster.

But she knew she couldn't stall much longer.

Ellen couldn't help tensing and squinching her eyes shut as she heard the familiar whistle of incoming. Followed by the boom of impact. Another one had gotten by her.

She twisted round, gazing over the park and up Library Street. A column of ruddy flame and smoke rose from the town center. That one must have landed somewhere on the commons. There wasn't much left on the green to destroy, save a spectacularly ugly fountain that would no doubt survive the entire war.

The Roses fired canisters of wizard fire that exploded into wildfires. Squads of sorcerers were kept busy all day and night, putting out blazes, else the town would have long since burned to the ground.

But some of the missiles were booby-trapped, spewing *gemynd bana* and worse when approached by the fire teams. Those who weren't killed were disabled for days. And they couldn't afford the loss of a single hand.

Ellen preferred to face her enemies sword-to-sword, on the ground. This faceless assault from the air was unnerving. She took a deep breath and forced herself to look across the black abyss of no-man's-land, to where spots of light moved like fireflies atop the wizard wall. Wizards readying the next onslaught. It was her third night in a row on the perimeter, and she was exhausted enough to make mistakes. But the work she and Jack did on the wall kept the bombardment somewhat in check.

Across the way, one of the fireflies brightened—a wizard gathering power, preparing to fire. Ellen fished a throwing star from the pouch under her arm and sent it whistling off into the dark, then rolled sideways, banging her elbow into the wall as a blast of fire came toward her.

Across the way, someone screamed. The firefly launched awkwardly from the wall, spiraling down into the darkness to be extinguished at the base of the wall.

"Catch a falling star," Ellen muttered, blotting blood from her elbow and looking for another target.

Off to her left, an enormous gout of flame and smoke signified that Seph was at work. Several times during the night, he'd spun past her, the hot ripple of magic in his wake identifying him. He was constantly on the move, scouring the wizard wall clean of bombardiers, providing cover for the warrior patrols between the walls. Blasting ruinous holes in the wizard wall opposite.

Ellen and Jack and Iris Bolingame and some of the other wizards helped, but Ellen had to admit that so far it was Seph that kept the Roses at bay. They'd soon be forced to make repairs to their wall, which was beginning to resemble sinister black Swiss cheese.

Let them try, Ellen thought, peering through the embrasure to the ground below, judging the firing distance to the base of the wall. They'd be ducks on a pond.

Why don't they try to breach the walls? she thought. We're totally outnumbered. What are they waiting for? How long could this bombardment go on? How long would the Anaweir stay on the Sisters before the Roses became aware of them? Before they ran out of food?

A slight sound behind her caused her to swivel, gripping the hilt of her knife.

"Whoa. Don't stab the messenger." It was Fitch, still in his Resistance garb. He shoved a parcel into her hands. "More stars." And another. "Midnight snack."

The Weir had laid a scaffolding over their wall on the sanctuary side, to allow the Anaweir to navigate it. The wall itself was still invisible to them.

Ellen ripped open the package of throwing stars and poured them into her pouch. "Tell Mercedes thanks." And turned back to her work. She wouldn't let another one past her, not if she could help it.

Fitch put his hand on her arm. "Jack says he's got the wall, so take ten to eat."

Ellen looked down the curtain wall to where Jack must be. She missed his solid presence at her side. It would've been great to have him next to her, but this way, if her position was hit, only one of them would go down.

Fighting always made her ravenous. She slid into a sitting position and unwrapped her dinner, resting it on her knees.

Fitch held out a water bottle filled with green liquid.

"What's this?" she asked suspiciously, turning it in her hand.

"Some kind of power-ade potion Mercedes whipped up."

"No dope," Ellen said, trying to hand the bottle back to Fitch.

"I don't think it's dope, exactly," Fitch said, with a what-do-I-know shrug. "Just like—you know—an energy drink."

"Hmpf." She took an experimental sip. And then

another. It tasted like fresh air in some unsullied part of the world.

She drained half the bottle, set it down, and bit into her sandwich.

Fitch still hung on the scaffolding and pulled out a digital camera. He took several photographs of Ellen.

"You're photographing me eating my *dinner*?" She waved a chicken leg at him. "That's exciting. What for?"

"Somebody has to do it," he said, gazing out at the fires beyond the walls, his face solemn and ruddy in the sanguineous light. "Like there was this photographer during the Civil War. Mathew Brady. He was assigned by the U.S. government to document the war."

"Fitch, you are such a nerd."

He said nothing.

She finished the sandwich and wiped her mouth with the back of her hand. "You think we're going to lose, don't you?"

"What makes you say that?" he said.

Ellen noticed he didn't deny it. "Because the winners always write the history. You want to make sure something survives. Of us."

He smiled at that, looking a little embarrassed. "Even if it's only digital."

❧ CHAPTER THIRTY-FOUR ❧
THROUGH ENEMY LINES

It was that breathless hour before sunrise. Up on Booker Mountain, Maddie might be preparing for the breaking of light to the east, for the reliable hills shouldering forward out of the dark.

But Maddie was not on Booker Mountain. She was creeping through the underbrush of Perry Park, following Jason Haley, wondering what kind of fool's errand she was on.

For a city boy, he was sure-footed in the woods. Maddie had only to follow his illuminated form, like a cloud that had passed in front of the sun.

Now she could see lights bleeding through the trees up ahead. Jason paused, waiting for her to catch up. "Camps of the Rose armies," he whispered in her ear.

Here the underbrush thinned as they entered a decimated grove of old-growth forest. Ancient oaks lay toppled—wizards had knocked down trees, creating scattered clearings where they could raise their pavilions and post wards and guards against their brethren.

A great bulking mass rose above the trees beyond the camps, blotting out the dying stars. "What is that?" Madison whispered, conscious of the surrounding wizards.

"That's the wizard wall," Jason muttered.

"I don't get it. Why can I see it?" She was familiar with Weirnets, which captured the Weir, but were invisible to anyone else—the Anaweir and elicitors.

Jason shook his head. "I was hoping you could just walk through it. It's not a Weirnet, it's a wizard wall. It's built by wizard magic, but constructed of stone, like any fortress. This complicates things. We'll have to go in through the gate," he said, glancing at her, then away. He'd been doing a lot of that slide-away looking, lately.

She said nothing, waiting for him to go on.

"So there's a chance we'll be caught. If that happens, can you just trust me?"

"What?" Her voice rose, and Jason flinched, putting a finger to his lips to shush her. She continued, in a hoarse whisper, "What kind of a question is that?"

"I'll get you through, I promise, but . . . just . . . play along, okay? Can you not ask questions?" He actually looked embarrassed.

"Um. Okay."

And so they went on, Madison turning over what he'd said and wondering just what she'd committed herself to.

The closer they got to the barrier, the more difficult it became to remain undiscovered. They had to stop a hundred yards from the gate. Their cover was gone—trees had been cleared close in to the wall. Wizards massed around the gate, seemingly in preparation for imminent battle.

Munitions masters passed out backpacks, armor, and supplies to the gathered troops. Flaming missiles arced overhead, disappearing behind the sanctuary wall. The ground shook as they struck their targets. Smoke and flame roiled into the sky. Trinity had been transformed into a fortress during her absence.

She could feel the seductive pull of the Dragonheart from within the walls. Her own heart beat faster—fear and dread warring with excitement.

Jason danced restlessly in place. "We're running out of time. Guess we have to take the direct approach." He grabbed Madison's hand and bulldozed through the jostling crowds of wizard soldiers and support staff.

In all the chaos and confusion, no one seemed to notice them until they were within a few paces of the gate. Then a half-dozen wizards in Red Rose livery stepped out of the crowd and surrounded them, shields fully raised. Madison drew closer to Jason, remembering what he'd said.

"Haley? It *is* you. The famous Dragonheart thief." The speaker, a tall, scarred wizard, looked vaguely familiar.

Jason studied him a moment, as if debating the possibility of denying it, then nodded grudgingly. "Wylie."

Wylie grinned. "This *is* a surprise. Wandering through enemy lines, are you? I knew you were foolhardy, but it seems you have a death wish." He glanced at Madison, then did a double-take. "I know you! You were the girl at Second Sister. With McCauley."

Madison blinked at him and opened her mouth to reply, then flinched in surprise as Jason draped an arm around her and pulled her in close. He gripped her chin and turned her face up, kissing her convincingly on the lips. Still holding her tight, he said, "She's with me now."

The Red Rose wizards laughed, elbowing each other like high school boys bs-ing under the bleachers.

Maddie wanted to stomp on Jason's foot, wriggle free, and ask him what he thought he was doing, but the rigidity of his body was a warning.

"What do you mean? I thought she and McCauley were going out," Wylie said.

"*Were*," Jason said, grinning.

Madison bristled. They were talking about her in front of her, like she was deaf or stupid.

Her mood must have shown on her face, because Jason looked at Madison and shook his head almost imperceptibly, then turned back to Wylie. "Anyway. Great to catch up. But we've got to get going."

Two of Wylie's companions took hold of Jason's arms. "Oh, no," Wylie said, getting in Jason's face. "You're both coming back with me. You're going to tell me all about the Dragonheart and what's happening in the sanctuary." He smiled savagely and patted Jason on the cheek. "I'm really looking forward to our conversation."

Jason jerked his head away. "Didn't Dr. Longbranch tell you?"

Wylie's smile faded fast. "What do you mean?"

"Ask her. It's all arranged. She'll explain."

Madison looked from Jason to Wylie. If it was a bluff, it was a good one.

Wylie went white with anger. "The hell I will. You're my prisoners, and . . ."

Suddenly they were surrounded by a full dozen White Rose wizards.

"Mr. Wylie, sir, Dr. Longbranch is waiting for these two," one of them said.

There was nothing to do but be hustled along toward an elaborate peaked tent flying the banner of the White Rose. Wylie and his wizards trailed unhappily behind. Jason stared straight ahead, but kept a hard hold on Madison's elbow. Madison couldn't help looking back at the gate. What was Jason thinking? Did he really think he'd have better luck with Longbranch?

Dr. Longbranch's tent was guarded by a dozen more wizards in White Rose garb. One of the guards disappeared inside. He returned and nodded to Jason and Madison. "You two. Inside. The rest of you stay out here."

Wylie watched sullenly as the guards ushered his prisoners in.

Inside, it was as much like a palace as a tent can be. Fancy rugs were spread over the ground, and velvet and satin hangings draped the walls and curtained off a sleeping area on one side. At the other end of the tent, chairs were gathered around a conference table. Wizard lights cast long shadows. Soft music floated in, somehow countering the sounds of the battle at the wall, and incense burners obscured the reek of warfare.

Madison just had time to take this all in before a tall witch-woman swept toward them, the velvet hem of her gown sliding over the carpets. She had green eyes and a long fall of pitch-dark hair. Ignoring Jason, she gripped both of Madison's hands and looked into her eyes. Unlike most wizards, she seemed to have no fear of Maddie's touch, but was careful not to let any Persuasion trickle through.

"Madison," she said. "I'm so pleased you've come. I'm Jessamine Longbranch."

"Hel . . . hello," Madison stammered, while her mind raced a mile a minute. *She knows who I am. She was expecting me.* She glanced over at Jason, who was all stony-faced except for his eyes, which glittered in the wizard light.

"I understand you're an artist," Longbranch continued.

"Yes, ma'am," Madison said, reclaiming her hands.

"I'm something of a patron of the arts myself. Perhaps I could make some introductions."

"Well. Sure," Madison said. "That'd be great." All of a sudden, everyone was interested in her art. Because they had another agenda.

"But first, we have to end this war," Longbranch continued. "So much bloodshed. So unnecessary."

"You're getting ready to attack?" Jason asked.

"We are." Dr. Longbranch nodded. "We were waiting for you."

"Right," Jason said, squeezing Madison's arm: a warning. "So we'd better get going."

Dr. Longbranch raised her hand to quash any notion of an imminent departure and turned to Madison. "The rebels won't surrender as long as they hold the Dragonheart. That's where you come in." She paused. "Jason says you can go into the sanctuary and bring it to us."

It was like a punch to the gut. "What?" Madison looked from Jason to Dr. Longbranch.

"Hey, Maddie. You know. The stone we talked about, remember?" Jason said quickly, facing Madison and putting his hands on her shoulders, looking intently into her eyes.

"All we have to do is bring it to Dr. Longbranch, and the war's over. We'll have more money than we'll ever need. We can go wherever you want. Paris. London. Bali. You can paint full time. We can be together." And then he kissed her again, probably to quiet her mouth.

Dr. Longbranch laughed. "You are a piece of work, Haley. Does McCauley know you've stolen his girl?"

Everybody's crazy, Madison thought, as Jason released her. But it doesn't matter. I have to get into the sanctuary. And if this is the way to do it, well . . . She'd have to make it up as she went along.

"Seph never had any time for me," she said, wishing for the hundredth time she'd inherited the lying gene. "It's his own fault if someone comes along who knows how to treat a person." I sound like Mama, Madison thought. Always trading the devil she knew for the one she didn't.

"Right," Dr. Longbranch said, smiling. "It *is* his own fault."

"Should we go, then?" Jason asked, jumpy as always when he had to wait.

"Yes and no," Dr. Longbranch said. "Madison will go and get the Dragonheart. Haley, you'll stay here to make sure she comes back."

"What?" Madison swung round and glared at the wizard. "No way. I'm not going without Jason." She latched onto his arm as if the two of them were soldered together.

At a nod from Longbranch, two White Rose guards stepped out of the shadows and grabbed Jason's arms, pulling him free of Madison's grasp. "Take him to our detention area and keep him close," she ordered.

She turned back to Madison. "My dear, be reasonable,"

Longbranch said. "Go and get the Dragonheart and bring it to me. Your young sweetheart will be free in a trice, and you'll come away with a fortune in walking-around money. Refuse, and I'll kill him now."

"Go on, Madison," Jason said, giving her a *Shut up* kind of look. "I'll be fine. The sooner you go, the sooner you'll be back."

"Just be sure you give the stone directly to me," Longbranch said. "We don't want it falling into the wrong hands."

Madison looked from Jason, who jerked his head toward the gate, signaling her to get moving, to Longbranch, whose cold, direct gaze said Jason would pay in blood for any kind of double cross.

One thing was clear: Jason Haley had been lying to her since the moment he set foot on her porch. Was he really plotting with the Roses? Or had he decided to sacrifice himself to get her into the sanctuary?

Madison threw her arms around Jason's neck as if she couldn't face being parted from him and whispered fiercely in his ear, "You lying lunatic bastard. They're going to *kill* you."

"I love you, too," he murmured. "Go find Seph. Help him."

She let go of him and turned and stalked toward the gate, flanked by a wedge of White Rose soldiers, oblivious to the chaos around her.

It was a mess. An absolute, total mess, since no matter what she did, she'd end up with blood on her hands.

Because there was no way she could bring the Dragonheart back to Jessamine Longbranch.

Geoffrey Wylie watched as White Rose soldiers escorted the elicitor Madison Moss toward the gate, hands twitching as he fought back the impulse to incinerate them. Moments later, more of Longbranch's wizards hustled Jason Haley off the other way, toward the middle of the White Rose camp.

The stench of betrayal was in the air. And it centered on Haley, the girl, and the Dragonheart. He could feel power building behind the walls, like a cataclysm in the making. What would happen if they breached the wall? Would they be vaporized, annihilated in an instant?

Longbranch was up to something, and Wylie didn't plan on being the sacrificial lamb.

He turned to his Red Rose captain, Bruce Hays, who stood, awaiting orders. "How many wizards do we have?"

"For the Red Rose?" The officer considered. "About three hundred, give or take a few infiltrators and spies for the other sides."

Wylie smiled. Three hundred wizards was an army larger than any seen since the Wars of the Roses.

"Here's what we'll do. Collect the Red Rose wizards and get them to the gate. We're not waiting for Longbranch's signal. The White Rose can fight the rebels while we go after the girl and the Dragonheart."

Longbranch's jailers didn't seem to consider Jason much of a threat. Though they clapped *sefa* manacles around his wrists, they didn't bother to disable him or search him for heartstones before they hustled him between the tents.

So he figured if he was going to make a move, he'd better do it before they threw him in whatever dungeon

Longbranch had contrived. He had a feeling it was the kind of place it'd be hard to get out of. But he didn't want to tip off Longbranch before Madison was well away.

The camp had been emptied out, most of the soldiers having deployed to the wall in preparation for the upcoming assault. Just as Jason and his guards reached a secluded spot where he thought his escape might go unnoticed, the White Rose wizards on either side of him crumpled silently to the ground and a band of Red Rose liveried wizards jerked him around and dragged him back the way they'd come.

Jason felt like the fricking princess in a video game.

"What's going on?" he demanded.

"Wylie has some questions for you. Now shut up." As they neared the boundary of the camp, shouts erupted behind them. The White Rose had discovered that their prisoner was being stolen.

The Red Rose wizards let go of Jason and turned to defend themselves. As the shields went up and charms began to fly, Jason left his captors behind and charged toward the gate.

⫷ CHAPTER THIRTY-FIVE ⫸
A HOUSE DIVIDED

Fitch peered down through the witch's brew of smoke and flame into no-man's-land, rubbed his eyes, and looked again. Yes. There was furtive movement at the outer gate, the shapes of several dozen figures crossing the open field.

He wiped his sweaty hands on his jeans. Was this it? The assault they'd been waiting for? It wasn't exactly an army. But a few wizards could do a lot of damage. He squinted through his field glasses, picking out the White Rose emblem on several of the invaders.

He turned, looking for Will, and saw that his friend had fallen asleep, leaning against the scaffolding at the end of the curtain wall. Fitch couldn't remember the last time they'd slept, other than accidentally.

"Hey, Will," he said. "Wake up."

Will instantly came awake, pulling hastily away from the wall. "What? I was just resting my eyes."

"Go tell Jack. Something's going down." Fitch pointed off the wall with his chin.

Will crept forward on his hands and knees and peered over the battlement, then scrambled backward like an over-size crab. Giving Fitch a thumbs-up, he picked his way along the scaffolding and disappeared into the darkness. He could be amazingly quiet for a jock.

Fitch resumed his surveillance, feeling like a member of the INS border patrol. He fished the remote out of his pocket and clutched it in one hand. He'd laid explosive devices all along the outer wall, in a modern-day version of the method medieval sappers used to undermine a fortification.

The first party was midway across the field when another, larger group poured through the bad-guy gate, following the first wave of White Rose wizards. From what he could see through his binoculars, this second group seemed to be Red Rose wizards.

The White Rose advance party didn't notice them at first. When they did, they didn't seem happy about the rein-forcements. After a moment's jostling confusion, half the group continued on, increasing their pace, while half hung back, turning to confront the oncoming army.

When the two groups came together, wizard flame erupted all along the line. The Roses were fighting each other!

Fitch fingered the remote nervously. If this was the assault they'd been anticipating, it was show time. But he didn't know what to make of the events on the ground.

Seph had found a quiet place from which to monitor the boundary of the sanctuary in one of the many drum towers Mercedes had built into her elaborate wall. It was good to be enclosed in stone, since he tended to set things on fire other-wise.

There he hung silently like a bat in a cave, his magical sonar lightly fingering the concentric walls of the inner fortress and the outer wizard wall, scouring the disputed space in between. He'd been on the wall for three straight days—putting out fires and creating conflagrations of his own.

Con-fla-gra-tion. A perfect word for a perfect storm of death. His enemies vaporized like mosquitoes who'd blundered into a high power line.

What time was it? He stood, stretching his overused muscles, massaging the base of his spine. He rubbed his grainy eyes and tried to spit out the awful taste in his mouth. Failing that, he pulled the flask from his pocket and washed it away with a long swallow of flame.

He had no idea whether he was really addicted to the stuff or if pain and exhaustion had made it temporarily necessary. At one time that distinction would have seemed important. If Mercedes wouldn't make it for him, there were plenty of sorcerers who would. They'd seen what he did on the wall. They knew he stood between them and hundreds of wizards, and they knew what would happen if he failed.

The flame coursed through him, and he was okay again. Totally. In fact, he felt almost giddy. Impervious. There was another perfect word.

The world crowded in and he welcomed it, each tiny blade of grass and leaf of tree and power-crazed wizard. Once again, he felt embedded. Connected.

Somewhere behind him, the Dragonheart throbbed like a toothache. His own heart seemed to keep time. He was the energy that connected and destroyed.

He sensed the intruders before he saw them, felt the raw

power of hundreds of wizards exploding through the wizard wall and streaming toward the sanctuary.

Leaving the drum tower, Seph ghosted forward until he could look over the curtain wall. The sun had not yet crested the horizon, and no glimmer of dawn had penetrated between the walls.

I know you're down there, Seph thought, pushing back his sleeves. Did you think I wouldn't notice? He was primed, bristling with power. They'd be history before they ever made the wall.

They came in two waves, the one rapidly overtaking the other.

Flame erupted between the walls as they came together, a ragged line spewing a fume of ruddy smoke like lava hitting the cold sea. Wizards were fighting each other down below. But a handful of invaders came on, heading for the Weirgate. Too close.

Seph lifted his hands, meaning to send flame roaring into the group charging for the gate. And stopped, sensing a familiar tear in the fabric of magic. A memory.

Instead, he launched a rippling arc of light into the sky. It illuminated an apocalyptic scene.

Hundreds of wizards battled each other between the walls. Most bore emblems of the Red or White Rose. Near the gate, a small group of White Rose wizards had stalled, stymied by the barricade. And, amid them, Seph saw someone that stopped his heart.

Madison.

She was at the center, carried along by the flow of bodies like a chip of wood on a flood, buffeted and jostled by the wizards around her. Her hair glittered in the wizard light, twisting in the hot winds generated by the flames. Was she a prisoner? Hostage?

Seph vaulted over the battlement, landing halfway down an interior staircase that led to the courtyard at the bottom. Then raced down the steps, his feet touching every third or fourth one.

"Commander! Sir! Wake up!"

Jack surfaced from sleep, wondering who the commander was and wishing he'd respond so he could go back to sleep—until he remembered that *he* was the commander. He sat up, banging his head on the bunk above. It was the first time he'd actually lain down in a bed in a week, and now . . .

"Will's here." It was Mick. The tall Irish warrior had been assigned to be his bodyguard.

Will Childers pushed past Mick. "Jack. They're coming. They're attacking. Or something. Hundreds of them. Heading for the gate."

Jack had yanked on his boots and was on his feet before Will finished speaking.

"They're ready for you, Commander," Mick said.

"Where's Stephenson?"

"She's out there in the middle of it."

"What's she doing?" Jack snatched up his baldric and strapped it in place. He pushed his way out of the tent and loped toward the gate, leaving Mick and Will to catch up as they might.

The *plan* was, there'd be no heroic sorties outside the wall, where their small numbers would put them at a disadvantage. Instead, they'd line the top of the Weirwall and rain destruction down on any among the enemy brave enough to approach it.

Ellen was the strategist. What was she thinking?

They were waiting for him, his ghost warriors. They'd trained for months for this moment. Somewhere out there in the dark were Ellen and her hundred. Against hordes of wizards pouring into the gap. Why would she leave the relative safety of the sanctuary and wade into an unwinnable battle?

"They're already hard at it, sir," Brooks said, scraping his hair into a ratty-looking queue and tying it off with a strip of leather. "It's a melee."

Outside the Weirwall, Jack could hear the thud of bodies colliding and the cries of the wounded. It seemed like a lot of noise. Even given the fact that Ellen was involved.

"Why'd she go out there?" Jack demanded. "Why didn't you stop her?"

Brooks spat on the ground. "Have you ever tried to stop Captain Stephenson from anythin'? She was looking off the wall and she seen somethin' out there, and went out after it. The others followed." He paused. "We need to go after her, I reckon. She wouldn't go out there 'athout good reason."

It was what Jack wanted to hear. He tried to close his mind to the possibility that he was putting his warriors in danger in order to save Ellen's life.

"All right, I'm going out after Captain Stephenson. If anyone wants to come with me, they're welcome, but it looks like a bloodbath out there."

His warriors crowded forward. All of them.

"Well." Jack tried to swallow down the lump in his

throat. "Um, at least half of you need to stay here and hold the walls."

In the end, he had to force them to count off. Brooks was selected to stay behind, but he called in a gambling debt and joined Jack in the barbicon.

"Let's go." Jack and his fifty passed through the long tunnel of the gate, under Mercedes's murder holes, and waded into chaos.

Visually, it was a sea of bodies—some jammed so closely together it was impossible to swing a blade, let alone tell friend from foe. Other twosomes danced and dueled, as oblivious to the battle raging about them, as if they were all alone on the practice field. Wizard on wizard, warrior on wizard—but no warriors on warriors since none were fighting for the other side. Flames spiraled into the sky and roared along the ground like a seriously malfunctioning fireworks show. Some of the fighters were clearly marked with emblems of the Red or White Rose, yet they seemed to be doing their best to kill one another.

Which was a blessing, because otherwise it would already be over.

All around, Jack heard the meaty thwack of metal against flesh, the explosion of air as blows hit home, the polyphonic roars of his fellow warriors. Then he was engulfed by the fighting and gave himself up to it for a while, using Shadowslayer to create a path ahead. He was still looking for Ellen.

He heard a distinctive yodeling war cry and turned to see Brooks standing alone atop a small hill, bleeding from a number of wounds, armed with shield and his trademark tomahawk, under attack by four wizards. Bodies were scattered all around his feet, and Jack wondered how many were theirs.

Brooks was losing strength. He parried the wizards' assaults clumsily, staggering from stance to stance as the wizards closed in, smelling blood. No doubt he would have been down already, but they wanted to take him alive.

Jack was still a hundred yards away when a bolt of wizard flame hit home, striking Brooks in the chest, bringing him to his knees. The wizards charged, and Brooks raised his ax with both hands, spewing eighteenth-century oaths and insults, probably hoping he could goad them into killing him outright.

Jack fished in a pouch slung across his chest and came up with a throwing star, something from Raven's Ghyll. He had no idea what it might do. Desperately, he sidearmed it at the wizards bearing down on Brooks.

It scissored into their midst, and two of them went down, shrieking.

Jack parried several blasts of flame and then he was into them, sweeping his blade from side to side, driving the wizards back. Hot blood spattered his face and hands. Someone stepped, hard, on his foot, and actually muttered, "Sorry."

Brooks writhed on the ground, still trying to stick the wizard leaning over him. Jack heard an immobilization charm uncoiling, as if in slow motion, and he shouldered into the source, slashing blindly with his belt knife. The wizard fell.

Jack knelt next to Brooks in one of those tiny bubbles of time that probably last a half second, but seem to go on forever. "Come on, Brooks. Up. Let's get you to Mercedes."

Blood dribbled from the warrior's mouth. "I'm done, Jack. But I took ten of the bloody bastards wi' me, and that's something." He gripped Jack's hand, as if looking for confirmation. Jack could only nod. "All the tournaments I won, all the poor warriors I put down . . . not half so . . . satisfying."

Jack could scarcely speak. "Up you go," he whispered, brushing away tears with his gauntlet. "Quit malingering."

"Tell the girl, when you find her . . . she has talent," Brooks gasped. "She's a fine fighter. Always was." And the warrior closed his eyes.

Jack remembered a sunny morning in Cumbria, Brooks charging at him across the grass, beaded hair flying, his moccasins wet with the dew, a tomahawk in each hand. More alive than any ghost had a right to be.

He stood, looked around. The center of the battle had moved a hundred yards off. Ellen. He had to find her. He cut a path through the mayhem, swinging his sword with deadly efficiency.

Eventually, he extracted himself long enough to note a clutch of White Rose wizards hard by the gate, seemingly in a furious pitched battle against some Red Rose wizards. And in the midst of it all, he spotted Ellen and what was left of her patrol—maybe twenty bloodied warriors fighting for their lives.

Ellen was her usual army of one, laying about her with Waymaker, smashing blows aside with her shield, rallying her depleted troops, making life miserable for anyone who came within her reach.

Jack bulled his way toward them, wondering why warriors would insert themselves into a battle among enemy wizards. Then he saw someone familiar among the White Rose wizards against the wall. Her studded denim jacket splattered with blood, blue eyes wide with fright, she was secured behind a phalanx of wizards and warriors.

Madison?

So focused were the Red Rose attackers on their intended that Jack cut down a half dozen before they noticed he was there. Even when he could no longer be ignored, only a few wizards turned to deal with him while the majority continued their relentless assault against the White Rose. They cut down one of the wizard defenders and stepped through the gap, only to be driven back by Ellen's fierce counterattack.

They're after Madison, Jack thought, his mind grappling sluggishly with the evidence before him. And the White Rose is defending her?

Perhaps the Red Rose had been instructed to take her alive, or maybe they were well aware of the consequences of attacking Madison with magic. For whatever reason, they were all doing their best to kill everyone around her while leaving her untouched.

Wizards poured onto the field in a seeming unending supply. There were wizards behind them. Wizards on all sides. Red and White Rose wizards. Unlabeled wizards. It was as if all the repressed fury of the past centuries had been unleashed in this single battle. If there hadn't been so much confusion on the field, Jack would've been dead long before he ever got close to Ellen.

One by one, the small party of White Rose wizards was eliminated, until it was just Ellen standing between the Red Rose and Madison Moss. She was already bleeding from several wounds, but she wore that familiar stubborn "Try me!" expression as she faced down a half-dozen wizards. She reached back behind and extended a dagger to Madison, hilt-first.

Jack's throwing star caught one of the wizards behind the left ear, and he pitched forward. Ellen's sword took out another. Now it was four to one, even odds where Ellen was concerned.

She looked up at Jack, scowling through the blood and dirt on her face. "Will you tell them to open up the bloody gate long enough to poke her through?"

Jack realized that she'd been maneuvering closer to the Weirgate, and now it was just behind them. But the defenders would never open it with hundreds of wizards just outside. They'd have no idea who Madison was.

"Mick! Go tell them to open the gate." He jerked his head, directing the warrior that way. Then, jostling past several wizards, Jack took his place by Ellen's left side, where his southpaw swordplay would cover her nondominant side. He could tell she was injured by the way she moved, and her tunic was stained dark with sweat or blood, he couldn't tell.

"Take Madison in," he suggested. "You're all beat up."

She shook her head and drew herself up. Jack caught movement out of the corner of his eye and turned. A wizard had somehow slipped in behind them and was closing on Madison, who was trying to hold him off with Ellen's dagger. It was young Devereaux D'Orsay.

"Devereaux! Come away from there!" A tall wizard sprinted toward them, trying to get between the two warriors and the boy. Claude D'Orsay.

While Madison was distracted by D'Orsay, Devereaux made a grab for her.

Jack took two steps, but Ellen was there ahead of him. "Hey!" She shouldered the young wizard out of the way. The boy turned, grinned, raised his hands. Too close to miss.

"No!" It was like one of those dreams where you're frozen, unable to run. Only a few yards divided them, but Jack couldn't cross the distance in time. Flame rippled from Devereaux's hands and slammed into Ellen, lifting her off her feet before she toppled backward onto the ground.

"That's one!" the boy crowed, then reached toward Jack, a greedy smile on his baby face, his pale eyes alive with delight behind round glasses. "Who would've known that warriors die so easi . . ."

Shadowslayer ended it. The boy died with a smile on his face.

Someone screamed "Devereaux!"

Jack turned. It was Claude D'Orsay, his face twisted in grief and rage. It was the icy Master of the Games as Jack had never seen him.

"You killed him! You cross-whelped barbarian, you've killed my son!" D'Orsay came grimly forward, driving a vast wall of flame across the battlefield toward Jack, apparently unconcerned who else he incinerated as long as Jack was numbered among them.

Jack stepped in front of Ellen's prone body, knowing there was no way he could stop what was coming. He raised Shadowslayer, said a prayer.

D'Orsay was so focused on his intended victim that he didn't see the person that materialized behind him. Jack blinked in disbelief. It was Jason Haley, with a dagger in his manacled hands.

Jason charged into D'Orsay, knocking him off his feet. They rolled across the ground, trailing a wake of flame. Jason came up on top. He gripped the hilt of the dagger with both hands and drove it home. D'Orsay screamed, a high, keening note, then sent flame ripping into Jason, nearly cutting him in two. D'Orsay pushed Jason's body aside, tried to rise, then fell flat on his face and lay still.

The onrushing flames hesitated, piling higher and higher, like a giant breaker hitting a reef, then collapsed and dissipated. D'Orsay was dead.

"Jason!" Madison screamed, and tried to push past Jack to where Jason lay next to D'Orsay.

Jack threw out a gauntleted arm, blocking her path, and thrust her behind him. "No! Please, Madison."

Ellen lay where she'd fallen, but Jack could not get to her. Wizards kept coming after Madison and dying on Jack's sword as fast as they came. Mick shouted at them from the Weirwall gate, gesturing at them to come ahead. But there was a sea of wizards between them. Madison stood frozen, eyes closed, fists clenched, as if to shut out the horror all around.

Jack saw movement on the battlefield, a kind of rippling, as if a snake were furrowing through the tall grass of humanity.

It was Seph, all smoky-eyed and dripping power, clearing the path to the gate. Ignoring the enemy wizards who did their best to kill him, he gripped Madison's hands, leaning close and speaking into her ear. Wrapping his arm around her shoulders, he turned her toward the gate. He looked back at Jack. "Come on, Jack. Leave it. Bring Ellen."

Jack's throat was raw with grief and smoke. "Seph. Jason's down." He pointed.

"Jason?" Seph's head came up and he went very still. "But he isn't even . . ." He turned and handed Madison off to Mick. "Take her in for me. Now."

Madison screamed and tried to twist free and return to where Jason lay, but Mick picked her up and carried her toward the gate. Seph went and stood over Jason, head bowed, like a great black bird with drooping wings. Crossing himself, he removed his coat and wrapped his friend in it. He squatted, rolled Jason into his arms, and stood. He looked back at Jack, his eyes like great bruises in his pale face. "Let's go." And he walked toward the gate, back straight, shrugging off a hundred flaming attacks from the Roses.

Wizards swarmed into the gap behind him. Jack knew there was no way he could carry Ellen and keep Shadowslayer in play. He'd be down before he went a dozen yards. But he had to try.

Mick had just reached the gate with Madison. Jack saw someone slip through the narrow opening and run toward him, nimbly dodging bodies and debris. A small wizard, but powerfully lit, in a pink sweater and blue jeans. Flame erupted from her fingertips, roaring convincingly across the field into the phalanx of Roses that threatened to engulf Jack. The charge faltered, slid back.

She came up beside him. It was Alicia Anne Middleton.

She sent a concussion of air into the oncoming wizards, bowling them back like tenpins, and put up a barrier to turn their fire. "Jackson. Are you going to take her in or what?" Her voice broke over the words, and she blinked back tears.

Jack thrust Shadowslayer into his baldric. Inclined his head to Leesha. Then knelt and slid his arms under Ellen. And stood, cradling her close, breathing her in. Her clothes still smoked from the wizard's assault. But to him, she always smelled of flowers.

He walked toward the gate, with Leesha covering him.
This was the scene he'd seen in his mirror, all those many
times. He was the last warrior standing, carrying his fallen
comrade.

They passed under the vaulted stone ceiling of the gate, and Madison wondered why she could see it. It was a Weirweb, and if so—it didn't make sense.

The world spun like a kaleidoscope as Mick carried Madison through the trees. An icy mist hung waist-deep, swirling as they passed through it. The sun was just clearing the horizon. It was like a dream sequence in a play Madison had seen once.

A nightmare. Jason was dead, because of her.

Mick's steel grip relaxed a bit when she finally stopped struggling. Her entire body tingled, thrummed with power. The source of it lay somewhere ahead, within the sanctuary. The Dragonheart, far more powerful than she remembered.

Seph smoldered behind her and to the right, impossibly brilliant through tear-smeared eyes. Strangely intensified. She remembered what Jason had said. *He's been using wizard flame.*

The healers had set up a triage center in one of the

pavilions in the park, where they received casualties. Mercedes met them at the door, somehow forewarned of tragedy. There was a hurried conference, and then Jack and Seph followed her inside, carrying Jason and Ellen. They laid them on cots in the center of the room.

Mick finally set Madison down just inside the door, keeping one arm around her. Madison didn't know whether this was to prevent flight or prevent her collapsing on the stone floor. She shuddered, her body shaking with great, silent sobs while Mick awkwardly patted her back and soothed her in Gaelic.

Leesha stood a little way off, pale as paper, eyes fixed on Jason's body.

"Where are the rest?" Madison whispered, trying to collect herself, gesturing toward the makeshift hospital. For all the bloodshed outside, there weren't many patients.

Mick shook his head. "Either they're dead, or they've been healed and went back to fight," he said.

"If . . . if ghost warriors are killed, can they come back?"

He shook his head again. "Not if they're done in by wizards."

As they watched, Mercedes bent over Jason, laying her hands on his body. She closed her eyes and remained that way for a long moment, her tears falling onto Seph's cloak.

"You be at peace, now, boy," she said. Then she straightened and turned toward Ellen.

As soon as Mercedes moved away, Leesha crossed to Jason's bedside and freed his hands from their bindings. Still holding his hands, she leaned down and kissed him on the lips while tears streamed down her cheeks.

Jack and Seph came toward Madison and Mick. "I'd

better go back," Jack said gruffly. "They'll need me at the wall. I think we lost half our warriors in that . . . that . . ." His voice trailed off.

"I should go, too," Seph said. "But . . ." He looked at Madison, as if he had no idea what to do with her.

"You all stay. I'll go to the wall."

They all turned to look at Leesha, who was suddenly back with them, her face streaked with mascara. "I mean, we're *so* going to lose, anyway. You two can stay here long enough to . . . to get some news."

She took Mick's arm. "Come on, Mick. Let's go fight somebody in a lost cause. I'm tired of being on the winning side."

Mick and Leesha set off for the wall, back to the work that wouldn't wait. The rest of them collected around a picnic table outside the pavilion.

Jack couldn't stay still. He paced back and forth, looking as pale and bleak as Madison had ever seen him.

Seph stared straight ahead, his lean, muscular body extended, his long hands clasped in front of him. His tumbled hair softened the hard architecture of his face and shadowed his eyes. Madison's fingers twitched. She longed to paint him like this—to somehow preserve what would soon be lost to her forever.

He'll never forgive me for what I'm about to do.

And then, without looking at her, Seph asked the questions Madison had been dreading. "What happened, Madison? What are you doing here? How did you get through the Wizard Gate?" His voice tremored slightly, reminding her that he was just seventeen.

She'd been working over what to say, but still she

stumbled. "I . . . Jason came to see me on Booker Mountain. He . . . he said you hadn't been able to get near the Dragonheart, and thought I might be able to help. So he brought me back up here."

"I told him not to get you involved," Seph said, brushing his hand over his face as if he could wipe away pain.

"We were caught trying to get through the lines. He told them that if they let me go, I could bring them the Dragonheart. So, they sent me through the gate with some wizards as escorts and kept him behind as . . . as a hostage. He must've got away."

"The Roses were fighting each other." Seph glanced up at her quickly, then away.

"That witch-woman—Dr. Longbranch—said I should bring the Dragonheart to her. Some other wizards came after us. I guess they wanted it for themselves."

Seph nodded, swallowed hard. "Jack. How did . . . What happened to Ellen and Jason?"

With a few spare words, Jack explained what had happened to Ellen and Devereaux D'Orsay. "Then D'Orsay went berserk. He would've killed me, but suddenly Jason was there. He nailed D'Orsay and saved my life. But D'Orsay . . ." His voice trailed off.

"So D'Orsay's dead, too," Seph murmured. The sounds of battle came to them, carrying through the still morning air. Flames arced up over the trees. "Not that it'll do us much good." He looked tired, worn down, suddenly shaky. He slid his hand inside his shirt and pulled out a bottle, making no attempt to hide it. He uncorked it with his teeth, took a swallow, shuddered.

Madison took a deep breath. "Maybe—if I saw the

Dragonheart—I could see if it could help us somehow." She intentionally kept her eyes averted.

"All right," Seph said, wearily. "It's worth a try, I guess. But we'd better hurry. I have to get back."

"If it's still at the church, I could go on my own," she offered, hoping he'd accept.

Will Childers burst into the clearing, breathless from running. "Where's Ellen?" he demanded. "I heard she was hurt."

Jack looked up at him, then back at his boots, pressing his lips together. Will sat beside him, put his hand on his shoulder. "The Roses have started a full scale attack on the wall," Will said. "Fitch is on his way. He's coming after he blows up some wizards."

This brought a faint smile from Jack.

Just then Mercedes emerged from the pavilion, her expression grave. Everyone turned toward her. Jack remained seated, as if he thought he should take her message sitting down.

"Ellen's alive," she said, and a kind of whoosh went out of them, like they'd been holding their breath. "But she's in bad shape. I suspect a wizard graffe, like Barber used on Jason. But it's layered over with charms, so it's hard to diagnose or treat. I can't even find the entry point; it's like it keeps shifting. Diabolical. She needs to be churched."

"What?" Madison blinked at her.

"We'll take her to St. Catherine's. The overlay charms are superficial. Hopefully they'll fade in a consecrated church, and we can see what's what." She turned to Jack. "Can you and Will bring her?"

"We'll all go," Seph said, glancing at Madison. "The Dragonheart is there."

"But what about the wall?" Madison stammered. "Don't you ... shouldn't you ... ?" She preferred that as few people as possible come to the church.

Seph's hand on her shoulder directed her out of the pavilion. His green eyes were bleak. "If we can't use the Dragonheart, we'll lose anyway. Whatever I do. Jason called it. He knew the Dragonheart was our only chance. That's why he brought you here."

And now Madison was going to betray Jason, along with everyone else.

The procession to St. Catherine's had the cadence and demeanor of a funeral march, each participant a prisoner of his own thoughts. Jack and Will carried Ellen on a stretcher. Fitch joined them somewhere along the way, fading in from a side street as if he were a ghost himself.

A lot had changed since Christmas.

Trinity was like a familiar painting in which major features had been daubed over badly. The areas closest to the Weirwall were the most intact—the angle of fire made it difficult for the Roses to hit them from outside the walls. There the streets were eerily the same—except no children played in the yards and playgrounds; no shopkeepers swept leaves from their sidewalks; no high schoolers flirted on street corners or waited for rides in front of Corcoran's. No fire trucks screamed by to tend the blazes that smoked all over town. Madison imagined the people of Trinity being led, lemminglike, under the lake.

The town center looked like pictures she'd seen of bombed-out European capitals from the last world war. Although the stone buildings of the college resisted burning, they'd been heavily damaged by smoke and explosions. The picturesque square was scorched and pitted with craters, the ancient oaks splintered and charred, denuded of leaves. Sorcerer cleanup crews shoveled rubble from the street and applied magical patches to broken water mains.

Seph had been remade, too, in Madison's absence. People made way for him on the streets and put their heads together, whispering, once he'd passed, like he was a celebrity or a saint.

Seph seemed oblivious to them, as if the real business of the day was going on in his head. Sometimes he flinched and sucked in a breath, his eyes going wide as if reacting to some private pain.

"Are you okay?" she asked, then thought, Stupid. Really stupid.

He hesitated, as if debating how much to share. "I feel it every time somebody dies," he said finally.

She shuddered. "Can't you shield yourself somehow?"

"Not if I want to know what's going on."

She was glad he couldn't reach into her mind. Glad her own thoughts were private. She had to focus on the way ahead or lose her nerve.

They turned up Maple, heading for the lake. She could feel the Dragonheart, dead ahead, warming her, as if she'd turned toward the sun in some tropical place. Seph said little but directed her mostly by the burn of his hand on her elbow.

At least the hex magic inside her seemed totally gone. Not that it mattered anymore.

They reached St. Catherine's. The ghost warriors who guarded the door had already heard about Ellen. They removed their various period headgear and stood silently by as the solemn group entered. Jack and Will carried her up through the nave and into a side chapel where they laid her on the altar like a corpse on a bier.

Ellen lay, still and cold, wearing the mute evidence of battle—scrapes and smudges on her face and arms. Mercedes ran her capable hands over Ellen's body. They stopped just above her waist. "Ah. Here we go. That's where it went in."

Jack stood at the head of the altar, holding Ellen's hand and speaking to her in a low voice. Will and Fitch lingered in the entry of the chapel so they weren't in the way as Mercedes bent over Ellen.

"Mercedes," Madison said diffidently, touching her arm. "Maybe I can do something."

The healer glanced up in surprise, hesitated, then stepped back. "Be my guest, girl."

Here it is, Madison thought. A tiny gesture to set against a huge betrayal.

She slid her hands under Ellen's jacket, pressed the tips of her fingers into Ellen's skin, and felt the malevolent heat of the curse. Madison drew on it, sucking the dark magic into the hollow that always existed inside of her. It was a small curse next to Leicester's, but deadly all the same.

Ellen's body went rigid, bucking under Madison's hands. She cried out and her eyelids fluttered. When Madison could no longer feel the heat beneath her fingers, she drew her hands back and shrugged.

Ellen's face was shiny with sweat, contorted in pain. She lay restlessly now, moaning, taking quick, shallow breaths. Her helmet of hair shone in the light from the candles that stood in tall sconces to either side.

"She's fighting now," the sorcerer said, looking more hopeful than before. "That's good."

"Madison. Let's go downstairs," Seph said, turning away abruptly.

They paused at the top of the narrow stairway so that Seph could disable the magical traps that he'd put in place. Then they descended the uneven steps to the crypt.

Seph kindled a row of tall, beeswax candles that had replaced the electric lights. Electricity came fitfully from a generator, now, and it was a precious commodity. The flames flickered in the draft from the stairwell, alternately concealing and revealing the names on the occupied crypts.

In contrast to the dimly lit corridor, the niche at the end of the row was brightly illuminated. A hunched figure sat on the floor next to it, wrapped in a shawl, seeming asleep.

"Nick?" Seph whispered.

The old man raised his head at their approach. Madison was stunned at how much—and how badly—Nick had aged in the time she'd been gone. He'd morphed from a vibrant old man of indeterminate age to someone who looked like he'd outlived the most ancient of the patriarchs.

Still. Why was he here, and not out on the battlefield?

"Ah." Nick nodded, as if they were expected. "You've come."

Seph looked a little confused himself. "Um. Ellen, Jack, and the others are upstairs. Ellen's hurt. Madison came to see if she could do something with the Dragonheart."

"Yes. Of course." Nick smiled, as if Madison were the answer to a prayer. "My dear, I'm so glad you're here."

But Seph still hesitated. "Nick? You all right?"

Snowbeard closed his eyes, as if too weary to hold them open. "Yes. I believe all will be well, now that you've come."

Maybe the old man was losing it. Madison glanced at

Seph, then back at Nick, receiving no guidance from either. "Okay, then. I guess I'll just see."

Cautiously, she approached the niche. Who knew what the rules were here? Slitting her eyes against the light, she stepped inside.

The stone was brighter, more alive than when she'd last seen it. Flame and color swirled beneath its crystalline surface, casting moving shadows on the walls, so she had the feeling of floating underwater. It was very much like standing next to a hot coal stove. Only, there was something else, something beyond heat, some other challenge to be met. It brushed her consciousness like a feather, a certain . . . skepticism. She extended her hand, then jerked it back when someone spoke.

"Careful," Seph said from the doorway. "It blistered my hand when I tried to touch it."

Madison swallowed hard. She wrapped her jacket around her hand and extended it again, gritting her teeth, half expecting to be flamed alive. A weapon, they called it, more powerful than any ever seen before. She dropped the jacket over the stone, slid her hands underneath, wrapped the cloth around it, and lifted it from its stand like it was an egg that might break.

Nothing happened, except she felt dizzy and overheated, confused and conflicted. A voice whispered in her head, but it was too faint to make out the words. At least the stone didn't explode.

She turned toward Seph, who stood watching her, a puzzled frown on his face. "So?" he said. "Anything?"

"Maybe," she said, swaying a little. Somehow, she needed to get the stone out of the church. "Only . . . I'm a little woozy. I need to get out into the air."

Madison pushed past him, protecting the stone with her body. As she emerged from the niche, Nick looked up from his seat on the floor. "Unwrap the stone, Madison," he said sharply. "Take it in your hands."

"Y'all just wait here. I'll be back in a minute." She stumbled for the stairs, thrusting the jacket with the Dragonheart into her backpack.

"Madison!" She was nearly at the top of the stairs when she heard Seph's quick footsteps behind her; she put on speed. To the landing, through the door, and out into the sanctuary. Past the side chapel where Will and Fitch hovered in the entryway, their pale, startled faces turned toward her. She heard Seph behind her and broke into a flat-out run up the aisle. There was no way she'd outrun those long legs from dead even, but his confusion had given her a head start.

She clutched the backpack close, worried about jostling it, and reached the double doors at the front thirty feet ahead of Seph. Then ran smack into Jack Swift, which was a lot like running into a brick wall.

"Hey!" He took hold of her shoulders to keep her from bouncing back onto her rear. "Madison? What happened? Where're you going in such a hurry?"

She tried to twist free and slip past him, but Seph shouted, "Grab her, Jack!" and then it should have been hopeless, but she kneed Jack hard, like Carlene had taught her, and he was so startled he let go. But he was still blocking the door.

She ran down the side aisle. It dead-ended into a small chapel. But there were stairs leading up, so she climbed them, knowing she was probably heading into another blind alley. They let out onto the balcony, and she ran across, hoping to slip down the other side. She met Seph coming up, and Jack was behind her, so she ran to the railing and dangled the backpack over the stone floor of the sanctuary far below.

Seph came from the right, Jack from the left.

"You get back or I'll drop it," she warned, giving the backpack a shake.

"Madison?" Seph halted a few feet away, his dark brows drawn together. "What's going on? What are you doing?"

"I need the Dragonheart," she said. "Go away and leave me be."

"Don't drop it," Seph said soothingly. "It might break. Or explode." He resumed his careful approach.

Madison seized the top rail and climbed over, clinging to the outside. "You come near me, I'll jump. I mean it. I don't care what happens to me."

Jack and Seph both halted again. "Does this have to do with the Roses?" Seph asked, reaching for some explanation for her bizarre behavior. "Do you think you can buy them off with the Dragonheart?"

"You can't give it to them," Jack put in. "You can't trust them. They'll kill us."

"It's not about the Roses." She couldn't seem to control her breathing. It came in great, shuddering gasps.

"Then what's this all about?" Seph asked, clearly clueless.

"It's . . . it's about Grace and John Robert. Warren Barber has them. He'll kill them if I don't bring him the Dragonheart."

Understanding flooded into Seph's face. "Maddie. I'm so sorry."

"Well, sorry won't do any good. I am not going to lose them, do you hear me?"

"You can't give Barber the Dragonheart. You must know that."

"I'm going to do whatever it takes to get them back."

"That won't get them back. Please, Maddie. Let us try to help."

"You have a whole town to save. And all the underguilds. Grace and J.R. can't be your priorities. But they're mine."

And, somehow, Jack leaped across the space between them and tried to grab hold of her backpack. She let go of the railing and clutched the backpack to her, and she was falling, and then Seph's hot hands grabbed her wrists and yanked her up over the railing with inhuman strength, and they were all three rolling on the floor, fighting for the backpack. Jack or Seph or someone nearly wrestled it away, but she got the backpack half unzipped and plunged her hand inside, groping for the stone, knowing it was now or never.

The jacket slid away, and she felt its smooth surface under her fingers. She pulled it out, clutched it to her chest, and backed away, vaguely aware of the staircase behind her. "I'm warning you. Stay away."

They came at her from two directions, the sound of their breathing competing with the drumbeat of her heart. Something exploded just outside. The building shuddered, plaster cracking and sifting down from the ceiling, the great chandeliers swaying uneasily.

She turned and leaped down the stairs, rammed into the wall at the turning, and fell down the last few steps. She sprawled out onto the floor of the sanctuary, curling herself around the stone to protect it. She lay on her back unable to move. The stone between her hands flared and pulsed, the light penetrating skin and flesh, revealing the bones beneath like the Visible Woman in the science lab back home.

She blinked and squinted against a brilliance that flooded the nave, driving the shadows from the uppermost vaults. From far away, someone was shouting, *Madison!* A name that seemed familiar. The stone under her fingers became more malleable, the hard surface dissolving like spun sugar. Power slammed into her like Min's medicinal apple brandy, rendering her drunk and helpless, the room spinning until she thought she might be sick. An unquenchable flame burned at her center and rippled under her skin, threatening to split it open. Someone was screaming, and she realized it was her.

The stone was a flame between her hands. And then it was gone, wicked into her body until she was lit from within.

She remembered something Hastings had said.

Elicitors draw all kinds of magic.

From somewhere close at hand, the sounds of battle intruded. The Roses must be inside the walls. There was no getting away now.

She'd destroyed her only hope of saving Grace and J.R. She wished the flame at her core would just burn her up so that nothing remained but ashes.

Pressing her hot palms against the cool floor, Madison sat up, scooting back until she leaned against the wooden pew. She illuminated the entire sanctuary, driving out shadows like the rising sun. "It's gone," she said, hopelessly. Tears sizzled on her cheeks, evaporating as soon as they emerged.

"Not gone," someone said.

Madison raised her head. Snowbeard shuffled up the aisle, gripping the pews on either side, a smaller man than she remembered, his lined face brutally revealed in the bright nave. The heat within her fractured and split. She retreated without a fight, shoved aside by another presence under her skin.

"Madison," Seph whispered. Jack came up behind him, and they walked toward her, as one might approach an explosive device or a demon. Will and Fitch followed at a discreet distance, no doubt drawn by the noise of the chase. Mercedes stood frozen in the doorway of the side chapel, unwilling to leave her patient.

The stranger within her stirred, seizing control of her body. Madison gracefully levered herself to her feet, seeming to extend herself as she did so, until she towered over them all. Her arms trailed light, resembling wings. Her skin reflected light like glittering scales, and her eyes changed, her pupils becoming vertical slits. She was beautiful and dreadful, and somehow no longer Madison Moss.

"No," Seph looked up at her, eyes wide and horrified. "Please. Maddie . . ."

A powerful intellect pressed against her. A rush of memory and emotion, sorrow and pain overwhelmed her, punching into her mind like a sword through paper. She was with the Lady, she *was* the Lady. She reverberated from one to the other.

She was a dragon, armored in shimmering plates of ruby, emerald, and gold, her long, narrow head questing toward Seph and the others, her glittering wings folded tight against her body to avoid colliding with the walls of the church. Another shift, and she was Madison again. Sort of.

The Lady's memories claimed her, and she looked through dragon eyes. The church retreated, was replaced by a rugged green landscape studded with rocky outcroppings. Nicodemus Snowbeard had changed, morphed into a much younger man, handsome, beardless, with black raptor eyes and hair Jack's redgold color. Seph and the others stood in a circle, frozen like standing stones, hemmed in and overwhelmed by the Lady's will.

Madison looked down at them from a great height. She extended her long neck toward them, and they shrank back, afraid.

"Demus!" The Lady spoke through Madison. "Nicodemus Hawk." Her voice rang out among the peaks, so startlingly loud that birds exploded from the trees.

This younger Nick fell to one knee, bowing his head. He was dressed expensively, in fine leather and silk, the cut of his clothes revealing a soldier's build. "My Lady Aidan Ladhra."

"Nick," Jack said, his hand on the hilt of his sword. But Nicodemus Hawk Snowbeard raised his hand and shook his head. There was something in Demus's face that might have been hope.

The Lady's memories rolled through Madison's mind like bright pebbles in a stream while Madison cowered in the corner.

"You betrayed me," the Lady Aidan said.

Demus's forehead touched the ground. "Yes, my Lady." He changed again, reverted to the familiar old man with the white beard. But the eyes—they were the same.

"I've slept away the years," she said, sounding slightly amazed. "While you've grown old."

He did not flinch. "Yes, my Lady. It's been over a thousand years. They call me Snowbeard now."

"That's fitting, old man," she said sardonically. "Have you grown wiser as well as older?"

Demus flinched. "One hopes, my Lady."

"Why did you dig me out of the mountain?"

"You promised to intervene if we broke the Covenant."

"I promised nothing. The Covenant was your creation, not mine. Your lies, not mine."

Nick raised his hands, palms up, a supplication. "The Covenant stopped the wizard wars. For a time."

Madison/Lady Aidan yawned, spewing flames all the way to the end of the valley. "Kill each other off, for all I care. The world will be better for it."

"We need your help," Nick persisted.

"Then be creative. Use my name, if you want. You have been, for years. I'm going back to sleep. I've had the most wonderful dreams." She closed her eyes, as if meaning to retreat to that place of dreams and leave Madison behind.

"I've made mistakes."

The eyes came open. She studied him dispassionately. "Perhaps you *are* wiser. You were arrogant, before. But, really. Was it at all fair to use an elicitor to draw me out?"

"It's a good match, my Lady. She's a painter, a lover of art. And shiny things. Like you."

"No one is a good match for a dragon. We are, apparently, meant for solitude." She paused, closed her eyes, and Madison felt the intensity of her scrutiny. "Madison Moss. What a peculiar name. She's hungry in the way of dragons, full of desire. She has more pictures in her mind than she can paint in three mortal lifetimes." She opened her eyes. "She loves the boy," the Lady Aidan said abruptly, glaring at Seph.

Nick nodded. "Yes."

"He'll betray her," the Lady said, flaring up dangerously, reaching for Seph with her taloned hand. Seph stood frozen and closed his eyes.

No! Leave him alone! Madison struggled clumsily with the Lady within her, trying to wrest control away from her.

"No!" Nick said quickly, morphing once again into the young Demus. "He loves her, too. He is, I believe, wiser than I was." He paused. "I know you are tired of life. But there is hope in the young. I think they'll find their way to peace."

The Lady Aidan looked them over, her gaze shifting from Jack to Seph—who still shivered under her glittering scrutiny. "The boy is damaged," she said, curling her lip back to reveal razor teeth. "He's using flame."

"He is desperate to save the ones he loves. He would trade his life for theirs."

"Hmmm." Shifting back into Madison form, she reached out her hand and touched Seph in the center of his forehead. His entire body relaxed, his hands unclenched, and the pain and exhaustion and need in his face fell away. Seph dropped to his knees on the turf, head bowed. "M . . . my Lady," he whispered, his voice catching in his throat. "Madison—is she—all right? Please. She never wanted any of this to happen. Don't take her. Take me instead."

She gazed down at him a moment, leaned down and kissed him on the top of his head. She turned to Demus.

"What is it you want me to do?"

"Put an end to this conflict. Sort out the Roses."

The Lady bristled with fire. "I never wanted to rule over you. You, of all people, should know that. I wanted an academy. Collaboration among peers. Meetings of the mind and communion of the heart. Philosophy and discourse under the trees. And yet you led a conspiracy against me."

Demus didn't answer for what seemed like a long time, and when he spoke, his voice fractured. "I am . . . so tired . . . of trying to make things right. If I could undo it, I would." He shifted back to Old Nick. "If you will not mediate this dispute, then take back your gifts. The Weirstones."

She gestured toward Seph and the others. "You've lived a long life, but they are young. Their Weirstones are a great price for them to pay to cleanse you of guilt." She smiled sadly and extended her hand. "Nicodemus. The age of dragons is past. I'm going back to sleep in the mountain. Come with me and rest."

"The Roses will annihilate or enslave the other guilds." Nick met Madison's eyes, then looked away. "Then they will murder each other. They'll destroy the world."

The Lady shrugged, as if to say, *Who cares?* Then she seemed to take pity on Nick. "It's too late, anyway. I have abdicated in favor of the girl," Lady Aidan said.

Nick's head came up. "What?"

"The girl is a blooded descendant of the Dragonguard. She wears the stone of that lineage. I name her the heir of the Dragonheart, the giver and taker of power. If you want someone to rule over you, she can do it."

Now, wait just a minute, Madison thought, rattling against confinement like a marble in a jar. Who's this girl you're talking about?

Nick cleared his throat. "But . . . so much power in the hands of one person."

The Lady Aidan shrugged carelessly. "She does not want it, either," she said. "And that is a hopeful sign. Let's trust her to make good use of it, shall we?"

"But, my Lady . . ."

The Lady drew herself up. "Good-bye, Demus. You know where to find me." Madison felt the touch of the Lady's mind as she departed—and was suddenly and terribly alone.

The green landscape faded, and the stone walls of the church closed in again. The others stirred, as if a spell were broken.

Madison looked down at herself. Her vision swam, and she knew she must be hallucinating. Her skin still glowed, and she seemed to morph subtly from one shape to another—from a girl in jeans and a denim jacket to the Lady with jeweled skin to something more dragonlike. Her skin glittered when the light hit it just so, and flame seemed to trail her gestures.

Seph gripped the end of a pew and pulled himself upright. "Madison?" he said cautiously. "It's really you, isn't it? But, you're . . . shifting." He reached for her hands, and when Snowbeard said, "Careful!" he ignored it.

It was like gripping a live wire—power mingling and colliding in their fingertips. Seph's touch seemed to anchor her, and she held on tight, gazing hungrily into his face. His green eyes were clear now, no longer muddy with pain. He leaned down and kissed her, another exchange of potent power, leaving Madison overwhelmed with guilt and gratitude.

He knows what I did, he knows what I am, and he doesn't hate me.

"Nick. So it was *you*." Jack's voice was icy cold.

Madison turned. She'd forgotten anyone else was there.

Jack slid his dagger free and pointed it at Nick, his blue eyes brilliant against a face pale with anger. "You were Demus—the wizard who established the guilds, who . . . who wrote the Covenant."

Nick was silent for so long that Seph thought the old wizard would not answer. When he spoke, he could scarcely be heard. "Yes. I led the original conspiracy against Lady Aidan. It was a long time ago, Jack. I was . . . very ambitious. Very full of myself. I saw no reason we should answer to a dragon, no matter how wise and virtuous she was. The price of living so very long is that one sees the error of one's ways."

"And the tournaments? They were your idea, too?" Jack's voice shook.

Nick bowed his head against this assault. "I did not antic-ipate the level of destruction that resulted from putting such devastating power in the hands of flawed human beings. It was not only the Weir who were dying, but thousands of Anaweir, in battles that raged all around the globe. We were destroying the earth, as well—poisoning the atmosphere, sul-lying our waterways, drenching the ground in blood.

"So. With the help of some confederates, I wrote the Covenant, convinced representatives of the guilds to sign, and persuaded the nation of wizards that magical disaster would strike if we did not adhere to it. I created a legend and enforced it with magic. Those who violated it paid the price.

No small feat, but then, I was in my prime." He looked up at Jack. "I know this is difficult to believe, but the Game saved thousands of lives."

"Just not the lives of warriors," Jack said bitterly. "We're expendable."

Snowbeard slumped into the nearest pew, his eyes still fixed on Madison. "At one time, that seemed . . . a reasonable trade-off."

"A reasonable trade-off?" Jack's voice rose. "And now Ellen's lying out there with a mortal wound—"

As if to add punctuation to this statement, a flaming missile smashed through the stained-glass window above the altar, sending shards of glass flying toward them. Seph put up a hand, and the shrapnel dropped to the floor as if it had hit an invisible barrier. "They're getting close," he said. "We'd better go."

But Madison put her hand on Nick's shoulder. He flinched violently when she touched him, and she pulled back her hand. "What changed you?" she asked.

He smiled, his face crinkling into familiar lines. "Why, my dear, I fell in love. One of your May–December affairs, my . . . fifteenth bride. I was totally smitten. I had no idea she carried warrior blood. When our son was born a warrior, I tried to conceal him. When the Roses took him for the Game, I—ah—freed him and fled to America. That was in 1802." He rubbed his hand over his face. "Jack, your great-great-grandmother Susannah was my many-greats granddaughter."

Jack stopped pacing and swung round, looking not a little horrified. "You mean you're my . . . grandfather?"

"So to speak. With a great many greats. I very much

resembled you as a young man. Though not quite so . . . muscular." Nick shook off the memory. "In recent years, I've tried to remake the hierarchy of the guilds, but found I'd lost power over it. My power has waned, while the system has taken on a life of its own. When Jason brought the Dragonheart, I was hopeful that it might be a link to the lost Lady. A last chance."

"What . . . was it, exactly?" Seph asked. "The Dragonheart, I mean."

Nick shrugged. "The Dragonheart is the Lady's encoded memory. Both her essence and the source of power given up by the Lady to the Weirguilds."

Outside, the fighting rolled toward them, its advance marked by the percussive tread of explosions. Flames flickered outside, casting bizarre shadows on the walls and floor, and thick smoke seeped in around the windows.

"Well, none of this is going to matter to any of us before long," Seph said. "They're in. Obviously."

"So. I guess this is the end, then," Fitch said, pressing his fist over his heart. "I have to say, it's been really . . ." He swallowed hard. "I wouldn't have missed it," he added, his voice faint in the cavernous sanctuary.

Seph reached into his jacket and pulled out the bottle of flame. He gazed at it a moment, then opened his hand so that it fell, smashing on the stone floor.

"Listen," Seph said. "The rest of you, get Ellen and go down in the crypt and out the tunnel to the lake. They won't know how many of us there are. They've broken through the walls, so there may be a way out."

"And what will you be doing?" Will asked suspiciously.

"I'll hold them off as long as I can. You know, to give you

a head start with Ellen. Then I'll come meet you," Seph said lightly.

"Right," Will said, not buying it. "Not a chance. We all go, or nobody goes."

"This is my fault," Madison said. "I am so sorry. I was just . . . just trying to save Grace and J.R., and I've ruined everything. You had one little chance, and I wrecked it. Now Jason's dead and Ellen's hurt, the Dragonheart's gone, and they're coming for us."

"Madison," Seph began, but she knew better than to look at him.

"Anyway, you all go on. I'll go out there and see if I can suck the power out of some of them. It's worth a try."

"Madison." This time it was Nick. "That won't work now. Not in the way you mean. You don't *draw* power anymore. But . . ."

"Don't argue with me; my mind is made up." She felt almost peaceful now that she'd made her decision.

"No," Seph said. "You didn't want to be involved in this in the first place. We pulled you into it, and now . . ."

"Listen to me!" Nick Snowbeard's voice boomed out with something of its old force, and everyone stopped talking. "Madison," he continued in a softer voice. "You do indeed have the means to save us all, but you must act quickly and with intelligence. I can teach you some things, but there's not much time."

"How? With what?" She looked around at the others, who seemed as puzzled as she.

"With the Dragonheart."

She looked at him as if he'd lost his mind. "The Dragonheart is gone."

"You are mistaken." Nick stood, and pressed his fingers to the base of her collarbone. "The Dragonheart is here."

"What?" Madison looked totally bewildered.

Nick smiled grimly. "Madison, like it or not, you are, shall we say, the Dragon Heir."

When it came down to the final assault, Jessamine Longbranch was surprised at the lack of resistance at the wall. After the days and weeks of siege warfare, it seemed the rebels' strength was far less than had been believed. In fact, the Roses had taken their greatest losses outside the perimeter—from inter-House battles and a diabolical series of nonmagical mines and explosive devices that infested the ground between the walls.

It was a mark of ill breeding for wizards to use such tactics against their fellow gifted.

In the end, they sliced through the Weirwall in three places. When the armies poured into the town, the rebels dissipated like smoke. The Roses sent flame howling up the streets and alleys of Trinity, but it was like hunting stardust.

Still, Jess was unsettled by the fact that Joseph McCauley, Jack Swift, and Ellen Stephenson were conspicuously absent. Her greatest fear was that somehow they'd found a way to escape with the Dragonheart and were even now making their way to a rendezvous with Hastings and Downey.

No sign of Madison Moss, either. But there could be no doubt that the Dragonheart was still close by, somewhere near the center of town. Now her objective was to get to it ahead of Geoffrey Wylie and the Red Rose.

So when she came through the wall, she did not linger to finish off the last defenders. Leaving the cleanup to others, she led a score of her most trusted lieutenants toward the source of the power that welled from the city core.

The town was in ruins. Its once-picturesque square fumed black smoke into the dawn, surrounded by blasted storefronts and littered with broken glass. Its gingerbread Victorian homes were ablaze. The streets were deserted, the Anaweir residents nowhere to be seen.

Jess saw movement off to her left and right, a flash of red livery. Not rebels, but some of her purported allies. She sent flame spiraling out in both directions and heard screams as they connected. She could do with a little less competition.

She quickened her pace to an undignified trot. If she could find the Dragonheart, so could anyone else.

She rounded a corner and all but skidded to a stop, swearing forcefully. Ahead stood a large stone church, like a great ship swimming in a sea of wizards—Red Rose, White Rose, and some brave indeterminate fools who had taken the new ecumenicalism to heart.

She was late. She took a quick count and shook her head.

Geoffrey Wylie greeted her on the church steps, a big smile on his ugly face, his shields firmly in place against a surprise attack from the sanctuary. Or his allies. "Jess! So glad you could come. We've demanded the surrender of the Dragonheart and are awaiting the rebels' response."

Jess shook back her hair and delivered a withering sneer. "Really, Geoffrey. Why are you even negotiating with them?"

The smile did not falter. "Once we have the Dragonheart in our hands, we will, of course, renegotiate. Watch and learn."

As if called by their conversation, the boy wizard Joseph McCauley emerged onto a second floor gallery, dressed all in black, glittering with wards. A few over-enthusiastic wizards (mostly Red Roses) directed a smattering of fire at him, which he brushed aside contemptuously. The boy surveyed the assembly as one might an infestation of fire ants— unpleasant, but, for the most part, manageable.

He was admittedly handsome, though he'd already mastered his father's habit of squinting down his long nose at his betters. Too bad he carried so much bad blood.

I should have kept hold of the girl, she thought. Perhaps McCauley still could have been turned.

The boy's voice rang out over the churchyard. "We've discussed your proposal," he said. "And we have a counter offer." He paused, as if to assure that he had everyone's attention. "We propose a new Covenant of peace and forgiveness. If you all go back where you came from and swear off violence, coercion, and attack magic, we will allow you to live."

For a moment, Wylie couldn't conjure a response. "Are you out of your mind?" he sputtered. "What kind of proposal is that?"

"If you refuse," McCauley continued, unperturbed, "we'll strip you of magic and leave you Anaweir."

A buzz of outrage erupted from the assembled wizards.

Jess couldn't help but admire the boy's arrogance. Apparently McCauley had also inherited his father's inability to recognize when he was beaten.

Wylie was less impressed. "Why, you self-important young . . ."

"A *generous* offer," McCauley's voice boomed out again, drowning out the commentary from Wylie and the rest of the crowd, "given the other crimes committed by some of you. Including the murders of Jason Haley and Madison Moss." His voice trembled a bit at the end, whether from rage or grief, Jess couldn't tell.

Jess was finally goaded into speech. "The girl's dead?"

"She was killed by falling debris during the attack."

Jess sniffed. "Haley got what he deserved for not delivering what was promised. And if the girl is dead, it's your own fault, for resisting."

McCauley went very still. "Well, she's still dead, isn't she?" he said softly. "And if not for you, she'd be alive."

"Enough of this posturing," Wylie said. "Give us the Dragonheart."

McCauley inclined his head, and came up smiling, an awful smile. "Be careful what you wish for," he said. He turned and looked back into the church. The windows kindled, illuminated by a light so bright Jess had to shade her eyes.

There was movement in the doorway: a long, sinuous neck uncoiling, wrapping itself around the tower of the church, a glittering body following, an armored tail clattering against the stone walls, the suggestion of wings that remained imprinted on Jess's vision when she closed her eyes. Slate roof tiles clattered down, followed by a gargoyle downspout, as the beast settled itself into the architecture of the building, its serpent's head questing out toward the wizards on the ground, its clawed forelegs gripping the stonework over the door. Wizards toppled, landing hard on the pavement of the parking lot, driven down by raw and irrresistible power.

Dragon! The word rippled through the crowd.

Jess managed to remain standing, though just barely. The apparition was so bright, it was difficult to look at for any length of time. The image wavered, and for a moment coalesced into a human figure, a woman, tall and terrible, with brilliant blue eyes and a cloud of glittering hair. She had a rather startled look on her face. Jessamine frowned, thinking she recognized her from somewhere.

Wylie had fallen. Now he gathered himself, forcing himself upright. "We've seen this before," he gasped, his face a fish-belly white. "At Second Sister. It's just a shade. A . . . a glamour. N–nothing to be afraid of." He sounded totally unconvinced.

Jessamine was filled with a cold and consuming dread. This was different from Second Sister. Horribly different. Raw power pulsed from the beast, pounding against her consciousness like storm-driven surf.

A dozen wizards surged forward in a charge across the cobbled square. Flame erupted from the ragged line, arcing toward the beast coiled around the base of the church steeple. The gouts of flame connected, but it was the wizards who went down screaming.

Another wave of twenty wizards washed forward, attacked, and went down.

After a moment's hesitation, the remaining wizards on

the plaza turned and scrambled for the perimeter. Only, Jess had a bad feeling that she still had a principal role to play.

"Geoffrey Wylie," the monster said. It was a female voice, softly cadenced, oddly familiar. Wylie flinched and covered his head with his arms, as if he might hide himself from view. The erstwhile Procurer of Warriors for the Red Rose rapidly back-pedaled until the dragon fixed him with its serpent eyes. Then he stood frozen, as a mouse caught in a snake's gaze.

The dragon shimmered, coalesced once again into the Lady, dressed in what looked like a rough-spun monk's robe, her brilliance making it impossible to make out her features. Slowly she descended the church steps, fabric whispering over stone, stopping three steps above the bottom. "Come forward," she said in a terrible voice.

Wylie shuffled forward, eyes downcast.

"You have perverted and slandered my gift to you," the Lady said, almost gently. She extended her hand until she touched Wylie's chest. "And so I take it back."

Wylie stiffened, eyes widening until the whites showed all around, gripped the Lady's arm with both hands, and tried to shove it away. Then he screamed, a high, wailing, desperate note, and collapsed to the ground, weeping.

"You are now Anaweir. Your link to the Dragonheart is broken. Live on in the knowledge of what you've lost."

Jess had nearly made it to the shelter of the alley before the Lady called her name.

"Jessamine Longbranch!"

Jess turned to run, but something slammed her to the asphalt. "Leave me alone! I've done nothing wrong." She tried to scramble away on her hands and knees, but the Lady's voice froze her.

"Come."

The link between them drew her forward. Unable to resist, Jess turned and stumbled back across the plaza to where the Lady stood.

"You are a murderer, a slavemaster, a ruiner of lives," the Lady said. "Jason and—and Maddie are dead, and Ellen's hurt, and believe me, I've about had it up to *here*." The Lady paused, as if to collect herself. "You have desecrated the gift of power. And so I take it back."

The Lady reached deep inside Jessamine, gripped her Weirstone, and pulled it free, as one might remove a pit from a cherry. It felt to her as if she'd been disemboweled, though her skin was unbroken. Jess rolled onto her back, screaming in agony.

"You are Anaweir," the Lady said.

Jess looked up at a world that had been drained of all color. She wrapped her arms around herself, breathing in great, heaving gasps as if she could somehow fill the void inside. She was a magical eunuch, exquisitely aware of what she had lost.

Jess felt the touch of the monster's mind, and another wave of terror rushed over her. Over her rage and pain, Jessamine heard the Lady say, "Now the rest of you had all better go on home and change your ways and preach to your friends and pray I don't call your name."

Wizards stampeded out of the churchyard. They didn't stop to help their fallen comrades.

Madison was just so full up with anxiety that she was afraid if she opened her mouth, the worry would spill out and make all the possibilities real. So she kept her mouth clamped shut and looked out the window, the familiar landscape blurring with speed and unshed tears.

Seph was just about as quiet. Now and then he asked a question about the road they were on, or how much farther it was to Booker Mountain. She could feel the tension in him, could see in the set of his jaw and the way his hands gripped the wheel that he felt entirely responsible for what she'd become and what she stood to lose.

Everything had changed. She'd lost the raw craving in her belly that she hadn't recognized until it eased. Seemed like an elicitor is just an empty vessel, always hungry for power. *Raggedy mad*, she'd called it. She couldn't help wondering if it was Seph's gift that had attracted her to him in the first place.

She and Seph were still circling each other, wary as stranger dogs. She felt a connection with him that hadn't existed before. His power was linked, entwined with hers. No one who hadn't experienced the flow of power from within could understand its intoxication. But she was like a child with a powerful weapon, the safety off: all crammed up with power and no idea how to use it, which Seph immediately pointed out.

"Try to settle," he said, resting his hand on her knee, forcing a smile. "You're sparking. We'll have to walk the rest of the way, if you short out the electrical system."

"You should talk."

"I'm just saying."

"Then teach me." She couldn't help herself. Madison was desperate for knowledge in a way she'd never been about anything except painting.

Seph removed his hand from her knee. "I told you. I will. But you can't learn it overnight. I was a disaster before I was taught. You're a lot more powerful than me, so more can go wrong."

Seeing his pale, haggard face, she felt a rush of guilt. "You should be going after your parents."

"I will. When this is done." He paused, groping for the right words. "At least they're grown-ups. They can defend themselves."

Truth be told, she was glad he'd insisted on coming. She would have welcomed an army at her back. Anything to bring the kids home safe.

If she was really any kind of dragon, she would soar over the blunted hills of home and swoop down on Warren Barber, lift him high in the air, then drop him off the nearest cliff after she'd wrung from him the whereabouts of Grace and J.R.

But she couldn't control that metamorphosis, any more than she could control anything else. Her dragon self was like someone else's memory that surfaced unsummoned and unannounced.

And then she saw it, the yellow ribbon fluttering from the branches of a twisted pine. "Here! Turn here!"

Seph made a hard right, skidding a bit, fighting to keep the car on the pavement. "You have to give me a little notice."

"This is Booker Mountain Road," Madison said, wondering if Barber meant to meet her on her home ground. "Where could he be keeping them? There's just my place. And the Ropers'." She would not—could not—entertain the idea that they were already dead.

"What did he say when you called him?"

"He said to follow the yellow ribbons. He'd make contact."

It was nearly dark. The light from the dashboard illuminated Seph's features and glittered off the amulets he wore around his neck. The air from the open window tumbled his hair into thick slices of dark that sluiced against his pale skin.

Time was she had thought she'd die of embarrassment if Seph saw where she came from—the Booker house, all shabby grand and fading; her mother, Carlene, much the same. Her brother and sister living like young savages on the mountain—resistant to their big sister's notion of civilization. Now she wanted to breathe them in like the scent of wildflowers rising off a sunny field.

Seph felt the intensity of her gaze and glanced at her questioningly, then looked back at the road—which was no longer there, just open space where the bridge used to be. Seph stomped on the brake and twisted the wheel. The car careened sideways, rolling once before it landed heavily on its wheels in Booker Creek. For an instant, Madison was fighting with the side airbag, and then it was gone, and her right arm that she'd flung out in front to keep from going into the dashboard was gashed deep and dripping blood.

She looked over at Seph, who lay unconscious, draped across the steering wheel, a purple swelling rising over his right eye. She pressed her fingers against the side of his neck. His pulse thudded against her skin, and she knew the key to keeping him alive was getting away from the car.

She squirmed out of her seat belt, forced open the door with her good arm, and slid out into the creek, which fortunately was just knee deep in this spot.

"That's the thing about wizards," Warren Barber said from the bank. "They're not used to having to be clever. All you ever need is one trick."

And all Madison had was one trick, the one Nick had taught her at the church. It would have to be enough. "You *idiot*," she said, more to herself than to him. "You could have killed me. Then you'd never get your hands on the Dragonheart."

The pale brows drew together. "I told you to come alone."

"I needed a ride."

"So you asked *McCauley*."

Madison took a deep breath, fighting for control. It wouldn't do to play her puny hand too soon. "Who else do you think would be willing to drive me all the way down here?"

"You think he'd let you hand the Dragonheart over to me?"

"He doesn't know I have it. I was going to split away before we met."

"So where is it?"

"I'll show you once I've seen Grace and J.R."

He shaded his eyes as if she were too bright to look at. "Show me the stone first."

"I don't have it on my *person*."

Barber kind of rocked back on his heels. She could tell he wasn't used to being said no to. "You'd better not be lying to me." He slid down the bank, landing lightly on his feet, and walked toward the car.

"Leave him alone," Madison said sharply. "He's out cold."

When Barber leaned into the window, she added, "You so much as breathe on him, and the deal's off."

Barber straightened and squinted at her uncertainly. "What's up? You seem different."

"I just want to get this over with. Come on. Let's go."

Barber's Jeep was parked at the foot of a gravel road that snaked over the shoulder of the mountain above the Roper place. They hairpinned up the slope on a road better suited for the plodding gait of oxen hauling overburden and pig iron. Madison knew then where they must be headed.

Coalton Furnace was a short-lived enterprise of her great-grandfather's. He'd built the stack of sandstone lined with firebrick and dug iron ore from the mountain and made charcoal from the groves of hardwood trees. The furnace produced ingots of iron that were floated down Booker Creek and eventually to the Scioto and the Ohio River.

The furnace stack remained against the shoulder of the mountain, though the company store, church, and school had long since slid away, victims of erosion and the cutting of trees. Brice Roper knew about the furnace. He must have suggested it to Barber as a place to keep his young captives.

They had to hike the last few hundred yards over rubble and rock, since the wagon track was too treacherous and unstable for them to proceed farther.

The retaining wall that kept the mountain at bay had collapsed, so the stack was half buried on three sides. Saplings sprouted out of the chimney where they'd found a little dirt between the stones. Someone had affixed a cast iron door to the stack to keep vandals from getting inside and damaging the historical ruins. The door was still firmly in place, padlocked and half buried in slag.

Madison swung around to look at Barber. "Where are they?"

He shrugged and pointed to the top of the chimney. "I dropped them in from the top."

"You *what*?" Madison scrambled up the unstable slope next to the chimney, rocks sliding away from beneath her feet, gripping the chimney with one hand to keep from sliding down herself. At the top, she could look down into the black interior of the stack. "Grace? John Robert?"

For a moment, nothing, and then she heard movement down below. She caught a whiff of foul air, what you might expect when two kids had been penned up together for days.

"M–Madison?" It was Grace, her voice uncharacteristically reedy and thin.

"Gracie? Is John Robert with you?"

And then they were both shouting and crying and calling her name, as if they thought she'd forget about them and go away if they let up.

"You just hold on, I'm getting you out of there."

She looked down at Warren Barber from her perch high on the slope, thinking she'd like to throw the mountain down on top of him and wondering if she could. But first she needed him to do something she hadn't the skill to do.

"You open up that door," she said, fury overcoming whatever fears she had. "Do it now."

"First the Dragonheart."

"I haven't seen those kids yet. I don't know that they're all right." She fetched up a first-sized piece of slag and winged it down at him, striking him in the shoulder. Stupid but satisfying.

He rubbed his shoulder, his lips pulling away from his

teeth in a snarl. "You're going to pay for that."

And she knew that she might, but she didn't care.

Madison slid down the slope, landing next to him in a shower of stones. "I want to see for myself that they're not hurt." She wished she knew how to focus her mind the way the wizards did to make him do what she wanted. Instead, the force of her will slammed against him in an indiscriminate way.

Barber squinted at her, fisting his hands at his sides, twitching with frustration. It was almost as if she could tease out the gist of his thoughts. She was proving unexpectedly stubborn, and right now neither one of them could get at the kids, so he couldn't use them to get her to do what he wanted. So.

"All right," he said, with a smile that froze the blood in her veins. "Whatever you say." He thrust his hand forward, palm out, and a concussion of air struck the cast iron door, bowing it inward. Rocks bounced down the unstable slope and landed at their feet.

"Will you be careful?" Madison hissed.

Barber stared at her. "What's with your eyes?"

She realized she was sparking again, as Seph put it. Settle, Maddie, she said to herself.

"Hurry up!" she said aloud.

This time, Barber ran a line of flame around the outside of the door like a cutting torch. He poked it with a fistful of air, and the door fell in with a clang.

Again, a rush of stinking air. Followed by Grace, blinking in the moonlight, her face streaked with soot and tears. She ducked through the doorway and stepped over the jagged metal threshold, lifting John Robert after her.

"Now," Barber said, reaching for Gracie. "Playtime's over."

"Run!" Madison shouted, slamming her shoulder into Barber's midsection. They tumbled downslope, Madison groping for his Weirstone as Nick had taught her; but then her head struck a rock and she saw stars for a moment, and when she regained her wits, Barber was gone, charging across the side of the mountain after Grace and John Robert. If he got hold of them, he'd have control of her, and he knew it.

Madison stood and almost fell again, her head spinning, then staggered after them.

John Robert's feet slid in the shale and he fell, and Barber had him, dangling him in space, his arms and legs pinwheeling as he struggled to get free. Grace went to turn back, and Madison, coming on, yelled, "No, Grace! Run!" and Grace turned to run.

Barber extended his arm, and Madison knew he wouldn't miss as flame streaked from his outstretched hand. Madison screamed as it slammed into Grace and kept coming and coming, an unrelenting river of flame squeezing out of his body.

Understanding and then horror flooded into Barber's face. "No!" he screamed, dropping John Robert and trying to rip free of Grace.

J.R. scrambled on all fours toward Grace, who stood like some kind of avenging goddess, her dark hair flying in the wind, until Barber wilted and toppled off the mountain into space.

It was almost as good as dropping him off a cliff.

It probably never occurred to Barber that if magical gifts

run in families, then so must the ability to suck magic out of a Weirstone.

Nicodemus Snowbeard died the day after the siege at Trinity ended, at an age variously estimated to be 600 to 1000 years old. They buried him at Dragon's Ghyll (which had reverted to its original name), before the cave and under the Dragon's Tooth, where he would be close to the Lady he had loved and betrayed.

With the end of the D'Orsay line, Leander Hastings and Linda Downey moved into Dragon's Ghyll Castle. No one seemed interested in contesting their claim.

Jason never went back to Britain. They buried him in the churchyard at St. Catherine's, his mother's amulet in his hands. They raised a stone, and on it was engraved *Draca Heorte*, Dragonheart. Mercedes and Leesha planted rosemary, for remembrance, and vines climbed over his stone, and flowers bloomed summer and winter over his grave.

Trinity suffered through a siege of confusion and investigations, invasions by government agents, and talk of terrorist plots. But it is difficult to get at the truth when a whole range of possibilities is off the table and those few who know something aren't talking.

Ellen was a terrible patient but fully recovered, except she had a new set of scars like a soldier's tattoos. Jack and Ellen and even Leesha Middleton threw themselves into the rebuilding of the town, an effort led by Jack's mother, Becka, who knew how to get things done and would make sure they were done right. Leesha's aunt Millisandra was a major donor.

When summer finally came, Madison Moss went home to claim her inheritance.

She could sit on her front porch and hear Booker Creek and look down the long slopes to the river, glinting in the slanted sunlight. And in those hills she saw the reflection of other hills, slashed by ghylls, set with jeweled meres and standing stones.

She could paint if she liked and sleep in the sun if she liked, something for which dragons are well suited. But what she liked most was tromping along Booker Creek with Seph McCauley, who seemed as at home there as anywhere.

People in the county said Madison Moss was different—somehow changed by her time up by the lake. She looked you in the eye more, and her eyes were different, too, almost mesmerizing. And sometimes her skin seemed to glitter and spark when the sunlight struck it just so. Everyone knew you didn't mess with Madison Moss. You never could tell what that girl would end up to be.

Brice Roper's murderer was never identified. The Roper mine eventually played out and closed, and Bryson Roper, Sr., went off someplace where there were other fortunes to be made.

Seph didn't know the ways of dragons, but he knew the ways of magic, and so he and Madison sorted some things out together and left others alone. And if sometimes they drifted on to other, more interesting topics, they could scarcely be blamed.

They'd lie in the hammock that swayed over Booker Creek and stare up at the canopy of leaves and dream dreams that they hoped would come true.

Among the Weir, legends about the Dragon Heir that appeared in Trinity spread, becoming more and more elaborate, fanned by certain storytelling factions among the various guilds. No one knew where the Lady had gone or when she might reappear. Wizards pressed their hands anxiously against their breasts and tossed and turned in their beds and wondered what it would be like to be Anaweir. And behaved; temporarily, at least.

Around the world, the magical guilds celebrated—all the while knowing that fear of dragons can't last forever.